The Ghosts of Arasur

Other titles from INDIAN WRITING

Aadhavan
I, Ramaseshan
Paper Flowers

Ashokamitran
Star-Crossed
Today

Hephzibah Jesudasan
Lizzy's Legacy

Indira Parthasarathy
Krishna Krishna
Wings in the Void
Into This Heaven of Freedom
Ashes and Wisdom

Indumathi
Surrendered Dreams

Jayakanthan
Love and Loss
Once an Actress
Rishi Moolam

Kausalya Saptharishi
The TamBrahm Bride

Neela Padmanabhan
Where the Lord Sleeps

P S Sri
The Temple Elephant

Sa Kandasamy
Sons of the Sun

Sivasankari
Bridges
Deception

Vaasanthi
A Home in the Sky

Vijay Raghavan
Twice Born

Yuma Vasuki
Blood Ties

The Ghosts of Arasur

Arasur Vamsam

Era Murukan

Translated from Tamil by
Janaki Venkataraman

INDIAN WRITING

The Ghosts of Arasur

A novel in Tamil by Era Murukan

Translated by Janaki Venkataraman

Pages 336, Price Rs 250

INDIAN WRITING - 20

ISBN 978-81-8368-582-5

An INDIAN WRITING publication

Published in India by New Horizon Media (P) Limited

33/15, Eldams Road

Chennai 600 018, India

Phone: +91-44-4200-9601/03/04

Fax: +91-44-4300-9701

Email: indianwriting@nhm.in

Website: www.nhm.in

Publisher: Badri Seshadri

Chief editor: V Ramnarayan

Editor: Shalini Umachandran

First published in Tamil in 2004

INDIAN WRITING translation first published in 2007

PRODN /03/12 - 07

About the author

Era Murukan (Murugan Ramasami) is a noted novelist, short story writer, poet, columnist and translator from Malayalam besides being a writer on information technology in Tamil. He is the recipient of numerous honours including the prestigious 'Katha' and 'Ilakkiya Chintanai' awards for literature.

Era Murukan belongs to the rare breed of Tamil authors who have made their mark in both mainstream and experimental fiction. He has published 18 books so far and his works have been translated into Malayalam, Hindi, English and Telugu. A senior management professional with an international IT organisation, Era Murukan is widely travelled and till recently was based in Edinburgh, Scotland. He (for the present, he notes) is a quiet resident of the noisy T' Nagar area of Chennai.

About the translator

Janaki Venkataraman is a Chennai based freelance writer and journalist whose contribution to the city magazine ASIDE as its editor made her a household name in the 1980s. She writes in both English and Tamil and has translated fiction and non fiction in both languages.

Introduction

Time is not Lord Rama's arrow* that returns to its quiver of space. Man has not the ability, yet, to stop, or even pause, the progress of time.

Writers have often not only expressed amazement at the swiftness of time but also yearned to bring it under their control.

Shakespeare, the father of incomparable literature, says, 'But thought's a slave of life, and life's time's fool, and time that takes survey of all the world, must have a stop.'

Writers have always tried to use their words to pause, reverse or advance time. *Arasur Vamsam* is one such effort. This novel is based on the belief that the seeds of the future lie in the past. Murukan's language facilitates this fancy. The Banian Brothers, the chief facilitators of the novel, are symbols of Time. They run backwards and forwards to impress the signs of the future on the past. By the same token, they drag the remains of the past to the present. The pages of this novel reinforce the feeling that the energy of life comes from memories. The pages fly, not like Snehamba's father, dashing against each other, but swiftly.

The Arasur family prospers from the trading of tobacco—they grow in wealth and stature before the eyes of the king in the neighbouring palace. The king, at first, envious of their prosperity is later reconciled to it. The tobacco merchant, Subramanya Iyer, has two sons—Swaminathan, an erstwhile Vedic scholar who loses his mind and has a sexual relationship with a woman who lived three hundred years before him; and a younger son, Sankaran, who looks after the family business and, like many young men of his age, has erotic urges that make him do things like peeping at bathing women. When the family accompanies Sankaran to meet his prospective bride in Kerala, their house in Arasur catches fire, killing Swaminathan.

Sankaran goes to Madras to expand the tobacco business, but ends up learning more about the business of sex than about that of tobacco, his teachers being the white women he meets on a ship. After he returns to Arasur he marries Bhagavati, the girl he is betrothed to, and his family grows. The king's palace turns into a store house for tobacco. The queen, who has been barren so far, conceives a child and the king's line gets an heir.

Within this fictional framework are amazing characters and events. The ever auspicious Subbamma who echoes the disasters to come, Swaminathan's ghostly lover, a woman whose spirit wanders restlessly across time, Kitta Iyer, who converts to Christianity, Vaithi who drowns his ego in onion sambar, his wife Gomati, the multi-talented Kottakudi dasi—these and many other characters swirl within the story, as deities swirl within yantras. With them are the Banian Brothers and the ancestral spirits, who appear frequently to share the events of the past and the future. This novel makes use of words and moods not normally found in 'Brahmin' stories. The point of such usage is obviously that culture comprises both good and bad, sweet smells and foul odours.

A fine writer creates an individualistic world which is smaller and simpler than the real world. Occasionally there appears a great writer who succeeds in creating an imaginary world that has all the dimensions, the reach, the encompassing embrace, of the real world. And then, it reaches further and surpasses reality. Harry Levine said this of Shakespeare. You will be able to decide which category Era Murukan falls into when you have finished reading this novel.

P A Krishnan

* Rama's arrow: in the epic, the *Ramayana,* it is said that Lord Rama's arrows had the ability to return to his quiver even after they struck their mark.

Author's Note

There are some questions which have no answers. Why I wrote *Arasur Vamsam* is one of them.

It started as a little family history. The information that encompassed two language belts had many gaps in it. Those who could have filled the gaps were long dead. From the known, a little leap to what could be understood, and from that to what could be sensed, could these justify the writing of a novel? Was it not enough to write a piece of social history instead?

Perhaps I felt like telling a story, a long story with a little reality and a lot of imagination, stringing together a series of events. Could this be called an effort at writing a novel or did it fall into the danger of being labelled a tall tale?

Was I trying to show the world that I could write magic-realism? If magic-realism is attempted in Tamil it should of necessity be incomprehensible and boring to the point that the writer should rest happily between words, sighing, 'Oh good, this is so difficult to understand!' If I were to write magic-realism that was also easy to comprehend, was I trying to compete with Gabriel Garcia Marquez or Gunter Grass? In that case should I write this book in

Spanish or German or at least, Malayalam, so that it could eventually be translated into Tamil through English?

Although none of these questions was answered, *Arasur Vamsam* got written. I still wonder what exactly motivated me or persuaded me to write it.

The bits and pieces of information on my family's roots form the framework of this novel. But whatever urged me to write it, pushed me to expand that framework and go beyond it—about 150 years before my time, in fact. I was no longer myself but had morphed into a tobacco merchant, a cook, a Brahmin-Christian, a snuff-trading Muslim, a depleted and powerless zamindar, an astrologer, a clerk of the Sarkar, a temple priest, a child, an old man, a dasi, a controlling and controlled wife, an abandoned woman, an ancestral spirit, a ghost. I entered houses of marriage and death, travelled on ships and bullock carts. I was part of all these experiences, I was also their observer. When I finished writing the 52 chapters, I felt an extraordinary sense of contentment and joy.

If this novel shares a little of that happiness and contentment with you, that would be reward enough.

Preface

'Write about Arasur,' urged my ancestors. 'Write about us.'

They surrounded my table, clinging to its corners like swirls of smoke as they tried to persuade me. They spread themselves across my computer screen like mist. Their smells—a melange of tobacco, sacred ash, turmeric, menstrual cloth, rice cooking in cauldrons, sesame seed sweets, sacramental appams in churches—hovered in my coffee cup.

They gathered in the corners of the room and watched me.

'Write about Arasur's history,' they insisted. 'Write about us.'

'Us' were tufted men, shaven-headed widows, goggle-eyed boys clad in veshtis that did not quite reach their calves, nervous little brides in sweat-stained wedding saris with turmeric and vermilion smeared across their foreheads, their huge nose rings obscuring their faces, their palms cupping balls of cow dung that they meant to flatten into dung cakes, some wore little crosses round their necks... All of them spoke to me, some in loving voices, some in commanding ones, others in plaintive tones.

I heard the approach of sandaled feet and turned to see the Banian Brothers. My ancestors shifted to make space on the ground for them to sit. The Brothers smelled of fresh cigarette smoke, as if they had lit up just five minutes ago.

The Banian Brothers said, 'Write.'

'What shall I write?'

'About these people. About us. About Arasur.'

Well, yes, I suppose I could. But what history does Arasur really have? Just as the Banian Brothers are not really brothers, Arasur has no real history, which is not to say they do not exist. Oh, they do. The Brothers, zipping through the narrow lanes of Arasur in a hundred-year-old car, ever on the lookout for a chance to dupe the foolish and the slow-witted. Arasur too, exists, geographically.

There is the Aatha temple with its four surrounding streets, the Ayya temple with its four streets, and between them the meandering market road. There is Raja Chatram, the guest house built by the kings of old, a maternity home, a tank with sweet water, a photo studio, a radio repair shop, a temple tank, a school surrounded by casuarina hedges, a bonesetter's clinic, a stone platform where the satyagrahis held a demonstration during the freedom struggle, Kamalamba Coffee House, the Munsif court... all these are part of Arasur. There is a palace too, not a large one but a palace nevertheless, with a king and a queen, horses, swords, shields, broomsticks, cockroaches, revenue registers, clerks, bunches of plantains ready to be given as alms to priests during death anniversaries, the huge stone on which fish are de-scaled, soap-nut powder, a handmaiden, a palanquin... there is space for everything in this little palace.

We have even visited it.

It was the Banian Brothers who started it all. One short and stout, the other tall and thin, both dressed identically in their pristine white veshtis and the trademark banian vests from which they draw their name, the Brothers went to the palace, ostensibly to collect money for the temple festival.

'Isn't it over a hundred years since the palace was inhabited,' I had asked them. 'From whom could you have collected money?'

And they had replied, 'Who said the palace is deserted? There is a king there. And a queen.'

CHAPTER 1

The queen had a complaint.

Someone was spying on her while she was bathing.

As she voiced her complaint, the king looked up from the pallanguzhi board, his fingers pausing in the act of distributing cowries in the hollows of the board.

She was a pretty queen, although a little past her youth. Her breasts were beginning to sag, her waist was widening, yet she was queenly. And, compared to the king, who was on the wrong side of fifty, she was still quite young.

Nevertheless, why would someone look at her while she was bathing? It occurred to the king that he himself had never done so. As he began spreading the cowries on the ground beside him, one of them rolled away towards the door. Ah, thought the king, his ancestors wished to communicate with him. One of them had definitely entered the cowry.

The king did not appreciate the interruption. He and his wife were just beginning an intimate conversation, they hardly needed their ancestors or descendants—the palace astrologer or the vegetable vendor for that matter—to intrude. It was not polite behaviour.

The king knew that his descendants would leave at once if he complained, but his ancestors paid no such attention to his feelings. They expected, nay demanded, respect from him. They felt they had the unquestionable right to enter his life at any time to advise, bully or guide him along what they felt was the right path. They were hardly likely to let trivial matters like the queen's complaint stop them from saying what they had come to say. The white cowry shook with their urgency.

The queen, however, did not like being interrupted. Stopping the quivering cowry with her right toe, she said, 'Every day when I bathe in the palace tank, someone watches me from above.'

The king looked in the direction she pointed. Through the window, he could see the new building that had come up on the northern side of the palace. He had heard that it had been built by a tobacco merchant, who traded across the seas. His family had bought a large tract of land and built the four-storeyed house with many rooms and a big garden. In one of those many rooms, was a gramophone that played dirge music endlessly.

The family had far more wealth and influence than the king. They also had the gramophone, something the king did not possess. The sad music it played melted his heart; the king often stood by his window, lost in the funereal tones of the music.

The gramophone, however, could not possibly make the tobacco merchant superior, or even equal to the king.

The queen picked up the cowry and put it to her ear. The ancestors were beginning to chat with her. For some reason they never got annoyed with her, even when she tried to trample them underfoot. Even the ancestors loved the queen more than they did the king. Did they also gaze on her while she bathed?

'No,' said the queen. 'They belong to the generations before mine. To them, I am a child. Besides, none of them is as young as some of the members of the tobacco merchant's family.'

Ah, so it was one of the tobacco merchant's children. Trying to placate her, the king said, 'They are children after all. Why worry if they look at you? Do they bother you, throw things at you?'

Although he had no children, the king understood their ways, their mischief and games. He could even understand, if not condone, the impudence of the little boys who urinated in great arcs outside their homes just when the king's palanquin passed them during his monthly procession of the village. The men behaved no better, he thought. They seemed to make it a point to ignore him as he passed—they chewed betel leaves, gazed out of the window while tightly, and obviously, embracing their wives, cleaned fish on the stones outside their homes or, worse, got oil massages squatting on their thinnais wearing only their loin cloths. The women hardly paused on their way to the river to wash clothes or even looked up from their household duties as his palanquin passed them.

The king knew that his subjects no longer respected him. 'King' and 'queen' were mere titles of convenience, as his ancestors liked to point out. The Sarkar had given him the title of 'zamindar' or 'mittadar' to mark him out as a land holder. The villagers had started calling him as 'king' and the name had stuck, although it was now a joke. As he was childless, the title would vanish with him. Perhaps his line would not disappear if he took the trouble to look at the queen while she was bathing, thought the king.

'We will see to that later. What are you going to do about the tobacco merchant's boys?' demanded the queen. 'They are not children. They are strapping young men with thick moustaches.'

The cowry leapt from her hand to the floor and began rolling towards the door. The strains of a dirge issued softly from it. Perhaps the ancestors had also been moved by the tobacco merchant's gramophone.

'Tomorrow, I will send the palace manager to their house to make enquiries. As a precaution, you need not bathe tomorrow.' The king smiled kindly at the queen, pleased with his decisive announcement.

'Enquiries! Just enquiries! By that aged and decrepit manager!' spat out the queen. 'Act like a king!' she screamed. 'Order that the house be demolished!'

The king rose to placate her, and stroked her hair fondly. It was still damp from her bath and smelt comfortingly of soap-nut and other herbal powders. Should he carry her in and bed her right now? It was possible that this would result in an heir.

But his ancestors would not approve of sex in the daytime. 'There is a time for everything. Will you shit in the middle of the night?' they would admonish him. The Sarkar too might disapprove of daytime sex as an unhealthy practice and stop paying his pension.

It angered the king that he needed permission even to make love to his wife. He flung the cowry down petulantly. It rolled away, screeching, 'Bhogam! Bhogam!'

'Right now is when I want it!' retorted the impatient king.

But the king's desire dissipated quickly, in the face of more urgent concerns—he had not yet had breakfast. One could hardly gratify the flesh on an empty stomach. The palace cook had been late and had not yet prepared the king's porridge. The king continued to stroke the queen's hair, feeling the grainy residue of soap-nut powder on the strands. She slapped his hand away impatiently, caught a louse crawling down her neck and squashed it against the wall, drawing a bloody line.

The king hastened to soothe her, 'Look, we don't have to send the manager. I will go and make enquiries myself.'

There was a reason behind this offer. If he could visit the house, he might get to see the gramophone—and if he was lucky, he might even get to listen to one of the dirges.

The queen thought little of his offer. 'You are a king!' she shouted. 'They are merely your subjects, cheap merchants who sell tobacco for a coin here and a coin there and build their homes brick by brick. That is how they live! How can you even think of visiting them? Summon the owners to your court and order them to vacate the house at once!'

The cook arrived with the king's porridge on a brass plate and tamarind gravy in an earthen pot to go with it.

The king thought he should postpone holding court and making enquiries. These things took money, and the Sarkar might not allow it. There were only two courses of action left to him: one, stop the queen from having a bath the next day, and two, eat his porridge. It would be nice, of course, if she joined him for the meal.

The queen did not think so. She shook her head and walked away in disgust.

The cowries moved on their own and filled the hollows of the pallanguzhi board. The runaway cowry paused, and returned hastily to the board. The king was relieved — the ancestors had begun to play the game, the queen had left, he could eat his porridge in peace. It would be nice if the gramophone played a dirge now, a soothing accompaniment to his meal. Was there anything more comforting than eating a tasty meal to the accompaniment of sad music?

There were many robust men with bristling moustaches in the tobacco merchant's house. Which of them played the gramophone? How could the queen's aging, soap-nut scented nudity compete with those melting, timeless dirges, wondered the king.

The king wondered if they made millet porridge in the tobacco merchant's house. They might, of course, be rice eaters. Perhaps if you ate rice thrice a day, your mind told you to go to the terrace of your house and gaze into the neighbour's bathroom. The king was thoughtfully pouring the gravy on to his plate, when he heard the trumpeting of an elephant outside.

The Banian Brothers had arrived.

CHAPTER 2

The Banian Brothers wore the four-yard veshtis that the king's subjects now seemed to favour.

The palace manager once returned from a trip to the Malayalam coast to report that even the women there wore such veshtis—and nothing on top. If they wore an upper garment they were taxed—that was the law.

The queen's reaction was an angry 'What injustice!' The king was quick to agree, but privately he decided to travel to the Malayalam coast to take in the sights.

He was not very mobile; his left leg was partially paralysed. Chariots had disappeared two generations ago. Horse or bullock-drawn carriages were the preferred mode of travel now, but these were for the general public, not for royalty. He had his palanquin but it required four robust men to carry it, and four more to replace the first lot when they grew tired. The men had to be paid and fed. The grant from the Sarkar allowed him only one palanquin ride a month around the village.

Last month the king had taken his ride at night during the full moon. It was cool and pleasant, and he did not have to encounter his impudent citizens, as he did during his customary daytime rides. He had climbed into the palanquin after a satisfying dinner of crab in gravy, turkey curry and brown rice.

The king was proud of his procession—a runner sprinted ahead with a flaming torch, an attendant walked before the palanquin, beating a drum to announce the arrival of the procession, four muscular men carried the palanquin, their footfalls, firm and resounding on the ground.

As the palanquin passed his neighbour's house, the king first heard the dirge playing on his neighbour's gramophone. The song was in an unfamiliar language, but its inherent sorrow was understandable and strangely soothing. The king wished he had heard this melody while partaking of the crab in gravy. It would have been a memorable experience.

There was no money in the treasury for a gramophone. If he wished to listen to dirges, his pension allowed him only to hire some dirge singers for the day. They could not provide the smooth, uninterrupted flow of music that emanated from the gramophone. The voices of the live singers would waver, they would cough, they would stop to chew tobacco or go out to urinate and when they returned, their voices would sound lifeless.

The king wondered if he could improve his finances by levying a tax on citizens wearing upper garments, as they did on the Malayalam coast. But there would be furious protests—the queen would be the first to cast off her upper garments and stand on the terrace of the palace in her semi nude state, flagging off the protest against the tax. The fact that she came from a line of militant, anti-Sarkar, anti-establishment landlords made the possibility very real.

Lost in thought, the king forgot to wave to his lackadaisical citizenry, as they stood gossiping, snacking on peanuts or urinating by the roadside. His full stomach and the soothing dirge music made him drowsy, and he curled up in his palanquin to take a nap.

The palace manager, who was accompanying the procession, looked at the sleeping king carried by four men, and, realising that it looked very much like a funeral procession, wisely ordered the procession to turn back immediately. As a result of the swiftness of the return journey, all the torches went out and the king was carried back into the palace in darkness, smelling of the hot oil of the doused torches and the strong scent of night jasmine. How livid the queen had been! The king could still remember her angry tirade.

It was obviously impossible to journey to the Malayalam coast in the palanquin. The Banian Brothers frequently tempted him by offering to take him there in a car, an Austin.

The Brothers belonged to a generation that came well after that of the king. Although this modern vehicle, the car, had been in use in Europe even during the king's lifetime, it had been introduced into this country, only much later.

An iron monster of a machine on four wheels, trumpeting like an elephant, the king thought the car and his neighbour's gramophone must be one in spirit. It was the Banian Brothers who had first told the king the name of the music box—gramophone. The music box too came after the king's time. The Banian Brothers said they had procured it for the tobacco merchant.

'It does not take up an eighth of the space of the Austin,' they told the king, adding that they could get him both a gramophone and an Austin.

'Where was the money for these things?' the king thought sadly. If one had the money, one could travel back in time and do whatever was needed to make one's life pleasurable. The king had once turned to his ancestors for suggestions to enhance his finances. It was a death anniversary and a priest had been invited to recite mantras for the spirits of the ancestors. The ancestors, however, had other ideas. They told the priest, 'Brahmin, take your alms and leave. We wish to speak with our great grandson.'

The priest paid no heed. He made balls of boiled rice and handed them to the king, bidding him to sprinkle water and sesame seeds on them and offer them to the ancestors.

'Sesame seeds don't agree with us,' said one of the ancestors. 'Why don't you offer us chicken? We would appreciate that.'

'This is the right offering to make to enable you to reach salvation,' the priest snapped. 'If you don't believe me, I can bring the books to prove it.'

The ancestors asked the king to give the priest alms of four pumpkins, onions, cabbages, potatoes, turnips (which the Banian Brothers brought from the future) and four gold coins, and send him away.

The priest said the only way he could help the ancestors attain salvation was by offering them rice balls sprinkled with sesame seeds. Receiving no reply from either the king or the ancestors, he left in a huff with his vegetables.

When he had gone, the ancestors gathered around the king urging him to be thrifty. 'You don't need a new fangled vehicle or music box. 'Nor do you need to travel to the Malayalam coast to ogle bare-breasted women. Do you know how angry those women are at being humiliated? Their feelings will scorch you, reduce you to ashes.'

The ancestors also warned the king about the Banian Brothers. 'Don't trust them. They come from the future.'

The king had a ready answer to this: 'You come from my past. Do I not trust you? Why should I not trust those from the future?'

The retort offended the ancestors. 'Such impudence is a sure sign of Kali Yuga,' they said, and vanished.

The king was sorry he had let them go before asking for a new chariot, but they were hardly likely to provide him one when they were against the very idea of his travelling to the Malayalam coast. He thought of the Banian Brothers again.

He summoned the Brothers. All he had to do was think of them, and they appeared before him immediately. The Brothers had taught him this trick. They had told him about a communication device from their time that made use of wires to carry voices over long distances. The wires had to be strung between iron posts erected across the countryside. The king told the Brothers that the new-fangled system seemed too complicated. The real reason for his reluctance to install the system was that he could not afford it. Even if he found the money to erect posts and string wires between them, his poverty-stricken citizens would most uproot the posts and sell them for rice.

When the king mentally commanded the Banian Brothers' presence this time, they were unable to come at once. They were collecting funds for the local temple's flower festival. The king had started the festival in his time—he had arranged for cartloads of flowers to be brought from the countryside and had the priests shower them on the idol of the goddess. The king and queen had stood outside the sanctum sanctorum watching as the white jasmine, yellow chrysanthemum and fragrant screw-pine were offered to the deity. His citizens stood outside, on the bare red earth of the temple grounds, fidgeting and waiting for the real celebrations to begin. These were heralded by the arrival of more bullock carts (after the worship of the goddess was over) bearing huge earthen pots of toddy. The king bought liquor for the entire village, and ensured that there was enough for every villager to get four glassfuls of toddy.

As they no longer had a king, the Banian Brothers said that they conducted the flower festival themselves. They could not fund it, and so they roamed the countryside to collect money. The king was saddened. He offered to send over four pots of toddy, but the Brothers said this was impossible.

The queen did not trust the Banian Brothers. Even the ancestors, who had entered the cowries when she played pallanguzhi that day, felt the same way about the Brothers, she said. They had told her: 'These two are sly and crafty men. Beware of them.'

Nevertheless, the king was partial to the Brothers as they had promised to take him in the Austin to the Malayalam coast where the women were so uninhibited. He heard the Brothers arriving. They must have come to speak to him about the journey.

The king peeped into the front room. The queen was fast asleep. Her handmaiden was fanning her. The king looked at the woman and wondered if he could sport with her after he had finished with the Banian Brothers. He hoped the maid would continue to fan the queen diligently so that she would not wake.

The king chewed betel nut contentedly as he walked towards the entrance of the palace to meet the Brothers.

CHAPTER 3

Subramanya Iyer gratefully escaped the humidity of his house for the airy spaces of his thinnai.

His house was stiflingly hot that morning and the smells of perspiration, turmeric and sandalwood were overpowering. There were too many women inside, laughing, singing and talking.

They were worshipping their female ancestors, perhaps the only function in which the women of the family were the main participants. The men were sidelined; they had to wait for the ceremonies to end and for the women to eat lunch before they were served. Brahmin women of all ages, relatives who had come from far and near, thronged the house.

Iyer looked at the upper storey of his house and thought of the twenty baskets of tobacco stocked there, waiting to be transported to Dhanushkodi by bullock cart and then by boat to Jaffna. Although the store rooms were locked and screens hung in the doorways, the smell of tobacco wafted down like a thin thread.

Tobacco trading was hardly a Brahmin's sanctioned occupation. A Brahmin was supposed to carry bundles of darbha grass wrapped in a water-stained upper cloth and go from house to house performing priestly duties. He was to live on the alms given to him by householders for the rituals he performed for the salvation of their ancestors, alms that consisted of no more than a few coins, pumpkins, plantains and rice which he would have to carry home in the noonday sun.

His thin wife, in her threadbare sari, would be waiting for him, eager to start cooking with what he brought back. If the children clamoured for food, she would cook in haste, not separating the sesame seeds from the rice, and the smell of fragrant sesame-flavoured rice, served with hot, thin soup, would fill the air.

Subramanya Iyer's ancestors had not insisted that he stick to the priestly profession. There had been no priests in the family for the last three generations, they had been cooks, village revenue clerks, and even went to school. Subramanya Iyer's father, Sankara Iyer, was the first to break away from tradition entirely and start trading—and in tobacco. He was bold enough to take the tobacco by boat to Jaffna and then by road to the tea estates in the hills beyond.

The money had poured in, and with far less effort. One did not have to sweat and suffer like a cook bullied by every wedding party in the region, nor persuade reluctant tax payers to pay their dues to the government. The humiliation of waiting outside a defaulter's house at dawn, following him as he went to the fields to relieve himself and even acceding to his saucy request to 'Pour some water from that pot, Iyere, let me wash my arse,' all to collect three and a half annas of kisthi.

Tobacco trading had its drawbacks—the nauseating smell of the leaves for one. But it was a smell one could get used to. Eventually, one began to deify the baskets of tobacco leaves as the divine provider of endless wealth—an avatar of Goddess Lakshmi. Everything Subramanya Iyer owned—his sprawling mansion, the diamonds in his wife's ears, his shop—came from tobacco.

The weed was also a curse. Upstairs in a locked room, was Iyer's eldest son, Swaminathan, certifiably mad. He had been an intelligent child but had grown crazy and now lived alone in his room. The villagers believed that Swaminathan's madness was a result of the Brahmin taking to selling tobacco. The murmurs reached Iyer's ears, sending flashes of guilt and pain through him.

Swaminathan, despite being isolated from his family, had a constant stream of unusual visitors. There were the Banian Brothers, some men who wore scarlet upper cloths, dark-skinned men who spoke in strange tongues... Iyer's ancestors said these visitors came from a time that was well after his own.

When he was not entertaining, Swaminathan listened to music from the odd music box with a trumpet like an open mushroom. Discs that rotated ceaselessly on the surface of the music box sent out the music. Iyer thought the discs looked like the lac plates in Chokkanatha Chettiar's home. Swaminathan only played dirges, music so mournful that it would fill anyone—living, dead or unborn—with grief. The music disturbed Iyer when he sat down in the afternoons and evenings to recite his mantras, it stirred his loins uncomfortably when he squatted in the backyard (sacred thread neatly tucked behind an ear) to relieve himself.

Iyer had bought the accursed music box, paying the Banian Brothers four gold coins for it. They kept bringing Swaminathan more of those wretched discs with those awful dirges, and Iyer had to pay silver coins for them. If he refused to buy them he had to contend with Swaminathan, who came crashing downstairs and threw unbearable tantrums.

Iyer looked up the stairs; there was complete silence. Swaminathan must be asleep or perhaps he was discussing something as esoteric as yogic sexual practices with his ancestors.

The ancestors suggested that Swaminathan be married. It would straighten him out, they claimed. Instead of debating the efficacy of yogic sexual practices, he could practice them on a woman in a nine-yard sari who would be next to him. It was difficult to find a bride for Swaminathan. Iyer's brothers-in-law had refused to give any of their daughters in marriage to Swaminathan, but were willing to accept Iyer's second son, Sankaran. Offended, Iyer swore to look for a bride for Sankaran outside the family circle.

Sankaran had slowly taken over Iyer's business. Iyer only went to the shop for a while every evening to check accounts or offer advice. Whether Sankaran followed the advice or not, business was booming, and Iyer had no cause for complaint.

They had not yet opened the shop this morning. The women would not let anyone leave the house until the function finished. The men sat around, waiting for the women to finish eating so that they too could eat and go to work.

'Sankara! ...Sankara!' Subramanya Iyer called for his son after a while. He had not seen him for a while.

Sankaran was engaged to be married to a girl from a family in Ambalapuzha. The formal engagement ceremony was to take place next month. Today's function was connected to Sankaran's forthcoming marriage. Iyer's wife, Kalyani had suggested they have the function.

Where was Sankaran? Had he slipped away to the shop? He must have remembered that the tobacco had to be sent to Dhanushkodi today.

A loud voice raised in song floated out from the house. Iyer recognised it as old Subbamma's. She had the gift of persuading the spirits of female ancestors to appear before her. She was begging them to appear and bless the family.

Subbamma was familiar with the women of the last seven generations. Perhaps this made composing and singing the songs easier. Her songs were reverential, funny or personal and involved events from the family's history. It was believed that the ancestors had given her the gift of assimilating the language of any place she visited and singing in that tongue.

Twenty years ago, she accompanied a group of ten families from the village, led by Iyer's father-in-law, on a journey to Kasi. It took them seven months to reach Kasi, and seven months to return. They travelled by bullock cart, changing bulls and carriages several times along the way. Seven or eight members died during the journey. Those who returned looked weak and exhausted, but Subbamma remained fresh and energetic.

Subbamma went to Kasi, not to bathe in the Ganges or worship Lord Viswanatha, but to track down her husband, who had left her a year after marriage to travel to the north in search of enlightenment. She heard that he was with a group of Gosai hermits in Kasi. Some said he stood on one leg in penance on the ghats, and his penis had grown so long that it touched the ground. They also said that he took the half-burnt corpses floating on the Ganges to the funeral ground, roasted their flesh on burning pyres and had himself a feast.

Subramanya Iyer's father maintained that a Brahmin would never eat meat, even if he had become a Gosai. He wanted to visit Kasi to see if such corpse-eating Brahmins really existed but the tobacco business and his health—he was fighting consumption—held him back.

Old Subbamma and the ten families started their Kasi pilgrimage in the month following Iyer's father's death from consumption. When she left on the pilgrimage, the spirits of her ancestors took the form of birds and snakes and followed her, singing through Subbamma in voices other than her own. When she tired of singing, they entered the tongues of others in the group and continued singing. Even Subramanya Iyer's father-in-law was not spared. When he began singing in a high-pitched female voice, Kalayani Ammal, Iyer's wife, recognised the voice and said, with pleased surprise, 'This is my grand aunt Salatchi! She was married into a family in Nannilam.'

As the ancestors' spirits remained with Subbamma throughout the journey, she could speak each of the languages of the regions they passed through. Subramanya Iyer's father-in-law later recalled that when the group reached Kasi, Subbamma began singing Hindustani. She sang so melodiously in Hindi on moonlit nights on the ghats along the banks of the Ganges that crowds of families and ascetics gathered to hear her sing. A famous Muslim musician declared her music divine.

Subbamma could not find her husband in Kasi and finally gave him up for lost. While the others gave up jackfruit, beans, gourds and similar things that they loved, Subbamma let go of her husband. While the others were unhappy at having to renounce things they were fond of, Subbamma had no such regrets. She had long forgotten her husband. The feel of his mouth sucking her nipples was a faded dream. It was many years since her breasts had shrunk and flattened out.

Today too, Subbamma, old and frail, sang energetically. She sang about the twenty-odd women in the last four generations of the family who died before their husbands and had thus attained divine status. She would not stop singing until the women finished eating, and they seemed to be eating extremely slowly. It was the astrologer, Annasamy Iyengar's wife who finally urged them to eat faster. 'The men have been starving since morning. Let us eat quickly so that they too may eat and get on with their work.'

Iyer wanted to thank her.

Someone was walking down the stairs.

It was Sankaran.

'I called for you. I thought you had gone to the shop,' Iyer said. Sankaran smiled.

With his heavy tuft and flourishing beard and moustache, Iyer thought he looked more like a Kshatriya than a Brahmin. He would look much nicer if he shaved off the moustache and beard and retained only the tuft... but if a Brahmin could sell tobacco, why couldn't he have facial hair?

Suddenly, Subbamma stopped singing and yelled in a strange, thick voice, 'Listen, everybody!' An ancestor was speaking through her. She began reciting, in a sing-song manner:

Should you look at bathing women?

Should you bend down and look at bathing women?

Their half-concealed breasts,

Their pretty waist belts,

Their thighs as smooth as plantain stalk,

Their rounded shoulders,

Is it right to look at them?

Is it right to peep at bathing women?

Her words were so powerful that all the women began repeating her words—but none spoke in her own voice.

Every voice was that of an ancestor—a chorus of spirits.

CHAPTER 4

It was noon when Sankaran reached the market street.

Normally, Sankaran told his assistant to mind the shop while he took a short nap in the storeroom in the back. But today he was late and there was a lot to be done. It would be evening by the time he could rest. It was not auspicious to lie down in the evening, the goddess of poverty and unhappiness, Moodevi, would move in with you if you did so. 'What is it?' she would come close and ask.

Sankaran could answer, 'Nothing. Come and lie down beside me.'

She would oblige. Her mountainous tits, two on her chest and two on her back, were too large for a man to cup with his hand. She would snake down his body, ready to snatch his loin cloth away with any of her four hands. A waist belt covered her middle. But even Moodevi would have only one vagina... Raucous laughter from the ironsmith's shed broke into Sankaran's fantasy.

'Look at the size of this mother fucking bull's penis!' the men in the shed pointed at the nether parts of the upturned beast onto whose hooves they were hammering iron shoes.

There were several carts parked nearby, the bullocks had been unyoked and stood patiently chewing hay. In the cloth shops, customers stood around, examining, buying. In the oil vendor's, the owner dozed, a man with a huge paunch leaning against a large pot of oil. At the ironsmith's, one of the men fitting the shoe on to the bull's hoof said, 'But I am sure it is not long enough for Kottakudi dasi. She'll probably need a yard more!' He stopped short when he saw Sankaran, waited respectfully until he had passed, then began laughing again. Sankaran wished he could have stood listening to them. He loved to hear about Kottakudi dasi.

This was fodder for his fantasies. Until the girl from Ambalapuzha became his wife, he could only fantasise about what he saw and heard until, at night, his loin cloth turned damp with his desire.

Except for these odd moments of levity and ribaldry that he witnessed, Sankaran's life was dull. He spent all day writing accounts, arranging the dispatch of tobacco to various places, supervising the retail sales of betel nut and tobacco to customers who paid in small coins. He always kept an eye on the street, watching out for anything interesting.

Occasionally the Kottakudi dasi would visit the market to go to the goldsmith's shop. So would young women who came clinging to their elders to get bangles or nose studs.

Kottakudi dasi never looked at anybody. She never lifted her eyes from the ground when she walked on the street. But Sankaran gazed at her spellbound when she passed and focussed on the undulating movement of her buttocks. That image stayed with him even when he met the gaze, for a split second, of one of the girls in the goldsmith's shop or when he peeped into the palace bathroom from his terrace.

What if Kottakkudi dasi walked by right now? Sankaran thought with yearning. He looked up the street. It was deserted.

Sankaran reached his shop and stood outside, loosening his tuft and wiping the sweat off the back of his neck with his upper cloth. It was unbearably hot this summer.

Sankaran took the lid off the metal pot in his hand and took long draughts of the jaggery-flavoured water in it. He usually brought plain water with dried ginger in it but today the women had sent jaggery water that they had prepared for the function. It was cool and refreshing.

Sankaran's eyelids began to droop with sleep—the result of an abnormally heavy lunch. Sankaran began humming sleepily as he opened the planks that formed the door of the shop:

Should you look at bathing women?

Should you bend down and look at bathing women?

Their half concealed breasts,

Their pretty waist belts,

Their thighs as smooth as plantain stalk,

Their rounded shoulders,

Is it right to look at them?

Is it right to peep at bathing women?

He remembered how all the other women had unconsciously followed Subbamma and sung the song. They stopped short and began giggling when they realised how ribald it was. Encouraged by their embarrassment, Subbamma began singing more suggestive lines:

In the quiet of noon,

Thaiyyu draws the goldsmith into her house.

She leads him to the dark corridor

And asks him to measure her neck

For a gold coin necklace...

The other women realised that Subbamma's singing was getting dangerously smutty, and one of them stopped her, saying, 'Enough! There are men outside and that boy, Ambi, is also listening.'

Only when the singing stopped did Sankaran realise that the earlier song had referred to him.

Should you look at bathing women?

Should you bend down and look at them?

How did old Subbamma know? Had somebody told her? Who else knew? Had the ancestors told her?

Well, so what? Sankaran thrust his chin out defiantly.

As he entered the shop, the song seemed to float around him:

Their half concealed breasts,

Their pretty waist belts,

Their thighs as smooth as plantain stalk,

Their rounded shoulders,

Is it right to look at them?

Sankaran felt at once humiliated, joyful and frightened.

When the house was being built, Subramanya Iyer had sent Sankaran to apprentice with his uncle, Sabesa Iyer, at a tobacco shop beyond Dhanushkodi. Sankaran learnt to write letters and keep accounts, things he should have learnt in school but had not.

His teacher, Subburaman's vile tongue had not been conducive to easy learning.

'It must have been an inauspicious time when your father took off his loin cloth, you dolt! Have you no brains? Do eight one-sixteenths make two? In which whore-filled place did you learn that?'

Subburaman was still around, enfeebled by age. He came to the market occasionally, clutching his cane, his veshti stained and his upper cloth torn. Sankaran always brought him to the shop, took his blessings and gave him a gift of betel nut and leaves if he saw his old school master. He wished he could tell him he knew that the eight one-sixteenths make an half. He could even tell him how the Kottakudi dasi's trim waist was sending him crazy—Subburaman was now stone deaf.

'Master, the bullock cart is here. Shall I load it up?' asked Ayyanai, a labourer.

'How many baskets of tobacco, Ayyanai?' Sankaran opened his heavy accounts book to note down the details. A line of verse popped into his mind, 'Should you bend down and look?'

When he looked, the sheer abundance of those breasts mesmerised him. The first time, it had been an accident. After that, it had been a planned daily occurrence. He looked away hastily when the lady looked up angrily. He left the terrace quickly, yearning for the next morning's sighting.

He knew he was wrong. Even the ancestors came into the tobacco store rooms with their moist smells and told him it was wrong. Today they had entered old Subbamma's voice and warned him again. They were making fun of him and warning him.

'Damn you! I haven't any respect for you in any case. You are dead and should stay dead. Why the devil should you keep hanging on here?'

With a small sharp noise, the nib of Sankaran's wooden pen broke, the ink splattering across the page.

'Master, this is not an auspicious sign. Shall we send the tobacco later?' Ayyanai asked politely.

'Should you bend down and look?'

'Why not? You should look!' Sankaran said aloud, puzzling Ayyanai.

CHAPTER 5

Sankaran laughed. 'What have omens to do with business?' he asked Ayyanai.

Ayyanai brought a handful of fine chaff from the shop and sprinkled it on the page to absorb the splattered ink.

'Write on another page, master,' he suggested.

Sankaran felt sleepier. Perhaps he could take a nap once he had sent Ayyanai away.

'There are thirty baskets of tobacco inside. Load them up,' he instructed Ayyanai.

Then he began making an entry in the accounts book four pages from where the nib had broken and splattered ink: Thirty baskets at the rate of one and a quarter annas per basket.

Below that he wrote: Received from R M Thekkur two rupees, five annas and six paise. Advance: one rupee and eight annas. Arrears...

Sankaran wrote swiftly, his words looping into each other. The previous week, his cousin Parasuraman on a visit from Ambalapuzha had looked at his handwriting in the register and burst out laughing. 'I can hardly make out the words! Is this how you people write accounts?' he asked. In Ambalapuzha, they wrote in carefully penned Malayalam, the words and figures separated neatly. There were Nair clerks to write the accounts.

Parasuraman was fun; he mimicked the accents of a Nambudiri Brahmin, a Nair, the Mopla Muslims who lived in the hills and so forth to entertain Sankaran.

Ayyanai reported, 'Master, I have loaded the thirty baskets. I will run home to collect the betel nut and leaves that the elder master asked me to take from him. I'll be back in no time.' He tied his turban around his head and ran out into the noonday sun.

Few customers would visit the shop now. It was too hot. They would come only around the time the lamps were lit in the evening.

Sankaran lay on his back on the floor next to his desk. He was drowsy. He sensed a female form lying on his body, one much older than him. He loved her eyes, her breasts, his arms rose involuntarily to embrace her. All around him gathered the smells of tobacco and tobacco estates. He dreamed he was in Sabesa Iyer's shop in Jaffna. It was over a year since he had returned.

Iyer had sent Sankaran to Sabesa Iyer's shop in Jaffna when the boy was thirteen and doing badly in school. In Jaffna, Sabesa Iyer called himself Sabesa Pillai as the Saiva Pillai community controlled all the business in the area. Brahmins were only employed as clerks. Sankaran was renamed Sankaralingam to give him a Pillai identity, but he could do nothing about Sankaran's strongly Brahmin-accented Tamil.

Sankaran went on a trip to the hills with Sabesa Pillai. He was struck by the sheer greenery of the gardens. All the workers were Tamils from India. They chewed betel leaf and tobacco ceaselessly and sang the songs they had sung when they worked in the paddy fields in the plains of the Tamil country. They drank arrack and tipsily sang the songs usually sung drawing water from the wells in their native land. Sankaran was sad to think they would never sing those songs to the rhythm of drawing water from the wells and pouring it into the channels in the fields.

But he was only there to sell tobacco, introducing another unhealthy addiction into their impoverished lives. He sold baskets and baskets of tobacco. He made permanent contracts for the supply of tobacco to the workers through the overseers. 'Besh, Sankaralingam Pillai,' Sabesa Iyer congratulated him, slapping him on the back. Four years later, when he left Jaffna and returned to his native village, his father had built the house.

It was an impressive house, much bigger than the zamindar's mansion next door. The outer walls had been painted with bold stripes of whitewash and terracotta, adding to the majesty of the house. The house did not have the grace of the stone architecture of the zamindar's mansion, but it scored because of its size and height.

Subramanya Iyer's old house, the one in the Agraharam, had been turned into a school of Vedic studies. Iyer had done this to make amends for the sin of selling tobacco.

Sankaran went around the house and finally walked upstairs. At the bottom of the staircase, Subramanya Iyer said, 'Go upstairs and see your elder brother. On some days he speaks well—do you know, even people who live three or four hundred years after us, come to see him? We have erected a special staircase in the front for the use of his visitors. But today is full moon day. No one will come to visit him. But go and see him. He might act a little funny. Just let him be and he will be all right.'

Despite the warning, Sankaran was shocked. Was this his Swaminathan? The intellectual of the family, expected to become a great Vedic scholar? There was no sign of the clever, enviable elder brother he remembered. Swaminathan was skin and bones and had a racking cough. He stood naked in the middle of the dark room, masturbating and laughing. In the background was a strange music box from which emerged the strains of a depressing dirge.

'Brother, our entire clan is being destroyed before our eyes!' Swaminathan said and moved forward, wiping the drops of sperm on the floor with his toes. Sankaran backed out of the room in alarm, slammed the door shut and locked it.

He wanted to weep. As the wail of the dirge from the room became louder, he wanted to wail too.

Swaminathan was not an average scholar. 'He is as bright as the sun!' Iyer was fond of saying. Swaminathan had studied the *Vedas*, especially the *Sama Veda*, deeply and was ready to graduate as a Vedic scholar—there had been just a month of tests left—when his mind went awry.

Sankaran had been in the last year of school.

No one quite knew what went wrong with Swaminathan. But old Subbamma, in one of her spells, sang that he had gone crazy because he had the impudence to grab the spirit of an ancestral woman who had died a virgin long ago, during a family ceremony when all the ancestors had gathered in the house, and by means of his mantras had kept her bound to him and had sexual intercourse with her during the day. The spirit of the virgin had cursed him and Swaminathan had gone stark raving mad. When old Subbamma sang loudly of this, the family told her to shut up.

When Sankaran left for Jaffna, he only dimly understood why his brother had begun behaving strangely.

During the next ceremony in the house, Subbamma sang again; this time the virgin, who was no longer a virgin, entered Subbamma and cursed and swore so viciously that Subramanya Iyer decided to build a new house and move. But the spirit had followed the family. So Iyer conducted special ceremonies for twenty days to ensure that the spirit took birth in this world again. But there were complications: Swaminathan had impregnated the virgin and the ceremonies had to include the arranging of the rebirth of the foetus too. All this cost a lot of money. Sankaran heard about this from Sabesa Iyer in whom his father had confided.

After the ceremonies Swaminathan's spirit-world paramour disappeared. She was so pleased with the arrangements for her rebirth that she blessed Swaminathan with knowledge of Western logic, philosophy and science, but on full moon days, Swaminathan's condition took a turn for the worse.

Sankaran left Swaminathan's room and opened the door of the store room opposite, where the tobacco was stocked. He was hit by the moist, musty smell of tobacco, reminding him instantly of the tea estates that he had recently left. Trying to recall the lines of the songs the estate labourers sang as they worked, Sankaran left the room by a door that led to the terrace. And that was when he got his first look at the bathing woman next door. She looked up at the same instant that he looked down. Sankaran felt the gaze of her kohl-lined eyes piercing his body. She wore a thali, the pendant of a married woman and she looked older than him.

As Sankaran climbed hastily down from the terrace, he felt as if her gaze was still upon him.

He made his trip to the terrace a daily ritual, except for three days in the month, when the queen did not come there to bathe. Sankaran left for work a little late every morning so that he could spend time on the terrace. He refused to feel guilty about going late to the shop. He could always make up for it by returning later at night.

'Should you look down?

At women?'

Then one day cousin Parasuraman came up to the terrace looking for Sankaran.

'What are you doing here, Ambi? Are you saying your mantras?' he asked as he walked up to him. He looked down.

When the queen saw the two pairs of eyes looking down at her, she lowered her gaze and never raised it again.

'Ambi,' Parasuraman had suggested gently, 'Why don't you come to Ambalapuzha with me?'

Now, as he dozed, Sankaran thought he could hear Parasuraman call out his invitation.

He should go. Would there be a terrace there, he thought sleepily.

CHAPTER 6

It was early morning in Ambalapuzha.

KittavIyer's ears were assaulted by the high-pitched screeching of the squabbling women of his family.

What was it with women? If they were around, there was never a dearth of yelling, laughing, weeping or quarrelling.

'When my father came here from Alapat, he brought a four anna coin tied securely in a corner of his waist towel. Now he finds that his clothes are intact, so is his towel, but the four anna coin has vanished! Where has it gone? I have known of all kinds of thieves, but none as clever as this—this one could probably rob you of a five paise coin if you stick it up your arse hole!'

It was Kitta Iyer's wife Snehambal. The quarrel that had been brewing between her and his brother Duraisamy Iyer's wife, Kamakshi, had bubbled over this morning.

When he could bear it no more, Kitta Iyer yelled at Snehambal, 'Good for nothing! Stop finding fault with people, munde! Why can't you get along with your sister-in-law?'

'I have never heard a husband calling his wife a munde—is that not great?' retorted his wife. 'Compared to that, our quarrel is nothing. This is none of your business. I don't want your advice. Who do you think you are anyway? The Diwan of Travancore?'

Kitta Iyer stormed out of the house. His elder brother Duraisamy Iyer had gone to Mainagapalli to offer condolences to their friend Kurup's bereaved family. Duraisamy would have rebuked his wife in the same way Kitta Iyer had.

The women quarrelled all the time, but by noon they would be best friends again, visiting the temple together, sitting companionably on the veranda, cooking together, sharing jokes and chatting at night until they fell asleep. The next morning, though, they would start screaming at each other again.

'My father brought the money to buy sweetmeats for my children. He was so careful with it too, feeling the coin in the towel all the time, as he lay down to sleep at night. Now it's gone! How terrible he must feel! Oh God!' Snehambal began to weep loudly.

Kamakshi disregarded the weeping and said loudly, 'That man! He sleeps on the terrace till the sun is sharp enough to prick your eyes, and he sleeps so soundly that he does not even know that his veshti has come undone. If an elder sleeps in this disgraceful manner, he will lose not only a four anna coin but his veshti with it!'

'My poor father! He is old and ailing—he coughs all night long and falls asleep only at dawn,' she said tearfully.

'I am sure he is wide awake through the night,' Kamakshi retorted, certain that Snehambal would eventually accuse her of stealing the coin. 'In the middle of the night he stands by the parapet wall and pisses what seems like four potfuls of urine. If someone were to walk by below in the night he will definitely be blessed by the dousing from your father's sacred water. I can guess what might have happened. Somebody, walking that way at night, and showered by this sacred water, must have looked up and thanked your father and asked for his blessings, and this old man must kindly have thrown the four anna coin at him!'

'How can you insult an elder like this, you bitch? No wonder you haven't had children all these years! My father is only guilty of pissing. What about your sister's husband who came to visit from Bhoothakulam? Remember how he sat around the whole day staring at the women and tried to get fresh with Kalyani Kutti who came to sweep and clean? Remember what a scandal that was?' Snehambal was pleased to have remembered the right detail at the right time.

'What rubbish! He had weak eyesight, poor man! He came here for treatment for that. It was only because my voice and Kalyani Kutti's resemble each other that he...' Kamakshi stopped short, realising that she had said too much, but the damage was done.

'So that was the devil's play! It is your hand that your brother-in-law wanted to grab! During the day it is your hand that he grabs—at night it is everything else, right?' Snehambal's voice rose with happy self-righteousness, thrilled that she'd scored another point against Kamakshi.

'You have a dirty mind, Alapat girl! What else can one expect from someone who comes from a family of sorcerers and men who increase their numbers by copulating in the afternoons?'

Snehambal's family in Alapat was renowned for its men being scholarly astrologers, one of the reasons Kitta Iyer's family had chosen a girl from it for him. In Kamakshi's rage-filled mind, the astrologers had turned into sorcerers. As for the other reference, Snehambal, in an amiable moment of confidence, had told

Kamakshi the funny story of a grandfather who had married late and been unable to keep his hands off his wife even during the afternoons. Now Kamakshi used the story to make all the men in Snehambal's family sound like sex maniacs.

'You talk as if you were standing by fanning them when they were copulating. What else can be expected of someone who steals a four anna coin from an old man's waist towel?'

Ah, now Snehambal had launched a direct attack. Kitta Iyer realised that if he did not intervene now, the women could squabble till afternoon, forgetting their daily chores. Kitta Iyer shouted, 'Stop this right now, Snehamba! I am telling you, stop it!'

Although the order was directed at Snehambal, it was also meant for his elder brother's wife, whom he could not scold directly.

Kamakshi understood this and departed reluctantly to bathe, but not without murmuring, 'Am I crazy to put my hand into the piss soaked waist towel of that old man for a four anna coin—just thinking about it makes me want to puke!'

While Kitta Iyer had no great regard for his father-in-law, he felt it might be true that his four anna coin had been stolen, but surely not by Kamakshi. This constant quarrelling and screaming was unsettling—a man could hardly concentrate on anything while the fights were going on. If there were no women in the house, how quiet it would be! The noise came from the fact that different kinds of men, women and children lived together under one roof. Kitta Iyer shook his head and began to think about the many things he had to do that day. He had to be in Adichanallur by the evening.

'Soman!' he called. 'I can't find the iron frying pan. Look for it in the backyard.' He began stacking all the brass cooking cauldrons he needed in the bullock cart.

'Ramendran took all the frying pans with him when he left last evening, Anna. He has also taken the long iron ladles that you need for making sweets,' Soman, or Somanathan, ran out from the house, tucking a wad of tobacco into his mouth.

They were going to cook at the wedding of Krishnanunni Nair in Adichanallur. Krishnanunni was marrying the second daughter of Rajasekhara Kaimal, a government servant. Krishnanunni had not asked for any dowry. He was happy that the girl, Sridevi, was a healthy, voluptuous lass who would work in the fields with him, look after the cows, cook simple meals and practise the religious rituals of his family. His only request of the girl's father, Kaimal, was regarding the wedding feast. He insisted that the cooks be from Ambalapuzha Iyer's family because no one could cook a wedding feast like them.

Kitta Iyer was starting out on a long journey. After the Kaimal family wedding, he had an assignment in Punalur at the celebration of a girl's coming of age, then he had to go to Karunagapalli to cook for a sixtieth birthday celebration, and finally to Karunakara Menon's house-warming ceremony.

Everyone wanted Kitta Iyer or his brothers to cook for their celebrations—no one made eriseri, puliseri, milagoottan, sambar, laddu, jangiri or vadai quite like they did.

All of them waited hungrily for Kitta Iyer.

CHAPTER 7

Kitta Iyer's family had been cooking and catering for family functions and feasts for three generations. Known as the Ayyanmars from Pandi, the family was famous for its culinary skills all over Kollam. Although they were settled in Kerala, the family still spoke Tamil at home.

They were three brothers and three sisters. The eldest, Kuppusamy, took over from their father when he died. Kitta Iyer, the youngest brother, had been just ten. Shortly after their father's death, Kuppusamy married Visalakshi and Duraisamy, the middle brother, married Kamakshi. Both weddings took place in Alapuzha. As if she had been waiting for her daughters-in-law to arrive, Kitta Iyer's mother died shortly afterwards.

The eldest sister, Echumi was only a year older than Kitta Iyer and Alamelu was his younger sister. Last of all was Bhagavati, who had only recently come of age, but the pretty girl had already received several offers of marriage. They had settled on one from a family of tobacco merchants in Arasur in Pandi. The family was distantly related to them through his mother's side. The boy was said to be very enterprising and had been to Dhanushkodi and beyond to trade in tobacco. Kitta Iyer's cousin Parasuraman, who went to Arasur to acquaint himself with the boy, had only good things to say about him.

Kitta Iyer was glad Bhagavati was marrying someone who was not a cook. His other sisters had been married to cooks who, although they came from far away, now worked with Kitta Iyer. Ramendran was Echumi's husband and Somanathan was Alamelu's. Both sisters had been married at the same time the previous year.

'Soman, did Ramendran send word from Adichanallur? He promised to get some herbal medicine for Alamelu to help her during childbirth. Did you find out from Echumi?'

Somanathan shook his head to say no. Kitta Iyer hitched the bullock to the cart.

Ramendran had gone to Kaimal's house a day earlier to make arrangements for the wedding feast—plantain leaves, vegetables, sugar and wheat had to be bought, a hundred other things had to be done before one could actually start cooking.

'Anna, there are eight long ladles, four pots, twelve brass pots, two lead vessels, three copper cauldrons and thirty four tumblers. Would you like to count them?'

'No, Soman. You keep track of them and load them in the cart on our return. There will be less confusion that way.'

Soman seemed pleased to have been given the responsibility. He wiped his face with his towel and tightened his tuft.

'Right. Hop into the cart and start. I will go to the market and get some tobacco and snacks and join you soon.'

'All right, Anna. I'll just fetch a palm leaf fan from the house.' Soman ran into the house.

Kitta Iyer knew that Soman had gone to take leave of his wife Alamelu. The elders claimed that the Sastras said it was not proper for husbands to take leave of their pregnant wives directly.

'Come quickly, Soman. It's getting late. Ramendran will be worried,' Kitta Iyer called.

'I'll be right back, Anna!'

Sometimes Kitta Iyer felt bad about making the sons-in-law of the family work for him, but they did not seem to mind. Working with Kitta Iyer's group, which was quite large and hired many assistants, travelling all over the region, and learning to make new sweets and savouries with every assignment, gave the sons-in-law valuable experience. In a couple of years they would be able to start their own catering services. Separate homes would have to be set up for Echumi and Alamelu.

That would probably have to be done anyway. The house was certainly getting overcrowded. The three brothers and their families lived downstairs and the two sisters and their families lived upstairs. Bhagavati, being unmarried, lived downstairs with her brothers.

At night, all the men slept on the terrace, while the women and children slept inside the house. There was an unwritten rule that each woman slept only in her allotted space. The reason was obvious—at night, after the children slept, the men would slip into the house and quietly wake up their wives and whisk them off, either to the storeroom near the kitchen or to the granary. It had to be really quick because one could never tell when one would be interrupted and by whom. Sometimes the delay caused in getting the sleep-dazed wife into the storeroom or granary, led to the ardent husband having a premature ejaculation and the whole exercise turned wasteful. 'It's okay. Go back now,' he would tell the wife and walk back to the terrace, disgusted with himself. Sometimes even as they were trying to wake their wives, their children would wake up instead and ask for something to eat. If Bhagavati or any of the other women were having their periods and had been banished to the courtyard, one would have to walk past them silently and make love so quietly that they would not hear. Sometimes, when the men went to the well in the backyard to clean themselves afterwards, they ran into each other's shadowy forms.

Once a rat ran across Kitta Iyer's bare backside as he lay over Snehambal in the store room. Another time, forgetting that his wife was having her periods and had been isolated in the backyard, Kitta Iyer went to her usual sleeping place, and by mistake, embraced Kamakshi Manni instead. The memory of that momentary embrace never left him. He had grown up on the assumption that your elder brother's wife was like your mother. His momentary lapse therefore seemed unpardonable. Now and then while trying to sleep in some strange place where he had gone to work, the memory would return to trouble him and he would get up and utter the *Gayatri mantra* a hundred and eight times to calm his mind.

His elder brother Duraisamy was as yet childless. His wife Kamakshi had had several miscarriages. Kitta Iyer's father-in-law, the astrologer, had suggested, during his last visit, after checking their future with his cowries that Duraisamy and his wife should go on a pilgrimage to Rameswaram. To thank him Duraisamy Iyer had given him a tray of betel leaves and nuts and four annas. The old man had, however, refused the money, taking only the betel leaves.

Kuppusamy's wife Visalakshi had borne him a daughter, but the child had died of small pox four years ago. The only children in the house at present were Kitta Iyer's two daughters.

The children were still asleep. He should start before they woke up or they would not let him go. The younger would weep; the elder would ask a thousand questions.

Kitta Iyer loved his daughters, but he didn't get to spend much time with them. He was away on work most of the time. He always brought back little gifts for them, particularly the boiled sweets they loved. Snehambal objected, saying the sweets were probably not prepared hygienically. 'Why should my daughters eat stuff prepared by some fellow who probably doesn't wash his hands after cleaning his arse, and come down with diarrhoea and vomiting?' she would complain.

To avoid such complaints, Kitta Iyer once brought back wooden dolls for them. Snehambal had looked around to ensure that there was no one with them and then, passing her hand over her breasts slowly, told him, 'If you keep touching and stroking them only once a month, they might forget they are alive and turn to wood like this doll's tits.'

Perhaps he should bring back a couple of gold bangles for her this time. Gold pleased a woman, not in the same way that sex did, but it gave her comfort nevertheless.

'Anna, shall we start?' Soman ran out of the house holding a palm leaf fan. Alamelu had apparently bitten his upper lip. It was red and he was soothing it by flicking his tongue over it. Kitta Iyer wondered if he too should go in and fetch a palm leaf fan. He decided against it—Snehambal had buck teeth.

Besides, the children might wake up and make a fuss. You had to be lucky in these things.

As they were leaving, Visalakshi Manni walked out of the house, her hair still wet from bathing, its ends tied in a knot. She was on her way to the temple. As she passed by them she smiled a small, quiet smile that was like a blessing that their trip would be successful.

'What a good omen, Anna,' Soman observed happily and set the cart rolling.

CHAPTER 8

The day moved slowly, according to the rhythms of the vegetables being sliced in the cutter, the slow swirling of the coconut oil heating in the frying pan, the boiling of the jaggery syrup in the cauldron, the steady grinding of the lentil dough being prepared for making vadais.

It was unbearably hot and humid. Since morning Kitta Iyer had bathed four times, pouring whole pots of cold water over his head to cool down, but it had made no difference. He felt completely drained, exhausted.

Never mind, he thought. The money would compensate for the discomfort. When the Kaimal family wedding was over, he would get a generous fee. There would be enough for him even after he paid everyone off. And then, of course, were the assignments in Punalur, Kollam and Karunagapalli.

Money was necessary. For gold bangles and boiled sweets. What about wooden dolls? No, he would not buy them. He wanted the real thing, to stroke and fondle and shudder in ecstasy and, as a result... a son. To have the space and privacy to do all this at leisure, money was needed.

He needed the money to get Bhagavati married and to celebrate the coming of age of his elder daughter, when the time came. Before he could blink, the younger one would also grow up and be ready for marriage. When all his responsibilities were over, he needed a small house with Mangalore tiles on the roof, a small patch of land, a garden with palm and areca nut trees. He also wanted a son. That had been his prayer since morning. Kitta Iyer poured another pot of water over his head. He loosened his tuft and washed his hair. As he was tying it again, he found a long strand of silver hair on his fingers. He paused, a little upset. Was he growing old? He was just thirty five. That was hardly old.

If Ayyappa, the presiding deity in the Kulathupuzha temple would bless him, surely he would have a son by the following year. A son to do the rites that would bring salvation to him and all his ancestors.

'Anna, why are you bathing every other minute?' Soman whispered as he walked up to him. 'It's time to put the rice on to cook.'

'Let's go,' Kitta Iyer agreed and started back, his wet veshti sticking to his body like a second skin.

'Anna, you have always said it is not auspicious to set the rice to cook while wearing wet clothes.'

'I know. I just couldn't bear the perspiration, Soman. Get me a towel.'

Soman brought back a towel and a dry veshti. Kitta Iyer dried himself, changed his clothes and entered the cooking tent erected in the garden, next to the regular kitchen. To his surprise, it was empty. 'Where has everyone gone?' he asked as he looked around the place, seeing only an elderly helper who was cutting a pumpkin. Just then Kitta Iyer noticed the commotion out front. There was the sound of heavy strides, as if people were running. There was a chorus of singing in deep, harsh voices.

When Kitta Iyer came out of the house to look, he saw ten or fifteen strange-looking ascetics running around carrying iron pestles. They sang and danced wildly together:

Dheere se bol

Zor se bol

Subha tak rat,

Viswanath!

They paused between the lines to hit themselves on their chests with the iron pestles. Their chests were scarred with hardened blisters. The long, dark-coloured pestles were frightening.

Who are these people? Kitta Iyer shot a questioning glance at Soman.

'They are Bairagi ascetics from the North. They have been to Rameswaram and are now on a pilgrimage in the land of Parasurama.'

Even as Soman was speaking, one of the Bairagis drew close to Kitta Iyer, rolled his eyes at him and laughed loudly. Little wasps buzzed around his matted hair. He was over six feet tall and next to the short Kitta Iyer, he looked like a giant.

The Bairagi ran past them, singing and slamming the pestle against his chest. To the scared Kitta Iyer, it seemed as if he would grab him any moment, slam him against his thigh, throw him high up in the air, play with him as if he were a wooden doll. He might hurl him to the ground and stomp so hard on his penis and balls that they would be squashed and Kitta Iyer could never ever hope to have a son. Kitta Iyer hugged his arms to his middle and stood there shivering with fear.

The Bairagi came close again, hit the pestle against his own abdomen and said something gravely in Hindustani. Somanathan translated, the Bairagi was hungry. Soman was acquainted with the language as he had accompanied a group of Nambudiris, as their cook, on a pilgrimage to Dwaraka and Mathura.

How did the Bairagi know he was a cook, wondered Kitta Iyer. What could Kitta Iyer give him? He was on assignment in Kaimal's house. There was nothing here that was his to give. The Bairagis would probably eat what four ordinary men ate, follow it up if still hungry with the pestle and digest everything with a pot of ginger water.

The Bairagi planted the pestle between his legs like an extended penis and continued to speak. The other ascetics continued to chant loudly, 'Viswanath! Viswanath!' The wasps flew out from their matted locks and fell to the earth and, having shed their wings. In the still quiet of the morning, Kitta Iyer thought he could hear the sound of the wasp wings falling off.

Would the Bairagis eat rice? Would they have the patience to wait until the rice cooked? If they did, perhaps he could ask Kaimal to offer them food in a separate enclosure and invite them to eat before the other guests. It would be good for the young couple to be married with the blessings of these ascetics who cared nothing for the comforts of this world. Kitta Iyer wondered if they would wait until the rice cooked. But Soman said, 'Anna, these people will not eat food cooked by anyone else. All they need is rice or wheat flour. They will retire to a quiet place outside the village and make their own food.'

Kitta Iyer hastily made his way to the makeshift store room and kitchen to get the provisions. The old man he had seen earlier was still cutting vegetables. He seemed to be shaken by a wracking cough. Kitta Iyer frowned and called out to him, 'Why don't you have a drink of hot water and rest for a while before getting back to work?'

The old man was one of the helpers they had recruited from the local Brahmins. Such helpers would be fed three times a day and given betel leaves and nuts and when the wedding was over, they would be given a few small coins. Kitta Iyer had to walk by him to reach the sacks of rice and wheat flour. As he began measuring wheat flour into a large cloth bag, Kitta Iyer suddenly paused and stared at the old man. He thought he had seen him before.

'Hey, aren't you from the other community in Savakkadu?' he yelled.

The old man stood up trembling. His cough became worse. 'I am also a Brahmin, Anna. Please have pity on me. I will do a few odd jobs. It is enough if you feed me. I can't bear the hunger.'

He held his sacred thread between his fingers and desperately prostrated before Kitta Iyer.

Kitta Iyer knew that the old man was a Christian. He and his brothers knew all about the Brahmins of Savakkadu who had converted to Christianity, after being brainwashed by a white man in long robes, who had descended from a ship to tell them that he had brought them news of the real Vedas. His name was Thomas and strange tales were narrated about him. It was said that when the Saivite Brahmins of Savakkadu were sprinkling ritualistic water, he made the drops of water hover without falling to the ground, to prove the superior power of his mantras. The Brahmins went with him, saying, 'You are the sun of knowledge. You are the origin of the Vedas. You are our guru.' They became Christians but did not cast off their sacred threads.

But the community of Brahmins would have nothing more to do with them. They were isolated, and had remained that way for many generations.

'What matters it that we belong to a different way? Are we not of the same clan?' the old man reasoned desperately. 'We still wear the sacred thread. We do not eat meat. We too meditate only on the vision of the ultimate as pure light. There are those among us who too are landlords, clerks and accountants, music teachers, interpreters and such, just like other Brahmins. Of course, there are others like me who have fallen on bad times and are impoverished. When I went to the Padmanabha Swamy temple to see if I could get fed on the offerings to the deity, I swear I prayed only to that deity. But someone identified me as a Savakkadu man and they chased me and broke my leg. Why, I have even enlisted as a helper with your father's group…' the old man's words poured out miserably, between fits of coughing. His eyes continued to plead with Kitta Iyer.

Kitta Iyer was not willing to show mercy. 'Oh, don't I know that? I even know that my father's friend Sivaraman beat you up so badly that you ran for your life—that was in Tirunelveli, wasn't it? Thirty years ago, that was. Do you remember?'

'Master, your father was a saint, Sivarama Iyer too. My time was bad, it always has been. What can I do? Is it my fault that I was born in Savakkadu?' The old man was shaken by a fit of coughing.

'Don't give me these stories. You are bad enough as you are, and you have a disease.'

The old man clapped a hand over his mouth in an effort to stop the coughing and stood up. 'Ayyo! This is a dry cough, Anna, nothing catching. Hunger is my only disease. I will be your slave, Anna. It is enough if you feed me just once a day. Even if you throw the food to me like you throw rice for the dead, I will be happy and bless you, holding my sacred thread.'

'Why does a man belonging to another religion need a sacred thread? Why do you pose as a Brahmin, you thieving dog?' Kitta Iyer stepped forward and tugged at the old man's sacred thread so that it snapped, and slithering down across his thin, heaving chest, fell to the floor.

Dheere se bol,

Zor se bol.

The Bairagis had entered the kitchen tent.

Somehow that made Kitta Iyer even more aggressive about getting rid of the old man. 'Edo, old man, leave before I beat you to a pulp. Only Brahmins can do this job. Otherwise the ancestors who come down for the auspicious occasion, will curse us all.'

'Anna, I am dying of hunger. I tell you, I am also a Brahmin. Only my holy book is different. What does that matter?'

'What does that matter?' an angry Kitta Iyer repeated. 'The Brahmins who went after that Thomas are all dead and gone. You are a Christian!'

'All right. I am a Christian Brahmin. An orphan and a destitute. I am hungry and am begging you for your mercy.'

'You impudent rascal, how dare you go on saying the same thing? Run away, you worm ridden old man, or I will beat you up!'

Kitta Iyer pushed the old man with such force that he fell against the grinding stone on which the ground pepper still lay in a mound. Blood appeared in a thin line on his forehead.

The Bairagis stopped as one, and folded their hands in supplication to the old man. Then they turned and walked away, empty handed.

'Wait!' exclaimed Kitta Iyer. 'Take this rice, wheat flour and jaggery. It is for you.'

But they did not look back.

Dheer se bol

Jhor se bol!

Above their chanting and Kitta Iyer's exclamations came the sound of the old man's plaintive weeping. Kitta Iyer went blind with rage and kicked the old man in the stomach with all his might, and dragged him and threw him out.

In the distance the Bairagis were raising a small storm of dust as they ran, beating their breasts with their pestles.

A wasp flew from them towards Kitta Iyer and settled on his thigh. It moved upwards into his veshti and loin cloth and stung him viciously on the tip of his penis.

From the distance, one of the Bairagis looked back and yelled, 'Your entire line will become Christian!'

'Soman, what is the Bairagi saying?' Kitta Iyer asked, through his terrible haze of pain, clutching his throbbing, swelling member. 'Did he curse me?'

'I didn't hear it clearly, Anna,' Soman replied, looking after the tottering old man, limping away from them. He had heard the Bairagi's every word.

CHAPTER 9

The king had walked to the large pavilion outside the palace before he realised that he wasn't wearing his sandals.

'Who's there?' he called.

He knew that there was no one within hearing distance, other than the maid who was fanning the queen. He knew her name—Muthamma—but it seemed undignified for a king to call a maid by her name.

Muthamma walked towards him slowly, lethargically. Even discourteously maybe, the king thought, but he couldn't expect his underpaid servants to run to do his bidding. He was quick to forgive Muthamma—after all, she never displayed the sullen temper or listlessness of the menopausal queen in sexual matters. A lot happened when the queen took her afternoon nap, as she did today. The king's attentions allowed Muthamma to fantasise that she was the queen. The ardent king sometimes pressed her feet while she fell asleep on the long swing in the hall.

'So what do you want?' she asked, drawing close and gently tugging at the ends of the king's moustache. If he pulled her on to his lap, then maybe afterwards she could order him to press her feet till she dozed off.

But the king was not to be tempted. He said sternly, 'Where the devil are my sandals, girl? Don't you know that it is not seemly for a king to walk barefoot to meet his visitors?'

The girl, clearly disappointed, walked back muttering to herself. While he waited for her to return with his sandals, the king sat on a wooden plank, leaning against the wall. Plaster was coming off the walls in great patches. He had sent for the palace mason ten days ago but he hadn't turned up yet. The palace was slowly disintegrating.

The masons would have been there in a flash if there was money. Then again, if he had the money, why would he renovate this old pile? He would have torn it down and built a brand new palace with giant pillars to support the ceiling, and an enclosed bathing pool for the queen, so that she need not worry about prying eyes.

Nadi and Angamuthu, the palace masons, were quick to grasp new ideas. But a mason had to be paid at least a rupee and a half every week, less than half that for the chief helper and a quarter of that for the second helper. If they could not be paid in cash entirely, they would accept half the wages in cash and the rest in paddy, but there wasn't enough paddy in the palace to feed the inmates. The palace manager had brought dismal news last week from his inspection of the king's agricultural land: there would be practically no harvest this year as the rains had failed.

Money troubles plagued him—and now the Banian Brothers here to see him. What did they want? Then the king remembered that it was he who had commanded them to appear at the palace.

The king checked to see if the rock salt he kept tied in a little knot at the waist of his veshti was in place. It was a talisman against the Banian Brothers' psychic powers. He'd discovered the rock salt's properties by accident. The last time the Banian Brothers had visited him, the king had been about to eat his millet porridge and discovered that the cook had forgotten to add salt to it. With oaths and curses, the cook was commanded to fetch the salt. When he finally returned with it, the king picked up a pinch of rock salt, with more threats and curses, only to realise that the porridge was cold. He told the cook to take away the porridge, reheat it and bring it back. The man grumbled and went back in, carrying the pot of porridge in one hand and the salt jar in the other.

The king heard the Banian Brothers call from the entrance. Tucking the pinch of salt in his hand into a little knot at the waist of his veshti, just beneath his formidable paunch, he went out to meet the Brothers. Strangely enough, the Brothers were hardly able to read his mind, as they usually, and annoyingly, did. They merely suggested that the king plaster the peeling wall above the entrance. The king agreed that it had to be done, and if he had the money, he would rebuild the entire palace with pillars as smooth and big as those in the palace at Madurai. When he thought of the pillars, the king was reminded of the thighs of his first lover, Shenbagavalli. Usually, when such erotic thoughts crossed his mind, the Banian Brothers also seemed to catch it and give him knowing smiles. But that day they had remained oblivious to his memory of Shenbagavalli. The king decided that it was the salt that was protecting him from the Banian Brothers.

They continued to talk about the king's new palace. The cook brought the reheated porridge in twice and was ignored both times. He retired to the kitchen and went to sleep. Meanwhile, the king and the Brothers spoke about the large, well-ventilated rooms the new palace would have. There would be a large courtyard in the centre where the king would hold performances. He would hold wrestling matches there as well as dance performances by nude white women, he would arrange music concerts for pipers and veena players, he would also get the unusual performers from Persia who could make music from their controlled farting. He would get erotic poets to read their verses not only to titillate but also to initiate discussions about matters sexual. The Brothers laughed slyly at this. Whereupon the king, speaking expansively because he was sure they had not read his mind, asked them, 'Tell me about the comforts that houses in your time provide. I could incorporate them in the design of the new palace.'

The Brothers suggested lavatories adjoining the bedrooms. The king was taken aback at this obscene suggestion and promptly vetoed it, saying that just because an idea came from the future, it was not necessarily good or hygienic.

The Brothers had not returned since that day. The king wondered why. Would they talk about the plan to take him to the Malayalam shore? The king had reservations about the whole idea now. Perhaps, as he stood mesmerised by the bounteous breasts of the women there, these two would creep up on him from behind, strangle him and run away with his jewellery. The king looked at his strong shoulders. These fellows were weaklings—he could tackle them if they tried anything funny. Nevertheless he decided not to talk to them about the trip to the Malayalam shore. Instead, he could discuss setting up a more private bathing space for the queen. He was not worried about the Brothers reading his thoughts on the queen's large breasts and her decreasing sexual attraction as he was protected by his pinch of rock salt.

Where were his sandals? 'How long will you take to bring my footwear?' he scolded the maid and gave her a love bite when she turned up with his sandals.

'If you keep biting me like this wherever and whenever you fancy, I'm going to tell the queen!' she complained. 'This month, you haven't paid either my salary or my daily allowance.'

The king took a silver coin from his pocket and tossed it into the maid's cleavage. She drew quickly near and kissed him on his lips, her breath smelling of the dried fish curry she had eaten. Then she ran back to continue fanning the queen.

The king wiped his lips and walked out to the pavilion in front where the Banian Brothers were waiting for him. When they saw him, they stood up and greeted him with folded hands. The elder handed him a lemon. The king hesitated, but the Brothers said, 'Sir, this is a token of our respect. Please accept it.'

When the king lifted the lemon to his nose to smell it, he thought of his ancestors. He felt some of them would enter the lemon and begin telling him things. It was so quiet here at this time of the day that even the ancestors might nap to escape the afternoon heat, but they would definitely comment on the Brothers' visit, if not now, later. They would be angry, but he would have to find ways to placate them.

He asked the Brothers to sit down, and took care to seat himself on a higher one. The elder Brother brought out an intricately carved black box containing the lac discs that played dirge music on the tobacco merchant's music box. The king asked them, 'Did you bring these for the boys who live next door?'

The Banian Brothers smiled meaningfully.

CHAPTER 10

The king could guess what the black trunk contained—those black, shellac music discs, which made such heart-rending, unbearably sweet music once they had been placed on the gramophone with its mushroom-shaped speaker, and the handle had been fully cranked.

The king knew he could only gaze on these discs, never possess them. He would have to yearn for them to be played on his neighbour's music box, just as the young men next door probably yearned for the sight of the queen bathing in her tank.

They had so much money, those young men, enough to buy so many records from the Banian Brothers. They could listen to music day and night, while they were cleaning their teeth, eating, sleeping or even while they were peeping at the bathing queen.

The queen was nothing to men of their means. They could get more voluptuous women to gaze at from close quarters, or even cohabit with—all this, while listening to the music or as a prelude to the music.

The king laughed self-pityingly as he said to the Brothers, 'There are music discs in there, right? I'll see them later. They are about as much use to me as a breast cloth to a eunuch.'

'Why do you say that?' the Brothers retorted. 'If you wish, Your Highness can buy thousands of music discs and breast cloths. You are too hesitant to spend money!' The taller of the Brothers took back the lemon from the king as he spoke. This practice the Brothers had of handing a lemon or a garland to a person of higher social status and taking it back from him after a while, fascinated the king by its sheer meaninglessness. No doubt it was a mysterious custom from the future.

The Brothers tried opening the trunk to show the king its contents but the lock would not give. After a couple of unsuccessful tries, the shorter of the Brothers picked up a dagger from the many swords on display on a wall nearby and prised open the lock.

The ancestors would not be pleased with the irreverence shown to the palace weaponry, the king thought. 'Is it seemly that some fellow on the street should use the dagger that we put down rebels and enemies with, to hack open the rusted lock of a stupid trunk?' they would chide him. 'And if that rogue does not have better sense, should you not stop him? Where are your brains? Curled up in your balls? If only you had something more productive there, you would have produced an heir by now.' The king was sure they would scold him thus tomorrow when he sat down for his morning worship, or the next day, which was the day of the new moon. Well they might not, as the priest had left the palace in disgust over their behaviour the last time, and might not come to perform the ceremony for the dead on the new moon day which, in turn, meant that the ancestors could not descend to earth.

The elder of the Brothers took the music discs out of the trunk and held them out to the king. He took one, brought it close to his nose and drew a deep breath. The disc had the sweet smell of death about it. How wonderful that they had been able to capture the heart-wringing sadness of death in the grooves on the disc. If only he could squeeze himself into those grooves.

The king returned the discs to the elder of the Brothers reluctantly, wondering when he would ever get to hear the music in it. His gaze, beggarly and yearning, turned involuntarily towards the neighbouring house.

The shorter of the Brothers placed a heavy book in the king's hands. The king knew about books—that they were printed in the land of the white men, in their language, that most of them were about the science, mathematics, philosophy and literature of that land.

Ever since the Sarkar came to this land, they insisted on the palace accounts being written on the bundles of paper supplied by them rather than on palm leaves, as used to be done earlier. The practice had apparently caught on with the general public too. On his visits to the market place, the king had seen shopkeepers write their accounts in note books of bound paper.

The king also knew that the white people put paper to another use—they wiped their soiled bottoms with it. The Brothers had informed him that the English nobles spent all their time reading printed matter, unless they were in the pleasant company of their ladies. It seemed only right that while the ladies were busy wiping their bottoms with paper, their men spent their time reading printed paper.

The king himself had no great use for paper. He could not read the white man's language. As for accounts, his manager looked after that. The king used a pot of water to clean his behind. What did he need paper for? These books would better serve the young men in the wealthy tobacco merchant's house. The king handed the book back, unopened. The taller Brother opened it at a particular page and returned it to him. Curiosity made the king look at the images. He held his breath—these were pictures of men and women having sex in a variety of postures. So many white women… in their midst was a nude man with vacant eyes and long hair covering most of his face. The king could not tell whether he was Indian or a foreigner. These women… perhaps, after wiping their bottoms with paper, they would bathe thoroughly, wear perfume and then engage in sexual play. The king turned the pages to see if he could spot a music box playing by the side of the naked bodies. He could not find one. Instead there was picture after picture of white women enjoying sexual pleasure.

'Please keep it and look at it in leisure. We will take it back next time we visit you. This sort of book is very much in demand in your neighbour's house!'

The king shook his head and returned the book. If the queen ever caught him with it, he would be humiliated. If the ancestors saw it, their ire would probably burn the book. The king did have a couple of questions regarding the book for the Brothers, though. How could the artist paint such pictures and why were they all in black and white? The brothers laughed.

'These pictures were not painted or drawn,' they said. The shorter of the Brothers removed a tripod from the trunk and then another contraption that looked like a lamp and fixed it on the tripod.

'Does this make music too?' the king asked.

'No. It takes pictures.'

'What do you mean, 'take pictures'?'

'It will capture your image, just as you are now, seated here.'

'If I call the palace artist, he will mix a few paints, smear them all over a canvas and make me believe it is my likeness. Why do you need a machine for that?' The king's tone was dismissive.

'This is different. This will picture reality. If you agree, it will record your picture as you are now, in five minutes!'

The king looked at the contraption uncomprehendingly. What were these rogues saying—that he and the queen should do all the things the white men and women were doing in this book and the Brothers would capture the scenes in this machine? He instinctively touched the rock salt tied in his veshti, wondering what his erstwhile lover, Shenbagavalli, would have looked like, in the pictures made by this machine. She had died of old age seven or eight years ago. The king picked up the small dagger that lay on the ground beside the trunk. It turned in his hand and drew a line of blood on his skin. The ancestors were here.

'When we were at your age, our minds were engaged in pious thoughts and plans to improve the lot of our citizens. You spend your time listening to dirges, and contemplating sex or massaging the feet of the maid. Now you have this decadent book.' The dagger squirmed in the king's grasp as the ancestors continued to scold him. The king wiped his hand on his veshti and handed the book back to the Banian Brothers. 'Put away that picture making box as well,' he instructed them. 'And that tripod.'

The brothers took it well. 'It's all right,' they said soothingly to the king. 'We just wanted to show it to you and chat about the new palace you might be building. Then there is your trip to the Malayalam coast. If you do not wish to travel by car, we can take you by another vehicle: a smoke-belching carriage called a train. It will be very comfortable to travel in. The Sarkar are planning to introduce it here in a few years.' The Brothers stood respectfully as they said all this. The king thought wryly, 'It would be better if they could bring along the silver and gold money that the Sarkar have introduced as well! But then these rogues will probably do that nevertheless —they'll mint coins of copper, coat them gold or silver and pass them off as genuine!'

The king slipped the dagger into its sheath and replaced it on the wall. A shield slipped off its hook on the wall and rolled, clattering to the floor. The Banian brothers observed in subdued tones, 'This is not a suitable time, we see. We'll come back on another day.'

The king removed two silver coins from the knot in his veshti and handed them to the Brothers. They bowed low before taking the coins. They brought back two bottles of foreign liquor from their vehicle that stood at the gate and gave them to the king.

There was a clamour from the ancestors. 'Is it not the new moon the day after tomorrow?' they enquired eagerly. 'Won't you offer this to us then?'

The king wondered how the priest could possibly send liquor to the ancestors. Besides, he had no idea whether the priest would turn up at all.

Just then the queen, fresh from her afternoon nap, sauntered out into the hall, asking, 'Has it never occurred to you that you could use those two rogues to burn down our neighbour's house?'

CHAPTER 11

It was well past noon when old Subbamma climbed the stairs, carrying a silver bowl in one hand and a small pot of hot cumin seed water in the other.

She noticed that the door to Swaminathan's door was ajar. It saved her the trouble of setting down her bowls, knocking on his door and waiting for it to open. The smell of the hot, soft rice in the tumbler would attract the crows from the terrace. They would hop over and ask her in their own language, 'Give us some, old woman.' And she would reply, 'Only if there is any left over after the child has eaten.'

They would cackle loudly and fly out screeching, 'You call him a child who was trying to fuck a woman who was four generations his ancestor? Watch out, Subbamma. Keep a tight hold on your own sari!'

'Go to hell!' Subbamma would curse them, but not in her own voice. By then the ancestors would have entered her voice and altered it to resemble their own. They would also grab hold of her hands and legs and try to pull her back. 'Don't go in there, Subbamma,' they would cry.

Despite all this Subbamma liked going upstairs because it was the only part of the house where she could nap undisturbed. As she entered Swaminathan's room, his voice greeted her with a simple question. 'Have they all gone?'

'Who are you referring to—our neighbours or visitors from other villages?'

'I asked you if they have all left,' his voice sounded stronger now, angrier.

Subbamma could not tell where his voice came from. She was distracted by the soft, sad music playing in the background. It was at once comforting and fearful, not the sort of dirge women should listen to.

'I did not ask about the women from the neighbourhood. I know that they would have stuffed themselves and taken snacks home for their children. Let them go in peace and make more children. They have the blessings of Sage Swaminathan, they have the blessings of the whoring Swaminathan.' He began to laugh loudly. He coughed and laughed again. Then he continued, 'My respects to the women who have visited us from above. They are the ones I fear. Pretty angels, don't torture me. Instead piss and shit in this old woman's mouth and amuse yourselves!' His laughter now became a high cackle. Subbamma could sense that he was somewhere close to her, watching her, perhaps fearfully.

Subbamma chuckled a little as she said, 'All those who came from above have left.' She wished she could set the vessels in her hands down somewhere.

'You are lying, old whore! I know that they are standing there behind you just outside the door. I know it!' Swaminathan laughed his frightened laugh again.

'Let them stand, then. Why are you worried? Don't call your grandmother a whore, child. Some evil spirit has climbed on to your tongue. These are not the kind of words you would ever use.' Subbamma's anguished voice travelled vaguely in his direction in the dark. It was the same every time. He would curse and abuse her and then calm down and call her patti and say affectionate words. It seemed that despite his chaotic mind, he never forgot the love with which she had reared him.

'Don't want an evil spirit on my tongue as well! I have enough trouble with the one who comes to me during the day and forces me to fuck her endlessly and in every possible way. Spare me the pleasure of having another rub her behind on my tongue!' he said and laughed again but this time the laughter was lighter.

'Saama, your mother told me that you have not eaten for the last two days. Why? Your health will suffer if you starve.'

She had been upset when Swaminathan's mother, Kalyani had told her that he had not eaten for two days. So many people came to this house to eat feasts. Yet the eldest son of the family had been starving. Subbamma mashed some hot rice and rasam and took it up to her Saama.

Saama's room was the only place in the house that the spirits of the female ancestors, who haunted her at all times, did not enter. They drove her crazy trying to fulfil their own urges and wishes through her. Sometimes they made her menstruate all over again, imagine, an old woman like her. And she had to wash the bloodied cloths surreptitiously. Sometimes they would force her to smear kohl on her eyes like a young woman, lift her sagging breasts and wiggle her buttocks as she walked. When she was with other people they only expressed themselves in harmless songs. But when she was alone with them they drove her insane with their demands on her body. But they were frightened of Saama's room. They would try their best to pull her back, and after she had gone in they would hover outside, wringing their hands. Subbamma did not care. She needed somewhere quiet to sleep a little. And Saama would never hurt her. Of that she was sure.

Subbamma's eyes had got used to the dark and she could see the gramophone with its huge, brass speaker, shaped like an open mushroom. Next to the gramophone was a cot, and on it lay Swaminathan. He was thin to the point of emaciation, his ribs protruding pitifully. Around his middle was a single piece of cloth. His hair and beard were wildly overgrown. He gestured vaguely for Subbamma to sit.

Did those who visited him from three or four hundred years later in time, also have to hold conversations with him in this dank, dark atmosphere? As if he could read her mind, Swaminathan laughed. 'When they come the place becomes clean and well-lit on its own,' he told her. Subbamma nodded as if she understood.

'Eat, child,' she told him, 'I have mashed the rice with fragrant ghee and hot rasam. Eat it Saama. It is very good.'

'Why do I need ghee, patti? When we go to Guruvayur to feed my baby rice and ghee, I will have a little then.' Saama had obviously begun to hallucinate again. Subbamma knew how this would end—Saama would start weeping after a while and ignore the food. Desperate to make him eat, Subbamma urged him, 'Saama, stop thinking about the past. I believe you have some new kind of music? Why don't you play it for me? I am so old and tired. Can I rest here awhile?'

'Of course, patti! Stay here by all means. Look, this is the music they play in Abyssinia during their death ceremonies!' Saama picked up a record and brought it to her, eager and enthusiastic. Subbamma slipped a handful of rice into his mouth. As he chewed, she wondered what Abyssinia was.

A breeze entered the room. Swaminathan seemed not to notice. 'Patti, did you know that the earliest men had a simple way to deal with the dead? They ate them—end of problem. In some parts of the Malayalam coast, they buried the dead in the garden and planted a jackfruit tree over the grave. Later, when the tree bore fruit, they would sit down as a family and eat the soft flesh of the fruit, a ritual that came from the earlier one of eating the flesh of the dead. All this is written in my English books. Shall I read it to you?'

'What do I need all this information for?' Subbamma replied, noticing that Swaminathan had eaten all the rice in the bowl. 'I'll be happy if you are in good health and eat and dress well. Here, drink a little water. Then lie down and sleep. How cool this breeze is!'

She lay down on the floor and was asleep in minutes. She dreamt of a drought-ridden village with a ruined temple. A young boy and girl had taken refuge in the temple. They looked as if they had been starving for days. Bats flew by their faces. The girl, who looked no more than fifteen, nodded at the bats and said, 'If we had been meat eaters we could have eaten these.' The boy, who looked a few years older, replied, 'Even meat eaters will eat only birds, not bats.'

'Well, all those who have fled the village obviously could not get even bats!' the girl retorted.

Perhaps he was her elder brother. He looked at home in the temple, as if he conducted the worship there. He lit a torch and held it close to the idols of the deities. 'Take a good look at them for who knows when we will return here?' He began to sob. The girl too began to weep. 'Both Amma and Anna have gone. Perhaps it is time we left too.' A bat, flying close to her head, lost its balance as the light from the torch hit it, and crashed down dead on her lap. The girl lifted it without any revulsion and flung it away. Falling to the dry and cracked earth, the bat suddenly opened its wings wide and, baring its fangs, dove straight at Subbamma's chest.

Subbamma could feel the bat stroke her breasts. Her breasts rose, youthful and firm, her legs parted and her vagina spread wide. The bat slithered downwards, past her waist.

'Subbamma, it's me. I have had enough of being a Gosai. I am here. What is this? Why are you moist?'

'Those ancestors—they're making me bleed again.'

'I'll make them stop it. I'll get rid of all of them. Lie down now. Shall I loosen your clothes? Do you feel the cool breeze?'

Subbamma squirmed and rolled on the floor, crying, 'No! No!'

Suddenly the young girl, sitting on the temple steps, stood up, and walking over to Subbamma, stamped hard on her vagina. 'Stupid hag! Why are you lying here with your legs spread out? Saama and I need to play. Get out of here, bitch!'

Subbamma vaguely saw Swaminathan standing there completely naked. At a glance, he resembled Subbamma's long lost husband. Was it him? What, then, was the bat, slithering and burrowing into her waist?

The ancestors began screaming from outside the room. 'Subbamma, run out! The priest's daughter has become a demon. And look at his member—it's rising and stiffening. In a little while the smell of intercourse is going to fill this space and choke you. Throw that bat away and run out. We'll teach you new songs!' they cried desperately.

CHAPTER 12

Kalyani screamed when she saw old Subbamma.

'Aunt Subbamma, what happened to you?' she cried, running to the old woman as she tottered down the stairs and collapsed near the storeroom. Kalyani's scream woke the entire household from its post-lunch somnolence.

Subbamma was trembling and piteously begging unseen forces around her to let her be, please, please...

Subramanya Iyer asked if Saama had turned violent. He thought Saama's condition was getting worse—formerly he turned violent only on full moon days but now it seemed to occur at any time. He needed to be taken to the temples in Kerala where they cured the demented. He needed to be taken to the Nambudiri doctors in Chottanikkara who would set him right in two or three months with their oils and decoctions. The family from

Ambalapuzha who had come to seek an alliance for their daughter with Sankaran had told him this. But who would take Swaminathan there? He was too old. Sankaran was too busy. Iyer had been considering sending old Subbamma and the servant Ayyanai with Swaminathan.

But now Subbamma was in this state. What had Saama done to her? Did he slam her head against the wall? Why was her hair standing on end? Did he kick her in her stomach? Was that why she was holding on to her abdomen below her waist and sobbing? A terrible thought occurred to Iyer. Had Saama…?

No, no, Saama was not like that, except on that one abnormal occasion. Good god, it was a sin to think of Saama like this. Saama was a Vedic scholar, an evolved soul—surely all his learning, his intelligence would save him from sinking to depravity?

Then Subbamma spoke. 'Saama didn't hurt me in any way. He is my child. I fed him some rice. He drank a few sips of water and went to sleep quietly. And then I also lay down to nap…'

Suddenly Subbamma screamed. When she spoke, her voice had changed entirely. 'My husband and I will stay only here,' she declared harshly. 'Who cares about old and young or that we belong to different generations? He is a man and I am his woman. Enough of suffering the drought and falling into empty wells to die. We have no intention of going anywhere else. Our life is here. We have got used to eating flesh. I care as much for the drought as for the hair on my…'

Subramanya Iyer turned away in embarrassment. But Subbamma would not stop. 'Bring me roasted birds to eat. If you can get bats, that is even better. After we have eaten, Saama will touch me here and I will spread…'

Subramanya Iyer ran. Kalyani quickly prised Subbamma's fingers from the sari at her waist and set her clothes right. One of the guests who had stayed back after the function because she had had her period early came running with a small pot of Ganges water to sprinkle on Subbamma as she observed the staining of the old woman's sari. 'What sort of a curse is this? Aunt Subbamma is menstruating again!'

Subramanya Iyer heard all of this from the next room with mounting horror. Had the spirit of that ancestral woman who had cohabited with Saama in broad daylight, returned? After all those expensive rituals to drive her off to her next birth? When she had left, she had seemed so content and had blessed Saama with the ability to learn any foreign language he desired and to converse with scholars of the future on matters of great importance. On moonlit nights, he had stood quietly at the door of Saama's room and heard him lecture his unseen guests on matters of such seriousness that his heart had filled with pride. If the Englishmen could have heard Saama they would have whisked him away on their ships to London to impart his knowledge to them. But poor Saama was not lucky enough for that recognition. And now, after all this time, had that female spirit returned to harass him? Who was she? Did she belong to this family or was she an outsider? How could she be expelled again? Should we plead with the spirits of the female ancestors through old Subbamma to intercede with that wicked woman on their behalf? But Subbamma herself seemed now to be under her influence. As a muddled Subramanya Iyer walked out, he could hear Subbamma begin singing, in her normal voice. Obviously the wicked spirit that had descended on her had left. Subramanya Iyer prayed silently and devoutly to all his female ancestors to protect Subbamma from the influence of evil spirits.

Subbamma sang in her normal voice but she sang about a man and woman copulating in broad daylight with all the doors to their room open. Kalyani was trying to divert her by saying 'Aunt, sing devotional songs, not songs like this. Come, let us go to the backyard.' She tugged gently at Subbamma's hand to raise her to her feet. But Subbamma resisted her, saying, 'I will not go to the pollution room[1] at the back. I will sit here and sing you pretty songs!'

Kalyani tugged at her hand more forcefully, ordering someone at the same time to bring some cow dung and clean the place where Subbamma had sat. Finally the old woman gave in and went with Kalyani, laughing all the way to the backyard.

Subramanya Iyer tightened his veshti around his waist and walked out of his house. He did not normally step out dressed like this, in a four-yard veshti, with a towel thrown around his shoulders. He usually wore an eight-yard veshti in the panchakaccham style and a crisp white upper cloth, fringed with gold lace. If he needed to meet someone important, he wore a turban and sandals. But he was in no mood to worry about his sartorial inadequacy now. It didn't really matter what he wore in this village where everyone knew him and how wealthy he was. No one would stare at him even if he walked around in his loin cloth. When your wealth covers you like an unseen robe, there is no need for anything else.

As he walked, he glanced at the palace that spread across half the street. It was dilapidated and housed a thoroughly useless zamindar. The fellow must be the same age as Iyer. He remembered the zamindar being carried like a corpse on a bier by his palanquin bearers because the idiot had dropped off to sleep in the middle of the procession last month. Just thinking about it made Iyer want to laugh.

After the Sarkar took over the administration all the chieftains and landlords had lost their power. But this man's condition was even worse, as his family had become insolvent two generations ago. Now he had to depend on the pension from the Sarkar for his every need. Not a soul in the village had any regard for him. Iyer was quite prepared to pay him handsomely both in cash and tobacco if he let him use the palace for storing his tobacco but the man wouldn't oblige. Iyer's own house had no more storage space. He had another house in the village that he had given for the running of a Vedic school. Taking it back to store tobacco might attract censure from his ancestors. What with that evil woman returning to haunt Saama and Subbamma, he needed all the help his ancestors could give him. It would not be wise to offend them.

Iyer's thoughts turned towards other business matters. Last week Sankaran had expressed a desire to travel to Madras to begin negotiations to trade in snuff. Pichai Rowther, a close business associate of Iyer, had brought him some of that powdered and processed tobacco that, he said, was such a rage in London, and asked him to try it out. Iyer had inhaled a pinch of snuff, was overcome with sneezes and had to blow his nose on his upper cloth thereby staining it a distasteful brown. 'Dost, when you get used to it, a pinch of it can zoom you to heaven, you will be in the company of angels and djinns!' Rowther enthused. Iyer felt no such enthusiasm for snuff, but what did that matter? If this powder was going to make him more money, he was willing to sell it to all those halfwits here who wanted to ape the white man's habits. Perhaps Sankaran should go to Madras the next week.

There was also the matter of Sankaran's marriage. The horoscopes matched perfectly. As a token of the auspicious event to follow, the propitiation of the ancestors had been held today. The bride's family was keen to hold the wedding the coming month. Perhaps Sankaran should leave for Madras only after the wedding. If the trading in snuff began, he would need more space to store the stuff. It would be nice if the zamindar let him use the palace. But the fellow was hardly likely to allow that, whatever royal blood was left in his veins made him a snob.

If old Subbamma continued to stay in his house (and that would be a very good thing because she could look after Swaminathan), Iyer could perhaps use her own house in the village to store the tobacco and snuff... As he mulled over these issues and reached his shop, in his home, he imagined with discomfort his wife Kalyani demanding angrily of no one in particular, 'Did my father give me in marriage to this family only to wash old women's menstrual cloths?'

CHAPTER 13

In Ambalapuzha, Kuppusamy Iyer was returning home. It was mid afternoon. His body felt scorched, from both the sun's heat and the accumulated heat of one month of cooking on giant stoves.

It had not been easy, this tour. It had been difficult to find assistants, those who did not dip into the sacks of cashewnuts and put handfuls into their mouths. The young men who came to work with him had a flippant attitude towards everything. If you gave one of them a yam to cut, he would cup it in his hand and stroke it, as if it were a breast, giggling all the while. If you asked one to peel a coconut, he would stand suggestively smashing the coconut on the upright, sharp, iron rod of the peeler, while his audience guffawed and passed lewd comments.

Pleased to see a bunch of men cooking, the women of the family that hired him would walk in, inspect the food and give advice. His young male assistants would be distracted by the teenaged girls who walked in with their mothers or aunts.

Kuppusamy ran a hand over his jaw, feeling the roughness of the four-day-old stubble. He needed to go to the barber, Velayudam, to get a shave and all the village news.

He would have time to relax over the next two months as there would not be too many weddings. He looked forward to the prospect of home-cooked food. Most of his work this last month had been for Nambudiri Brahmin families, who, until lately, had considered Tamil Brahmins not good enough to cook for them. But Nambudiri cooks were hard to find, so Tamil Brahmin cooks were being hired, but they were not treated well. The Nambudiris paid badly, seeming to think that the honour of cooking for them was payment enough. While the Nambudiri Brahmins looked down on the Tamil Brahmins, they also envied them their lifestyle, principally their being able to marry and have wives with them all their lives. In the case of the Nambudiris, only the eldest son was allowed to bring home a bride. The other sons had to be content with transient relationships with the women of the taravads. Consequently, it seemed to Kuppusamy, their mind was on women all the time. He remembered the dance performance he had attended the night before he left for home. The dancer was a dasi and her movements were sensual and suggestive. Sangunni, his friend, translated the bawdy Malayalam lyrics to Tamil, thereby titillating him. In the audience were several Nambudiris whose yearning for the woman was obvious. It was only then that Kuppusamy began to think of his wife, Visalakshi, with a ferocity that was both thrilling and disturbing.

While walking back from the performance that night, Kuppusamy could not stop thinking about his wife. He hoped she would not be menstruating when he reached home, he yearned for her cooking, he grew excited about the fact that both his brothers were away, which meant that he and Visalakshi would have the store room to themselves for several nights, he thought of his wife's breasts and how he could rest his face between them through the night. Even as he wiped his perspiring face with his upper cloth, and walked faster through the sarpakavu, a fisherwoman emerged from behind one of the trees and stopped him. Her breasts were so bountiful that Kuppusamy could not help looking at them, in his mind ran erotic lines from the song to which the dasi had danced at the performance. Kuppusamy prayed to all the gods to save him from this woman who could easily be a yakshi or neeli, in which case, he was done for.

It turned out she was neither. She was just an ordinary woman who had stopped him for some information. Her daughter had come of age the previous Tuesday. Was that an auspicious time? She was obviously too poor to consult an astrologer to cast the horoscope of her daughter. Kuppusamy looked obviously Brahmin and most Brahmins were learned—so perhaps he could tell her whether her daughter would be lucky as a woman. Kuppusamy was not an astrologer, but he knew a few basic astrological calculations—he did these mentally and, looking resolutely downwards, told the woman that her daughter had indeed come of age at an auspicious time. She began searching for some coins in the cloth bag at her waist to pay him, but he refused it quickly and walked on.

He heard the sound of hooves. Moments later he saw a white, Christian priest riding towards him, along with a number of others. When they passed each other, the priest looked at Kuppusamy and the latter shivered involuntarily. 'I had no evil thoughts regarding that woman,' he told himself, for he feared that the priest, although he was of another faith, had the power to curse him. Didn't these Christians regard every human being a sinner? At least, that's how they began every address to the public.

When Kuppusamy reached home that afternoon, there seemed to be no one there.

'Visalakshi!' he called, 'Visalakshi! Visalam!'

There was no reply. Perhaps she was napping. Where were his brother's children? And where on earth was his brother's squeaky-voiced wife? The doors were all open. Where had they all gone, leaving the house open like this?

He walked to the backyard to wash his feet and look for the family. As he was drawing water from the well, a shadow, like that of a giant bird, passed over the water. Kuppusamy turned back to see what it was. Kitta Iyer's father-in-law, the old man, was levitating and was floating downwards from the terrace. When he reached the depth of a foot from the ground, he began treading air towards the coconut trees at the back of the yard.

CHAPTER 14

'Now that you have visited the backyard and had your breakfast, why don't you bathe? More importantly, why don't you go to Velayudan and get a shave?'

Visalakshi said this to Kuppusamy as she stood there drying her hair. It seemed to Kuppusamy that her skin glowed, as if the radiance came from within her. He could feel the glow of contentment reflected in him as he recalled their uninterrupted night of joy.

'Why didn't you shave? Your stubble hurts,' she had mumbled shyly against his chest at one point during the night. At another she had gently complained, 'Is it not enough that I suffer mosquito bites, must you also bite?' But there had been laughter in her voice. With her, Kuppusamy forgot all about the dasis and their erotic dancing, the bawdy chatter of the cooking assistants, the fisherwoman's breasts. As she stroked his jaw, his cheeks, she laughed softly, feeling his hair stand on end. Her breath smelled sweetly of cardamom and clove, transporting him to a world of pure sensuality. Now, as he watched her standing there, freshly bathed, her clean perfume seemed to spread in every direction.

He looked at her and murmured, 'You look like a beautiful yakshi in the grove.'

She playfully tossed hair over her face and queried, 'Shall I then fly like Snehamba's father?'

Visalakshi laughed at the thought, but Kuppusamy regarded the issue more seriously. Snehamba's father was turning into a nuisance. He recalled watching the old man float down from the terrace the previous afternoon and, still floating, reach the garden in the backyard and pee in a circle there. His eyes were half closed as if he was in a trance. When he had finished, he floated right back to the terrace. Kuppusamy was sure some mischievous ghost had entered the old man's body and was making him behave in this fashion. As he walked back into the house, thinking about the old man, he knocked his head against the top of the doorway and bit back a cry as the pain rammed into him. By now everyone seemed to have returned home—the women, children, even his younger brother Duraisamy Iyer.

'Where did you all go, leaving the house open?' he asked them sternly. 'And Durai, what are you doing here? Aren't you supposed to be cooking for the Adichanallur wedding?'

'Anna, Kittan has gone there. I went to Mynagapalli to cook for Kurup's father's obsequies. Only when I reached there did I find that his aged mother had also passed away four days earlier. Kurup postponed the observance of the obsequies so that they could be held together—such a miser! I had to demand a quarter of my fee for the moment. I'll go back later.'

Why hadn't Durai gone to Karunagapalli from there and helped out Kittan? It was obvious. He wanted to get back home to Kamakshi, before any of his brothers returned, the lusty idiot.

'Same as you!' Visalakshi's eyes seemed to say to him as she laughed softly.

'But where were you all right now?' he asked grumpily.

'We attended the Sri Rama Navami puja in Rama Sastri's house, Anna. His wife begged us to attend. We closed the door but it must have opened with the breeze,' Bhagavati said.

Rama Sastri was a Telugu who had migrated here just a few years ago. He and his wife taught music—vocal music as well as the veena—to the young women of the village and had made enough money to buy the house they had first rented. Kuppusamy had no further interest in Rama Sastri's hospitality to his family than to find out if there was any food for him in the house. He was ravenously hungry.

'So you did not cook at all?' he asked, dismayed. The children began running around the house, playing and raising a clamour. Kitta Iyer's wife, Snehamba, said quickly, 'I'll cook rice and rasam in a moment, Anna. There is no need to bother Manni. Kamakshi, keep an eye on these devils,' she instructed Duraisamy's wife, and hastened into the kitchen. Duraisamy said, as if he had just remembered an urgent chore, 'I am going out for just a bit. I need to collect all the brass pots that are being coated with lead at the iron mongers.'

Echumi and Bhagavati walked into the kitchen after Snehamba. It was obvious that they all wanted to leave Kuppusamy and Visalakshi alone for some time. Between then and in their conversation after lunch in the backyard, it was Visalakshi who told him what had transpired with Snehamba's father.

'He's been this way for the last ten days. He sleeps all day. When he gets up he starts floating. He doesn't fly like a bird; it is more like the leaping of a cockroach or a hen.'

Kuppusamy wondered if the old man was afflicted by an evil spirit. If evil spirits had entered the house, it would not be wise to cohabit with Visalakshi that night. The spirits might get up to all sorts of tricks.

'Snehamba says her father is merely weak of body. But do all weak people float? I think this is just his karma, poor man,' said Visalakshi.

At first they had all been scared by his behaviour. They were wondering whether it was appropriate for them to call in a witch doctor while the men were all away from home. But by the time Duraisamy Iyer returned home they had got used to the old man's floating. Duraisamy took it in his stride. 'Let Kittan come and decide what to do—after all, he is his father-in-law. Besides, he just sleeps all day and as for his floating, he only does that between the terrace and the backyard, he doesn't venture out of the house, does he? So it's not dangerous.'

When Duraisamy put it like that the women felt even more reassured. Still, it was embarrassing that the old man's granddaughters had to stand in the backyard and threaten him with a stick to make him float back to the safety of the terrace.

'What is Snehamba doing about it?' Kuppusamy asked his wife.

'What can she do? It is her father after all. She is diligent about taking him food twice a day and making sure he eats it.'

They didn't refer to the topic again that night. There were better things for them to do.

Now Kuppusamy stood up and tightened his veshti around his waist. He leaned towards Visalakshi to take in the perfume of her wet hair.

'Don't touch my hair,' she said coyly, moving away from him. 'You haven't bathed yet. And I have to go to the temple.'

Again he said, 'You look like a yakshi.'

'I heard you,' she replied. 'And didn't you hear my answer? Should I fly like Snehamba's father? If I were to sleep naked the whole day like he does I'm sure you would find that very convenient!' She made as if to fly away.

'Fly!' he replied. 'Wherever you go, you will come back here! I'll take care of your impudence after dusk today! But what is bothering you? You want to tell me something?'

Even as he spoke he knew what it was—Kamakshi and Snehamba had been quarrelling again.

At dawn Visalakshi had come to the store room to wake him. 'Get up!' she had whispered to him urgently. 'What will people think if you sleep so late here? Everyone will know we have spent the night here!'

'Let them know!' he had replied sleepily. 'It's nothing they don't do! Shut that door and go!'

Even as he dozed off he could vaguely hear the voices of Kamakshi and Snehambal raised in a quarrel in the kitchen. Visalakshi now wanted to tell him about the cause for the quarrel—it involved the old man, of course.

Early that morning Kamakshi had gone to the lavatory in the backyard. The roof of the lavatory had many gaps as most of it had been blown away by the last monsoon. As there were no tall houses nearby, and the men of the house were away all the time, the roof had not yet been repaired. Hardly had Kamakshi squatted in the lavatory than she looked up to see Snehamba's father floating down from the terrace and eyeing her. This was her complaint. Kuppusamy was forced to side with the old man. 'That poor fellow's eyes are closed most of the time. Besides who would want to look at a shitting woman, however beautiful she is?'

'You may be right,' Visalakshi agreed. 'But Kamakshi is bent upon sending the old man back to his home in Adichanallur. This incident is her excuse for insisting that he go back. Snehamba, however, is not giving in that easily. She says that only upon her husband's return can anything be decided, as only he can accompany her father back to his village.'

'Why, Duraisamy can go with him!' Kuppusamy suggested.

'He can, but you know that he is too lazy to do such things. If he works for ten days he has to sleep for ten days, either with Kamakshi or without.'

'Lucky fellow!' Kuppusamy sighed and looked at his wife with fresh yearning. His lust threatened to get out of control.

'Oh, your brother is a very lucky man, indeed!' Visalakshi laughed. 'So lucky that when he was making love to his wife, someone dashed against his back and that too, while floating half a foot above the ground! Can anything be happier than that?'

Kuppusamy could hear her derisive laughter long after she had gone.

CHAPTER 15

The king dreamt that he was dead and had been laid out on a beautiful bier. It was an ornate, bamboo one, with satin spreads and pillows, and surrounded by fragrant strings of jasmine, tube rose and vettiver. There were polished copper steps leading up to the bier which rested on four huge wheels. It was a horse drawn bier but the horses could not be seen. There was a fine muslin screen between the driver's seat and the rest of the contraption. Further away, some men were digging the grave. The king saw that one of the grave diggers was the shorter of the Banian Brothers. He spat on his shovel, flung it away, pissed into the grave and said, 'Time to lower that whoreson into the pit.' The taller of the Banian brothers played a record on the gramophone. The king, on the bier and listening to it all, thinks it would be nice to lie in the warmth of the grave and listen to the dirge. Although the dirge is in some strange language, the king knows that it is announcing his death to the world.

'The millet porridge is ready. But I haven't salted it. He has some rock salt tied in a pouch at his waist. Let him use that,' the cook says, tossing a spatula into the grave. Imagine using that to dig a pit, the king thinks angrily. What a lousy worker! The king gets angry. He'd like to get up and kick the cook's balls to a pulp. But he cannot rise, he is so tired. Besides, something about the music makes him even more lethargic.

The queen's handmaiden gets on to the driver's seat. She is nude. Then she pushes back the muslin curtain and kicks the king. The skin on her heels is cracked. Her anklets brush against the fine hair on her ankles as she kicks him in his face. The kick lands on his eye, hurting it. Yet there is a faint pleasure in that pain. He smells her feet as she kicks him, they smell headily of sweat, of tamarind and salt, the dust from the corridors of the palace, fish scales from the kitchen, horse manure from the stables, and that special smell of a woman who has just finished her periods and had her ritual bath...

'She will also lie down in the grave,' the taller of the Banian Brothers says, stepping forward and squeezing her breast.

'Don't touch her, son of a bitch! I'll curse you so your genital hair gets scorched!' the king swears.

The maid is now kicking him in earnest below his waist. It makes him go all moist.

The king woke up with a start. It was early morning. The queen was pummelling him to wake him up. He could feel his veshti fall loose around his waist, and the spreading moisture around his penis. He felt proud. There was some stuff left in him still. Perhaps the queen could be impregnated even now. But would the queen lie with him in the grave? Where was the maid? What fragrance would the queen's feet have?

The king closed his eyes again, upon which the queen lost her temper and yelled, 'Why are you closing your eyes again? How long must I spend waking you? How can someone sleep so deeply?'

The queen's voice woke him up fully and he discovered that he was not dead, nor was he lying on a bier. He had merely slept and dreamt. The queen looked a sight. She had not bathed and wore an old sari. The kohl in her eyes had run on her cheeks. There was yellow matter at the corners of her eyes.

'My father is dead. We just got a message,' she informed him, and launched into a full scale lamentation. It did not fail to occur to the king that there was something singularly atonal about her loud sorrow. She should have listened to the dirges from the gramophone. That would have made her wailing more tuneful. The king couldn't help feeling a fierce stab of pleasure at the news of his father-in-law's death. He was a nasty fellow who seemed to have moved over from his distant village to live close to the king for the express purpose of needling him. Whenever he sighted the king he never failed to ask, with a sneer, 'When are you going to place my grandson on the throne?'

It was when the king decided he couldn't bear him anymore that the maid brought him the complaint that the bushy moustached old man was harassing her repeatedly to perform 'lip service' to him. The king warned the old man of dire consequences if he tried to get fresh with the maid again and expelled him from the palace.

That had been three months ago. 'You are not courteous to my father. That is why he will never come here as long he lives,' the queen complained accusingly. 'I care a hair!' muttered the king in retort.

'He was a brave man, capable of leading a thousand soldiers!' the queen wailed in exaggeration. 'Now he's gone, alone at the time of his death. I wonder what he thought as he was leaving. I wonder if he thought of me!' the queen began her wailing again.

'What do you want me to do?' the king asked her petulantly.

'Should I tell you even this? You must set forth at once to participate in his funeral, in a manner that befits your station and your relationship with him. All my brothers would have gathered at my father's home by now. Only we are still here!'

The king had a problem with starting at once. He needed to finish his morning ablutions, he needed to be shaved, he was hungry, he needed breakfast. He was thinking longingly of dosai, egg gravy and coconut flakes mixed with jaggery. 'Wait a bit,' he tried to reason with the queen. 'We'll start before the sun gets too hot. We should consult with the priest about what we should carry for the occasion.'

'May you rot in the sun!' the queen burst out. 'Are you coming right now, or shall I leave?'

To placate her, the king ordered loudly, 'Who's there?' Prepare the palanquin. The queen needs to leave at once.'

'No need for any wretched menstrual blood imbiber to come with the palanquin! I know how to go!' the queen shouted and swept out of the room. A few minutes later the king saw her and her maid climbing into the bullock cart. The cart driver cracked his whip and they were off like lightning.

The king relaxed. Should he have a little nap? Why weren't his neighbours playing their music box today? On second thought, the nap did not seem such a good idea. He had, after all, promised the queen that he would start while the day was still young. And he had so many things to do before that. The king walked to the kitchen and yelled for the cook, 'Palaniappa!'

As if he had been waiting for the call, the cook brought a silver tray on which was placed a banana leaf cup full of vallarai lehyam and a silver tumbler full of hot water. The lehyam and the hot water kept the king regular, the royal intestines well plumbed.

The king felt kindly disposed towards the cook this morning. 'Have you been drinking toddy so early in the morning, you rogue?' he enquired smilingly.

'No, Highness, nothing like that. I haven't taken a drop of toddy for years!'

'Then you should have some today,' the king replied and flung a coin at he cook.

As he went past him to the backyard, he didn't forget to give him the menu for breakfast.

In the backyard, a servant already stood ready with a pot of water for washing the royal behind. Some distance away, the barber was setting out his razors and cup of water, in the shade of a tree. It pleased the king to see routine restored to his life after the minor upheaval of the morning. Even the prospect of attending the bushy moustached old man's funeral did not seem too bad. It had been a while since he had taken part in the curious customs and practices that death entailed. Even as he was getting ready, the king remembered the contraption shown by the Banian Brothers. Why not ask them to bring it along? A picture of the bushy moustached old man's body could be captured with it and hung somewhere in the palace. It would please the queen.

'But don't come at once—come a little later,' he mentally commanded the Brothers.

The barber shaved the king's face and then asked, politely, 'Should I take off the hair below as well, master?'

The king would have preferred it, but as the region was still moist from his ablutions he refused the barber's offer.

CHAPTER 16

When the king reached his father-in-law's village, the farewell fireworks had started. The man setting them off on the open ground near the water tank was running away from the explosions in a haze of acrid smelling smoke. The drummers had begun their rhythmic music, leaping fervently to the beat.

The king was conscious of the fact that he was discourteously late for the funeral. He had not intended to be, but the cook was late with his breakfast, much of which was burnt in any case. The king had borne all these difficulties patiently only to set forth for the funeral quickly. Even so, he had been delayed, principally by that arrogant priest. It was obvious he had not forgotten the last incident at the king's palace during the performance of the memorial obsequies for the king's ancestors. The priest now took his revenge by mentioning, unnecessarily, several times that his son-in-law, who worked for the zamindar of Namakkal, had invited him to come and work there. The king knew that Namakkal was a much bigger town than Arasur and that the zamindar was far more affluent—the priest would definitely make a lot more money there and be treated with greater respect. 'The only reason I'm not going there immediately is that I have got used to our village and don't want to start all over again in a new place at my age,' the priest said pointedly.

The king stared at him for a while, then went into the palace and brought back a tray on which he had placed four betel leaves, a couple of betel nuts and a single gold coin that weighed a sovereign. He felt sad to part with a gold coin from the small but precious hoard he had so carefully saved, but then this was a crisis situation—he had to make sure that the priest did not leave his village.

It worked. The priest grinned and swore that nothing pleased him better than being the family priest of the mighty Emperor of Arasur. After all, his ancestors had all been priests to the palace. What could possibly tempt him at Namakkal, he wondered aloud, and laughed. The king laughed with him politely, wondering inwardly whether he could send a ruffian to assault the priest on his way back home, cut his sacred thread and grab the gold coin.

Another gold coin had to be spent on buying all the items the priest suggested the king should carry to the funeral. It was when everything was being loaded on to the horse carriage that the king remembered the Banian Brothers' camera. The Brothers did not answer the king's call at once. They took their time coming and said their car had broken down and had to be fixed before they started. They'd had to get petrol for the car and that was not easy to get as there was a war going on. The king could understand none of this, nor did he care, as the war and everything else was obviously much after his time. The only important thing was to get to the bushy moustached old man's funeral on time. He didn't fail to ask the Brothers whether they had brought the picture making machine. 'Yes,' they said. It was in the car.

'Follow me. I'll pay for everything at the village,' the king assured them and got into his horse-drawn carriage, although the Brothers offered to take him in the car. You never knew with these new-fangled machines. It might capsize on the way and, who knew, the king might himself need to be carried on a bier. Even as the horse carriage jogged along, the Brothers' car overtook it and zipped off like lightning. Let them go, the king thought. They could do nothing until he himself reached the venue and gave orders for the photos to be taken.

Along the way the king ate all the snacks the cook had provided and drank a whole pot of sweet jaggery water. This resulted in his stopping the carriage several times to get off and relieve himself by the roadside. Further delays occurred when the king's servants were dispatched to buy jackfruit and cucumber from the vendors along the way. By the time the king had polished off these, the carriage reached the village. As he got off the carriage, the ritual dirge singers turned up the volume of their singing.

Lotus in the water

Oh, mother.

Aavaram flowers on the ground,

Oh, mother.

Plantains for us,

Oh, mother.

Heaven for you,

Oh, mother.

The king nodded his approval as he stepped out and caught sight of the Banian Brothers leaning against their car and drumming their fingers on its roof in time to the music. The pipers began blowing on their pipes more lustily. The volume of the lamenting was stepped up. All this, the king knew, was a sort of welcome being accorded to him, a subtle acknowledgement of his presence.

Many of the dead man's relatives came wailing to the front door, in order to greet the most important visitor to the funeral. They were followed by the queen. She stopped at the doorway. She seemed irresistibly beautiful to the king. Her maid, peeping out from behind her, looked even more so. The king quickly shelved these thoughts as being inappropriate at a funeral. Just as the queen stepped forward, frowning, ready to complain about the delay in his arrival, the king was saved by the arrival of his two brothers-in-law. He warmly clasped their hands to convey his condolence and they nodded vaguely in acknowledgement. The king then began asking all those pointless questions that people ask at funerals: when did it happen? what time? What did he eat last night? How energetic the old man had been! And so on. Several answers floated around the king. The explosions of the fireworks began again. The men making the bamboo bier were sitting quietly in the shade of a tree chewing tobacco.

'Why have you brought these blokes with you?' the queen hissed angrily in the king's ear.

'To take pictures of your father,' the king replied proudly. 'The pictures can be hung in the palace and looked at till the end of life.'

'Whose life?' the queen retorted tartly. But the king had no answer to her question.

CHAPTER 17

The king lunched well that afternoon.

The chair on which he sat had a backrest flanked by two meticulously carved roaring lion faces. The effect was of the king's head being hemmed in by snarling lions but that did not dim his appetite for the endless courses of food served by the women of his wife's family. They served him without a word and without ever raising their eyes to his face—to behave otherwise towards the son-in-law of the family would have been impolite.

Six feet from where he sat lay the body of his father-in-law. Generous wads of cotton had been stuffed into his nostrils and mouth. Someone had placed a bunch of nauseating incense sticks near the head of the body. A couple of fat ants were making their way towards the corpse. A barber was meticulously shaving the bushy moustached old man's cheeks. As if realising that no such convenience would be available where he was going, the dead man seemed to accommodate himself completely to the barber's razor.

The sounds of the fireworks and drums came intermittently from a distance. All the female mourners had gone to bathe in the tank and bring back pots of water with which they would bathe the body. The king was anxious to finish his lunch before they returned. In a tent in the backyard, less important diners were being served lunch. Cooks were busy making other dishes a little further off. Many of them were sweating profusely. Possibly their perspiration would find its way into the dishes they made, after all, they were not finicky palace cooks. In any case one could not be too particular about these things in a crowd of this size. An old woman, who could take some liberties with the king because of her age, tipped four vadais on to the king's plantain leaf, telling him, 'Don't be shy! Eat well!' The vadais were full and round like a pregnant woman's breasts and glowed with an oily sheen. Have some more, urged the king's tongue. Oh please stop, said his stomach.

The king's brothers-in-law were busy organising refreshments for the mourners, including twenty pots of toddy. They were in a generous mood, happy that their father had died quickly, without troubling anyone. Now and then they approached the king, politely urging him to eat and drink more.

When the king was ready to get up from the table, he found he needed help. He would have preferred a young maid to help lift him but all he got was a couple of thin old men who struggled to get his considerable bulk off the chair.

A group of menials was awaiting the king at the backyard to help him wash his hands. One of them ran hurriedly towards the far off corner with a jug full of water, anticipating his using the lavatory over there. 'These fellows would even readily oblige with loosening my loin cloth if I intend to piss', thought the king with immense pride and satisfaction.

When the king returned after washing his hands, he saw a young servant woman, bending close to the old man's body, and wiping the edges of his mouth. The king wanted to warn her, 'Woman, don't get too close to that old lecher. He'll grab your hand and try to kiss you.' As if reading the king's mind, the woman looked at him and smiled. Then she stuffed fresh wads of cotton into the old man's mouth and nostrils and left.

The king wanted to see the bushy moustached old man from up close. He would cause no more trouble for him. Certainly, he would not be able to make nasty cracks about the king's virility. Just a little while longer. Once he was bathed the old man would have to go quietly to his grave.

When the king walked up to the body, he saw that the ancestors were there ahead of him, chattering among themselves. Some of them were trying to pull the old man's spirit from his body, but the old man stubbornly clung to his body.

'Why should you stay here and worry about anything?' they cajoled the old man. 'Your son-in-law will look after everything. You should come with us and see how much there is to enjoy in our world!'

'I can't do everything that the old man demanded!' the king exclaimed to the ancestors in alarm. 'I just don't have the money. You didn't leave me anything. The Sarkar doles out coin by measly coin.' The king was worried that they would egg the old man on to make unreasonable requests. They were bad enough, demanding foreign liquor. The old man would demand other satisfactions that the Brahmin priest would certainly not be able to provide.

'Shut up!' the ancestors chided the king. 'Here we are, trying to cajole him to come with us and you come along and remind him of pleasures that he will be loathe to leave behind!' One of the ancestors, in the form of an ant, bit hard into the king's ankle to express his anger. The king shook his leg to rid himself of the ant.

'We heard that they are bringing in the toddy. Ask them to bring the first pot to us. Let us at least smell the toddy. And at the next new moon get that good-for-nothing priest to offer us foreign liquor. Apart from us there's that stupid Brahmin woman from the tobacco merchant's who keeps demanding liquor for herself!'

The king shook his head and said, 'I don't understand you.'

'So what's new?' exclaimed his father-in-law, who now seemed to have ganged up with his ancestors. 'Is there any thing you understand apart from eating vallarai lehyam and squatting in the backyard? You can only eat and make out with the maid. To think that bitch wouldn't open her mouth to me!'

The old man had never spoken to the king in this derogatory fashion when he was alive. Perhaps death conferred on one the right to be insulting. The ancestors, however, did not allow the old man to speak further. They dragged him away even as he was asking eagerly about the spirit of the Brahmin woman who demanded foreign liquor. The king too wondered about her. Was she the one who was playing the dirges on the music box?

Even as the king was pondering this he heard the clearing of throats behind him. He turned and caught sight of the Banian Brothers. He politely asked them if they had eaten. They nodded.

'Did you find it difficult to drive this strange vehicle all this way?'

'Not at all,' they replied.

'Get your black box ready,' the king instructed them. 'We should get a fine picture of this old man.'

Following him, the brothers went up to their car and brought out the camera and tripod. The procession of women, returning from the tank, their clothes all wet, was approaching the house. Behind them came the pipe players and the men. The king wanted the brothers to photograph the scene. But when he turned to call them, he found that they had set up the camera near the corpse and were peering at it from under a black cloth that they had draped over the camera. The king was curious to know how the image of the old man would enter the black box, but felt it would be humiliating to ask the brothers who were little better than menials.

'What are those good-for-nothings doing here?' the queen whispered angrily into his ear. 'If we don't watch out they'll make off with the studs in my father's ears'.

'They are not rogues or thieves!' the king protested. 'Trust me, they are only engaged in taking a picture of your father.'

'Huh, they are not even capable of burning down our neighbour's house, that is, even if you could bring yourself to order them to do it!'

Just then, they saw a bullock carriage filled with garlands approaching the house. 'Oh, here come the flowers we ordered for father,' the queen said, pleased. 'I was very particular that they should be fresh. Why, you can smell their perfume even from this far!'

The king felt sad for the flowers, they would be wasted on that smelly corpse. A group of musicians approached the king and bowed low before him. 'We have come to sing dirges,' they said. The king enthusiastically asked them what songs they were going to sing, before turning to go in to see the bushy moustached old man prepared for his last journey.

CHAPTER 18

The hall was flooded as the women poured pots of water on the corpse of the bushy moustached old man. A fishy, unpleasant smell pervaded the air. Each woman tried hard to weep as she poured water on the body. The king, from his perch on his carved chair, watched the women with interest, belching loudly at regular intervals. One of the Banian Brothers, standing respectfully behind the king's chair, whispered, 'Shall I photograph this?'

'Why not?' replied the king. 'But make sure that you don't click your picture when the upper cloths of the women have shifted.'

Though the king was sitting there only to ogle at the women, he didn't want their exposed breasts to be recorded for posterity.

'If your Highness can ask one of the women to pose holding the pot of water above the corpse, it'll make a great picture,' suggested the Brothers.

So when the queen's maid came to pour water on the corpse, the king ordered her to hold the pose. She did so but was weeping quite genuinely. The king wondered what her tears were for: the husband who had deserted her after just one year of marriage, the many men she had consorted with thereafter, none of whom showed any lasting interest in her, the nasty, sexual demands made by the old man who was now dead, the fact that her salary was due for the last two months, or simply for her aching calves that had not been massaged by the king lately.

'Stop your wailing and hold that pot carefully over the body,' the king told her curtly.

She did as she was told, and the shorter of the Brothers got behind the black cloth covering the camera. A few seconds later, there was a pop and a flash of light from the black box. At the same instant the corpse rose vertically as if the bushy moustached old man were trying to sit up. 'Father, you are dead!' cried his sons and pressed the body back onto the floor, straightening it as they did so.

'It's done,' said the Brothers as one of them emerged from the black cloth. The queen, rubbing her wet feet against the wall behind her, gave him a sour look. The king ignored her. He was curious to see the photo—not for the corpse of the old man, but the shapely figure of the servant woman.

Now the men moved in. 'All women, leave the hall. We are going to strip the old man and dress him in new clothes. Don't want the virgins to see something they shouldn't see and get scared out of their wits!' commented a young man. The older women laughed. 'You are right, boy,' retorted an old woman whose ear lobes touched her shoulders. 'They know what their men have. They wouldn't want to measure them against what the old man has and feel cheated for the rest of their lives!' she joked.

'Grandmother, speak only about what you have seen, not about the rest of us!' replied a young man from the crowd.

'Hey, I've seen the lot of you with your bells ringing, carried you wet on my hips. I know enough about you!' the old woman went on and the other women broke into raucous laughter.

'Who is she?' the king asked the queen.

'One of my father's harlots,' the queen spat. 'Even when my mother was alive, he had a mistress in every town. After she passed way, this bitch moved in here and is hanging on to see what she can thieve. Whore!' the queen gnashed her teeth.

'I don't remember seeing her during our wedding,' the king said thoughtfully, recalling the scene from thirty years ago.

'Even if you had seen her, what would you have done? Laid her down and...'

Before she could finish the king moved away to stand closer to the Banian Brothers.

After the women had left the hall, the old man's grandsons stripped him and began wiping the body with a towel.

'Don't rub him too hard below the waist. He might get an erection and refuse to go into the grave!' joked one of the grandsons. Laughter swept the hall in waves, even the king smiled. Finally the old man was dressed in all his finery for his last journey, someone put stripes of vibhuti on his forehead, and someone dotted the centre of his forehead with sandal paste and vermilion. Still another brought some ghee to apply on his bushy moustache and twirl its corners upward.

Then the women returned to the hall. The old woman with the long earlobes placed the bushy moustached old man's head on her lap and began a loud and rather elegant lamentation. The king found it as beautiful as the dirges from the music box.

'Stop, Grandma! Listening to you, grandfather might come alive. Then you'll be in trouble, possibly pregnant!' the boys teased her. Now the rising laughter made even the old woman feel shy.

'This is what one calls a joyful death— we are all laughing all the time!' the king remarked and everyone agreed with him.

The taller of the Banian Brothers whispered to the king that he should allow him to take a picture of the corpse seated on a chair. The king wondered how the old man could possibly be made to sit on a chair. But his brothers-in-law thought it easy. They pulled and bent and finally pushed the body upright onto the chair and tied it with a rope to secure it there. Then they draped an upper cloth with gold lace on it across the thigh of the corpse to hide the rope. Someone brought mashed betel leaves and smeared the green-red paste over the corpse's lips so that it looked as if the old man was alive and chewing betel leaf. One of the grandsons told the photographer, 'The effect should be that of an elder who has led a full and satisfying life and is totally contented.'

'Of course,' said the Banian Brothers.

'Let the older grandchildren sit at the feet of their grandfather,' the king suggested. The queen forbade the younger children from assembling there, because they might get scared by their grandfather's corpse. The old man's mistress sat at his feet and rested one of them on her lap. There was a gap at the right corner, so the king asked the queen's maid to sit there. When all this had been arranged, the Brothers went behind the camera, there was another flash of light and a loud pop. Even as they all shut their eyes against the brief lightning, there was a loud noise. They turned to see that the bushy moustached old man's body had slipped off the chair and fallen on the servant woman's lap.

The astonished king couldn't help cursing the old man. 'Rascally lecher!' he swore to himself.

'Do you need to take the picture again?' someone asked.

'No, I have already finished,' replied the taller of the Brothers. He took his leave then and said he would bring the photos over the next week.

Then there was nothing left to do but place the old man on his decorated bier. There was some argument about whether they should wait for some cousins to arrive. But the queen put a stop to it by saying firmly, 'Let there be no further delay. Once the king and I have placed our jasmine garlands around his neck, he can leave.'

That was how the bushy moustached old man left on his final journey. But he had to have the last word. When the procession arrived at where the Banian Brothers had parked their car, it refused to move an inch further, however hard the pall bearers tried to move. Then the old man's grandsons smilingly whispered something to them, and they too laughed. They lowered the bier so that it was on level with the projecting, round, fat rubber horn of the car. The corpse's hand seemed to move towards it of its own accord. Then one of the pall bearers curved the hand around the horn, as if to stroke it and then squeezed it hard. There was a loud and joyous boom from the horn.

'Take him away,' said the king disgustedly. He privately worried that the old man should behave in whatever world he was travelling to.

CHAPTER 19

The king sat on a chair on the pyol of his late father-in-law's house and watched his eldest brother-in-law receive visitors who came to condole with him. The brother-in-law's head had been shaved as part of the mourning rites, and that, along with the absence of his moustache and beard, gave him a distinctly beggarly look. He was hardly impoverished, in fact. He had huge tracts of paddy land and plantain groves near the Tamiraparani river, all given to him as part of his wife's dowry. The king would have loved to marry that woman, except that she was filially related to him. If he had only been able to marry her he would have been a landlord and never suffered for money. But then, what charm was there in being a landlord when compared to the grandeur of being a king and ruling over a people? None at all, the king decided and shot his brother-in-law a kind look. After all, benevolence was a kingly attribute.

The truth was he was bored. He wondered if he should not make a trip to the sweet water tank outside the village. On his last visit the old man, his father-in-law, had taken him there. It was a pretty place with water lapping the steps of the tank and a small temple to Hanuman on the bank. The king remembered everything about that visit: the stone idol of Hanuman wearing a garland of vadais, the Kannada-speaking priest who offered the king some of the vadais as prasadam, the women who came to the tank to collect water and hitched up their saris as they climbed the steps of the tank with their pots of water—the king had watched their bare legs with absorption. Why not go there again?

Even as the thought crossed the king's mind, a servant brought him a tray of snacks. When the banana leaf covering the snacks was removed, the king was disappointed to see these were just more of the heavy, greasy snacks he had been plied with all day. Why, these rascals seemed intent upon feeding him to sickness! Still, it would seem rude to refuse to eat, so he began munching, after looking at the middle distance and ordering for a carriage to be brought round so that he could go to the water tank. In the time that it took him to demolish most of the snacks, word of his outing had reached the queen. She walked up to him and whispered, 'You can't visit a temple just after a funeral! Have you gone crazy?'

'I'm not visiting the temple,' the king placated her. 'I'm going up to the tank to take in some fresh air and walk for a while. I have been sitting down since morning. My buttocks feel as if they are wearing away!'

A horse carriage came up to the front of the house right then.

'Come back soon. Those who have come to pay their condolences cannot leave until they see you signal to them that they can go,' the queen said this loudly in a respectful voice. The king was pleased to note that she was always polite to him in public. He was slipping his feet into his sandals when a commotion broke out. His brother-in-law was angrily pushing away a relative who had come late to offer his condolences. 'Just go away, I don't want your sympathy!'

he shouted at the man, who cringed and said that he had been delayed because he was unwell. 'Rubbish!' exploded the queen's brother. 'This old fellow was drunk and rolling on the streets of Madurai! That's why he is late. Those who went to inform him of my father's death told me all about it.'

'How could I drink when I could not get up enough energy to squat and void my bowels?' the old man wailed. 'Some jealous motherfucker has lied to you!'

The king knew that the argument would probably last the whole evening. He could always watch the fun when he returned. So he set forth briskly on his little trip.

The tank and its environs were as pretty as ever: the gently lapping, tinted water, the banyan tree nearby, the birds flying overhead and the temple on the bank. But there was no one around, let alone women. The king sat under the tree and craned his neck in every direction, but he couldn't see a soul. Had all the women heard about his visit and decided to stay away?

The man who had accompanied him came forward and bent low. 'What is it?' the king asked.

'There is a festival in the Shiva temple. That is why no one is here,' the man replied.

The king was taken aback. How had the man read his mind? Had he been so transparent? The king smiled vaguely. An instant later he felt something creeping underfoot. He jerked his foot back and his sandal flew off and landed in the water. His escort clucked his tongue. 'How sad that the dirty sandal has landed in drinking water!' he said. The king was annoyed. A loyal subject should have jumped into the water and retrieved the sandal. The king swore loudly at him and walked back to the carriage. The man followed him carrying the remaining sandal. The king ignored him and let him run all the way back behind the carriage.

When they reached the house, the king was pleased to find the dirge singers performing in the courtyard. The men sat around them. The women were in the hall around the courtyard, modestly seated behind the pillars. In the light from the torches, all of them seemed like apsaras. As he sat down one of the young men went up to a singer and whispered to him. The singer looked embarrassed. A few more young men went up to him with further whispered requests. After some uncomfortable minutes the singer cleared his throat and began singing,

The ascetic's wife

Had the longest hair.

While tying her hair,

Along with the lice,

She tied in her secret lover.

When the time was ripe

She opened her hair.

And out jumped her lover.

She then cast off her breast cloth.

Her breasts hung like ripe fruits...

'Stop!' cried the old man who had been insulted in the evening. He seemed to be on stronger ground now. 'It is not seemly to sing such bawdy songs now,' the man admonished. 'You should sing only dirges or tragic stories. That is the tradition. Am I right or not?' he looked around him and everyone, including the queen's brother, nodded in agreement. The king was irritated, not only because the song had been stopped but also because the quarrel between the two men had obviously been resolved. He began to feel hungry. His escort to the tank walked up to him and whispered in is ear, 'What shall I do with the remaining sandal?'

'Toast it and bring it to me—I will eat it,' was the king's annoyed reply. At least a few people around him would have heard his words. His hunger was building up to something unbearable.

The dirge singers were saying, 'We will sing you a tragic tale now. Later, after the women have all gone to sleep, we can gather in the terrace, and we will sing you the story of the ascetic's wife.'

The young men hooted in agreement.

A servant came up to the king and whispered that his dinner was being served in an inner room. The king could have hugged him. As he rose from his chair to go in, the lead singer began his story. 'They say that there is going to be a terrible famine in the year of Dhatu. I do not know if any of us will be alive to see that. We have no words to speak of the happenings of the future. But I shall now tell you about a terrible famine that took place in the past. A hundred years ago, such a drought afflicted the land that people died of hunger.' The dirge singer was moving into his story of hunger deaths when the king began eating. On the plantain leaf before him was a satisfactory mound of steaming rice and curried plantain. The cook had poured tamarind gravy on the rice and spoonfuls of fresh, fragrant ghee. He seemed to be a better cook than the one in the king's palace.

The king continued to eat, listening to the story being sung by the performers in the courtyard. 'This is the tragic story of a young Brahmin girl and her brother, who left their village to escape the drought and reached another village only to fall into an old, disused well and perish. A story that can melt a heart of stone. Listen to it, O Masters!'

The drums rolled to heighten the effect.

'No rain, no water,

No trees, no plants.

Gazing upon the pitiless sky,

The dry fields wail.

The earth has hardened and cracked,

Only aloe grows along the dry river bank.

Suddenly another voice cut into the singing of the lead vocalist. 'Yes, it's true. There was no rain, no water. The fields had turned into hard earth. I did leave my village to escape the drought. I did fall into the old, dry well and die. Now I have come again. Very close. I am Saama's wife. Do you know the scholar Swaminathan? Oh, is it not seemly to utter my husband's name? Will it cut short his life[2]? What if it does? Did I not die young? But listen, you harridan! You enticed him to see so he noticed you. That's the end of the matter. If you even think of burning down his house, you will perish, along with your entire clan!'

The king, listening on, choked on his food. He could recognise that voice. It was the queen's.

CHAPTER 20

Sankaran's whole family went to Alapuzha to see his prospective bride. The mood was festive and they set off in high spirits. Subramanya Iyer's male cousins, their wives and children, the family astrologer, Subbamma and other relatives left early intending to stop at various pilgrimage spots along the way.

Subramanya Iyer, Kalyani, and Sankaran left just two days before the function and went straight to Alapuzha so that the shop would not have to be closed for more than a week.

Subbamma had to prepare carefully for this trip. She had begged the spirits of her ancestors to leave her alone during the trip. Subbamma's problems with the spirit of the evil young woman in Iyer's house had become so intense that she hardly ever visited Iyer's home, not wanting to embarrass herself. She pleaded with the astrologer,

Annasami Iyengar, to give her amulets and yantras to keep the spirit at bay. Given the persistence and ferocity of the spirit, the astrologer was compelled to create a copper yantra that was large and unwieldy in order to accommodate all the deities that were required to protect her from the evil spirit. When Subbamma first wore the long, rectangular plate of copper around her neck, her ancestors told her that the deities were scuffling to appropriate their rightful places on the yantra. Eventually they all settled down and they were able to keep the evil spirit away. But the weight of the heavy copper plate gave Subbamma unbearable aches and pains. She found it hard to urinate and her stomach started swelling. She often fell over because of the weight of the yantra. To counter this, Subbamma had a small wooden roller made, upon which she placed the yantra, attached the roller to her waist with a length of rope and dragged the roller behind her wherever she went. The first day she walked down the street dragging the roller with the yantra behind her, she drew surprised stares. The deities were not pleased with this arrangement. They said that being dragged around on wheels on the dust of the street was an insult to the yantra. Dogs followed Subbamma and sniffed at the yantra.This just won't do, they chided her. Subbamma's benevolent ancestors interceded on her behalf, after all, it would only be a short time before the effect of the yantra did away with the evil spirit altogether. Subbamma repeatedly fell on the dust of the street, paying obeisance to the various deities. Despite all this there were times when, pushed by her ancestors and pulled by the weight of the deities, she wept and wished she had drowned in the Ganges at Kasi—she would have been rid of all her problems that way.

Unfortunately, the yantra did not seem to be having any long term effect on the evil spirit. Once, when Subbamma, in a hurry to visit Subramanya Iyer's house (because the astrologer was there to compare Sankaran's and his prospective bride's horoscopes), forgot to drag the yantra along with her, the evil spirit promptly entered her again. Immediately upon entering Iyer's house, she began to yell at the astrologer. 'Is this soothsayer keeping you?'

the spirit demanded to know. Then she entered Subbamma who proceeded to kick and pummel the astrologer, yank open his tuft, spit on his face and attempt to tear off his sacred thread. Then, as if ordered by someone she leapt forward and tried to kiss the astrologer on his lips. The latter gathered his books together in a hurry, told Iyer that he would compare horoscopes on another day as today was obviously not auspicious, admonished Subbamma for having forgotten her yantra, and left quickly. Subbamma laughed raucously at his back, gestured towards the space below her waist and yelled after him, 'This is the right place to shove your yantra!'

After this, Subbamma stopped visiting Iyer's house. Still, when she was invited to go to Alapuzha to meet Sankaran's prospective bride, she accepted at once. Following the astrologer's advice, she packed the yantra in the cloth bundle containing her clothes and kept it with her at all times. She joined the group outside on the road, because she was worried that if she entered Iyer's house, the evil spirit would catch hold of her again. Ayyanai was to stay behind to care for Saama and his food would come from the school of Vedic studies. 'After all, that is the food he ate for five years when he was a student there,' Iyer reasoned. 'Maybe the food itself might cure him.' He fondly told Subbamma that he had given money to meet her travel expenses to the priest, Sundaram, who was organising the trip.

'What he hopes for his son will not happen,' Subbamma's ancestors whispered in her ear.

'I wish it would happen,' Subbamma prayed fervently to all her deities and waited at the crossroads for the bullock cart to appear.

By the time it came by, it was late and she was tired. The delay had been due to the astrologer, Annasami, who was very apologetic about it. 'At the last minute that idiot of a king sent for me and would not let me go,' he explained. 'He wants an exorcism done in the palace.'

'What for?'

'The evil spirit that haunts Saama has apparently wandered to the palace and travelled with the family to the home of the king's father-in-law, who died recently. She caused trouble there, despite their giving her the courtesy due to a Brahmin woman. Now they don't know how to get rid of her. I have promised to conduct propitiatory rites to get rid of her upon my return,' the astrologer said, unconsciously fingering the gold coin the king had given him in advance.

Then everyone climbed into the bullock carts and they set forth. Sundaram the priest advised them, 'Keep your jewellery inside your cane boxes for there may be bandits on the way.'

Subbamma smiled sadly as she touched her oil-stained earrings. 'I have no need to be cautious. These will not weigh even a quarter of a sovereign,' she replied.

It was evening by the time they reached Madurai. They visited the temple of the goddess Meenakshi and on the way back saw a Brahmin selling food[3] in a makeshift shop. For four coppers he gave a plantain leaf package of rice and vadais. A few Telugu pilgrims were sitting on their haunches enjoying the food. Sundaram slapped his forehead in disgust. 'A Brahmin selling food that should be given free to pilgrims! How much more sin can this world take?'

Despite his hot words, the priest wanted to taste the food. Subbamma's ancestors too insisted that they wanted to taste the Brahmin's food. So she sat down on the street and stubbornly demanded food. Sundaram gave her some money and said, 'Eat whatever you like and then come to the chatram at the end of this street. That's where we are staying for the night.'

If he'd stayed, he would have been disgusted by the speed and gusto with which Subbamma ate mounds of rice, vadai and poli. The Brahmin selling the food was dumbstruck at the sight. Thinking the devil had taken possession of the old woman, he took the coins she gave him, grabbed his empty baskets and ran home.

At the chatram that night, a group of Telugu pilgrims chatted through the darkness. Despite that, Subbamma's fellow travellers slept, exhausted by the day's journey. She alone stayed awake, her over-stuffed belly causing her acute discomfort. Strange visions passed before her eyes. Saama and a pretty girl ran in circles around her and engaged in lovemaking. A bat hovered overhead asking, 'Subbamma, can I come close?'

Children passed by, carrying a palanquin of bamboo poles and palm leaves. A young man with six fingers on each hand led the way. Subramanya Iyer's house appeared before her eyes, caught fire in an instant and burnt merrily.

Strange lac discs whirled in circles, creating the saddest dirge music –so sad it made her choke.

'God!' Subbamma held her little cane box close to her chest.

Her deities remained silent through all this. Had they gone to sleep? Or did they like the music? She did not know.

CHAPTER 21

Sundaram, the priest, was standing waist deep in the Vaigai river and pondering on life in general and his in particular.

There was not much water in the river, although the wet sand higher up along the banks showed that the river had been in flood sometime ago. Sundaram had finished his morning ablutions save bathing. He hated having to use the river to clean his behind—were not all rivers sacred? Why did he have to degrade them like this? He dunked into the water and pondered on the information that the Vaigai, unlike most rivers, did not flow into the sea but into some tank or lake. Annasamy Iyengar had told him this. Sundaram himself knew no geography. In the School of Vedic studies, such subjects were not taught. There was only the repeating of the four Vedas, until they became a part of your oral memory. Intonation and pronunciation were the most important aspects of learning. He remembered his teacher yelling, 'Can't you get the 'sh' sound right? You will only be fit to be a Brahmin mendicant at a funeral!'

Sundaram smiled at the memory. His teacher, Eswaran, had been violent in his efforts to get lessons into his pupil's head. This included grabbing hold of Sundaram's tuft and banging his head against the ground, as if to physically force knowledge into his skull. Yet when Eswaran died they could not find a single Brahmin mendicant to receive alms at his funeral.

'*Narmade, Sindhu, Kaveri...*' Sundaram murmured as he dunked his head underwater and rose to walk to the shore. As his body and damp clothes dried in the breeze, Sundaram applied the ritual stripes of vibhuti across his forehead, chest and shoulders. When his veshti dried he wore it in the panchakaccham style and got ready to walk to the Meenakshi temple. It seemed that most of his life was spent walking from place to place. He walked from village to village to perform his priestly duties. These duties seemed to pertain largely to funerals and annual obsequies. He could not afford to forget a single death he had attended, as his clients expected him to remind them about the annual rites. He was conscientious about reminding them and following all the rituals and restrictions that were enjoined on a priest performing such rites. It did not make for an easy life. He wondered when his ceaseless walking would stop and, if it did, who would preside over his own funeral. Perhaps he could just as well walk away from this life and become an ascetic. His mind wandered to the story of Sadasiva Brahmendra, saint and musician, who walked miles and miles in his adoration of the Divine. Why, it was here, on the banks of the Vaigai, that an angry king ordered that the saint's hand be cut off, for wandering into the king's harem. That the saint had been in a spiritual trance and was singing the most evocative songs, totally oblivious to his surroundings, had not helped. What was that song? '*Manasa sancharare...*' What was the next line? He knew it well, but could not recall it. The only things that came readily to his mind were the mantras accompanying funeral rites. Sundaram felt depressed. Why couldn't he be a priest who attended weddings, cradling ceremonies and festive homams? Why was he caught in the funeral rite warp?

It hadn't been his decision alone. His teacher, Eswaran, had repeatedly told him, during his last year at school, 'Child, it is easy to conduct a wedding or a festive function. Let the others conduct such rites. But you, you must do something much more difficult, something that requires perfect discipline and conscientiousness: funeral rites and obsequies. Without faultless mantras and rituals, the departed souls can never reach their rightful states or achieve the wisdom that comes only after death. A single mistake and they will be left in limbo, to rot in hunger and thirst. And their misery will reflect on the lives of the living they leave behind. So nothing is more important for a priest than these samskaras. It is in these I wish you to excel.'

Ever since, Sundaram's life had become inextricably linked with the raw plantains and sesame seeds[4] of obsequies.

'Samskaras', Sundaram said aloud, as he walked. A milkman driving his cow ahead of him turned at the word and looked curiously at the priest. Sundaram thought wryly, 'It's bad enough to be called the funeral priest. Soon I'll be called the mad priest!'

The milkman stopped. Sundaram drew near, touched the rump of the cow with his right hand and placed his hand reverently on his eyes. The milkman pulled some grass from a bundle dangling from his shoulder and respectfully handed it to Sundaram who took the grass from him and fed it to the cow. Sundaram wanted to laugh at the irony of feeding the cow the grass he had taken from its owner. The cowherd said politely to Sundaram, 'She hasn't been milking properly for the last four days, master. Bless her so that she may regain her health.'

Sundaram spoke the expected words of comfort. 'She'll soon be well. Do not worry. Do you feed her oilcake?'

'I can't afford that, master. The price of everything has gone up so much.'

Sundaram was not very sure of the price of anything. Perhaps the only monetary information he had was the price of conducting the obsequies on the new moon.

His cousin Subramanya Iyer kept inviting him to stay in Arasur and manage the School of Vedic Studies. Sometimes, Sundaram was tempted. Then he would remember his teacher's words and go on with his work. Besides, he had forgotten all mantras except the ones he used for work.

The milkman was telling him, 'Master, take a short cut through this ground. You'll reach the temple in no time. There's plenty of time for the morning worship.'

When Sundaram reached the temple, a group of singers, probably belonging to the silk weaver community were striding across the corridors of the temple, singing devotional hymns. In the quiet of the morning they sounded meltingly pure and sweet. As he stood listening to them, Sundaram felt a stab of envy: if only he too could be a part of this group and go wherever their legs and the singing took them. These people would, after they had finished singing, pray at the sanctum and return to their homes, content and resume their quiet lives in front of their looms. But he, once he returned from this pilgrimage, he would have to pick up his darbha grass bundle and resume his depressing duties... Suddenly the milkman appeared before him and, smiling, said to him, 'Master, take this...' handing him his severed left hand, all smeared with river sand. Drums began to roll in the temple and bells began to peal. A terrified, sweating Sundaram looked down at his hands. They were both there, healthy and safe. The apparition of the milkman had vanished. Sundaram drew a deep breath and folded his hands fervently towards the sanctum. 'Goddess, forgive me. I will do what it is my duty to do,' he prayed, closing his eyes. When he entered the sanctum, the adorning of the deity had begun.

CHAPTER 22

Ten days into her pilgrimage, Subbamma being driven crazy by her frequent visions of a burning house and the procession of children carrying palm fronds, accompanied by a smell of burnt bat wings.

She got no help from the spirits of her female ancestors who accompanied her everywhere. 'Look,' they said. 'This is entirely your problem and you have to experience it. The only thing we can do for you is not to trouble you in any other way. We will not ask you to sing or eat mounds of food at wayside eateries or ask you to thrust out your breasts when you walk. We will be with you always. Do not worry about anything.'

Subbamma had a premonition that something bad was about to happen. She knew that her female ancestors knew about it, but they wouldn't say a word.

The deities in the yantra were also of no help. When she asked Annasamy Iyengar about it, he replied that the deities in the yantra had no powers to deal with dreams and visions. If she had told him about this problem earlier he could have fitted in the appropriate deity in the yantra. Perhaps he could make a smaller yantra for this purpose when they returned to Arasur.

Subbamma had no more money to spend on Annasamy's yantras. It would not benefit anyone if she spent all her money on yantras and had no more to feed herself. Her female ancestors would not help with all these mundane problems. Besides, they might actually complain that they were hungry. 'We wouldn't do such a thing!' they said in hurt tones when the thought crossed her mind. 'We will never let you go hungry as long as you live.' Subbamma prostrated gratefully on the ground before them for this kindness.

As Iyengar had instructed her, she bathed the yantra every morning, first with water, then with milk, to satisfy the hunger of the deities. The milk she needed for the daily ritual was brought by the milkman who Sundaram had become acquainted with. Sundaram told the milkman that his face reminded him of the face of a clay doll of a snake charmer that was part of his collection of Navaratri dolls. This pleased the milkman greatly and he brought milk for Subbamma's worship everyday, free of charge. When Sundaram said the doll wore a green turban, the milkman listened attentively. The next time they saw him he too was wearing a green turban.

While Subbamma's worship was simple, it was also very effective. When she poured the cold milk over the yantra, it seemed to enter the metal in a flurry of sparks and smoke. Sundaram's wife, Nagalakshmi said it was as if the deities themselves created lamplight and incense smoke from the milk. She was a little envious of Subbamma's extremely simple form of worship, having been used to her husband's elaborate and involved pujas at home that usually kept her hungry until late every afternoon.

True to their word, throughout the pilgrimage, Subbamma's female ancestors did not trouble her. They entertained her with stories about places she had not visited and rituals she had not observed. They kept a close eye on her, pulling her back in time from the waves at Kanyakumari where she took a ritual bath at the confluence of the three oceans[5]. Despite their presence and that of the deities of the yantra, Swaminathan's spirit lover managed to approach Subbamma one day when they were in Sucheendram in the Thanumalayan temple. Annasamy Iyengar was recounting the history and legends of the temple. Pointing to a large uruli in the corridor, Iyengar was explaining that there was a practice in the temple of using the uruli to try Nambudiri priests accused of adultery. The uruli would be filled with burning hot ghee. Into the scalding hot ghee would be dropped a small, gold icon of a cow. The accused Brahmin would be ordered to dunk his hand into the hot ghee and recover the icon. If he was able to recover it without scalding his hand, his innocence would be established. Otherwise, he would be exiled from the village.

It was when Subbamma was looking at the uruli that she felt a hot breath on the nape of her neck. How could human breath smell of bats, Subbamma wondered and turned to see who was behind her. A beautiful girl, the daughter of the temple priest, stood there. But when she addressed Subbamma, it was clear that she was not, at least for the moment, the priest's daughter.

'It's me, Subbamma, Saama's wife,' the girl introduced herself. 'You alone can save me.'

Subbamma's alarmed female ancestors flew cawing like crows into the sky and circled the space above Subbamma's head. Subbamma had left her yantra in the chatram where she was staying, but she was not afraid of the girl.

'What do you want me to do?' she asked the girl reasonably. 'You are at least two hundred years older than me. And Saama is young enough to be my son. Does that not make him the same age as your great-grandson? Just because he was stupid enough to invoke you should you fornicate with him? And what about me? Have you not tortured me enough? Why should I spend all my money on a yantra that has to be carted everywhere? Aren't all my troubles due to you?'

'You are right, Subbamma. I should not have teased you thus,' the girl said contritely.

'Don't trust her!' screamed the female ancestors.

Annasamy Iyengar had already led the rest of the group into the sanctum. Subbamma sat in one of the pavilions in the corridor outside, arguing with the spirit.

The girl said, seductively, 'Do you know how wonderful it is to be naked and feel the body of your husband against yours? Do you not remember your husband's first embrace?'

'Subbamma, don't think about those things,' warned her ancestors. 'This spirit is trying to pollute your mind inside the temple. If only you had carried the yantra with you, none of this would have happened.'

The girl too seemed to hear them. She folded her hands respectfully in their direction and pleaded, 'Did you all not enjoy the pleasures of the flesh? Did you not spread your legs and enjoy the experience? Why is it wrong when I do it?' She started weeping piteously. Subbamma felt sad for her.

'They are going to burn the house down, with Saama and me inside it! Subbamma, you have to save us. Ask your ancestors to help too. If not for me, at least for the sake of Saama, you have to help!'

Just then the temple priests came out of the sanctum after the noon hour worship, and the spirit of Saama's lover vanished like a puff of smoke.

'Aunt Subbamma, are you tired? You have fallen asleep right here in the pavilion!' Annasamy's wife was shaking her awake. And Subbamma exclaimed, 'Save my Saama!'

Sundaram comforted her saying, 'We have prayed for the well-being of the entire universe. Lord Narayana will take care of your Saama too.' Subbamma could only hope he was right.

They reached Tiruvananthapuram late at night. The men ate at the temple kitchen and complained about the excessive use of coconut in the local cuisine. The women ate the sweet gram flour balls they had brought with them. Then they all sat in the chatram that was awash with moonlight and chatted for a while.

'If we go to the temple early we will be able to see the Raja of Tiruvananthapuram there,' someone said. 'He is a great patron of the arts; musicians and dancers from as far away as Thanjavur have migrated to his court.'

Subbamma's female ancestors said, 'We too should sing before such a king.'

Subbamma remembered herself singing in Hindi (which she did not know at all) on the ghats of Varanasi. She had no wish to repeat a similar performance here in front of a powerful king. She was saved by one of the ancestral women cancelling the engagement as she was having her periods and was shy of visiting the king's court in such a state. They made up for it later when Subbamma and her group had finished their pilgrimage and were leaving for Ambalapuzha from Trichur. They set Subbamma off as she sat in one of the bullock carts and made her launch into a bawdy lyric.

Thanaaro thannaaro thana thaanaaro thannaaro

Near the village of Pattambi

A Brahmin lady there she was.

When her husband, the Brahmin

was away travelling

A dog saw this bitch and ....

She sang the first few lines sending the drivers and torch bearers who obviously know the lyric very well into fits of raucous laughter. Hastily Annasamy's wife tied a towel around her mouth. Subbamma attempted to continue with the song even as she struggled to remove the gag. The cart drivers picked up where she had left off and started humming the tune as a chorus with gusto, much to everyone's discomfiture. Fortunately, just then someone yelled, 'We've reached Ambalapuzha!' And they all got off to enquire where Duraisamy Aiyyan's house was.

CHAPTER 23

Kuppusamy Iyer's house was full of the remains of the Ayyappan puja conducted that morning, as a prelude to Sankaran and his family meeting his sister Bhagavati. The afternoon was creeping in with the ants in the kitchen dragging tiny pieces of leftover sweetmeats and monkeys jumping around the branches of the mango trees in the garden behind the house. The air was thick with the cacophonous notes of a stubborn drunkard walking with unsteady steps down the mud road.

Sankaran and his relatives sat in the large hall where the puja had been held and waited for Bhagavati to appear. He and his parents had arrived in Ambalapuzha the previous day and had been staying in the Telugu music teacher's house. Subramanya Iyer spent most of his time sitting on the pyol outside the house, practising his Malayalam on everyone. Kalyani listened to the Telugu songs that the music teacher's wife sang, joining in now and then.

The second group of relatives, led by the priest, Sundaram, had also arrived and were now gathered in the hall. Sankaran had caught sight of Bhagavati the previous evening when she had come to the music teacher's house for her lessons. It was dusk when she came but Sankaran had seen her beautiful profile as she sat there strumming her tanpura. Sankaran wondered why the music teacher was making a pretty girl sing the rather militant sounding Atana raga. A graceful Vasanta, a seductive Kamas or a majestic Kalyani would have been more appropriate. It was not that Sankaran did not like to listen to Atana, but it invoked a feeling of worship in him that hardly suited his mood.

The Kottakudi dasi back home was said to have set erotic folk poetry to sensual tunes and danced to them for select audiences. Sankaran would have liked to see her dance—observe the circles of sweat under her arms as she raised them to hold a pose, take in the sweet redness of her betel-stained lips, the thrust of her breasts and nipples. He heard about these things from customers to the tobacco shop. He could have gone to the performances, of course, but that would have lowered his reputation among the villagers, and that would not be good for business. His father tapped him lightly on the thigh to bring him back to the present. He came to with a start and smiled vaguely at everyone.

Subbamma said loudly, 'Why not bring the girl in now?'

Snehamba and Visalakshi went into the room where Bhagavati was dressing. Bhagavati's sister Echumi and her friend Narayani had plaited her hair and adorned it with flowers and jewels. They held a mirror to her face and to her back so that she could see how she looked. Seeing Snehamba and Visalakshi, they chorused, 'She's ready. All she needs is a small black dot on her cheek to ward off the evil eye.'

'No black dot or dots of any other colour!' cried Bhagavati. 'They will take one look at my dotted face and run back to where they came from!'

Visalakshi thought Bhagavati looked like a child when she laughed. She had been a child when Visalakshi first came to this house as a bride. She had watched her grow up into a lovely young woman and had deep maternal feelings for her.

Bhagavati had been briefed: she had to walk in sedately making sure she did not trip on the unfamiliar sari, having reached the hall she had to pay obeisance to everyone gathered there, then move to a corner and sit quietly with head lowered modestly. If they asked her to sing, she knew exactly which song she would sing, the sober '*Nannu paalimpa*'. Bhagavati would have preferred something less classical, '*Omana tingal kidavo*', a pretty Malayalam lullaby. She wished she could spend her life singing songs like that and watching dance performances in the temple with her friends. None of that would be possible. She would soon have to go far away and spend her time in a kitchen in a distant household.

As they walked towards the hall, Visalakshi suggested, 'Child, lift up the hem of your sari, if you are afraid of tripping on it.'

'Lift it just a bit,' teased Narayani. 'Don't lift it up to your thigh. You can do that with your husband.' Bhagavati gave her a playful slap on the back and the girl ran laughing towards the kitchen.

Sankaran looked up as Bhagavati entered the hall. Her large, kohl-rimmed eyes drove every other thought from his mind. Bhagavati kneeled and touched her head to the floor in the direction of all the visitors. Before her bent gaze were a series of feet, many with split nails and cracked soles, but she could easily make out those dark skinned, strong and shapely feet as belonging to the man who would be her husband. The rest of him matched the feet—he was tall and well-built with strong shoulders. He had thick black hair which he had tied in a tuft. On his earlobes were winking solitaire studs.

As Bhagavati rose, Subbamma began to sing. Sensing her mood, someone tied a towel around her mouth. Bhagavati's family looked shocked but the astrologer, Annasamy, quickly explained, 'The spirits of seven generations of auspicious women in her family remain with her always. They bless all those around them. Sometimes their joy knows no bounds and they start singing jolly songs through her. What can be more auspicious for a home than the happy presence of such blessed spirits?'

Subbamma removed her gag and began singing a devotional song and the other women joined in. Subbamma then sang a simple Tamil song that melted their hearts. Visalakshi felt her eyes fill with tears. Bhagavati was transported to another world. The song ended and someone said, 'The bride-to-be should sing now.'

Just as Bhagavati launched into '*Nannu paalimpa*', Snehamba's father, the old man, floated effortlessly from the terrace of the house and out across the street.

CHAPTER 24

Swaminathan wandered slowly from room to room in the empty house.

Old Ramalakshmi, the cook in the School of Vedic studies, had left some lunch for him: bland rasam, rice and snake gourd curry in which Saama spied a long strand of white hair. He remembered this as food from a previous birth, although it was what he had eaten at school just a few years back.

'Oh Agni, listen to our prayers, as you sit with Mitra and Arya on your throne. You are as potent and strong as Indra. You were kind enough to incarnate on this earth. Then you leapt into space...' Saama could hear the lines of the Sama Veda which he had memorised so diligently in school. He is repeating them after his teacher. The sounds of chanting rise like flames from the sacrificial fire. His body glows with majesty. He grows wings and takes off into the sky. Men bearing red flags flank him. They have all come to speak with him—they are not from his time but from the future, a future in which everything would change. Men would be the most powerful beings on earth, not ghosts, nor gods. That is what these men believe. He does not know whether what they believed came to pass, but he looks at them with affection.

'O Agni, you are the true lord of my home, the teacher for my worship. Burn down our sins and faults. Stop us from sinning and lead us along the right path.'

'Why do you chant all this stuff, Saama? Why can't we be content with what we have? Cannot we be as we are?' Saama's lover embraced him from behind and whispered in his ear.

'No, Vasu, listen to me. Let me tell you about the Sama Veda. Do you know why these people are carrying red flags?'

'I don't want to know anything, Saama. Your body alone is enough for me.'

'No, Vasu, stop. O Agni… Damnation! Why do you want me on the swing?'

Saama could feel her hair brushing his lips.

'Vasu. Vasumati. Vasu, pasu, sisu…'

She laughed and covered his body with hers. She still managed to use one foot to keep the swing moving. The pressure of her body and the movement of the swing sent Saama into ecstasy. How wonderful if he could die this way!

'There's still time for that, you rascal!' she whispered in his ear, having read his mind. 'Come on, make love to me. And, this swing had better not stop moving, do you hear?'

Her sharp words only served to heighten his passion.

For the last two days she had been with him constantly. When old Ramalakshmi brought his food, she pulled at the folds of her sari mischievously and cackled. Ramalakshmi, however, thought her sari had come undone accidentally and ran out blushing. Vasu would not leave Ayyanai alone either. When he came in the mornings and evenings to enquire after Saama, she gave him resounding kicks on his back. But Ayyanai was a bold man and knew of her. 'I am being nice to you only because you are a Brahmin girl. Otherwise I will set my village deity, Muniyandi Karuppan, on you and reduce you to nothing!' When Ayyanai slapped his shoulders and yelled at her, she ran behind Saama and hugged his shoulders fearfully.

'Master, get rid of this nuisance and get married like your brother,' Ayyanai advised Saama before leaving. Once he had left, Vasu climbed on to Saama's lap and chatted cheerfully with him, bringing to him visions of what was happening with his family members on their travels. There was Subbamma, gagged with a towel. There was the priest, Sundaram, standing on the riverbank after his bath, dressed in nothing but his loin cloth. A Brahmin vendor sold packets of food from a roadside eatery. A milkman, wearing a green turban, drove his cow ahead of him. An old man floated in the air and stopped to relieve himself. A young woman sat in front of Sankaran and sang a song.

Vasu bent over laughing.

'Why have they gagged Aunt Subbamma?' Saama asked her as he draped one of her legs around his neck. She told him why and he laughed. Even before he had finished laughing she said to him urgently, 'Come to me.'

Sometime later, Saama wanted to know why the old man was floating in the air. 'I don't know,' she replied. 'Can we give reasons for every happening? Why did I come when you called me? Why are we like this as if fucking is the only end of life?'

Swaminathan had no answers. He followed her as she led the way to the kitchen. When he realised her intent, he objected. 'Not here!'

'Why not?' she retorted. 'Is it not clean and neat? See how cool the floor is, scrubbed with cow dung.'

He sat down with reluctance. His whole body ached. If only she would let him rest a while. She would not. 'Come here and look,' she invited him to another vision: a man and a woman were copulating in a granary. 'I don't want to see,' he demurred.

'They belong to the family into which your brother is going to marry,' she enlightened him. 'And look at this old man! What is he doing, floating into the granary when these two are fucking? Look, he is dashing against the man's bare buttock! Don't laugh! What if it happened to you? Would you like it?'

'Why do I need that old devil? I have enough of a devil in you!'

She embraced him so tightly that Saama felt as if the ground was disappearing under his feet and he was drowning in a velvety darkness.

'Let's go upstairs,' she invited him after some time.

'Why, are you tired of the kitchen already?'

'No, but we need to go upstairs now. Only then can we be ready.'

'Ready for what?' he asked.

'For that which will happen. I did beg everyone possible to save us. But no one has helped.'

'What did you ask? And what did they say?' Saama pulled her to him as she was climbing the stairs ahead of him and, turning her around, kissed her on her mouth. Her breath smelled of meat.

'Do you eat flesh?' he asked her.

'I could eat anything, even...' she pointed teasingly to the spot below his waist. He clapped a hand over his penis and threw back his head and laughed.

'Where is your veshti, you rogue?' she asked him. He looked back and saw it lying crumpled on the swing.

'You are a fine one to ask me that question!' he replied. 'Are you dressed decorously?'

'But I belong to a time when we dressed differently, that is, two hundred years before your time,' she said to him.

'Then why did you come to me? Am I not the same age as your great–great-grandson?'

'I did not come to you, you rascal! You called me! I was just a spirit hungry for food and came to your house to eat the leftovers from the srardha meal. I just happened to wander upstairs. And what did you do to me, you rogue?'

'This, just this,' Saama replied and became one with her. As he lost himself inside her, he wished he could this instant dissolve and become nothing.

'O Agni, do not come here. I will myself turn to dust and vanish. I offer you my obeisance. O Agni, take our prayers to the gods. What is my prayer? That I should stay locked in my Vasu's embrace through the night. Just that.'

When darkness fell heavily into the room, Saama got up and stumbled to the table where he cranked up the music box and began playing the dirge music on it.

'Are you hungry?' Vasu asked him gently.

'No. I feel neither hunger nor thirst. My heart is full of joy. Vasu, do you know what this is?' he pointed to the music box.

'No. Am I as educated as you? I only know that a soul, as disturbed as I am, is sitting in it and wailing.'

So Swaminathan told her about how the music box really worked, then he told her about the other wondrous machines of the future: the box that could make pictures of reality and machines that could type words on paper. He also told her about the terrible war that would come, and the fireball that would rise to the skies in the shape of a mushroom and destroy lakhs of people.

Vasu listened to all of it and said, 'Why do I need to know all this? All I wanted were a few grains of rice to eat everyday. If I had been given that I would have led a normal life, reached old age and died like everyone else.' Tears were streaming down her face as she said this and Saama reached up to wipe her cheeks.

'Come with me. I will ask those rogues who bring me these music discs to carry us away to the future. All my friends are there—the ones who speak English and wear strange clothes. They will look after us well. Shall we go?'

She looked at him sadly and replied, 'We can go nowhere, Saama. We have to vanish as we are, right now.'

Even as she spoke, a flaming torch landed inside the room from outside the window, then another and another. Swaminathan's table caught fire and the flames spread an eerie light in the room.

'Vasu, you look as beautiful as Menaka,' Saama said, his eyes drinking in every aspect of her form.

More burning torches fell inside the house.

'How bright it is, as if it were Deepavali, or Kartikai!' Saama exclaimed with joy. He felt like dancing.

'Get up, Vasu! Look how beautiful this is!' he cried.

'No,' she said.' Lie down on me. This is the way I want to go.'

When he raised his head for the last time, he saw the flaming disc in the music box rotate furiously, spewing sorrow and then come to an abrupt stop.

'I am Agni, the pure. All knowledge belongs to me. I am the breath of life, I am wind, I am the sun.All sacrifices are made to me.'

Saama remembered the lines from the Sama Veda for the last time.

'All sacrifices go to you,' he thought. 'So do I.'

He embraced his lover tightly.

CHAPTER 25

The king woke up smelling smoke.

Something was burning somewhere or someone was being burnt. The king thought he could smell a number of things burning: flesh, guava tree, bricks and tiles, basil plants, cloth, leftover food, shit and urine—everything was being reduced to ashes.

In his sleep-hazed state, the king wondered if it was the body of Bushy Moustache, his father-in-law. Had he been up to his tricks even from beyond the grave? Perhaps his relatives had decided that as long as the old man had a body, his cock would always be stiff and that the only way to stop all that would be to dig up the body and burn it to ashes. Even as the thought occurred to him the king brushed it aside as being completely ridiculous. He was awake now and realised that this was his palace and the old man had been buried near the waste land used as an open air toilet by one and all, a wretched location far from this place. Why should anyone bring the corpse here to the palace and burn it?

The king got up from his bed and walked to the window. He could see fire and smoke. People were rushing to and fro trying to put out the fire with pots of water. The tobacco merchant's house was going up in flames! The king felt sad that he would no longer be able to listen to music from the music box.

Calmer now because he knew the location of the fire, the king urinated into the copper pot that was kept near the bed, covered it with a palm frond and went back to bed. The copper pot was an innovation that was necessitated when, owing to lack of funds the king had to dismiss his night watchmen. They usually accompanied him to the backyard when he visited it during the night, lighting his way with torches. It was not safe to visit the backyard at night without the protection of the watchmen. The dismissed watchmen had taken up other means of livelihood: one of them sold jackfruit in the market place, another sold vials of peacock oil, a potent aphrodisiac (he was also rumoured to pimp for the Kottakudi dasi—an apt extension of his trade). The king had a soft corner for them and gave them a few coins whenever he saw them in the market (that every time he saw them, he unconsciously felt an urge to piss was another matter).

As he lay down again, the king glanced at the queen by his side, sleeping soundly with her mouth wide open. In the light of the oil lamp she somewhat resembled her clean shaven brother at her father's funeral. Why had she opened her mouth so wide as if preparing to scream?

The king sat bolt upright as the image of the queen screaming in the voice of the Brahmin girl at Bushy Moustache's funeral came back to him. For a while the entire household had been wrapped in a ghostly silence. Then the dirge singers had started singing in a loud voice about the Goddess, and the other women had lit camphor before the queen to calm whatever spirit had invaded her. The queen had then fainted. By the time the king, who was having his dinner, had come running, his hand still squishy with food, his brothers-in-law's wives and maids had lifted the unconscious queen and laid her on the floor of the courtyard close to where her father's corpse had been laid. The king tried to kneel down and fan his wife but his weight would not allow him to bend his knees and he ended up standing and waving the palm frond hand fan uselessly, creating more breeze for himself than the queen.

'It is a house of death, there are bound to be a few ghosts moving around until all the rites are over. We have to be careful,' said one of the old men. The queen's brothers agreed.

'Your highness, the food is drying on your hand. Please wash it,' the old man's aged mistress said respectfully, bringing the king a pot of water. The king would have liked to finish his meal, but that would not have been polite.

The queen fell asleep. The dirge singers moved out of the house and sang the epic of the ascetic's erring wife in soft voices to applause from the young men. The king would have liked to join them, but he was swamped by the presence of his ancestors. 'It matters little who this Brahmin girl is,' they advised him. 'What matters is that our child should be more careful.'

'Which child?' the king asked, confused.

'We are referring to your wife.'

'What should she do?'

'It is enough that she does not do anything. Things will happen of their own accord.'

'Are you saying she should not bathe?'

'Tell her to bathe within the palace.'

'I will, but the mason says that to build a bathroom inside the palace, it will cost me ten rupees. Where will I go for that kind of money?' a pleading note crept into the king's voice.

Before his ancestors could answer, the spirit of Bushy Moustache intruded. 'I want liquor, I want cigars, I want snuff…' he ordered the king, trying to grab his hand. 'Arrange for all of it on the final day of my rites.'

'Why don't you pay lip-service to me, you whoreson?' retorted the incensed king.

That invitation for fellatio set the old man off. He fired a volley of unrepeatable words at the king. The latter's ancestors scolded the king for aggravating the old man. Then they dragged the old man away and disappeared in a puff of smoke.

As the king recalled this, he gazed at his sleeping wife and wondered if she was responsible for the fire. There was no way of knowing. It would not be right to wake her up and ask her. He got out of bed again and wandered outside. Well, what if she had arranged for the fire? Could there be a bigger sin than spying on an honourable woman while she was bathing? The fire seemed an appropriate punishment for such a sin. With the men in that house disposed towards degrading themselves, some curse or calamity had to befall them. If it was not the queen they were probably spying on the women bathing in the village pond or tank… but the ponds were all dry because of the drought. No one could bathe in them and provide entertainment for the tobacco merchant's boys.

The king would have liked to enquire about the fire from the people trying to put it out, but he didn't want to take the chance of receiving a rude answer. Perhaps he could walk to the palace priest's house and ask him. This was the priest he had given a gold coin to make a yantra to ward off the Brahmin girl's spirit. The priest said he needed a certain poem in Sanskrit and Tamil to be inscribed on the yantra. He would write the Sanskrit poem but the king would need to find someone to write the Tamil poem. The only person in the village who could compose excellent Tamil poetry metered perfectly was the Kottakudi dasi. The king toyed with the idea of inviting her over to the palace in the afternoon when the queen napped so that she could compose the poem and…

but there might not be much time left over for other things after the dasi had carefully worded her poem. Now that the tobacco merchant's house had burnt down, there was no need for the dasi to compose a poem or for the yantra to be made.

The girders of the tobacco merchant's house came crashing down, sending up huge sparks of fire. The spectators scattered in panic. The crowd was rushing towards the palace. The king walked back into the palace, not wishing to be caught gawking. He wished he had not wasted a gold coin on the priest.

CHAPTER 26

'So while the old man was floating all over the place, you were sitting at home gorging yourselves on kesari and vadai?' Sangunni Nair teased Kuppusamy Iyer.

They were meeting four days after the Arasur family visited Kuppusamy's house to meet Bhagavati and the two families had exchanged betel leaves[6] to clinch the betrothal. The visitors left immediately afterwards.

'That was completely chaotic,' Kuppusamy agreed. 'My poor brother Kitta Iyer had to spend a lot of money on his father-in-law because of all this.' Kuppusamy spoke as he sliced a betel nut in half in his nutcracker.

'Why must this old man float and fly at his age? What use is that of to him like a hen sporting tits? If it had happened to you or me it would have helped us travel faster to earn money!' Sangunni joked.

Kuppusamy nodded vaguely. The acidic betel juice in his throat was giving him a warm feeling of contentment and joy. He would be happy to sit here, chewing betel leaf and listening to Sangunni's chatter. The fellow could tell very funny stories about Nambudiris. Kuppusamy was just asking him to tell him a new one when Sangunni's servant, Kesavan, walked over and spoke to him.

'I'll be back,' Sangunni excused himself and accompanied the servant.

Kuppusamy closed his eyes and let his mind wander to the events that took place on the day of Bhagavati's betrothal. Young Bhagavati's fiancé was a handsome man, he thought, dark skinned, yes, but his features were handsome. That was exactly his wife Visalakshi's opinion. Visalakshi never seemed to have a bad word for anybody in any case. She was like that. There seemed to be so much love in her heart that she lavished it on the world around her. Even the beggar who passed their house every night, singing for leftovers, seemed to her a veritable musician. 'Only his body is weak,' she would say fondly. 'Hear how beautiful his voice is and how strong!' And she would fill his earthen pot with rice and vegetable gravy.

'Now that fellow is going to sit down on our pyol and eat and break out into such music that our Telugu teacher will despair of facing such competition and leave our village!' Kuppusamy liked to tease her, as he did on the night of Bhagavati's engagement, after he had come into the house and she had returned from feeding the beggar.

'Why do I tell you such things—you are such a dud!' she teased him back, rubbing him fondly around his waist. He felt an almost uncontrollable urge to bed her right away. He knew that there was no one else in the house right then as everyone had gone to the temple for Bhagavati's birthday. He pulled his wife to him, laid her down on the floor covered with scattered grains of yellow rice and bits of betel nut and flowers. Just then someone began banging on the front door.

'You do have a talent for getting the urge at all the wrong times!' Visalakshi laughed and moved away. He felt too irritated to get up and move towards the front door. He lay there while his wife went out. His gaze fell on the spot on the wall where, in the afternoon, that old lady from the Arasur family, whose mouth they had gagged, rested her head. There was an oily mark there now, shaped strangely like a black bat.

Visalakshi opened the door to find several men standing outside with flaming torches in their hands. Behind them had been set down a rope-strung cot on which lay a body that had been fully covered with a long piece of cloth. Leading the group was Narayanan, the son of the melshanti of the temple and his friend Parasuraman. Visalakshi peered at the cot. The body belonged to the old man, Snehamba's father. Visalakshi screamed so loudly that Kuppusamy came running. After he had taken in the scene he bent close to the old man and felt his pulse. He seemed to be alive.

'He's fine,' said Parasuraman. 'It's the man who sets off the fireworks in the temple during worship who has lost a toe because of him.'

Kuppusamy was amazed. They had locked the old man upstairs so that he would not cause trouble during the betrothal function. How on earth had he got out? Kuppusamy remembered how he had advised Kitta Iyer to take the old man back to his sons in Alapat. But Kitta refused, saying that the old man was being treated for his condition by the local vaidyan and that they could not discontinue the treatment.

Kuppusamy felt he had already lost the argument but he had tried again. 'Kitta, you know the people from Arasur are coming to see Bhagavati. What if he floats around the hall that day? His indiscriminate urinating in the backyard has made the place so smelly that no amount of washing can get rid of the odour.' Kuppusamy was upset, and annoyed that the old man's sons seemed unashamed to leave their father in the care of their sister's family.

At this point Visalakshi said, 'Let the poor man stay. We will feed him and provide enough water and close the door to the room upstairs so that he cannot leave. We can even leave a mud pot for him to urinate into.'

Snehamba hugged her in relief. 'You are as kind as the goddess in the temple,' she said, and eyes brimming, promised, 'I'll make sure he doesn't cause problems during the function.'

The old man had not floated downstairs or to the backyard. Instead, he had floated out of the house and away across the village.

After they had brought the unconscious old man into the house, Kuppusamy removed the dirty sheet he was covered with and wrapped him in a clean veshti. Visalakshi averted her gaze while he was doing this as the old man was perfectly naked under the sheet. Her gaze rested for a second on the oily stain on the wall, left by the old Arasur woman's head. It resembled a bat. Suddenly she heard a whisper, 'What a nuisance this interruption is! How fondly you were stroking your husband's waist! I was so hoping to witness the rest of it. And then this old man comes and ruins everything!'

'You dirty devil! The only reason I am pardoning you is because you came with that nice old lady!' Visalakshi heard her mind snap at the bat. She looked away from the wall in fear.

'What happened to the man who sets off the firecrackers?' Kuppusamy asked Narayanan.

'Ah, that's quite a story! When this old man floated across the streets all the women thought he was a ghost and ran home. The children ran after the old man. There was a strong breeze and the old man's veshti and loin cloth ripped away from him and landed beyond the temple. The old man was blown into the temple, where he landed with a thud near the flagstaff and urinated. The melshanti of the temple came running, yelling at the top of his voice. He locked the temple doors and went to the local astrologer to find out what to do to rid the temple of the pollution caused by the old man's urinating. He did not chastise or harm the old man, assuming that he was possessed by a ghost. The vaidyan, who was at the temple when the incident took place, tried to tell the melshanti and others that the old man was not possessed by any spirit. His floating was due to his extremely enfeebled state. 'Think logically, scientifically!' he urged. Instead, the melshanti lectured the vaidyan on the reality of ghosts, evil spirits and sorcerers. While the debate raged, the old man rose to the sky, floated into the temple again and landed where firecrackers are burst during worship[7]. The man who sets off the crackers was lighting one when the naked old man landed squarely on him. The cracker burst, scorching the man's hand and blowing off one of his toes. The vaidyan, meanwhile, procured a cot and placed the old man on it. The old man fell into a deep sleep on the way home.'

Kuppusamy thought the expense of treating the firecracker man would fall squarely on Kitta's shoulders.

Narayanan left, agreeing that the reason for the old man's tendency to float was probably due to his enfeebled health rather than the mischief of a ghost. 'But my father will not agree. I really don't know when people are going to reason things out,' he said.

The moment everyone left, the old man sat bolt upright and said, 'The house and everything in it has been burnt down!' His voice was loud and clear.

'Edo Kuppusamy, are you day-dreaming or sleeping?' Sangunni, returning from his errand, dug a finger into Kuppusamy's side to rouse him.

Kuppusamy opened his eyes and looked at his friend. A question scratched at his mind. 'Whose house had been burnt down?'

He would have liked to ask the old man, but his sons had arrived the day after to take him back to Alapat. The old man had stopped floating—he seemed completely cured and walked on his feet like everyone else.

He retained a lifelong fondness for urinating at the base of a mango tree in the backyard.

CHAPTER 27

Both Saama and the house had been reduced to ashes.

Until two days earlier, he had been alive—a human being who had imbued scholarship but had descended into a depraved existence, unaware of his nudity, finding joy only in listening to the most sorrowful music and pleasuring himself shamelessly. All that flesh and the joy it brought him now lay in blackened ruins under a dirty piece of cloth.

Behind Saama's body stood the blackened walls of the house.

Subramanya Iyer received the news of his son's death and the fire when he reached Madurai on his way back. His friend and former employee, Thanu Pillai waited for him on the road outside the town limits. Ayyanai had run all the way from Arasur to inform Thanu Pillai of the tragedy the previous day.

Thanu Pillai waited for his friend to arrive, sitting on a chair with a servant holding an umbrella over him to shield him from the sun. He got up as soon as Iyer's bullock cart came into view.

'Pillai, why are you sitting here just to receive me? Don't I know my way around Madurai?' Subramanya Iyer chided him, though secretly pleased that his former employee accorded him so much respect. He decided that if he started dealing in snuff, he would make Thanu Pillai the agent for Madurai.

Sankaran felt something was amiss. Why was Pillai sitting there craning his neck at the road like a pimp sitting outside a prostitute's house? Something was wrong. Had the financier to whom they had entrusted their cash died? Had the Englishman to whom he had loaned money returned to England without re-paying them?

Inside the carriage, Kalyani woke up and felt the dire need to relieve herself. She stepped out slowly and saw Thanu Pillai. She hoped they would stop at his house so that she could use the facilities in his backyard. Her abdomen felt as if it would burst.

Thanu Pillai stared at the three of them and did not quite know how to break the news. He called his servant, Veeran, and told him to take Iyer and his family to his home. 'Take them in my horse carriage, as that is faster. I will follow in their bullock cart.'

He walked quickly towards Iyer's carriage, leaving the others no option but to climb into the horse carriage. They reached Thanu Pilai's house in no time. Kalyani was surprised that her polite enquiries elicited only silent nods from the women of Pillai's family. None of them asked how the betrothal ceremony in Ambalapuzha had gone. She didn't pay too much attention as she was in a hurry to get to the backyard. When she had relieved herself, she bathed at the well. As she was re-entering the house in her wet clothes, she heard the loud, ugly wails of the men in the hall. 'When did it happen?' Subramanya Iyer cried. 'How? Why did no one tell us? There I was eating and making merry, while…' he broke off and began to sob.

Kalyani felt her damp clothes choking her. Water from them ran in rivulets on the ground where she stood. Intuitively, she knew what had happened. 'Saama!' she screamed. 'Swaminatha!' She stepped into the hall and Iyer wailed, 'Everything's gone, Kalyani. Disaster has struck our family!' Kalyani heard no more as she swooned and collapsed in a heap. The women of Thanu Pillai's family, themselves sobbing, rushed to her aid.

The men moved to the pyols outside the house. A crowd had gathered to offer condolence and help. Thanu Pillai was well known in the area and everyone knew that he respected Subramanya Iyer greatly. Their grief and desire to help was genuine.

Sankaran stood on the pyol leaning against a pillar. Their house was gone. So was his elder brother. He tried to seek out the positive aspects of the tragedy—they had not left any cash in the house, it was safely with the financier; he had not left a single basket of tobacco leaves in the house, he had transported them all to the agents. The fire would not affect their business. How much would it cost to rebuild the house? Why had it been burnt down? Who could have done it? Had they been careless in leaving only Ayyanai to guard the house and care for Saama?

'I told that wretch Ayyanai to stay with Saama! Did the rogue slip off to drink toddy, allowing my house burn down? May he never be rid of the sin of casting me into the hell of mourning my son?' In his sorrow, Iyer ranted and raved against his loyal servant. Thanu Pillai felt impelled to interrupt.

'Sir, do not blame Ayyanai, it was not his fault,' he said. 'He was there, sleeping on the pyol, when the house caught fire. Someone threw flaming torches into the house from outside. They had coated the torches with sulphur, so things caught fire quickly. Ayyanai rushed up the stairs but the whole place was already burning and the smoke was thick. Ayyanai managed to reach the younger master's room, but it was locked from the inside and he could be heard laughing loudly. It was all over before Ayyanai could get help. That old man ran all the way here to give me the news and ran back without pausing to drink even a sip of water.'

While the women of Thanu Pillai's household tended to Kalyani and sent for the vaidyan, Iyer and Sankaran left for Arasur with Thanu Pillai. Thanu Pillai assured Iyer, 'Sir, the women will look after your wife and when she is well enough to travel, my father-in-law or brother-in-law will accompany her to Arasur.'

Sankaran requested him to tell the women not to inform his mother that Saama was dead. 'It is enough if they tell her that he is unwell.'

'No need to tell them, Sankara. They know how to handle it,' Iyer said softly, wiping his eyes with his upper cloth.

As the carriage hastened towards Arasur, Iyer felt like a poverty-stricken Brahmin who had lost everything. He would become a pall bearer to eke out a living. A little later, he fell into a light sleep despite himself. By his side, Sankaran thought, uncomfortable though the thought made him feel, about Bhagavati. He remembered the smells of cardamom and clove and sandalwood and jasmine that had filled the house in Ambalapuzha. In this manner, father and son reached Arasur.

Ayyanai sat on the ground near the blackened feet sticking out of the stained sheet covering Saama's corpse. When he saw Iyer and Sankaran arrive, he rose and began screaming so loudly that all of Arasur came running. 'Master, we have been ruined!' cried Ayyanai, inconsolably.

CHAPTER 28

A crowd of mourners went to cremate Saama.

Not that there was much left to cremate. And no home left for the mourners to return to.

Alternative living arrangements were quickly made. Swaminatha Iyer owned the building that housed the School of Vedic Studies. The principal was asked to shift the school to Raja Chatram, a public guest house owned by the king. The king agreed to allow the principal to move the school there temporarily. The school building would be the mourners' home until their ruined house was rebuilt. Old Ramalakshmi, the school cook, struggled with damp firewood and a disused stove to cook a meal large enough to feed the students as well as Iyer's family. A few students carried the food to Iyer's home and left the dishes there, covered with plantain leaves.

'I have no wish to eat. Why can't I die right now?' wailed Iyer, as he sat disconsolately, with this back to the wall in their new home. Sankaran, however, was ravenous, so hungry that he was unwilling to consider anything or anyone, dead brother, wife-to-be, or mourning father, until he had appeased his hunger. He sat down, and serving himself, ate a huge meal. Watching him eat seemed to give Iyer an appetite and after a while, he put some rice on a plantain leaf and began eating it. 'Have some buttermilk, father,' Sankaran said gently and served him.

Iyer repeatedly imagined he had become a pall bearer. A pall bearer eating his frugal meal. After that, he would rest for a while at the pyol when someone would rudely wake him up – 'you wretched being, get up and come along. There is a corpse to be carried to the burning ghat'. Not a badly burnt corpse, it will be. The hasty signature that life had scribbled when leaving the body would still be visible on its face.

Thanu Pillai and the others from Madurai had left immediately after the funeral. 'Don't worry about your wife,' Thanu Pillai had reassured Iyer before leaving. 'The women in my family will look after her well until you are ready to come and fetch her.'

The students cleared the dishes away. Sankaran cleaned the floor on which they had eaten and went to the backyard to wash his hands. The backyard stank of urine, bushes had grown around the well, loin cloths still hung on the clothesline, vibhuti bags rested in the niches on the wall, reminding him that this was still the school and had not yet become his home.

As Sankaran walked back through the house to the entrance, he passed his father, fast asleep on the floor.

It was a humid night. When he came out to the pyol, there was hardly any traffic on the street. He wished he could talk to someone, anyone—the Kottakudi dasi, a cattleherd or the queen who bathed in view of his terrace. He suddenly remembered that he had forgotten about the queen over the last few days. Smitten by

Bhagavati's beauty, the queen, the dasi and every other woman had flown out of his mind. 'Isn't the queen someone else's wife, you rascal!' someone snapped at him, or so Sankaran thought he heard. He felt as if the cowherd had smeared dung on his face, or as if the masturbating Saama's sperm was splattering his lips. He looked up in panic. It had started to drizzle.

Now it would become even more humid. He thought he would walk by his old home and take a look.

What was left to see? What happened to the roof and the swing in the hall? What happened to the red spider that wove endless webs in a corner in the corridor where they left their footwear? And the face of the goddess Lakshmi that had been drawn on the wall in the hall? And the parapet wall on the terrace? What happened to them all?

The drizzle was stronger now. He walked slowly. When he reached the crossroads, his feet turned involuntarily into the market street where his shop was but he pulled himself back and walked on to his house. Who cared about the shop? Let it remain closed for a couple of days. He took a turn and the palace came into view. It was dark, except for the light from a single window. Perhaps the queen was trying to pleasure the elderly, obese king. When this difficult task was over, she would doubtless check to see if the oil, soapnut powder and other herbal powders for her bath the next morning were laid out properly. When she bathed the next day, Sankaran would not peep at her over the parapet wall of his terrace. She could bathe in privacy and climb the ruined steps of the tank back to the palace.

Sankaran reached the ruins of his house. The rain beat hard upon his face. Lightning made the blackened remains of the walls glow. 'Why have you all deserted me?' the house seemed to wail at Sankaran whose heart broke at the sight.

He entered the house in a trance. Without doors and windows to protect it, the house looked like an elderly woman who had been stripped naked. 'I will rebuild you,' Sankaran vowed fiercely. 'I will set you right within two months. When the temple chariot rolls along our street in the month of Panguni, the house will look normal and we will distribute buttermilk and jaggery water to the poor from our pyol. I will leave my sandals right here in this corridor. Even if that spider is dead in the fire, another will take its place and weave new webs. Upstairs in his room Saama will play his music box...' He caught himself short. No, Saama would never again play his music box. That would never happen. Sankaran shook his head to clear it and began climbing the staircase, lit as it was by lightning.

With every step upwards, the stench of bats and human sweat got stronger. For some reason Sankaran was sure it was the sweat of a woman, a woman who had pleasured her lover, climaxed, and in the aftermath, with sweat pouring off her body from her exertions, lay contentedly in his arms. A woman who ate flesh, the flesh of bats. Did people eat bats?

The staircase ended abruptly in empty space. Lightning criss-crossed the dark sky. Drenched to the skin, Sankaran climbed down the staircase and stopped short. On a rug on the floor of the hall below, a young woman sat singing a classical kriti. She stood up shyly when she saw him. Was it Bhagavati Kutti? No, this was another young woman.

'Come and sit next to me, Sankara!'

It was Saama, moving backwards and forwards on the swing in the hall. He looked absolutely dry, with not a drop of moisture on him.

'Did I sing well?' the girl asked as she approached the swing. The smell of old moss, as from a disused well, rose from her clothes.

'Sit, Sankara. She is your sister-in-law, my wife,' Saama introduced them, swinging harder.

'How will my brother-in-law sit on the swing if you keep moving it so fast?' the girl asked and laughed.

'Tell me, is my wife beautiful or the girl you went to see?' Saama asked him, and even as Sankaran was gazing at the girl in confusion, Saama pulled her to him and kissed her.

'I think my brother-in-law thinks only the queen, having her bath, is beautiful, even though she has burnt his house down,' the girl said, gently wiping her lips.

'That's a sin, Sankara. Looking on a married woman when she is in the nude is a terrible sin—at least that is what some worthless fellow has written in some godforsaken grantha,' Saama said in a stern tone, but his eyes were laughing.

'Oh, and is it not a sin to bed a spirit who just came down to eat rice at a srardha?' the girl teased, stroking Saama's waist. Sankaran turned his face away.

'Look at this girl, Sankara. She wants us to make love on the swing, while it is moving. Is that what a swing is for? Bitch! If you swing so hard, the swing is going to hit the face of Lakshmi painted on the wall. The goddess is looking at us.'

'Let her. And let my brother-in-law look too.' She laughed.

Sankaran ran out of the house. He could still hear the sound of the swing, despite the noise of the rain.

CHAPTER 29

They had told the king that the representative of the Sarkar would be visiting the palace early that morning. It was quite late and the king was still waiting.

The king hadn't slept well since he'd heard about the officer's visit. He dreamt that he was begging on the streets of London, extending his copper urine pot to sundry Englishmen. The king woke up in a sweat and was unable to go back to sleep. He paced the hall and the courtyard for the rest of the night.

The king knew the Sarkar representatives were appropriating fiefdoms that were without heirs. They had suffered terrible losses in a battle in Kabul and were resorting to all sorts of methods in the quieter South to make up those losses. Would the representative test whether the king would be able to produce heirs or would he grab his assets? The king hoped he would not come, but as he was dependant on the generosity of the Sarkar, he could not refuse to receive him.

He was beginning to feel drowsy. He was constipated as well, this disturbed him almost as much as the imminent arrival of the Company representative. He ordered another dose of vallarai lehyam and scalding hot water. He thought he had been having a variety of ailments ever since the burning down of the tobacco merchant's house. Had the Brahmin boy who died in the fire cursed him? Why should he do that? Why should he have cursed him with constipation?

No one blamed the king for the fire in the tobacco merchant's house. The palace manager informed him that although there was some resentment that the king had done nothing to douse the fire, no one linked him to it. There had actually been some rejoicing in the Brahmin Street. Many had resented the fact that a Brahmin had grown rich selling rubbish like tobacco. 'God has punished him for this sin by burning down his house and his eldest son,' people said.

The king felt sorry for the tobacco merchant. There was nothing wrong in selling tobacco; one must grab opportunities to make money in these difficult times, thought the king reasonably. He, unfortunately, was forbidden by tradition from doing anything lucrative. The Kottakudi dasi had her singing and dancing, Annasamy Iyengar had astrology, the Iyer had his tobacco trade—they were all lucky. He was forced to beg for his survival from the Sarkar. The Sarkar denied him the right to collect taxes from his people. If he could levy just a copper on each person who squatted in the wasteland adjoining the pond, he would be a rich man.

When the letter from the Sarkar informing him of the representative's visit arrived three days ago at lunch time, the king promptly lost his appetite (although the dried fish gravy was excellent that day) and had not regained it since. 'What has that Lord written—that his balls have descended and that he wants me to come and hold them up for him?' the king asked the manager resentfully.

'They are sending someone to oversee the palace affairs,' the manager replied.

What was left in the Arasur palace to oversee? the king thought angrily. He was in a state of penury, having spent much of his stipend on Bushy Moustache's funeral. He had wasted two gold coins on that astrologer. How was he going to explain the expenditure to the overseer who would go through the accounts? Would he himself come or send his Brahmin dubash? The king couldn't understand how Brahmins and the Sarkar were so close. Although the Sarkar seemed to keep all dark-skinned people at bay, they allowed Brahmins wihin arms' length, kneeling, of course. They were paid very well for all the kneeling and fawning.

The king suddenly realised that his ancestors had come down for a chat. It was most inopportune but who could tell them that? 'You fool!' one of them said conversationally. 'Not everyone who fawns on the Sarkar has good fortune. Why, the dubash who was working for them is now mortally sick. His heirs sell snuff and have gained fame as well as a mistress in every town they visit.'

The king snapped, 'So what? If it is not this dubash it will be another.'

He did not want his ancestors around when the representative of the Sarkar came to visit. If the man was insulting they would be witness to his humiliation.

As if reading his thoughts they said, 'Why are you so nervous? You have done no wrong!'

Old Bushy Moustache, now a part of the ancestor crowd, came forward. He had wrapped strings of jasmine around his wrists as if on his way to a dance performance and seemed happy and content. The king felt a stab of jealousy. Would he shit with ease?

'Only you stinking humans have those problems, not us!' Bushy Moustache laughed, but without rancour.

'Remember those pictures they took of him—have you got them?' another ancestor asked.

'What a sight that was!' remarked another. 'They tied you to the chair to get you into a sitting position, remember?' They roared with laughter at the memory. Bushy Moustache looked shy and moved discreetly back into the crowd.

A bat came flapping from nowhere, crashed into the king's chest and then against the wall. When it fell to the ground twitching, the ancestors all fell silent.

'Why don't you laugh now? After all, you burnt us down with the house, exactly as you wished, didn't you?'

The words came from a young woman the king had never seen before. Who, the king wondered, was she, this tall, willowy woman with brown skin and sharp features?

'Oh Brahmin lady, we beg your forgiveness. Our girl should not have done it. But what is done is done.' The oldest among the ancestors knelt before the woman as he pleaded for her forgiveness.

The woman took a step back as if ashamed. 'Please don't do this!' she said quickly. 'How can you elders kneel before me? I am a worthless, unclean creature. I have lost everything. Now they have taken Saama away from me too.'

'Who is this lady?' the king asked Bushy Moustache, unable to contain his curiosity, though he wished they would go away before the Sarkar representative turned up.

'Do you remember the music box you used to listen to?' Bushy Moustache asked him. 'This is the wife of the Brahmin who played the music.'

'Forgive me for interrupting,' the woman said softly. 'But you are not saying it in the right order.'

She came close to the king who involuntarily stood up.

'You remember the music that you loved, that you used to yearn to listen to, from your neighbour's house? The music that came from the discs that were brought by those two men who came in the strange vehicle—do you remember?'

'Yes, of course, I do,' replied the king. 'How long it is since I heard it!'

'Since the third day after the new moon,' the woman replied. 'The full moon has come and gone too and it is now the fifth day after that. It has been twenty two days. It was music that Saama played.' The woman began to weep.

The king felt his stomach lurch and churn. He felt the happy and urgent need to visit the backyard. As Bushy Moustache was asking the woman, 'Where is your husband then?' the king folded his veshti and hitched it up.

'His family did all the rites and uttered all the mantras to send his soul to join his ancestors. Only I am wandering around like an orphan. If I try to join my ancestors they chase me away. And here there is no Saama.'

A huge group of souls seemed to be moving up behind the king's back. He quickly unhitched his veshti and began walking towards the backyard.

Behind him he could hear the woman crying piteously, 'Saama, wait for me!'

'It is time for his monthly obsequies. That is why we are taking him there. You can't come there, you are polluted. Go away!'

The chanting of mantras rose in a wave, drowning out everything else.

The king, squatting and relieving himself contentedly, did not even notice the chanting. He felt euphoric. Who cared if the Sarkar representative or his whore's son came? He could handle anyone—his body was behaving once again.

'Your Highness!' his manager called urgently from outside.

'What is it?'

'They are at the outskirts of the village!'

'Let them be! You push that bucket of water inside!' the king ordered the manager in majestic tones.

CHAPTER 30

The officer of the Sarkar was rather aged. He seemed to be in a tetchy mood. Well, thought the king, he is so far from home at his age, no wonder he is in a bad mood. This explanation, however, did not comfort the king as he knew that whatever the mood of the visitor, his arrival only meant one thing: trouble.

The visitor sat on a chair with his legs crossed. His hat was on his lap and his pipe in his mouth. The dark smoke that rose from it irritated the king's nostrils. Four sepoys, dark-skinned and strong as mahogany, stood behind the man, their rifles in their hands. Their horses had all been tied near the entrance and were feeding on oats. Horse dung lay in small heaps on the ground.

Several empty coconuts lay on the ground near the visitor. He refused palm fruit, saying it tasted peculiar. Opposite to him, sat the king on his ornate chair. One of its legs was a little shaky (the palace carpenter refused to fix it before he left for more lucrative work in Chettinad, because he had not been paid for the last piece of work he had done in the palace).

The chair was not the only discomfort the king was forced to endure. He was dressed in a coat, a zari-bordered cap with tassels, trousers, a sash with his sword stuck in it, sandalwood paste and vermilion streaks on his forehead, as if he were posing for his portrait. The attar and javvadhu that the servants had smeared on his chest—following the queen's instructions—made his skin itch. The smell from the perfume made his head ache.

All around the hall, cuscus screens had been hung and these were periodically dampened to bring perfume and coolness to the air. The pulleys of the punkahs had been diligently oiled the previous day and the punkah pullers were tugging at the ropes briskly. Despite this, it was hot and humid in the hall—a fact that the visitor commented upon. That was the dubash's interpretation of his master's words, which sounded as if he was speaking with his mouth full of boiled yam.

The dubash looked smart and sounded impudent. The king tried to guess his community: perhaps a Muslim from Arcot or a Mudali perhaps. Then he said, 'The heat will get unbearable as the sun climbs higher.' He hoped this would make the visitor finish his work quickly and leave. The latter nodded vaguely and handed his pipe to the sepoy standing behind him. The sepoy took it to a corner of the hall and spilled the ash from it on the floor there before bringing the pipe back. The king thought spitefully that he was probably being paid extra for all these services—the government seemed to turn stingy only when it came to paying the king his grant. If he had known that this fellow was a smoker he could have got him some tobacco from his neighbour, the merchant. The devil take that thought! The moment it entered his mind, the visitor pointed at the neighbour's burnt house and said something. The dubash translated it, in commanding tones, as, 'How did that house burn?'

The king looked at his manager, expecting him reply. A strange peace descended on the latter's face. Obviously the Sarkar representative had not come to check his account books and torture him with questions. As for the fire, 'The king alone will have an answer to that question,' the manager said.

The king shot him a look of pure hatred and when he spoke to the dubash, his anger boiled over, 'It burnt down somehow. How would I know? Am I the king or this gentleman?'

The dubash took fright at the king's aggressive tone. This fat, richly dressed man was not an employee of the government like him. He was a zamindar, used to the respect of people from several villages. If the Sarkar were to leave this country suddenly, people like the dubash and the sepoys would probably need the zamindar to make a living. So he told the Sarkar representative, in respectful tones, that the king had been fast asleep when the calamity had occurred and had little information regarding it. He then translated what he had said in Tamil, for the benefit of the king. His words did not really offer any comfort to the king who now wished he had not been so hasty and yelled at the dubash . The man could, after all, attribute all sorts of statements to the king, and the latter would know no better. That might incense the visitor who would probably recommend to the government that the grant to the king be stopped.

While the king worried about this, the visitor got up suddenly. The sepoys promptly stamped their feet hard on the ground and pointed their rifles upwards, startling the king. 'Let a plague devour you, rascals', muttered the king visibly irritated.

'Let us go see the place,' the visitor said as he put his hat back on his head. His entourage moved after him. The king trailed behind them.

He could hear someone running after him—it was the queen's servant maid. The king thought embarrassedly that she should not expect him to spend time with her now. Perhaps later, when the queen was taking her nap. She paused by him and whispered urgently, 'The queen told me to tell you this. Say that you don't know anything about the fire, no matter what the visitor asks.' She then ran back.

The queen would not appear before strangers such as the Sarkar representative. Besides, she always said it nauseated her to be in the company of white people who were rumoured to use paper to wipe their behinds and never bathe.

'Well, what else can they do? They live in a cold country where their hands freeze if they touch water!' the king had told her only the previous night, adding that even if he too did not approve of their habits, he had no choice but to entertain them. Otherwise he'd probably have to go to their country and beg for money.

'And who do you think will fund your steamer ticket?' someone asked impudently.

It was old Bushy Moustache and the other ancestors. The king was actually glad to see them. Though they were not human, they were his people and gave the king strength.

As they stepped into the empty, blackened shell of the neighbour's house, it occurred to the king that this was the first time he was coming there after the fire. Next to him the visitor was sniffing and inspecting the ruins. 'Everything is gone in the fire,' he said and the king understood his words even without the dubash interpreting.

Later the visitor called the dubash over and whispered to him. The dubash, nodding his head, instructed a sepoy who immediately went out.

'There has been a complaint,' the dubash explained to the king. 'Subramanya Iyer has complained in writing to the Governor, informing him of the fire and of the loss of life and property. That is why this officer has come to make an enquiry.'

The king was frightened. He looked at Bushy Moustache who, along with the other ancestors, comforted him by saying, 'Don't worry. You will be fine. Remember to offer us liquor during the next new moon, though.'

'Liquor for me too!' the Brahmin woman piped in. The king nodded his head at her. Watching, the Sarkar representative looked at him queerly.

Subramanya Iyer, tired and frail, walked in with his relatives. Only he and his son came in—the others waited outside the house. It occurred to the king that he and the queen had not visited to offer their condolence. He tried to tell himself that he did not know where the family had moved but even he had to admit that in a place the size of Arasur that would not have been difficult to find out.

Subramanya Iyer folded his hands silently in greeting. His beard was white, like cotton wool. He did not look like a wealthy man at this instant. In fact, he reminded the king of mendicant Brahmins who offer to carry corpses to the cremation ground in return for small change.

The officer was offering Iyer words of condolence that the dubash tried to translate, but the officer stopped him, saying Iyer would have understood. Bushy Moustache translated this for the benefit of the Brahmin woman. The king marvelled at Bushy Moustache being able to understand the white man's language once he had travelled to the other side. He worried briefly that his late father-in-law, that utter lecher, should not bother the Brahmin lady. Otherwise that could become a big nuisance and he would have to spend all his money making yantras to stop it all. He wondered if the astrologer could make him a yantra that would take him far away from all this trouble, perhaps to the white man's land.

'What will you do there? Beg?' The king thought that was what the visiting officer was asking him but the dubash translated, ' Do you know how much loss this man has suffered because of the fire?'

'A great deal, I heard. I am very sorry about that,' replied the king, feeling truly sorry for Iyer.

Iyer's son yelled loudly, 'This is the man who set fire to our house!'

A chill went up the king's spine.

'What? I set fire to your house? What are you saying? I know you have suffered a great tragedy, but can you blame just anybody near the place?' the king's voice was overcome with emotion. He should have sounded brave and outraged but he did not feel it. He knew he was responsible for the tragedy in some way. The ancestors had not told him what exactly the queen had done. Yet something had happened behind the king's back.

'Don't talk rubbish, Sankara!' Iyer admonished his son. 'This is the handiwork of some business enemy of ours. It is to find out who exactly that I complained to the Governor.'

The king felt comforted that Iyer, at least, did not suspect him. He said to Iyer, 'If only you had told me, I would have sent my own men to get those rogues in a trice!'

Upon hearing this, Sankaran seemed to lose his cool completely. 'How dare you pretend to help us when it was you who burnt our house down!'

The officer directed his men to take the young man outside. Obviously he could not put up with the yelling. He handed his pipe to a sepoy who began cleaning it by the wall on which the face of the goddess Lakshmi had been painted. As the other sepoys passed by the king on their way out with Sankaran it seemed to the king that they gave him suspicious glances, as if seriously believing that he was the arsonist.

Then the visitor began speaking. 'It is your duty to protect the lives and property of your people. Consequently the government cannot give any compensation to Iyer. You yourself have to compensate him for what he has lost in the fire.'

The king went into shock upon hearing this. How on earth could he compensate Iyer? Iyer's property was probably worth more than what the king's family could save in four generations!

Outside, Iyer's son could still be heard shouting. Somebody was singing the dirges that had once played on Saama's music box. It was an old woman, leaning against a pillar on the pyol, singing in both male and female voices. The king looked beyond her. He could see Iyengar, the astrologer, carrying a large metal yantra into the palace.

CHAPTER 31

Everything about Chennai Pattinam[8] amazed Sankaran. The streets were countless, snaking across each other in complicated twists and always full of traffic. The smells of horse and cattle dung, jackfruit and roasted grain and jasmine, sweat and urine, mixed to produce a compound city smell that pervaded every lane and corner. And everywhere there were men busily going about some kind of business. The horse carriages of the white people ran on the wider roads and there were the more private, shaded roads where the western women walked, protected from the sun by their parasols. Then there was the Black Town where lived the families of Indians who worked solely and proudly for the white people—they and their children after them. Both Tamil and Telugu were heard equally frequently from the houses he passed. Eateries did brisk business at every intersection.

Sankaran had never experienced urban life of such a nature. He had seen Jaffna and Madurai, but they were like tiny villages compared to Chennai.

And then, there was the sea, and the immense stretch of the beach. After he got married, he should bring Bhagavati Kutti here. In her sixteen years, exposed only to the rivers and fishing boats of her home, she would have never seen anything like the vast beach of sand. He would like to walk with her on this beach, their feet sinking softly into the sand. When they grew tired of walking they would sit down and he would listen to her sing. Her voice would rise above the roar of the waves. Salt spray would sprinkle their faces and Bhagavati would lean her head against his shoulder. But would she be able to strike erotic poses like the Kottakudi dasi, a small voice inside his head asked him mischievously.

'Master Iyer, are you daydreaming? Are you making plans to build two huge buildings on the sand, one for selling snuff and the other for selling tobacco?' Karutha Rowther teased Sankaran and laughed loudly.

Karuthan laughed frequently and loudly. He was the son of Pichai Rowther of Bangalore, a good business friend of Subramanya Iyer.

'Karutha, I have told you so many times not to call me Master. Call me Sankara, or if that is difficult, call me Sankara Iyer.

'How can I call a Master anything but Master, Master Iyer?' Karutha laughed uproariously. Over the last three days, Sankaran had got used to his levity.

Subramanya Iyer had insisted that Sankaran go to Chennai. 'I can't bear to see you like this, Sankara. You are just sitting around moping. Saama is gone and will not come back. Those he has left behind have to get on with their lives. You haven't stepped into the shop and you don't talk to anyone at home. On four occasions Ayyanai has brought you back from outside the old house where you just stood staring at that burnt pile. This will not do. Go to Chennai Pattinam, Sankara. The sea breeze will do you as much good as the change.'

'What will I do there?' Sankaran had grumbled.

'Learn the snuff business. Pichai Rowther's son has opened a shop exclusively for snuff in the Ex… Ex... I can't pronounce the name of the place.'

'That is the Esplanade,' old Subbamma said clearly, adding, 'The ancestors have all come to bless you.'

Overcome with joy, Iyer folded his hands in obeisance to them.

Behind him, in an inner room, Kalyani lay moaning. She was bedridden since she had heard about Saama in Madurai. Her sorrow afflicted her in bouts. She would lie dead to the world for hours. Then she would suddenly sit up and plead loudly, 'Saama, my breasts ache, drink the milk from them, child. Saama, prostrate before the elders with your wife. Sit down on the swing. Somebody give the couple milk to drink and plantains to eat… Have the pillows for their bed been stuffed with the softest cotton?' She would ramble on loudly for a while. Then she would relapse into unconsciousness.

Iyer begged Subbamma to stay with them to look after Kalyani. She hardly had the heart to refuse, although her own sorrow over Saama's death was immense, compounded by the guilt that she had been unable to do anything to prevent it although that girl at Sucheendram temple had begged her for help. What could she have done or what could the ancestors have done? They could only record happenings or foretell them, not prevent them. They could bless the living, as they were doing now. If Sankaran went to Chennai, his health would improve, they said, and his business would expand and flourish. They said Sankaran's marriage should take place as fixed. When the priest, Sundaram, disagreed and said that it should take place only after Saama's first death anniversary, the ancestral women gave him a tongue lashing through Subbamma and sent him home.

Subbamma was relieved that the spirit of the young woman who had committed suicide was no longer affecting her. She did not need to carry the heavy yantra with her. She only bathed it in milk so that the deities did not go hungry. Sometimes at night she heard the deities quarrel, make up and sing together. She was not surprised they quarrelled. It must be difficult cooped up in such close proximity. 'What can we do about it?' she asked Annasamy, the astrologer.

He replied, 'I am making a special yantra for the good of the world and will establish it in the palace garden. I will provide room there for the deities in your yantra as well. But it is complicated work and I don't seem to have time for it—I spend my time consulting the cowries to tell the villagers where to find their lost buffaloes or preparing horoscopes for girls.' Annasamy consulted the cowries and told Iyer that it would be good for Sankaran to go to Chennai.

A long letter from Pichai Rowther helped Iyer make up his mind. Rowther condoled with him over Saama's death and said he would do dua for the good of Saama's soul. Iyer could not understand what dua was, but he certainly understood what came after. 'I have set up a shop for my elder son Karuthan in Chennai. He is a good businessman but not smart enough to write accounts. In Chennai it is easier to find Brahmin accountants who will do a good job maintaining accounts in return for Rs.4 a month. If you could send your son to Chennai he would be able to help interview and select the right candidate. They can discuss plans to expand the snuff business all over the south. I myself am unable to come to see you right now as my wife's sister is down with the pox.'

Iyer gave Sankaran the letter and five hundred rupees for expenses. He arranged for a further thousand rupees as an at sight demand draft from the moneylenders in Thambu Chetty Street. Sankaran was to stay with a relative, Vaidyanathan who lived in Nungambakkam. Sankaran's journey to Chennai was planned even before he decided to go. Finally he did go.

In the last three days, he had been interviewing candidates for the post of the accountant in Karuthan's shop. He asked Karuthan, 'When did that Telugu Brahmin candidate say he would come?'

'Who, Rao?'

'That's right. He seemed the brightest.'

'But Master Iyer, he is asking for a salary of six rupees a month! After I pay him his salary, taxes to the government and rent for the shop, nothing will be left for me!'

'Just because he asks, are we going to pay him six rupees? I'll speak to him tomorrow. Don't say a word while I am talking to him,' advised Sankaran.

'If you could only pay his salary as well, that would be a great help!' winked Karuthan.

'You are a smart Turk[9], Karuthan! But Rao said he lives in a village somewhere. We have to find out if he can commute early enough from there to open the shop and to stay on till after the shop is closed.'

'He lives in the village of Guindy. That's not far. He needs to take two jutkas and he can reach Esplanade.'

'Whatever. Let him come by carriage or let him walk. It will be fine if he turns up for work for the three and three quarters of a rupee you are going to pay him!'

'He is not three quarters, Iyer. I am!' Karuthan said, pointing mischievously below his waist.'

'Why can't you leave that poor thing alone? Why circumcise it?'

'You should ask my father that!'

Sankaran laughed with him. His heart felt lighter than it had for weeks.

'Karutha, we need to go to the moneylender in Thambu Chetty Street tomorrow, to exchange the at-sight bill and pay for the snuff I mean to take back with me. Without the money you won't give me the snuff!' Sankaran joked.

'With or without money, my snuff in full, half and three-quarters are all yours!' Karuthan said with a straight face.

'Thank you, but I don't want your three-quarters. Isn't there someone at your home who might want it?'

'That's right. I have been quicker than you in this matter, Iyer!' Karuthan laughed, adding, 'Let's go. It's getting dark. My wife is pregnant and will be expecting me back early. I promised to get her some halwa from the north Indian sweetmeat shop on the way.'

Sankaran thought, 'I too should get Bhagavati halwa when the time comes. I should feed it to her, then kiss her and suck the halwa back from her mouth...'

The small voice inside him spoke in the tones of the Kottakudi dasi, 'Will you refuse the halwa, if I give it to you in the same way?'

CHAPTER 32

Cousin Vaidyanathan's house in Nungambakkam was modern and convenient.

Vaidyanathan was elder to Sankaran by several years. Almost touching forty, he looked it, with his rising paunch and growing baldness. Everyone in the neighbourhood respectfully called him 'Saar,' a form of address Sankaran had not heard before. It was popular in Chennai Pattinam as he understood, a spin off from the English term of respectful address, 'Sir'.

Vaidyanathan was a government servant. He was a Port Navigation clerk and his office was in Fort St George. He told Sankaran proudly that nothing or no one, including Sarkar lords and ladies, could travel by sea to or from Chennai without him knowing about it. He kept all these records and accounts in English, of course. Sankaran was impressed. He asked him, 'Vaithi Saar, is it very difficult to write and keep accounts in English?'

'No, not if you have learnt the language at school,' replied Vaithi. His father, Ramanatha Iyer, who had been a court official in Chennai, had sent him to a school where English was taught. Ramanatha Iyer had even arranged for him to go to England to study for his BA but that plan had fallen through because the local orthodox Brahmins and priests declared that if he crossed the seas to a foreign country, he would be excommunicated[10]. Vaithi was forced to forego his foreign education and be content with finding a job as a clerk in the Fort.

Sankaran was surprised to hear that there were Brahmin priests in this crowded city. Both in the Black Town and elsewhere, the streets were so crowded that it was impossible to walk without rubbing shoulders or hips with someone of another caste or community. How would Brahmin priests manage in this situation, since they were required by orthodoxy to bathe every time they were touched, even accidentally, by a member of another caste or community? They probably spent all their time bathing, Sankaran concluded. 'How did they find the time and energy to find out about Vaithi's plans to go abroad and threaten to excommunicate him?'

'If I had been born later, I could have gone to college here itself. The Sarkar have set up a university here, but there was no such facility when I was your age. One must appreciate how much the Sarkar have done for this country. If it weren't for them, you and I would not be sitting in this lovely house and having this relaxed conversation!'

Sankaran thought about this. Sarkar or no Sarkar, he would have been making money selling tobacco, but Vaithi might not have been a clerk in the Fort and built this large, two-storeyed house with its lovely garden in Nungambakkam. What else would he have done? Been a priest or a lowly employee in the Munsif court or an accountant in a shop or run a snuff or tobacco shop... Suddenly Sankaran felt depressed, what had he gained from selling tobacco? It was a lot of hard work—procuring it, storing it, transporting it properly, collecting payments... And after all this, they seemed to be only suffering loss of property and life. His house had been much larger than Vaithi's but it had been destroyed in the fire. Perhaps if he hadn't been selling tobacco but had a job under the Sarkar, life would have been easier. Listen carefully, Bhagavati Kutti, we have to educate our children in English, no matter what the cost. Close the door and come here. I'll get you cart loads of halwa or anything else you desire, even if it is something that they sell in the European shops. Do you know about the Navigation Record Clerk? Let's lie down and I'll tell you all about it. You don't want to lie down? Why not? This is an auspicious hour.'

The Kottakudi dasi appeared suddenly, pulling off Sankaran's loin cloth and laughing as she pretended to speak English. 'Why does this woman chase me everywhere, like that girl Saama liked to fornicate with?'

'Sankara! Sankara, you're lost in thought! Is something wrong?' Vaithi was concerned.

'No, Saar, I was just thinking about the college, the port and the fort—these are all places that I am not at all qualified to visit. I was wondering if I could at least see them!' Sankaran said, thinking quickly.

'Oh, don't worry. I will take you to all these places,' Vaithi said affectionately. 'Come, let us eat.'

'I haven't yet bathed, Saar. You finish your meal and leave for office. I'll start out later.'

'It is Sunday, idiot! I don't have to go to work. How do you think I was able to fetch you when you arrived at Mambalam, last week? Only because it was a Sunday. If it had been a weekday I would have had to send a servant to fetch you. And that fellow would probably have missed you and brought home the first village bumpkin he saw with a kudumi. And this silly wife of mine would have bent over backwards to be hospitable to him!'

Vaithi laughed. His wife Gomati had just then entered the room with a bundle of darbha grass in her hand. She was scattering pieces of grass all over the house. As she passed him, she playfully flung one at her husband, saying, 'My brother-in-law is not an idiot nor am I. You are the only one who is!'

'Donkey! Did your father, the landlord Gopalan, get you married to me only so that you could call me an idiot?' Vaithi shot back, equally playfully.

'And did my father send me to you empty-handed? Three hundred sovereigns of gold jewellery, he gave me, and silver vessels and silks...' Gomati lifted the lid of the milk vessel and dropped a piece of grass into it.

'As long as you are tabulating your dowry, you may as well add to it my solitaire, diamond ear studs and also, the Colombo umbrella that was given to me during the wedding!' Vaithi teased her.

Vaithi was, in fact, very proud of the dowry his rich wife had brought. He did not mind the fact that next to his bulky physique, her reed slim form looked insignificant. Sankaran thought she was also a little taller than Vaithi. But what did that matter? She had borne him three sons. And her father had provided solitaire ear studs for them too.

'Ears are meant not only for wearing diamond studs, but also for collecting information—tell him that brother-in-law,' Gomati said archly.

Gomati had treated Sankaran like a brother from the day he arrived. If Saama had been alive and had got married, perhaps his wife too would have been as kind as this.

Sankaran remembered the young woman sitting in the hall of his burnt down house and singing, opposite the swing on which Saama sat. Was she his wife? Her song, the one that Aunt Subbamma sang, leaning on the pillar of the pyol (and shocking the visiting officer), and the songs that swirled out of Saama's music box—were they all the same?

'Your brother-in-law seems to have gone into a trance again,' Vaithi was saying to Gomati, as he shook Sankaran gently.

'Get him married to my sister and he'll be fine. He can run his business from this city, raise a family, build a modern house and lead a happy life. But nothing can change the fact that he has to starve this morning!' Gomati concluded.

'Manni, you are Annapoorani herself. If you give me food I will eat. If you won't, I can always drink the sweet water from your well and go to work. But don't starve my brother, poor fellow.'

'He's right. Don't you always make idlis on Sunday morning? Hot idlis with ginger chutney and onion sambar... aren't we getting any of that?' Vaithi asked yearningly.

'How will you get it? Don't you remember that there is an eclipse[11] of the sun today? Only after the eclipse is over, at ten thirty, can I bathe and start cooking. The eclipse is also affecting your birth star, so the priest will be coming over to do the propitiation. Stop complaining and get ready to bathe.'

'Oh, Annapoorani, at least give me a drop of coffee!' begged Vaithi.

Sankaran had fallen in love with coffee, a beverage he had drunk for the first time only here. He had travelled by horse carriage and bullock cart, via Karaikudi, Tiruchirapalli, Mayavaram and Thanjavur. At a wayside shack in Thanjavur he had first tasted coffee. The two Brahmins there had mixed a brownish liquid with boiling hot milk, added sugar and sold it to the long line of customers. Sankaran had found it wonderfully reviving. He usually never ate anything outside during his travels for fear of falling sick. He carried food, plentifully and carefully prepared by Subbamma and Nagalakshmi, with him. On the first day of his travel, he ate rice and dosai, on the second, third, fourth and fifth days he had to make do with various dry snacks and sweets, which, while tasty and filling, had completely constipated him. When Vaithi had spotted him in the crowd of travellers at Mambalam (easily, because he smelled so powerfully of tobacco, tamarind rice and oily snacks) and brought him home, the first thing Gomati had done was to extend a brass pot full of scalding hot, aromatic coffee. The moment he drank it, Sankaran knew his stomach was going to be all right, and he was so grateful for that. He decided at that moment that Gomati was smarter than her husband.

That had been exactly a week to the day. Sankaran said, 'Manni, give me a tumbler of coffee too. I don't care if Rahu and Ketu eat me up after they have gobbled the sun. If I drink this nectar I can handle anything!' Sankaran spoke in a pleading tone.

'This man is a rogue from Arasur!' Vaithi laughed. 'If you give your sister in marriage to him, he will run through her dowry by drinking coffee!' he said and tugged at Sankaran's tuft.

CHAPTER 33

It was late afternoon by the time Sankaran left Vaithi's house to meet Karuthan. He had meant to leave earlier, but had been delayed by the eclipse. Besides, it was Sunday and time had flown chatting and drinking endless cups of coffee with Vaithi. Sankaran noticed that if you had a cup of coffee, you wanted to sit back and chat or gossip. When you ran out of things to say, you wanted another cup of coffee.

Vaithi's children taught him some strange things that day. He found them playing with a bit of glass, blackening it by holding it against the flame of an oil lamp. Gomati scolded them, 'If you cut your hand or foot, the white doctors will amputate the hand or foot. Then you'll have to use a stick and go limping.' But they hardly paid her any attention. 'Our teacher told us we should view the eclipse through a smoked glass,' they said.

Sankaran wondered if all the teachers in Chennai were slightly crazy. Where he came from, education consisted of learning to read and write and do accounts and memorise all the important slokas. That made the children intelligent. What was this rubbish Chennai children were being taught?

Gomati strengthened his opinion by complaining, 'These Christian priests teach all sorts of nonsense. And we pay them so much for it. They hate our culture and religion so they teach our children things which are contrary to our beliefs. Would anyone seriously tell children to blacken bits of glass as a useful activity?'

It turned out, however, that there was a method to the children's madness. They took Vaithi and Sankaran to the terrace and urged them to look at the sun through the smoked glass. Vaithi obliged them and said in astonished tones, 'Sankara, you too should have a look! You can see how the sun has been engulfed by Rahu or Ketu. May God set things right again!'

'Appa, that is not Rahu or Ketu, just the shadow of the earth falling on the sun!' the children said.

'Oh yes, and tomorrow you will say that there is no Shiva or Vishnu, just because that teacher in long skirts tells you so,' Gomati chided them, adding, as an aside to her husband, 'Look, if you don't hurry and conduct the ceremony to make them wear the sacred thread, those teachers at school will probably make them wear skirts like them!'

The priest arrived to conduct the propitiation ceremony and Gomati and Vaithi went downstairs. Sankaran held the smoked glass in front of his eyes and looked at the eclipse. He saw the dark circle of the sun, with its circumference blazing. 'Are you well?' it seemed to ask Sankaran in Saama's voice. Then it added, out of the blue, 'Today your celibacy will end. You will know passion.'

Shocked, Sankaran dropped the piece of glass which smashed to smithereens on the terrace floor. He ran downstairs. In the hall, the propitiation rite for Vaithi was going on. The priest, who was drinking coffee, inclined his head towards Sankaran and asked Vaithi, 'Is that your brother?'

'My cousin,' replied Vaithi.

'Have you come because you have found employment in the Fort?' the priest asked.

Sankaran was embarrassed to say he had come to sell snuff. So he said he had come on personal business.

The priest said he lived in Mylapore and if Sankaran needed his services, all he had to do was come to the temple and ask for Vembu Sastrigal. After he had left, Sankaran asked Vaithi whether the priest was a learned man who was as well known in Mylapore as Vaithi was in Nungambakkam. 'Rubbish!' Vaithi laughed. 'He is just a wind bag! He was an impoverished Brahmin making a living by helping to carry corpses during funerals in Chidambaram. Now that he is in Chennai he pretends to be a big time priest. There are many of his kind in this city. That is not to say that there are no Vedic scholars here. There are many learned priests who are invited to preside over auspicious occasions, and they make huge amounts of money.'

Sankaran thought of Swaminathan again. If he had been alive and in possession of his senses, he could have been a learned priest in Chennai, made tons of money, built a house as big as this, married a nice girl and raised a family. Sankaran could have travelled between Chennai and Arasur, improving his tobacco business and had any amount of coffee to drink. Saama would have liked the taste of coffee too.

Gomati invited him to have lunch. Sankaran liked the taste of the all the new vegetables that seemed to be found only in Chennai and which orthodox Brahmin households in the South did not use—cabbage, turnip, onion… As he savoured Gomati's cabbage curry, Sankaran wondered whether he should marry Gomati's younger sister and settle down in Chennai to enjoy the urban lifestyle. He brushed the thought aside impatiently. What value had cabbage and coffee against the sheer beauty of Bhagavati Kutti?

Sankaran had not shaved for the last few days as he had been unable to find a barber and his beard had grown quite long. 'You look like a rishi, Sankara,' Vaithi commented as they ate.

'A rishi who eats cabbage!' Gomati teased.

'Do you know, rishis are said to have been meat eaters once,' Vaithi said. 'They ate mutton, chicken, even beef…'

'Stop!' exclaimed Gomati. 'No more of this nonsense while eating. Besides, the children should not be listening to this!'

After Vaithi had gone to take a nap, Gomati had gone to clean the kitchen and the children had wandered off to play, Sankaran set out to see Karuthan. Four streets from Vaithi's house was an intersection where you could wait for a carriage to take you to the Black Town. When Sankaran reached the intersection, there were four other people waiting for the carriage. Nearby, under the shade of a large tree, stood a fat man, wearing loose clothes, holding a cross and proclaiming 'Pray to Christ Maharishi! I will now show you the pictures of this great soul and his mother Goddess Maha Mary.' He pulled a large piece of paper from his shoulder bag and held it out for his audience.

Sankaran was not interested in the propaganda, but the large patch of shade in which the evangelist stood drew him. He wished the man would finish and leave soon, may his gods bless him, so that Sankaran could move into the shade of the tree. As his audience grew because no carriages had arrived, the waiting crowd listened to the evangelist for lack of anything better to do.

Sankaran began walking in search of shade. At the beginning of a street near the intersection was a locked house with a large pyol. Grateful for the shade and space it provided, Sankaran spread his upper cloth on the floor of the pyol and placing his shoulder bag on it, lay down. He reminded himself that he should make himself a coat like the ones Vaithi and Karuthan wore. Chennai was full of itinerant tailors who sat on pyols, cutting and stitching.

He dozed off and awoke to the sound of a strange vehicle stopping beside him. Two men got down from it. Sankaran recognised them as the two who used to visit Saama. They wore strange coats, but their clothes did nothing to hide the fact that they were thieves and rogues.

'Young master, do you want music discs?' the elder of the two asked Sankaran.

'No,' replied Sankaran, 'Why do I need them?'

'You have a snuff shop. If you play the music there more customers will visit your shop for the added novelty.'

'But this is not from my time.'

'So what? After all, the snuff is from your time!'

'No, I don't want it. Look, there is a man there preaching in the shade of that tree. He might want your music discs. All I want to do is take a nap. Leave me alone.'

'Well, never mind the music discs. Look at these pictures instead. These are really jolly.'

The shorter of the men came close, his breath smelling revoltingly of onions, and extended a book, the pages of which were open. Every page had a picture of white women engaged in a variety of sexual play. In their midst, with his tuft undone, was Sankaran.

CHAPTER 34

'Master Iyer! I have been expecting you since morning. There was no sign of you,' Karuthan greeted Sankaran.

'I was delayed, Karutha.'

Sankaran sat down on the plank that served as a sort of bench outside the shop. On the bench opposite him sat the Telugu chap he had interviewed the previous day.

'I believe there is some problem with the sun today, Master? They tell me that you people have to dip in the temple tank 151 times to pray for the sun to be rid of the devil afflicting it?'

'Which whoreson tells you all this nonsense?' Sankaran retorted.

'Do Tamil Brahmins perform a lot of rites in connection with the eclipse?' the Telugu employee-to-be asked.

This irritated Sankaran. He did not like the man to speak to him like this. He was, after all, just an employee. Sankaran would be one of his bosses if he became a partner in the business.

'When did you come? We told you to be here by noon!' Sankaran sounded unnaturally harsh.

The man got up and folded his hands respectfully. 'Forgive me. I have been here since early morning, before the shop opened.'

'Did you have a ritual bath after the eclipse? Or do you do that only if someone dies?' Sankaran asked sarcastically.

'We have ritual baths whenever necessary, Swami, not just for death. Every night after I reach home, I have a bath, perform rituals with a sacred fire and only then have my dinner. We have been following this custom for four generations.'

'Iyer, this man has been fasting since morning like we do for Ramzan. He would not even eat the plantains I wanted to get him from a street vendor,' Karuthan informed him.

Sankaran felt ashamed and angry with himself for having been rude. If he had not dozed off on that pyol, he could have reached the shop earlier. He decided to talk to the man and let him go home. Otherwise, he might fall dead from hunger and that sin would cling to Sankaran the way Saama's ghostly lover clung to him. If sin was a female entity perhaps he could cohabit with it.

Sankaran was uncomfortably aware of how much his mind was occupied by thoughts of sex. Perhaps it was because of that book that those rascally brothers had shown him. Was that real or a dream? Sankaran could remember the pictures vividly—white women making love to him. If the carriage going to Black town had not arrived at that point and disturbed his sleep, he would probably have dampened himself. That would have meant returning to the house for a wash and change of clothes. Why was his mind teasing him like this? The Kottakudi dasi was also entrenched firmly in his thoughts. Nothing could possibly help him except getting married to Bhagavati Kutti and laying her.

'Are you married?' he asked the Telugu.

'No, not yet. My family is looking for a bride for me. My mother wants me to be married by next year.'

'Give me four coppers worth of snuff, Saibu' a customer demanded. Karuthan dipped a ladle into the porcelain jar containing the snuff and carefully measured it out on to plantain bark packets. Looking at his careful movements, Sankaran asked the Telugu, 'So, if you get married will you take off from work for a couple of months or what?'

The Telugu smiled, as this line of questioning obviously meant he was getting the job, and answered politely, 'No, saar. I will be getting married in the city. I will need only three or four days' leave.'

Sankaran did not understand the meaning of 'leave'. He envied the man his knowledge of English, but it pleased him to be addressed as 'saar'.

'Salaam aleikum!'

The Muslim man who greeted them was a giant of a fellow, smelling strongly of perfume. He wore a cap with a border of gold lace. He sat down next to the Telugu who inched away from him.

'Oi, Iyer, don't move away. I am not bothered by the smell of your sweat!' the man joked. The Telugu remained silent. A sepoy carrying a rifle took some snuff and left without paying for it.

'Shaitaan ka bachha!' Karuthan swore after him.

'Why didn't you refuse to give him the snuff, bhai? What could he have done? Crushed your balls?' Suleiman, the big Muslim, asked Karuthan loudly.

'Why don't you shut up, Suleiman?' Karuthan chided him.

'Unless you keep these fellows in check, they'll make korma of us!' retorted Suleiman.

'Let him be. Now meet our guest. This is Sankaran Iyer, the son of my father's friend, the elder Iyer from Arasur.'

Suleiman rose and bent low towards Sankaran. 'Is he to be our partner? Excellent! Suleiman is so happy to have met you!'

Suleiman, who was Karuthan's cousin, was the third partner in their business. Along with his father, he had a variety of business interests in the city—from acting as tour guides to white people in the city to selling snuff, leather products and dry fruits. Karuthan told Sankaran that he gave Suleiman the money for the consignment of snuff that was arriving for him the next week.

Sankaran took the hundi for thousand rupees that his father had sent with him. 'I have been asking Karuthan, to encash the hundi at the money lender's in Thambu Chetty Street. He has been procrastinating, I'll see to it that it is encashed tomorrow and you get your money,' he said apologetically to Suleiman.

The Telugu interrupted, 'Why do you have to encash the at sight hundi? You can endorse it and hand it over to this gentleman. He can encash it himself. Or endorse it again and give it to the supplier from whom he buys stock. In the ledger we can have a separate column for dealings in hundi, apart from the regular income and expenditure columns. You can take payment in hundi form even from those to whom you will be supplying snuff. Thereby you can also avoid paying a lot of taxes to the government.'

Sankaran was astonished by the Telugu's smart thinking. He was ashamed that he had misjudged the man. He seemed to know so much. Even Karuthan and Suleiman looked at the Telugu with new respect.

'Swami, come to work tomorrow morning,' Karuthan told him, after fixing his salary at five rupees a month. 'Is it an auspicious day?'

The Telugu's perks included half-a-day's leave on Fridays, a full day's leave on new moon days, Deepavali and Ramzan. The Telugu informed them that he would come to work on Wednesday, which was auspicious. He left after folding his hands respectfully to all of them and taking an advance payment of five rupees, with which he planned to get some decent clothes to wear to work.

After he had gone Suleiman said, 'Seems to be a fellow who knows a lot of stuff. In a way it is good.'

'In what way is it bad?' Sankaran asked.

'That depends on how we use him, friend.'

Sankaran was relieved at the way things had turned out. 'Karutha, it is getting dark. Why don't you close the shop? We can go for a walk on the beach,' he suggested.

Suleiman quickly shook his head. 'Let Karuthan go home,' he said. 'His wife will have a baby any time now. He needs to be with her. I will take you to the ship. It has anchored only this afternoon.'

'Me? To the ship?' Sankaran wondered aloud.

'Why not? Are you afraid of being polluted? Doesn't that happen only if you go on a trip across the seas? What is the harm in visiting the ship? I have heard that you have been across the seas to Jaffna.'

'I was not thinking about pollution,' Sankaran replied. 'What will I do on the ship?'

'You can meet new people,' Karuthan said as he boarded up the shop.

Sankaran wanted to visit the ship to see the machines, the travellers and the conveniences that were available to them on board, but it was getting dark and he felt reluctant to go. Suleiman brushed away his hesitation saying, 'It will take us just ten minutes to get to the harbour from my house which is close by. Another ten minutes for the ride in the catamaran to the ship. We can leave the ship by nine and return home. I will drop you in Nungambakkam.'

Sankaran wondered if he could take a piss on the ship. It would be safer to do it in Suleiman's backyard before they set out for the harbour. Would the Brahmins of Chennai excommunicate him because he had visited a Muslim's house? Sankaran did not care. Let the priests of Chennai debate the point in their urine-smelling lanes. As for the priests of Arasur they could not care less what Sankaran did in Chennai. He could go back to Arasur and change his sacred thread at the annual ceremony and all the pollution would be removed.

'Let's go,' said Sankaran.

CHAPTER 35

The catamaran bounced along the waves. Half a mile more and they would reach the ship. They could see it standing there, as imposing and arrogant as the white men. 'Black dog!' it seemed to say. 'What kind of a harbour do you run that you make me wait here for hours without so much as someone falling at my feet and greeting me?' It was the same irrepressible arrogance that the white men displayed.

Here comes the white man!

Here comes the mother fucker!

The boatman from the catamaran next to theirs sang loudly.

Suleiman swore at the boatman's mother and sister in choice language. The boatman and his passengers laughed uproariously. Sankaran too felt laughter bubbling up within him. A wave slapped against his face. Suleiman swore at the wave, not only in Tamil but also in Hindustani. Sankaran loved the sound of the curses. He wished he could learn them and use them, in his own mind, against Vaithi or the Telugu accountant, if they tried to act too clever with their English.

The Kottakudi dasi knew Hindustani. She could compose Tamil verses, dance to erotic poetry and had so many other talents. She never chewed tobacco for fear it would stain her teeth. That would be bad for business. She had really nothing to buy in Sankaran's shop. So what? Sankaran wondered what 'Suar ke bachche!' meant.

'Hey, Iyer, want a pinch of snuff?' Suleiman asked, as he opened his snuff box.

'Do women ever use snuff, Suleiman?'

'Why does your mind always wander towards women, Iyer?' Suleiman slapped him hard on his behind.

In three hours Suleiman had become a closer friend to Sankaran than Karuthan. Perhaps because he was wealthy, Suleiman had a teasing, joking manner that Sankaran found very attractive. Karuthan was always respectful towards him and never overstepped his limits. But Suleiman recognised no limits. To him Sankaran was merely 'Iyer'. Sankaran would not have been surprised if he had begun to call him 'Sankara'. The familiarity came easily perhaps because he had ten times more money than Sankaran.

His father, Dastagir Rowther was the same. He sat in his large house, chewing paan and speaking of nothing but money to Sankaran in the short time he was there. He spoke about the tobacco agents in Tiruchi, Thanjavur, and Pudukottai, where they came from, how much money they made, how many mistresses each of them had and how much they spent on the women. Sankaran had listened to him politely, although rather frightened of the pigeons that flew across the courtyard, moving his shoulders frequently to avoid their droppings. He was saved by Suleiman who bellowed from upstairs, 'Sankar Iyer ! Sankar Iyer! Come upstairs!' Sankaran was shocked that the fellow should have the temerity to call him by name but his sense of outrage dissipated when he reached the first floor.

'Iyer, go in there and let it all out!' Suleiman instructed him pointing to a toilet inside the bedroom. Good god, this rascal had a lavatory inside the house! Sankaran was both shocked and fascinated. 'What is this, Suleiman... you have a lavatory inside the house!' Sankaran could not help laughing.

'What's wrong with that?' Suleiman retorted. 'Are we going to run a household from the bathroom or eat biriyani there? It's only for our convenience and it's in a corner.'

The bathroom had marble tiles and a toilet where one could sit on raised marble, shaped like feet, and relieve oneself. The room was sparkling clean and smelt fragrant. 'If one was rich would one's urine smell like perfume?' Sankaran wondered. He noticed that there was space to take a bath too.

'How long you have taken, Iyer, it's like you had to piss potfuls! Shall we go?'

Suleiman's voice was so loud that Sankaran was uncomfortably aware that his words could have been heard by the burqa-clad women downstairs.

When they came downstairs Rowther was smoking a hookah, making gurgling noises. On each of his shoulders sat a pigeon.

'Arre, munna, make detailed enquiries about all the passengers in the ship. I have to receive and take them into the city tomorrow. Don't forget to find out who is a little hard up for money. If this Iyer bachha knew some English it would be useful. Anyway, with his tuft and ear studs he looks very decorative. The white people like to see such people: snake charmers, magicians and Brahmin boys like this, provoke their interest.'

Sankaran resented the fact that Rowther was not seeing him as a canny and capable tobacco merchant from Arasur but as a curiosity on par with snake charmers and magicians. He vowed that he would succeed in business and one day build a bigger house than Vaithi's or Rowther's in Chennai. He would definitely have a toilet inside the house, however much the elders and ancestors disapproved of it.

Suleiman drove the horse carriage as if a demon possessed him. Pedestrians in the narrow streets cursed him as they narrowly missed being trampled by the horses or run over by the wheels. He swore right back at them and continued. The regular driver, a poor creature in worn-out clothes and a dirty turban, sat on the back steps of the carriage, chewing tobacco and looking relieved that he had not been asked to drive.

When the carriage came to a stop, Suleiman swore at the driver. 'Lazy fucker, look after the carriage and feed the horses. Don't nod off, you worthless piece of shit.'

Sankaran enjoyed all the swearing. He decided to learn all of it when he came to live in Chennai.

'Ahoy! Ahoy!' exclaimed a white man standing on the deck of the ship and looking at the shore with binoculars.

'Do they have a beach in London as well?' Sankaran asked Suleiman.

'No sea there. You have to go to Dover to see the sea. That's what my vaappa says. He is very good at geography. And these people are not English, they are American.'

'What's that?'

'America is a new nation, about a hundred-odd years old. They were also English originally, something like our Tamils going to Sri Lanka and settling there.'

Sankaran was a little disappointed that he was not going to be meeting Englishmen. But then what did it matter? A white man was a white man no matter which backyard he was born in.

More white people appeared on the upper deck. One was obese, another as thin as a stork, yet another had a luxuriant beard. There were a few white women as well, wearing long skirts and hats.

'Have you ever smelled a white woman, friend?' Suleiman asked.

'I haven't even smelled a local woman. The only smells I am familiar with are those of tobacco and snuff.'

'Come aboard the ship and you will experience everything,' promised Suleiman.

With that he sprinkled some perfume on Sankaran from a bottle in his bag. 'No, no Suleiman don't give me your Turk perfumes!' Sankaran protested, but he was secretly pleased to be smelling of attar. The white man on the upper deck yelled something at Suleiman who yelled right back. He gestured for them to come aboard.

'The mother fucker wants to know if we have brought any liquor. I knew he would ask. That's why I brought a couple of bottles in my bag.'

A large wave crashed against the boat and drenched them. 'Don't worry about it, I have two extra sets of clothes with me. You can borrow one,' said Suleiman.

Sankaran preferred damp clothes to wearing Suleiman's, so he remained silent.

Climbing the rope ladder to board the ship was a new and alarming experience for Sankaran. He climbed carefully, never once looking down at the sea. He kept his eyes firmly on Suleiman's behind, climbing ahead of him.

The moment they stepped on board, a bunch of laughing white women ran over to greet them. They looked like angels to Sankaran. Their colouring was paler than he liked, but he could find no fault with their generous bosoms and tiny waists, set off to advantage by their figure hugging gowns. Their hair was brown or red, like the waters of the pond after the rains and they had painted their cheeks pink.

One of them shook his hand and asked him something

'She is asking you if you have brought your snake along,' Suleiman translated.

'I am Sankaran, a tobacco merchant from Arasur, not a snake charmer,' Sankaran told her politely in Tamil. It was obvious she did not understand his words. Another woman, standing next to her, pulled at his tuft and knocked him lightly on his head. The women crowded around him and laughed.

Sankaran could smell their perspiration. He found the smell truly intoxicating.

CHAPTER 36

Suleiman mingled with the white folk as if he had known them from childhood. He used a mixture of pidgin English, Hindustani, Tamil and gestures to convey his meaning successfully. Abandoning Sankaran to the ministrations of the white women, he left in search of the ship's officials.

Sankaran did not quite know what to do with the women. If only they would leave him alone for a while he would be able to concentrate on business, but they seemed to have no intention of letting him be. They pulled at his tuft, stroked his cheeks, patted his back, pretended to pull off his veshti, tugged at his ear studs and treated him like a plaything.

In a little while, Suleiman returned following an elderly white man who wore white clothes and a cap. The man took off his cap and greeted the women and added some words that made them giggle and run downstairs to the cabins.

'Captain, this is a Brahmin,' Suleiman was telling the white man, gesturing towards Sankaran. 'He is my father's office clerk. See the tuft. See the thread. He is a Brahmin clerk.'

He was describing Sankaran as if he were a strange animal. Sankaran recognised the word 'clerk'. Vaithi was a clerk too, some sort of a clerk, he could not recollect exactly what. It seemed that Suleiman was introducing him to the white officer as a respectable man. If only he too knew English, he could hold conversations with this officer and with those women with tiny waists.

The white man inclined his head and said something to Sankaran. Suleiman answered for him, 'Father coming tomorrow. Clerk coming now.'

The white man chuckled.

Suleiman removed a large bottle of liquor from his bag and handed it respectfully to the officer.

'Thank you. Thank you so much,' said the officer.

Obviously these white men were so fond of liquor that they accepted it gratefully from whoever gave it to them, white or black. Did Vaithi also carry bottles of liquor to the fort on special days to present to the white officers there? Is that how he had made enough money to build his large house and eat onion sambar at leisure on Sundays?

When the officer had grasped the bottle by its neck like a hen and departed, Suleiman told Sankaran, 'That was the captain of the ship, the master of all those who work here. Tomorrow when vaappa comes to the ship, he has to get the signature of this man before he can do business with anybody on the ship. As long as the ship is berthed here, we supply the meat, vegetables, fruits, eggs and liquor. The captain has to pass the order to procure the provisions from us.'

'Will those women also hold the wheel and drive this ship?' Sankaran asked.

'Iyer, you have obviously become so besotted with the smell of white flesh that you cannot think straight! Those women are not employees of the ship. They are travellers, tourists. Of the three hundred people on this ship, only twenty or thirty are employees. The others are all tourists who have bought tickets to ride on this ship and see the world.'

'That's fine, Suleiman. But how are all these virgins travelling alone, without the protection of their parents?'

'They not only see the world, they might even opt to stay back here if they get a job in the government offices or hospitals or, if some of the white men here want to marry them, they will just extend their fingers for rings to be put on them. That's it—they are as good as wives once the rings are on their fingers. After that they will be quite willing to accompany their men to Calcutta or Rangoon.'

A crowd of white men came up to Suleiman. Just then, the catamarans reached the ship and porters, carrying sacks of liquor bottles clambered aboard. Removing the bottles one by one from a sack, Suleiman handed them to the white men, receiving pieces of paper from them in return. To each of his customers he said, 'Father coming tomorrow morning for document signing. Take rest. Take brandy.'

Sankaran took one of the pieces of paper from Suleiman and studied it. There was a picture on it of a man who had sunken cheeks and a moustache and a beard, his face looked like that of a rishi.

A white man told Sankaran, 'Lincoln. President,' and kissed the piece of paper.

Sankaran remembered the evangelist at the Nungambakkam intersection. He too was showing his audience pictures of some rishis—Sankaran had been too overcome by the desire to nap to look at them. Now he was being given a chance to see the picture of the lingam. This was all good. What did it matter if it was a white man or the priest Sundaram or the evangelist under the tree? They all spoke of good things.

Sankaran looked at the picture on the piece of paper with respect and handed it back carefully to Suleiman, who took it casually with his left hand and stuffed it into his coat pocket, shocking Sankaran with his irreverence.

More sacks came on board.

'Iyer, why don't you help me?' Suleiman asked him, explaining what exactly he had to do. 'Look,' he said, showing him one of those pieces of paper. 'This is a dollar. Two of these make an English rupee. If you give these men three of these liquor bottles you collect a dollar from them. Give them the stuff and tie the money safely in your veshti. I'll take it from you later.'

Arasur Subramanya Iyer's son was selling liquor! Subbamma's ancestors and angels, sleep quietly. This is just for fun. If Saama is with you tell him about it, he will enjoy it. For how long can I sell only tobacco?

In a few minutes Sankaran had learnt the knack of handing over bottle and collecting cash in one smooth movement. In no time the sacks behind him were empty. He could not see Suleiman nearby. Sankaran began to wander in search of him. Suddenly the white women spotted him and rushed over, squealing and giggling. They dragged him inside a dark room.

He was shocked to see that they too were drinking liquor. Was this the sign of Kali Yuga, that women too imbibed liquor? Sankaran tried to turn and run out of the room, but one of the women was quicker and bolted the door.

'Go sit there,' she ordered, pointing to a chair. Sankaran could understand what she was saying although he could not understand English. Sankaran sat down on the edge of the chair. Another woman poured out a drink in a glass and handed it to him.

'No! Not this! If Bhagavati Kutti ever comes to know she will castrate me!'

Someone pulled at Sankaran's tuft from behind and held his head, while another opened his mouth forcibly with a spoon. A woman sat on his lap and poured the liquid down his throat, like forcing medicine down an infant's mouth. The liquid burned its way down his gullet like fire. He pressed his chest with his hands. It hurt, it pleased, it frightened him out of his wits.

The woman on his lap was stroking his chest now, as she continued to feed him the liquor. If she went on like this he would soon be willing to drink all the liquor in the ship. Then he could cushion his head against her breasts and go to sleep.

He felt uncomfortable on the chair. He needed to sit on the floor. These girls could sit on the chair. They could kick him on his chest and back with their soft feet. They were all angels, apsaras. Bhagavati Kutti... why think of her now? If he survived this he would think about her. Those rascally brothers had warned him, had they not? Even Saama, peeping at him from the eclipsed sun had told him that he would lose his virginity, that he would know passion. Was this it? The smoked glass... it had smashed on the terrace. When Gomati manni went to the terrace to get the dry clothes off the clotheslines there, the glass pieces might cut her feet. But who cared about that now?

It felt so good to recline on the floor. The movement of the ship on the waves was pleasing too. Why is this woman pulling me to lie down on her? Will Gomati manni's sister have breasts as big as this one's? Will you make a fuss if I touch your tits? Do you know the love epic of Koolappa Naicken? Kottakudi dasi knows. And this is how she gestures when she dances to it. Don't laugh bitch! Fill my glass again. There was an eclipse today. If it affected your star you should have done a propitiation ceremony. You have to pay the Chennai priest a fee for that. I am not a priest, nor am I a snake charmer. I am a Brahmin who sells tobacco and snuff. A Brahmin should not drink liquor. But he can drink coffee. Can you make coffee? Why are you pressing your spit on my lips, slut? That is dirty, polluted. Never mind. Don't be angry. Actually it was rather nice. What is this, a plantain? Why does it smell so bad? But everything tastes good when you feed it to me! This is tastier than Gomati manni's cabbage curry. Suleiman, you rogue, where are you? Let's go. I have to get back to Nungambakkam. Have to get the hundi exchanged. Karuthan should be careful when dealing with that Telugu accountant. Don't pull off my veshti! Has anyone ever spied on you when you bathed? What do you smell of, attar or foreign perfume? Never mind, the smell of your body alone is attraction enough. Get me that glass, bitch. I'll drink as I lie down here. How can I drink if you rub your body against mine like this? Why are you all laughing? Do you know the sexual tactics that Kottakudi dasi practices? Princess, you can probably teach her a thing or two! I know that is a bed. You don't have to tell me.

If only the music box was here. The music from it would have made this even more pleasurable.

CHAPTER 37

At midnight, a strong wind began to rock the ship. It pulled at the ropes holding the anchor. It teased the waves so that they rose to angry heights. Overseeing the tumult was the cool, detached face of the moon. Looking at the moon as he walked naked on the upper deck, Sankaran felt as detached as the moon.

He did not know the time. What did that matter? Over and above the roar of the sea, his head was filled with the clamour of demons and angels, beasts and serpents. He could hear the angry shouts of Pichai Rowther, the priest Sundaram, Bhagavati Kutti's brother, Kitta Iyer, Thanu Pillai and the Telugu employee, they were all pointing to below his waist and shouting in a frenzy. 'Don't wander around unclothed, Arasur Sankara!' they were admonishing him.

Sankaran would, in fact, have preferred to be clothed, but he could not find his clothes. He would have liked to lie down with those white women again. One of them would have held the liquor in her mouth and then, kissing him, passed it on into his own as she had done before... the ecstasy of it!

'Stop! No more!' he had begged. 'Never say stop, idiot!' Saama had chided him. 'Find out instead if there is a swing here somewhere. To lay a woman on it as it moves, or to be laid, is wonderful!' In the salty waves, the queen bathed, the white patch between her breasts visible in the moonlight, the envy in her eyes, obvious. He would hear the music of the lac discs again, in Vaithi's voice,' Passion! Pleasure!' the voice would repeat, like a mantra. He would have liked to lie down again listening to it.

He wondered if it had all been a dream. He remembered getting off the bed and walking down a long corridor smelling of damp, candle smoke, liquor, meat, white women. Was it all a dream, even his copulating with those white girls? If it was a dream, where was his veshti? Why did his breath smell so foul? Why did his body feel drained one minute and fully alive and virile the next?

This was not the Sankaran who had sold tobacco in Arasur. This was a Sankaran who had come to sell snuff and learnt to drink coffee and swear in Hindustani. But these were not the things that drove him. That was his body—its desires were irresistible and its domination over him powerful. Now he had reached a stage where it mattered not that he was naked. His past life and its humdrum details seemed of no consequence to him.

He tripped over something in the dark. Was it a man, another reveller who had fallen down on the deck in a heap? How had he got here? Did those angelic girls bring and dump him here? Or had he found his own way? He could not remember. He looked at the mound near his feet. It was not a man but a large sack. Suleiman's sack, he thought. It would contain his spare clothes He could hear approaching footsteps. He needed clothes. He took Suleiman's clothes out of the sack. It was not a veshti but a loose robe of the sort Muslims wore. He put it on, looked into the sack again and found a pair of pyjamas that went with the robe. Where was his sacred thread? He could not find it. He wondered briefly around which of those white women's bountiful breasts the thread now lay looped. Never mind, he could always get a new one during the next annual sacred thread ceremony. The priest from the Vedic School would definitely ask him where his thread had gone. At that point he should definitely tell him about the breasts of the white women.

It took a while for Sankaran to get dressed in the unfamiliar, attar smelling clothes. But once he had them on he felt quite at home in them. His tuft had come undone and his hair swirled about his shoulders. Clothes made a man. Sankaran was no longer Sankara Iyer. He was Suleiman Rowther. Rowther, Iyer… these were just labels to comfort oneself. Even without these, Sankaran had received a lot of comfort last night from the white women who did not care about labels. He felt very sleepy. 'Let me sleep.' Even if someone clothed him in the robes of the Christian fathers while he was asleep, he could not care less.

Sunlight woke Sankaran hours later, burning his eyelids. He opened his eyes and found people walking on the deck. He could hear the singing of the catamaran boatmen. Sankaran went to the ship's railing and looked over it. There were at least fifteen catamarans there. In the first one stood Dastagir Rowther, his lips red with betel leaf, his posture authoritative. His secretary was standing behind him holding an umbrella over his head. Another assistant, an extremely thin man, was stacking sheets of paper in a cane box. Where on earth was Suleiman? Was he also lying drunk and naked somewhere? What did he do for clothes? Would he have Sankaran's veshti and sacred thread?

Dastagir Rowther looked freshly bathed and dressed. The ship's employees, dressed in immaculate white and walking purposefully, may also have bathed. Even those white girls might have bathed and wrapped their hair in towels and might be praying to their gods. Bathing, working and thinking purposeful thoughts would remove the taint of the previous night, no matter how dirty it was.

Sankaran too should bathe before the visitors boarded the ship. If only he could get some coffee. Coffee was beyond pollution. You could drink it without bathing. Sankaran saw a staircase leading down. He slung Suleiman's bag around his neck, walked down and found the toilet. This had a hole for a urinal, a tank of clean water and a mirror on the wall. Sankaran washed his hands, feet and face and brushed his teeth with his finger. He wiped himself dry by lifting the cloth of his robe and using that as a towel. As he did so, Suleiman's bag tilted and he saw a black fez inside it. Sankaran tied his hair in a tuft and looked in the mirror. With his moustache and beard, he resembled a young rishi, but the tuft and studs on his ears did not go with the robe at all. He removed his studs and put them in the bag. He thought for a moment and then placed Suleiman's fez on his head. He wondered afresh where the women were.

When Sankaran returned to the upper deck, he found Dastagir Rowther sitting there on a chair with the captain. The captain was signing some papers that Rowther had placed before him. A short distance away stood the thin assistant holding some more papers. When Sankaran's shadow fell on the captain, he looked up and sighting Sankaran, said, 'Your Brahmin clerk is now dressed in his proper uniform. It's good that he is not naked above the waist as he was when he came aboard last evening!' Rowther laughed as loudly as the captain. Then he signalled casually to Sankaran as if to say, 'Hey, come here!' When Sankaran went to him with humble steps and a servile attitude, he was himself reminded of the servility of the Telugu clerk and Vaithi towards their bosses.

'Did you stay here last night?' Rowther asked him. It seemed to Sankaran a superfluous question. Still, he was, as Rowther's employee, bounden to answer him. So he stared at the beach in the distance and replied, 'Yes, master. I had lain down here last night.' His voice and words were that of a servant.

'Well, don't stand there like a buffalo. Bring all those papers here!' Rowther ordered him. Sankaran took the stack of papers from the thin assistant and took them over to Rowther. The captain asked Sankaran to push the ink pot closer to him. When the pen fell to the floor Rowther asked Sankaran to pick it up and place it near the captain. When Sankaran did so Rowther admonished him, 'Don't you have any brains? Will not the pen have the dust of your feet on it? Wipe it on your robe before you return it to the table.'

When Sankaran had wiped the pen on his robe and, watching the blue-black stain it made on it, handed the pen to the captain, Rowther yelled at him again, 'How dare you hand it to the captain, idiot? Is he your brother or your friend? Place it on the table.'

Sankaran thought he deserved all the insults. He wished Rowther would scold him more, maybe the white man would even spit on him.

'Where is your son?' the captain asked Rowther.

'Useless fellow! He came here last evening without my permission or yours and brought along this scoundrel of a clerk with him. My apologies, Sir.' Rowther looked at Sankaran as if he were a worm.

'No. No problem. They were, in fact, really helpful.'

'I am glad to hear that my lord. Can we please have the passengers sign the immigration papers now? My head clerk is also present over there to help them.' Rowther pointed towards his thin assistant who greeted the captain as if his life depended on it.

'Sure. Sure,' said the captain and Rowther snapped his fingers at Sankaran.

'Go stand there to that side. The passengers will come one by one and you have to get their signatures on these documents. You should not miss even one. Do you follow?' His voice sounded unnecessarily harsh, but Sankaran nodded his head humbly.

He was hungry and yearned for a mouthful of coffee and a couple of idlis. He would have given his life for a spoonful of water, he was so parched. But the passengers who had now queued up did not need his life, they just needed to sign the papers he held out towards them.

It was a simple drill: dip the nib in the ink pot, wipe the pen carefully on one's robe and place it carefully by the side of the document on the table. Repeat the drill with the next passenger. A white woman wearing a large hat that concealed most of her face bent low to sign the paper. Had she sat on his lap last night, Sankaran wondered.

'Shaitaan ka bachha! Will you take all day? Hurry up!' Rowther yelled. When every passenger had signed, the thin assistant came forward and tied all the papers with a piece of hempen string. 'Hold it tight, Mudali. Otherwise they will scatter,' he told Sankaran. It felt strange to be addressed as a Mudali.

'Welcome to the ancient city of Madras,' Rowther stood on the upper deck and addressed the passengers, spreading his arms as if to embrace them. A short lecture on the merits of Madras followed. Sankaran stood behind Rowther, holding the stack of documents on his head.

The passengers left for the shore on sail boats. The upper deck was empty except for Sankaran, Rowther and his thin assistant.

'Mudali, place those papers in the box!' the thin assistant peremptorily instructed Sankaran.

Upon this, Rowther snapped at him, 'Hey, this gentleman is neither a Mudali nor our employee. He is Suleiman's business partner!'

Then Rowther turned to Sankaran and said apologetically, 'Iyer, don't be upset. The captain thought you were a clerk, so I just went along with it. These mother fuckers like to do business only with those blacks who bully their employees. That's why I pretended to yell at you. Don't take it to heart, will you? And from when did you start wearing robes and pyjamas? Suleiman told me that you had a veritable orgy here last night! Be careful, young man. If you indulge too much you might catch the clap, don't want your prick to rot and drop off do you?' Rowther laughed and began descending from the ship to the waiting catamaran. Sankaran found the thin assistant looking at him with newfound respect. He must be one of those men who stood on the shore and fantasised about the white women on the ship.

Sankaran scanned the sail boats and catamarans leaving with the passengers, trying to spot the white woman who had slept with him last night. There was something he had to ask her—where was his lovely white Salem veshti?

CHAPTER 38

Miracles still happened. What else could you call what transpired with that Brahmin-turned-Christian from Savakkadu?

The pitiable fellow whom Kitta Iyer had kicked out of his cooking tent not so long ago became a wealthy man overnight. It was said that he found a buried treasure. A big metal pot full of coins from the times of the Chera kings, jewellery, a marble vial and more.

The Savakkadu Brahmin-Christian was thrown out of his house because he could no longer pay the rent. The landlord, also a Brahmin who had converted to Christianity, showed very few Christian feelings towards his penurious tenant and beat him up before casting him out. The Savakkadu Brahmin had all along been treated like a worm by other Brahmins. The Ambalapuzha Brahmins, like Kitta Iyer, were worse. They would not even give him menial jobs like assisting in their catering contracts and no matter how hard he begged, they would not give him a morsel of food.

Driven out of his house he took refuge in a small piece of land that had been left to him by his ancestors. It had been left untended for so long that nothing grew on it. A small house, which was entirely open to the elements, stood at the centre of this patch of land on which people threw their rubbish. The Savakkadu Brahmin-Christian slowly removed all the debris from the ruins of the house and found there was nothing left there for him to live in. Without much hope, he begged the local carpenter to help him put up four pillars and a thatch roof. The carpenter agreed to help him, without any hope of remuneration.

After he had begun work, the Savakkadu Christian promised to give him the small piece of gold that he wore on his girdle. He promised to get the gold thoroughly cleaned before he handed it to the carpenter. The carpenter had to trust that his impoverished client did have a piece of gold on him. He could not pull off his client's veshti to check if he was speaking the truth.

While the carpenter was busy putting up the pillars, the Savakkadu Christian began to plan a vegetable garden on his dead land. As the carpenter watched, certain that the old man was out of his mind, the latter began digging. Suddenly the carpenter heard the sound of metal striking metal. Curious, he walked over to where the old man was digging and found him struggling to lift an ancient metal pot from the pit he had dug. The Savakkadu Christian had found his treasure.

'Why did you beat up that poor man? Look how rich he has now become while we will remain cooks for the rest of our lives!' Snehamba chided her husband in a loud voice, when she came to hear of the Christian's good fortune. Kitta Iyer felt bad about having humiliated the man. He did not know what had come over him that day. Why had he got so angry? He was not usually a violent man. Apart from the guilt he felt for having beaten up the Savakkadu

Christian, he was also very disturbed by the curses the Bairagi ascetics had uttered that day, the way the strange wasp had stung him on his penis. He wondered whether the sting had made him impotent. But Snehamba had missed her last period, putting his fear to rest. He was dismayed that he had made an enemy of a man who had zoomed from rags to riches.

Those envious of the Savakkadu Christian said the treasure did not belong to the old man and should be handed over to the government. The pastor set all doubts at rest by saying that by law and religion, the treasure belonged entirely to the old man. 'Let him who seeks be surprised and joyous when he receives what he seeks,' the pastor said, closing the subject. Most members of the congregation crossed themselves and accepted the pastor's judgement. Yet there was one persistent fellow, a man who had read the gospel of St Thomas forwards and backwards, who raised the question, 'Father, didn't St Thomas say this: 'Let he who seeks do so until he finds. When he finds what he seeks he will suffer great mental disturbance and his hair will stand on end with his astonishment?' Did this man too suffer from these signs?'

The pastor drew the sign of the cross on his forehead and replied gently, 'Even if things do not happen exactly by the book, they happen by divine will, do they not?'

His questioner knelt quietly before the father, folded his hands respectfully and left without further argument.

The pastor provided more information for his congregation: the Savakkadu Christian had undertaken to pay for the renovation of the church in Kodungallur with his newfound wealth.

It was also said that the Savakkadu Christian had found some ancient palm leaf manuscripts and a marble vial of some strange liquid. The manuscripts were given to a Tamil scholar to study. The latter could make little of it—his assessment ranged wildly from the plan for building a flying vehicle to the ground plan for an urban drainage system. The Savakkadu Christian put the manuscripts away, deciding to do something about them later.

The Savakkadu Christian spent some of his newly found wealth building himself a decent house. The rest he deposited with the money lenders, Peria Karuppan Chetty and Maliakkal Thomas. They paid him a handsome interest.

The liquid in the marble vial was strange. When the Savakkadu Christian accidentally rubbed a few drops of it on his head, his white hair turned black and glossy. The hair on the head of the man standing next to him began to drop in clumps. The Savakkadu Christian wondered whether he should drink a little of the liquid, but decided against it afraid that the man standing beside him might fall dead. On the advice of some learned people he invited the scholarly Nambudiri astrologer from Melamangalam to conduct a prasnam on the desirability of using the liquid from the vial.

On the day of the prasnam the Savakkadu Christian arranged for Kitta Iyer to cook for all the guests. Dressed in white silk and walking elegantly, the Savakkadu Christian came up to Kitta Iyer as he was stirring the ginger and tamarind gravy and barked, 'Hey there, how is it going? A great number of wealthy men are attending today's event. If your cooking is not to their liking, you will not be able to cook in this region again!'

Kitta Iyer could see the cruel glee on the man's face.

When the feasting was over, the astrologer studied his cowries and said that the Savakkadu Christian's trials and tribulations so far had been due to the effects of the planets, Mars and Jupiter. The bad phase had passed and the old man could expect good times. The vial, the astrologer said, contained nectar. He would have to place it facing east within a watermelon and worship it for forty days with prayers, the prayers could be directed to St Thomas or Jesus Christ. After forty days of prayers, if the Savakkadu Christian drank the nectar he would become young again. When the latter asked the astrologer if he could give some of the liquid to anybody else, he replied that it was not advisable. While the other person would not come to harm from drinking it, the nectar might make him begin to speak in faulty Sarkar language. 'This is a good time for you. Your future appears prosperous and happy. Why do you want to spoil it all by inviting the displeasure of the government by making your friends speak bad Sarkar language?' the astrologer asked.

The Savakkadu Brahmin did as he was told. He prayed to his God for forty days and sanctified the contents of the vial. He drank a little of the liquid from a cup made of a jack fruit leaf. He stood in front of his mirror every morning for the next two days to see if he was getting his youth back. Nothing happened.

The cow that ate the discarded jackfruit leaf cup he had drunk from began to moo and low in Sarkar language. The owner of the cow complained to the Savakkadu Christian, 'What have you done to my cow? Now she is insulting the government by making rude noises in governmental language. Who will buy her milk? No one will even want to touch her! Either change my cow back or buy her off me!'

The Savakkadu Christian did not reply. He paid the cowherd the price he asked for and tied the cow in his own cattle shed. All night she babbled in a strange tongue. Since nobody would buy her milk, her new owner boiled the milk until it became creamy, added jaggery to it and distributed the sweet equally between the local temple and the Kodungallur church. The pastor from the church came over to tell his Savakkadu parishioner not to keep such strange animals at home. Deliverance came in the form of the chief priest of the local temple who agreed to shelter the cow in the temple's cattle shed and use her milk for bathing the idol of the goddess. Many devotees, including Snehamba believed that the deity's face had acquired a special radiance after being bathed by the milk of the Sarkar language speaking cow. Snehamba said this to Kitta Iyer on a night when the rest of the family had gone to the temple to see a dance performance. She had decided to stay home because she wanted to have a private conversation with her husband.

As they cuddled that night, Snehamba whispered to her husband, 'Why don't you pay the Savakkadu gentleman a visit?' She tugged playfully at Kitta Iyer's sacred thread as she said this.

'For what?' her naïve husband asked. He wanted to kiss her on the lips but when he had done so the previous night her buck teeth had rubbed against his lips and made them sore. He settled for the region below her neck. Their little daughter, lying nearby, muttered in her sleep that she wanted a silk pavadai for her aunt Bhagavati's wedding.

'I will certainly buy it for you, darling,' Kitta Iyer told her, fondly stroking her head. The child went back to sleep.

'Is it true that your brother and you are planning to sell the land to fund Bhagavati's wedding?' Snehamba asked her husband.

'Yes. How else can we give her a dowry befitting our status?'

'You have sold most of your property to marry off your sisters. Before the rest goes, don't you think we should provide for ourselves?'

Kitta Iyer was intent on squeezing her breasts. He felt an urgency to take her into the store room and complete his lovemaking. It would not be long before everyone returned from the temple.

As he spread his body over Snehamba's on the floor of the store room that smelled of rice and sack cloth, she continued to speak, 'Let us sell your share of the land and borrow some money from the Savakkadu Christian. With the money we can open a small eatery, not here, but either in Alapuzha or Kollam.'

Even as they climaxed, they had no words of love for each other. The eatery loomed large in their minds.

CHAPTER 39

'Hey Nani, what is all this hustle and bustle in the temple?' Bhagavati asked her friend Narayani as they entered the temple that evening.

'Don't you know? They are going to perform the Chaakkiyar Koothu today, it's really funny. The performers make you laugh till your stomach aches. But then you and I can't enjoy it. Young, unmarried women are not allowed to stay in the temple after dark. So we don't get to see the koothu.'

Even the temple was not considered safe for young virgins, after dark. It was said that ghosts gathered around the sacrificial stone in the temple after dusk, begging for some of the offerings made to the deities during the evening worship. Some of these ghosts would love to get into the bodies of careless young virgins who hung around the sacrificial stone at this time. The ghosts were especially partial to virgins whose marriages had just been fixed.

Both Nani and Bhagavati came under this category. Nani's fiancée was related to her and would soon come from Ettumanoor to make her his wife. As for Bhagavati, her marriage was confirmed. There had been some doubt about it after the tragic happenings in the Arasur family. But just yesterday a handwritten letter had arrived from Subramanya Iyer, confirming the alliance and stating that the wedding would take place on the date that had earlier been decided upon.

'You are going to lie with the tobacco shop owner and bear him a son—the baby will arrive smelling of tobacco!' Nani teased Bhagavati.

'Well, what of your Nambudiri? He is so busy making sacrificial fires all the time. Your baby will probably come smelling of ghee and smoke from the homams!' Bhagavati retorted, giggling.

Bhagavati's family felt sad for the tragic events that had taken place in the Arasur family. They wished it hadn't happened just after the alliance with Bhagavati had been fixed. It was as if she was bringing them ill luck, but how could one blame her for the death of Sankaran's elder brother or the burning down of the family's house? Her horoscope was clear on this—she had a clear and lucky horoscope, as even the astrologer who accompanied the Arasur family proclaimed after studying it. This same astrologer had said that Duraisamy Iyer's house too was afflicted by ghosts and that he would make and bring a yantra to drive them away when he came for the wedding. If only he had made one right then and left it in the house, perhaps Snehamba manni's father would not have floated over the temple and caused all that trouble.

Nani had actually seen it. 'Poor old man,' Nani observed. 'Not only did we all see him fly, we also got to see him completely naked and pissing from the sky! Look, if you don't feed your tobacco man well, he too will become weak and float away one day. Tie a rope around his waist and hold on fast!' Nani added, breaking into giggles.

'Well, you hold on to your tambiran below the waist, Nani. Otherwise he too will fly and fall into some taravad!' Bhagavati laughed, as they entered the temple that evening.

'Bhagavati, is this the Chennamangalam Devi temple that you need to worship with laughter? What's all this laughing for? Is it because your marriage has been fixed and that of your friend's?' the chief priest of the temple chided them gently. He was a good friend of Bhagavati's family and she had known him since she was a child.

'Uncle, is our laughter making more noise than the clapping of your hands before you begin your worship?' Bhagavati asked him innocently. Then she burst out laughing all over again.

'How do you know about the rituals I conduct?' the chief priest asked with genuine surprise.

'She knows so much!' Nani said with pride. 'She is a Tamilian, isn't she? In their families they allow girls to get an education. That's how she knows.'

'Well, why don't you get educated as well?' the chief priest asked Nani. He wiped his sweating shoulders with his upper cloth and wondered where the temple cook had gone. He was not to be seen at the entrance to the kitchen where he usually lounged.

'Uncle, have you made up with your son? Do you speak to each other?' Bhagavati asked the chief priest.

'What quarrel have I with him?' the chief priest retorted. 'It was just that over the incident of that old man from your family flying over the flagstaff of the temple and polluting the temple space, we held opposite views. Anyway, all that is over. I hear that the old man has now stopped floating and walks normally—whatever the reason for his recovering his health, I am happy about it.'

Nevertheless, Bhagavati had heard the elders in her home say that things were not yet quite normal between the chief priest and his son. Narayani now said impudently, 'Sir, get your son married. He'll be fine then!' She laughed.

'If you did not have a fiancé already, you could have come to my home as my daughter-in-law, child. It's not too late even now. Ask your fiancé to look for a bride elsewhere and I'll get you married to my son. Then Nani Kutti need not leave her village at all,' the chief priest teased her.

'Wherever I go, Uncle, I shall still remain within the four walls of a house, and not see much of the world,' Nani replied, unsmiling.

'Hey, all that will soon change, child,' the chief priest comforted her. 'My son tells me that very soon Nambudiri girls will also get an education and come up in life. Perhaps he is right.'

The temple cook came out of the kitchen as a signal that the food for the deity was ready. The priest began walking towards the sanctum of the temple telling the girls, 'Let me begin the evening worship. Meanwhile you two can stop laughing and start chanting the names of the deity while walking round the sanctum.'

The firecracker man came up to him, holding out a small metal box. 'Something astonishing has happened!' he said.

'What wonderful thing have you seen in that box? I do not wish to look at anything ugly now,' the chief priest said hurriedly and walked away.

As they walked in the temple corridor, Bhagavati wondered what was in the box. Very soon the girls realised that it was getting dark. They would have to return home soon. In Bhagavati's hand was a plantain leaf cup with the prasadam from the sanctum. As she walked by the sacrificial stone in the northern corner of the temple, she heard the firecracker man speak loudly. He had obviously been following the chief priest. 'Tirumeni!' he called plaintively. 'Had we not put only one toe in it, Tirumeni? Now look at it, it has grown five whole toes!'

Bhagavati remembered that when Snehamba manni's old father had floated over the temple and fallen naked on this man, the impact had caused the firecracker in his hand to go off and sever his little toe. Some kind soul had picked up the severed toe that had been flung far from the temple and brought it back. The vaidyar had observed that it would not be possible to attach the ragged toe, as it was, to the firecracker man's foot. The Chief Priest, though the vaidyar did not agree with him, opined if the severed toe was soaked in a herbal liquid in a box and the box placed ten feet to the east of the flagstaff, it would, in due course of time, acquire enough flesh and muscle. That would enable the vaidyar to surgically reattach it to the man's foot (at a cost of seven and a half governmental rupees). That was how the severed toe had found its way into the small metal box.

The firecracker man placed the box containing his little toe on a mound of earth quite a distance from the flagstaff. The chief priest saw it there sometimes at night when all the lights had been doused and he was locking up the sanctums. It usually had a small flower garland on it. When he passed it, he would fling a few grains of rice from the offering to the deities that he was taking home. Perhaps the nourishment had made the toe grow and branch into five toes. Or so the firecracker man believed. Bhagavati heard him say that the toes had long, demonic looking nails.

The chief priest tried to comfort him saying the vaidyar could easily remove the required toe and attach it to the firecracker man's foot. 'But what shall I do with the other toes then?' the man asked.

'We'll talk about that after I have finished the last worship of the day,' the priest told him.

Bhagavati saw the firecracker man limp away towards the place where he set off the firecrackers during the evening worship. She walked into the space where devotees offered their obeisance to the deity and knelt down on the floor and touched her head to the ground. When she got up, she found that Nani was not beside her. She circled the temple more times than Bhagavati and therefore took longer. Bhagavati decided to watch the arrangements being made for the koothu performance that night while waiting for her friend. She moved out of the main temple and walked towards the pavilion where the performance would be held. When she passed the sacrificial stone on her way, she saw a young Brahmin girl standing there, beckoning her. As she drew close she inhaled the strong, mossy smell emanating from the woman.

'Bhagavati Kutti, God will bless you if you ask someone to give me some rice to eat. I am so hungry!'

How did the strange woman know her name? As Bhagavati looked at the woman in astonishment the woman's figure seemed to fade and become one dimensional. Was this a ghost?

As if reading her mind, the woman said, 'Yes. It is three hundred years since I died. I am the mistress of Swaminathan, the elder brother of Sankaran, the man you are going to marry. I am the woman who spread her legs and lay with his brother.' She started to laugh loudly.

Bhagavati Kutti sank to the ground, holding her head in her hands.

From beneath a nearby niche that held an oil lamp, a metal box moved, slowly and purposefully, towards Bhagavati.

CHAPTER 40

Kuppusamy Iyer folded his hands pleadingly towards his younger brother, Duraisamy Iyer, and said, 'Speak softly. It's been ten days since Bhagavati Kutti fell ill. Only now is she sleeping a little. I think the vaidyar's medicine is beginning to work only now.'

'That's right. There is no need to speak about all this now. Let my husband also come home. He has, after all, a share in the land. And I would also like my elder brother to arrive from Alapat before we discuss how to dispose of the land,' Snehamba said in a loud whisper. She had made sure to close the door of the granary before speaking. Inside, screened off from the grains, tamarind and jaggery stored there by a cane screen, lay poor Bhagavati whose face looked pale and bloodless.

For the last ten days Bhagavati Kutti's behaviour had been bizarre. She woke up at random, asked for food, but before Visalakshi or her sister Alamelu brought the food, she slipped into an uneasy sleep again. She moved restlessly in her sleep, muttering and moaning.

For the last ten days she had not eaten or bathed or performed any bodily function. Her family could hardly bear to see her suffer thus.

Her sickness began on the night of the previous Saturday. The chief priest and others had found her shivering and curled up in a foetal position on the ground near the sanctums. There was no way they could make her get up and walk. So they placed her on a cot and carried her home the way they had carried Snehamba's old father home after the incident he had caused in the temple. The firecracker man accompanied the little procession, carrying a lighted torch and limping all the way.

When the ghostly woman extended her hand towards Bhagavati begging for the prasadam in the leaf cup in Bhagavati's hand, the latter froze. Her tongue would not move to utter the names of the Goddess that might have saved her in this moment of need. When, involuntarily, she held out the leaf cup towards Swaminathan's lover, the metal box that had crawled towards her stopped at her feet and opened. From it the five-toed foot rose up, and crying, 'That's for me! For me!' kicked away the ghostly woman. The spectacle made Bhagavati's hair stand on end with fright. In her fear she dropped the leaf cup to the ground.

Little Bhagavati was the sole witness to the fight that ensued between the 300-year-old ghost and the severed, five-toed foot, over the morsel of rice in the leaf cup.

'You are just a lump of flesh. The man who owns you is over there firing crackers. When the vaidyar attaches you back to his leg you will be part of his maggot-ridden body. Why do you need to eat rice?' the ghost-woman screamed in frustration at the foot and tried to grab the leaf cup from its grip. The toes of the foot were trying to empty the contents of the cup into the box, but with the pull of the ghost-woman's hand, the leaf cup fell from the grip of the toes and rolled on the ground. Thereupon the raging foot, all shiny with herbal oil, tried to hop out of the box to chase the cup.

'Bhagavati, child, why should this lump of flesh be bothered if I beg you for food? Am I not related to you? What does it matter that Saama is not there anymore? What does it matter that I am a ghost wandering around in limbo and hungering for food? Are we still not related?' the woman wailed, but her voice was drowned by the loud singing from the koothu that had just then begun in the pavilion.

'Ayyo! That this beggarly bit of flesh should snatch the food from my lips! Won't anyone question this injustice? Oh ancestral women of the Arasur family! Oh deities of the sacrificial stone! Oh Bhagavati! Will no one help me? Oh Saama, you whoreson! Did you not lay me on the ground and enjoy me even during broad daylight? Now you have left me to suffer without a morsel of food! May even the place where the ashes of your phallus fell become barren and covered with poisonous plants and thorn bushes! May your lineage be destroyed!'

As the ghost-woman cursed and ranted, the firecracker man's foot ran, dragging the leaf cup into the darkness beyond the sacrificial stone. Bhagavati stood rooted, staring at the energetically moving foot. Then she heard a chorus of female voices singing. They sang that the Arasur lineage would survive, with fighting and peace making, with sickness and health, with desire and frustration, with passion and wealth, like every other human family, for many generations to come. It was sung with joy in the voice of that old lady who came with the Arasur family to see her and whose mouth they had had to gag with a cloth.

'I do not have a body, but I have life and therefore I hunger. You only have a body but no life. Why do you need the food? Don't drag it in the mud. Give it to me!' the ghost-woman wailed afresh as she went after the firecracker man's foot.

Bhagavati swooned and fell to the ground where the lamp by the sacrificial stone cast a long shadow. Since then, for the last ten days, she had been following the ghost-woman and the firecracker man's foot in her mind. She saw the ghost woman grab the foot and bite it and stand there with the herbal oil and the blood from the foot smeared around her grinning mouth. She saw the foot trying to wriggle into the ghost woman's waist cloth. 'Stop!' she heard the ghost-woman scream, 'Don't put your foot there Saama! No, you are not Saama. I would know the warmth from his body anywhere. You are part of a strange man. Sinner! Oh, Bhagavati, come and lift this wretched thing off me! Get up Bhagavati, child! I am so hungry! Eat a little for my sake, Bhagavati. Visalakshi Manni, Alamelu akka, Sneha manni, Echumi akka, bring some rice and lentil mixed with a drop of ghee. Just four morsels of it will do. A little water to drink and I am all done. There are so many sacks of rice and grains in that place beyond the screen—I know Duraisamy Iyer has stacked them there. Visalakshi! I saw you here that night with your husband. I brought the old man floating through the room but took him away before he could see everything. Get me some rice, Visalakshi, you have the kind looks of the goddess in the temple. Visalakshi, Visali, Salatchi, Salu, Salumma... look how fondly I call you, just like your husband Kuppusamy Iyer. I beg you, a little rice! I am so hungry!'

For every four sentences that the ghost woman spoke in her mind, Bhagavati herself repeated one of them, muttering the words faintly, 'Rice... lentil and rice and ghee...'

Hearing her Duraisamy Iyer asked his brother Kuppusamy Iyer worriedly, 'Anna, what is the vaidyar saying? Will she soon be well? If she is not better tomorrow should we take her to Alappuzha to the missionary doctor? God, what a mess this is, what with Bhagavati's wedding drawing near!'

'The vaidyar has said that she will be cured today. We have been giving her the medicines he prescribed every day without fail. We have to trust his methods. Without trust in the doctor how can expect a cure?' Kuppusamy Iyer replied.

Duraisamy Iyer nodded. He had called a meeting of his brothers so that they could discuss selling their land in order to meet the expenses of Bhagavati's wedding. But there was no sign of Kitta Iyer yet. Meanwhile the sons-in-law of the family, who had also come to attend the meeting, were getting impatient.

But Snehamba would not let them start the discussion without her husband. 'He'll be here, wait a little,' she had been saying since morning.

'Where has he gone?' they repeatedly asked her. 'We know he has no cooking contracts for today.'

Although she did not tell them, Snehamba knew where her husband had gone. He had left early in the morning to see the Savakkadu Brahmin-Christian about a loan. If he could find out how much he was willing to give him he would know exactly how much he should ask his brothers from the proceeds of the sale of their land so that he would have enough money to start his eatery. The Savakkadu fellow was asking for a steep rate of interest. But Kitta Iyer was going to get the loan without any surety, after all, what did he have that he could pledge? He was reluctant to pledge the small pieces of gold jewellery that his wife and children wore.

Two days ago Kitta Iyer had been to see the Savakkadu Brahmin for preliminary talks. The man, with his newly blackening hair, his fine silks and an air of supreme contempt, told Kitta Iyer, 'What does it matter that we belong to different religions now? We were once the same. Although you were cruel enough to kick me out without feeding me a morsel of food, and now have no compunction about standing at my door and begging me for a loan, I always say the same thing—I will give you money, whatever amount you ask for. Ask.'

Kitta Iyer replied respectfully, 'Sir, I plan to change my residence to Alapuzha or Kollam and there set up an eatery. I am tired of taking up cooking contracts and wandering all over the place. I will pay the interest on the loan you give me on every new moon day and in four years, I will pay back the principal.'

The man from Savakkadu listened to Kitta Iyer, as he crossed his legs comfortably and chewed betel leaf in a leisurely manner. He imagined how Kitta Iyer's new venture as a restaurateur would go, he thought of all the suhiyan, dosai, puttu, appam and ilaiadai he would make and dish out to his customers without caring what their caste was, careful only about whether they were paying. He would make his fortune slowly by copper coin and silver coin, never mind whose dirty fold of cloth they came from. His lifestyle would become better. Snehamba and the children would grow fat and prosperous. Soon a son would be born. Kitta Iyer would clothe him in silks and take him to the temple in Guruvayur for his rice-feeding ceremony[12].

'Kitta Iyer, come back on Thursday. I will then let you know how much money I can loan you.'

Today was Thursday. Kitta Iyer had left early in the morning to see the man from Savakkadu. After he returned the family would speak about the sale of their land and about Bhagavati's wedding. Kitta too would have something to say. Bit by bit their land had been sold to meet the expenses of the weddings of the two elder daughters of the family. Now they had to spend on Bhagavati. There was also the issue of farmers who were encroaching on their land and would soon probably claim it as their own. Before that happened it would be wiser to sell the entire tract of land and after meeting the expenses of Bhagavati's wedding, split the rest equally between the brothers. There was also the question of splitting the joint family in which they now lived. Kitta would soon be leaving the village. There was a lot to discuss, once Kitta returned home… Snehamba was lost in thought when they heard the cheerful sound of anklets from just outside the hall.

It was Bhagavati. She came in looking as if the darkness had lifted from her. Her hair was wet as if she had just washed it. She smiled radiantly at Visalakshi and said, 'Salatchi manni, I am hungry. Truly.'

CHAPTER 41

The noise and activity in the palace grounds were getting almost unbearable. Carpenters, iron smiths and masons were all at work. The king felt he could hardly differentiate the palace grounds from the noisy intersection in the market place.

The astrologer had also chosen just this time to erect a conical wooden base upon which he intended to establish the yantra he had made for the palace. He stood there taking measurements and correcting alignments.

The king's ancestors were so irritated by the doings of the astrologer that they said they would not visit the palace until the Brahmin astrologer left. 'It's impossible,' they complained. 'Whenever that Brahmin shifts the yantra this way or that, we feel a searing hot wind blow over us. We can't come here until that fellow leaves.'

The tobacco merchant's house too was being rebuilt. The masons had smeared milk white lime wash on those exterior walls that still stood and the sheer whiteness of those walls seemed to mock the run down palace.

All this harassment resulted from that old Sarkar officer's visit. The white whoreson seemed to fancy himself as faultless a judge as Vikramadityan[13]. And everything was being done exactly as per his orders which were as impudent (in the king's estimation) as the upright hair on the white man's genitals.

Two days after that disgusting fellow (may his balls swell and rot) decided that the king should pay compensation for the burning down of the tobacco merchant's house, the king's troubles began. A messenger from the government came the very next day to get the king's official seal on a document that was covered with crawling handwriting. The king inhaled the pleasing perfume of paper and ink and handed the document over to his manager for safe keeping. He thought the whole matter had concluded right there. He was mistaken. Apparently the devilish messenger had handed a copy of the document to the tobacco merchant as well. The merchant in turn egged his relatives and friends to go to the palace and meet the king for further action. The ragged group visited the king early the next morning.

The king was in the pavilion to the front of the palace when they came. He was half listening to the palace manager reciting the expenses of the previous month in a squeaky voice and half asleep from the contentment that follows a great breakfast. The peace was broken when Subramanya Iyer's supporters trouped in noisily. When he saw them the king gestured graciously but vaguely for them to be seated. He also called out aloud, 'Someone bring chairs for the visitors!'

Unfortunately, no one answered the king's call as it was Wednesday when all the male servants in the palace went to the local shandy to make a bit of money by selling dried fish or mangoes. The king felt bad about his servants' extra curricular activities but he could hardly object as what he paid them would hardly keep their bodies and souls together. Why could these Brahmins too not go to the shandy and engage in some lucrative trade instead of coming over to plague him?

Eventually two women from the queen's quarters brought the chairs and the visitors sat down. One of them began saying, 'I am a close relative of Iyer. I used to work in the courts in Madras Pattinam. Now I have retired and come to live here. My son is still in Madras, working in Fort St George.'

The Brahmin's introduction made the king nervous. It seemed as if, by mentioning the courts and the Fort and his son's clerical employment, he was trying to intimidate the king. Perhaps he was close to the government. Had the tobacco merchant sent him so that he could terrorise the king into signing over the palace to them?

Two other men had accompanied the court Brahmin, whose name was Ramanatha Iyer. One was fair and the other dark. The fair one turned out to be Krishna Iyer, a cousin of Subramanya Iyer and a wealthy landlord in a nearby village. The dark man, who stood respectfully behind the seated men, was also a cousin and a priest. His name was Sundaram. Upon being introduced, Sundaram uttered a short benedictory prayer in Sanskrit that so impressed the king that he stood and leaned over to touch the priest's feet.

'Oh king, do not touch my feet. You are our protector, a Kshatriya who deals kindly with his subjects,' the priest said, drawing his feet back hastily.

The king thought it might be good to be on the right side of this priest—he might decide how smoothly the discussion would go. So he said politely, 'You are learned in the four Vedas and the Sastras. How can I sit when you stand? Let me also stand.'

The king had unconsciously slipped into a faulty Brahmin lingo as he said this, driving his manager out of the room in an effort to contain his giggles. The priest sat down cross-legged on the floor and said to the king, 'Let me not be the cause of your discomfort. Please return to your throne.'

Forced to sit down, the king asked, 'What is the reason for your visit?'

'Zamindarval, Sir Horton has sent a document recording the orders he gave on his visit here. You too might have received a copy of the document, I think?'

'Oh yes, we did!' replied the palace manger returning to the pavilion at the wrong moment. The king could have sliced his tongue for speaking out of turn. Still, the damage was done, so the king merely looked at his visitors with a sad expression. It seemed as if the priest would have liked to ask him why he was looking so sad but in fact, he said nothing, closing his eyes as if he were going into a trance.

The king began to speak in a plaintive tone, 'What shall I say? The whole world knows in what terrible financial shape the zamin is. Any taxes we collect go directly to the white man. It is only because they send a little money my way that I am able to run the palace.' The king stopped and looked at his visitors. They nodded their heads sympathetically. The king wondered if he could continue his plaintive tale a little longer, serve his visitors coconut water and thus send them on their way. Perhaps he could give them a couple of gold coins to stop pestering him. If only things were that easy!

Krishna Iyer, the fair and wealthy cousin, began to speak. 'Zamindarval, Iyer does not expect any money from you.' Krishna Iyer paused to belch luxuriously. The king felt a stab of envy for the man who could belch so contentedly so early in the morning. Still his words were as music to his ears. Krishna Iyer continued to speak. 'Iyer will rebuild his house himself, you would have noticed that the work has begun. By god's grace he has enough money to spend on that. What he wants from you is a little help in the matter of his business.'

'If you tell me what it is that you want, we can easily do it,' the king replied, joyous that no money was expected from him. He was cut short by the imperious voice of the queen which interceded from behind a screen.

'What is it, queen?' the king asked graciously.

'Let Iyer's family members specify what sort of help they require, before you promise them anything,' the queen said in a low but clear voice. Suddenly it seemed the visitors were all looking at the screen behind which the queen stood, as if the focus of their discussion had shifted from the king to her.

'May the queen, the living goddess, be blessed,' the priest intoned.

'Can I ask for some fruit or milk to be brought for you?' the king asked the priest in particular. The priest opened his eyes slightly and, smiling kindly, said it was not necessary. 'All Iyer wants,' he continued, 'is that the king should be kind enough to give him a little space in the palace compound to stock his tobacco.'

As the king stared at him uncomprehendingly, the queen, who had understood the request at once, replied quickly, 'There is no facility in the palace to store tobacco, Sir. Besides, the smell of tobacco will be awful.'

Ramanatha Iyer, the cousin who had been a court employee, got up and went over to the screen. 'Maharani, we are not so unreasonable as to ask for room inside the palace. We just want a couple of rooms in the grounds and some space in the garden. Iyer will put up a shed there. We will make sure that the smell of tobacco does not invade the palace. Why, these two rooms here will be ideal!'

'Not so fast. Sir,' the queen replied. 'I will choose the areas you can use.'

'Why should you strain yourself, Maharani? The king can decide on all this,' Ramanatha Iyer interrupted.

The king nodded and told his wife, 'Don't worry yourself about these petty matters. Go and rest. Let the burden of palace decisions remain with me.'

They could hear the queen's chair scrape back angrily. Then she had swished out of the place into the interior of the palace. The king knew this was not the last he was going to hear about the matter from the queen.

In the end, the visitors got almost a quarter of the area of the palace to store the tobacco: a couple or rooms, the old stables, the chariot shed, the armoury, and a good portion of the garden. Ramanatha Iyer told the king that if he gave them the use of this area, he would write to the government about how generous the king was and recommend that his grant be enhanced. 'I can easily follow up on this through my son who works in Fort St George,' Ramanatha Iyer said. The king could hardly say no after that. The queen, however, returned to her perch behind the screen and said firmly that they could not have the armoury as it was sacred to her family, the weapons of four generations of kings having been stored there. The visitors agreed.

Two days later the dubash of the white officer returned with another document, stating that Iyer's family had a lease on the agreed upon portions of the palace for the next ninety years. Both the king and Iyer signed it.

Work on erecting sheds in the palace garden had begun, causing the king to be so hassled. However, there was very little he could do to stop it. So he just sat there and watched what was going on. Soon, it will be over, he told himself. 'Something else will begin then,' said a small voice inside his head.

'This is such a clean angle! Wonderful! This is exactly how the yantra should be established!' the astrologer's pleased voice rose above the noise and confusion in the garden.

CHAPTER 42

The astrologer was a persistent man, as the king found out, to his dismay.

'Only because of your support, Your Highness, has the establishment of this yantra been made possible,' the astrologer told the king politely. 'The yantra is being erected for the good of the world. So it is important that you actively take part in the puja that will consecrate the yantra.' The Brahmin's voice had a humble, pleading quality to it, making it difficult to disregard. The king was worried that his taking part in the consecration ceremony would involve paying more gold to the astrologer. He was keen to avoid this expenditure.

'I would be happy to take part, Iyere. But the area where the yantra is being established in the palace grounds now belongs to the tobacco merchant. You know that, don't you?'

'But he is only leasing it, Maharaja. You are the true owner of the land. Why, you are the king of this entire area!'

The king now had no doubt that the astrologer's invitation was a prelude to demanding more money from him. After all, everyone knew that the land belonged to the tobacco merchant for the next ninety nine years, at the end of which time neither the king, nor the tobacco merchant or the astrologer were going to be alive.

But the Banian Brothers would be around, interjected the king's ancestors. They were now visiting the palace as before and had followed the astrologer to speak to the king. Only the young Brahmin woman was no longer to be seen with them, which was, of course, a good thing.

The astrologer continued to plead with the king. 'Subramanya Iyer would also like you to take part in the ceremony. He is bearing the cost of the entire function. All that we want the king to do is to be there along with the queen.'

The king felt a flood of relief. Along with it came the pride at being accorded so much respect. If only the queen and he could die while still being so respected. They would be saved from the humiliation of having to beg in the streets of London in their later years.

'Shall we tell him? Shall we tell?' Bushy Moustache, the king's late father-in-law, asked the other ancestors. He was today wearing a long white robe like a Christian priest. He was also wearing a strange contraption, two round pieces of glass fixed on a metal frame, in front of his eyes. From a silken cord tied around his waist hung a watch. He looked so elegant that the king suddenly felt that there were many advantages to being dead. You could dress up in fine costumes, have knowledge of foreign languages, never suffer from bodily ailments, gossip at leisure... One could not get liquor to drink, but what of that? Was liquor everything?

Another ancestor told Bushy Moustache, 'No need to give the good news to your son-in-law right now. But you must insist that tomorrow, on the new moon night, he should tell the Brahmin priest to offer us liquor.' This ancestor stood very close to the king, so close that the king could smell the asafoetida and garlic in his breath. Perhaps the astrologer smelt it too. The king noticed that the Brahmin had taken his upper cloth to his nose, under the pretext of wiping his face, and was taking a deep breath through its folds.

'Iyere, let me know at what time the ceremony will be held tomorrow. If there is no urgent business of state to attend to at that hour, the queen and I will definitely participate. One more thing. As it is the new moon tomorrow...'

'Absolutely. That is why we are holding the consecration tomorrow! You can finish making offerings of water and sesame seeds to your ancestors early in the morning, before attending the consecration.'

'Water and sesame seeds are fine, Iyere, but my ancestors also want an offering of liquor,' the king said.

Even as the king spoke there was the loud sound of horns and the Banian Brothers' strange vehicle came to a stop in front of the palace. There they were, the banian clad rogues.

The king decided the Brothers were answering the call of his ancestors. 'Hey, someone bring me some salt!' the king yelled. The cook came running with a couple of pinches of salt which the king promptly knotted into his veshti. 'It was I who brought him running!' announced Bushy Moustache. 'He was cutting a chicken and I dragged him over!' The old man licked his blood stained forefinger the way children lick candy sticks. He added, pleadingly, 'Blessings will be upon you if, along with the liquor you also serve us some partridge meat.' The king wondered how it would be possible to make such offerings.

Reading his mind, Bushy Moustache said, 'Get the Brahmin priest to write down the mantras and methods for offering liquor to us. Then ask those rascals, the Banian Brothers, to do the actual offering.' Having said that Bushy Moustache rose like a white stork and began flying around the hall.

The king said hastily to the astrologer, 'Iyere, I will definitely be there tomorrow morning. There is something else I have to ask you. If you could come here after sunset today we can talk about it.'

'Of course,' said the astrologer and took his leave.

For the evening's consultation the king would have to pay the astrologer, after all it was at the king's bidding that he was coming.

'Uncle!' the king called out eagerly to Bushy Moustache. 'You said you had some good news for me—what is it?'

The Banian Brothers were just then entering the palace. In their hands were a couple of large, bound volumes. The king wondered if these were again those books on the sexual practices of white women.

'Your thoughts are always centred on the groin,' complained Bushy Moustache. 'You have to rise further than that!'

He was a fine one to talk, the king thought as Bushy Moustache flew low, his feet brushing the king's shoulders now and then. 'Right! We will leave now. We will talk later, after these fellows have left.'

'But uncle, you had something to tell me! What is it?' the king begged.

'It is good news. Don't worry about all the small expenses from now on. A mountain of good fortune is coming your way!' Bushy Moustache spoke like a soothsayer. Then he was dragged away by the others and the king was left alone to greet the Banian Brothers.

As the king gazed beyond them, he saw the chariot shed, the horse stables and the small stone outhouse in the garden. They were all now filled with baskets of tobacco. Beyond the palace walls he could see the renovated house of the tobacco merchant. It had been tall, double-storeyed, like the taller of the Banian Brothers, before. It was now short, single-storeyed, like the shorter of the Brothers. 'Come in'' the king welcomed the Brothers, making sure that the salt was firmly tied into the knot at his waist. 'What have you come to see me about?'

'You sent for us, do you remember, Your Highness?' the shorter of the Brothers reminded him and extended his customary lime fruit towards the king. The latter smelled the fruit and dropped it into the pocket of his coat.

'We had gone to Madras to collect money for the Flower Festival,' the taller of the Brothers said.

'But I am already conducting the Flower Festival! Why do you need to collect money?' the king asked, making the Brothers smile. It occurred to the king that he had said something silly. 'Ah, I forget! You are from the future. How can I be there to conduct the festival?' the king shook his head sadly.

'Even if Your Highness is not there, your descendants will be there, Maharaja!' the Brothers replied. The shorter one gave the king one of the books. The king opened it to see a large picture of the queen's servant maid pouring water over Bushy Moustache's corpse. These were the funeral photographs that the king had forgotten about. They were quite amazing. The king was open and generous with his praise. When Bushy Moustache came for his liquor the next day, he would be pleased to see these. The picture of the servant maid slipped down from the book. The king placed it a little distance away on the table. Then he went in and returned with a gold sovereign for the Brothers. He felt strangely elated and not in the least upset about parting with his gold. His ancestors had told him, had they not, that something wonderful was about to happen. He was sure that included a good deal of money.

He said to the Brothers, smiling, 'I need twenty bottles of liquor tomorrow night. Can you bring them?' He tossed the gold coin high and caught it. He felt like singing aloud. A passage from the dirge music escaped his lips sounding as if it were the happiest song.

'Liquor? No problem, Your Highness. We have bought a good stock in Madras and will bring it tomorrow,' the taller of the Brothers said, eyeing the gold coin fixedly.

The king gave him the coin and asked, 'What news from Madras?'

'We saw the tobacco merchant's son there. Apparently he is going to start trading in snuff.'

After the Brothers had left, the king wondered what inhaling snuff was like. Well, he would soon find out. After all, it would all be stocked right here.

The ancestors had returned. The pages of the album opened by themselves and the ancestors crowded round it, appreciating the pictures with great enthusiasm. Bushy Moustache bent low over the picture of the servant maid. The king snatched it and put it into his coat pocket. 'Hey, I was going to show it to you tomorrow, on new moon night. What's your hurry?' he asked all of them affectionately.

CHAPTER 43

Plantain leaf cups. They seemed to be everywhere, strewn indiscriminately all over the palace garden, the remnants of the morning's festivities. The leaf cups had been used to store all the requirements for the morning's ceremonies: sandalwood paste, ghee, a squash of banana fruit and jaggery, honey and many other ingredients. Now all the ceremonies were over and the leaf cups were the only reminders.

The king picked up the cups and put them away in a corner, his heart filled to bursting with joy. The day had gone well—in fact, it had more than gone, it had galloped like a horse, with the king feeling as if he had grabbed its tail and rushed behind it.

Since the previous day, the queen had not been feeling too well. She had an aversion to food and was sleepless. Despite that, the preparations for the erection of the yantra had gone well. A number of strangers had come to greet the king the day before, most of them had been from Madras. Among them were Vaidyanathan, the government employee and Suleiman Rowther, the tobacco merchant's business partner.

Vaidyanatha Iyer came across to the king as someone who was indispensable to the Sarkar in India. Every lord and lady who visited Madras had to be registered in Vaithi's records before they could step into the city, let alone conduct their business there. The king could not tell how true this claim was. Still, it was obvious that Vaithi could be of some use to him at some point.

As for Suleiman Rowther, the king liked him instantly. And he was not alone in this. Even the queen, who greeted everyone else sullenly, was truly pleased to meet Rowther. This may have been due to his bending his six foot frame low and salaaming her upon being introduced and saying, 'Sahiba, you look like my elder sister. If I gain nothing else from this visit, the joy of meeting you is in itself the biggest gain of my life.'

So pleased was the queen with this flowery greeting that she smiled warmly at Rowther. Later she asked the king, 'He does look like my younger brother Vellaiyan, does he not?'

The king saw no resemblance whatever, Vellaiyan being as short and stout as Rowther was tall and muscular. Still, to please the queen, he nodded his head. It occurred to him that whatever pleased the queen had perforce to please him.

Suleiman presented the queen with a vial of French perfume. She accepted it happily. She told Suleiman he could store the jars of snuff he had brought in a corner of the armoury. She asked the cook and the punkah puller to help carry the jars into the armoury.

'The snuff doesn't smell too bad. In fact, the smell will probably help to cure colds and migraines, as the vaidyar told us,' she observed to the king. Her words made the smell of snuff bearable.

After the queen had retired to her chambers, Suleiman brought out two bottles of foreign liquor and presented them to the king with great affection. 'Why did you go to all this trouble?' the king asked but accepted the bottles all the same. He thought with relish that while he would have to distribute the liquor that the Banian Brothers brought, Suleiman's gift was his alone to enjoy.

Suleiman suggested respectfully that if the king wished he could become a partner in his business of selling foreign liquor and snuff. The king graciously declined the offer saying that it was hardly the sort of thing a person who was engaged in running a government could do. That was not the real reason of course. The king was aware that by doing this business he would be able to earn much needed money. But he had no money to invest in the business—he did not want Suleiman to know that.

Besides, engaging in such business ventures might anger the government which in turn might lead to its stopping the grant it was currently giving him—as the palace manager pointed out after all the visitors had left. The ancestors also agreed that this was not the sort of thing the king should do. Nevertheless, they encouraged the king to trust the Muslim, as for the Iyer from the Fort, the king would do well to be cautious in his dealings with him. The tobacco merchant, however, was an honest man, the ancestors said, and could be trusted. The ancestors also gave the king some good news. This was regarding the letters the white official sent the tobacco merchant. The official had urged the merchant to pay a rent of thirty rupees a month for the use of the palace space—his own commission for arranging the storage space for the merchant was five rupees a month. The king could now expect the generous sum of twenty five rupees a month from the tobacco merchant. The king wished the elderly white official had sent him a copy of that letter. He had no objection to giving up five rupees from the rent to the white man. Perhaps get a copy of the letter from the tobacco merchant himself.

After the visitors had left the king went to the queen's quarters to find her lying on her bed feeling unwell. He sent for the vaidyar, who examined the queen and said he would like to check her pulse at dawn to diagnose her condition accurately.

That night, after he had drunk a little of Suleiman's foreign liquor, the king returned to the bedroom to find that the queen was not sleeping there. The maid said she had retired to her own quarters because she was not feeling well. 'Ask her to eat some fruit before going to bed,' the king sent word through the servant.

When the king awoke the next morning there was good news awaiting him—the vaidyar, who had returned to check the queen's pulse, announced that she was pregnant. A wonderful feeling of joy surged through the king and stayed with him through the day.

He looked with new respect at the copper yantra that waited to be installed on its tall pedestal in the garden. He had not the slightest idea why the astrologer had erected it but it seemed to have brought him good luck. Not that the yantra had anything to do with the queen being pregnant, the credit for that went to him and him alone. Could anyone deny that?

A little later the astrologer, dressed in a white silk panchakaccham, visited the king, greeted him with folded hands and asked him if he could bathe and get ready, so that they could begin the ceremony to install and consecrate the yantra. The king shared the happy news of the queen's pregnancy with the astrologer. 'It is due to the blessings of God,' the astrologer replied happily.

'Iyere, it is the new moon day today. Can we, on this happy occasion, give my ancestors what they asked for?' the king asked the astrologer.

'The Maharaja should not mistake me when I say that those offerings are forbidden to the ancestors,' the astrologer replied. 'The sastras are very strict about this. If they find these things in their world they may use them, but we cannot offer them these things from here.'

'Why don't you add a feature to the yantra to propitiate the deities for this lapse?' the king suggested. 'My ancestors have said that I should pay you one rupee a month for installing and maintaining this extra feature.'

It was a blatant lie and a bribe but it worked. The astrologer replied, 'Can anyone oppose Your Highness' words? I will do a small calculation and add the feature required. But, how can I handle those items…?' he ended reluctantly.

'Don't worry about that. I will get someone else to do the actual offering.'

'That's all right then. I will give you a consecrated loop of darbha grass. Anyone wearing that on his ring finger can make offerings to the ancestors. I will also write down the instructions for making the offerings on a palm leaf and give it to you,' the astrologer sounded enthusiastic now.

As he went off to bathe, the king thought that it was a good thing that Bushy Moustache had not asked for offerings of an erotic nature. That would have created insurmountable problems.

When he entered the palace garden later, dressed in ceremonial silks, he found everyone assembled there, waiting for him. The queen too was present, dressed in fine silk and wearing jasmine flowers in her hair and chatting happily with the other women.

The men were seated separately. Suleiman Rowther stood respectfully outside the garden, unsure whether he could join them. The king signalled affectionately for him to walk in and sit by his side.

On one side sat the tobacco merchant's family. Subramanya Iyer's son Sankaran too was there. The king noticed that ever since his return from Madras, he seemed to have a vague and lost look about him. His earlier expressions of anger and hate had vanished. The king signalled for him to come and sit by his side, but Sankaran made a gesture as if to say that he was content to be seated with his family.

As the king gazed about him, he caught sight of the old Brahmin woman from the tobacco merchant's family approaching the astrologer with a large cane box in her hands.

'What is the hurry for this mami?' the astrologer said to her. 'These deities can be put into the yantra later. You should continue to worship them for one more week. By that time I will finish making the required calculations.'

The old woman seemed very disappointed as she walked away with the cane box.

For the next hour the astrologer performed the ceremony to consecrate the yantra. He made marks with a bit of limestone on pieces of palm leaf and placed them in four directions. Every time he did so he instructed the king and others to make offerings of the ingredients in the leaf cups.

At noon, the astrologer signalled to the carpenter and he hefted the copper yantra on to its pedestal. For a moment the copper plate, etched with a complicated pattern of geometrical designs, rose towards the sky as if it were throwing up a challenge, the next it dipped as if in acceptance of a divine design. The carpenter installed four strong teak pillars to hold the yantra in place horizontally.

'The yantra has been installed,' the astrologer announced formally. 'In two hours there will be heavy rain in Arasur,' he added.

As the king picked up and put away the last of the leaf cups strewn in the garden, a drizzle began, just as the astrologer had predicted. Someone came rushing over with an umbrella to protect the king's head from the drizzle which could turn into a downpour.

The shorter of the two Banian Brothers, who had come by at the king's bidding, said, 'If the king so commands, we will make the offerings to the ancestors now.'

'That's right. If the offerings are done with, we too can get some rest,' Bushy Moustache said. For some reason he sounded sad.

'Why would he not be sad? The astrologer has sent that young Brahmin woman up and away through the yantra,' said another ancestor, as if in answer to the king's observation. He did not feel like asking where she had been sent.

The rain did not last. The drizzle petered out after it had dampened the grass and the strewn flowers in the garden. When the king went in to his bedroom he found that the queen had already gone to sleep.

He came out again to find the taller of the Banian Brothers waiting in the hall. He was telling the shorter brother, 'Start the vehicle. I'll be with you shortly after finishing with the offering.' The shorter brother left the hall.

'We can start now,' said the king.

CHAPTER 44

Another journey, more hassles and exhaustion, but he would have to go for Bhagavati Kutti's sake.

Sankaran was angry and ashamed at himself. It was four months since his trip to Madras—a trip made to acquire snuff but one on which he had acquired sexual knowledge instead. Sankaran was so ashamed of what had happened on the ship that he was unable to look Karuthan and Suleiman in the eye. He could not bring himself to chat with Vaithi or ask Gomati Manni for a tumbler of coffee. His eyes always seemed downcast and his mind in a constant state of confusion. The titillating memories of Saama and his lover had almost faded from his mind, replaced by images of the rounded breasts of the white women, the smells of foreign liquor and unmentionable food. The remembered smells made him feel so nauseated that he had to rush to the backyard to vomit.

Exhausted, he would sleep and wake refreshed, but the respite did not last long.

Karuthan asked Suleiman to accompany Sankaran when he left Madras. Suleiman knew what had happened on the ship but had not said a word to Sankaran. Sankaran wished Suleiman would talk about it so that he could confess everything to him—but he was not entirely sure what had happened to him on the ship.

Was it Sankaran who had acted as Dastagir Rowther's humble and faithful servant for a whole day or was it someone else? How many of those women on the ship had he slept with? Would they all have become pregnant? Would they throw him, the black dog who had dared to sleep with the white ladies, in prison?

If those women had complained upon disembarking, the police would have come to Vaithi's house and arrested him? That hadn't happened. So was his experience on the ship a dream? In that case, whom had Dastagir Rowther warned to be careful? Why would his phallus rot and decay? The thoughts chased each other endlessly in his mind.

On their journey from Madras to Arasur, Suleiman was careful to speak only about how to establish and expand their trading in snuff.

'Sankara, don't set up a separate shop immediately. Make space for these jars of snuff in your present shop. I will teach you and your shop assistants how to mix the snuff and pack it in plantain leaf packets. Until the business picks up, either Karuthan or I will come here once a month with fresh stock. You should also visit Madras frequently.'

Sankaran shook his head at the last suggestion.

'Hey, you don't have to go to the ship! You can stay with your relative in Nungambakkam. It is enough if you come to the shop in the black town.' This was the only time Suleiman even obliquely referred to Sankaran's experiences on the ship.

When they reached Arasur they found that the tobacco and snuff was to be stored in the palace. Sheds were being erected and work had started to rebuild the house. The house had been renovated, but the family was reluctant to return. Suleiman had no compunctions about staying in the house, but he could not relish the vegetarian food that old Ramalakshmi cooked.

'Sankara, I'm eating so much vegetarian food, I think I am growing a tuft!' he joked, pulling up a handful of hair at the top of his head. He was busy showing people samples of snuff in plantain leaf packets tied festively with silk cords. Sankaran accompanied him everywhere except to the palace, because he still thought the king was responsible for setting fire to his house.

When Uncle Ramanathan came to hear of this, he said mildly, 'Child, you are wrong in assuming the king set fire to your house. He is a bit of a brute but harmless and innocent.'

Suleiman laughed to hear Sankaran being called a child. Ever since his visit to the palace, Sankaran knew that Suleiman had adopted the queen as his sister. If only he knew that Sankaran used to peep in on this elder sister of his while she was bathing!

Suleiman also set up of a big, wooden doll outside the tobacco shop to attract customers. It could turn its head and blink its eyes, but whenever the doll rotated its head so that it faced the palace, it would freeze. Someone would have to manually turn its head to get it started again. Annasamy, the astrologer, discovered that the pull of the copper yantra in the palace garden made the doll freeze. As nothing could be done about the yantra, they adjusted the mechanism within the doll so that it did not quite face the palace.

On the night before Suleiman left for Madras, Sankaran spent time with his friend in the new house. All night they spoke about the business and other things. In the morning Sankaran's heart felt light. Suleiman had said something about the business that Sankaran felt applied to his life too: 'Think only about the future and how you can work to make it good.'

Once Suleiman had left, Sankaran felt a terrible emptiness. He felt his old depression return. That night he stayed alone in the new house. In the middle of the night, wearing the new coat he had got stitched in Madras, he went to visit the Kottakudi dasi.

She was alone that night or maybe her visitors had left. Although she seemed confused about who Sankaran was, she welcomed, brought him water to drink in an earthen pot and asked him what he wanted.

Sankaran felt compelled to introduce himself at great length, talking about the shop in the market with its fancy wooden doll, the amount of snuff he sold, the crowds who gathered at his shop, his impending marriage to Bhagavati Kutti. The Kottakudi dasi listened with complete attention and interest. From close quarters she looked older than he had thought. He expressed his desire to her. His body was hot for the experience that he had had on the ship.

'But you told me that you are going to be married?' the dasi asked softly, stroking his head.

'What does that matter?' he retorted. 'Right or wrong, my body is afire with desire. I have brought a lot of money. Look, this is the currency of America, a dollar. It is equal to two of the government rupees. Look.'

She took the coin from him, looked at it and returned it to him.

'You don't want to sleep with me?'

'I don't feel like sleeping with anybody these days,' she replied.

'Why?'

'I don't know. The astrologer took a poem from me to etch on the yantra he has erected in the palace. Ever since the yantra was erected, I have become like this.'

'But why should that be?' Sankaran asked, drawing her into his embrace.

'The yantra faces my house, especially my bedroom. Ever since then my mind swings between peace and despair. As for sexual desire, I have lost it completely.' She drew away from his arms.

'No. You are refusing to sleep with me because you know that I slept with many women on the ship in Madras. Did Suleiman tell you that? Don't believe him. My prick is not diseased or rotting. Shall I show you?' He began to undo the knot of his pyjamas. The dasi put out a hand to stop him.

'I don't know Suleiman at all. I have no desire. That is all. But you don't have to go away. You can stay the night here. You can talk to me and I will listen. I can't sleep in any case.'

Sankaran leaned his head against her shoulder and began telling her everything, starting from the eclipse. Now and then she would stop him and make a small poem about what he had just said. He was amazed by her talent.

An hour before dawn, Sankaran left the dasi's house and returned home. He turned his cot so that it faced the yantra in the palace. Immediately, he fell into a peaceful sleep. He worked hard all day long and slept undisturbed at night. Just when he began thinking this would be a good way to spend the rest of his life, Subramanya Iyer brought up the matter of his marriage again.

'Why should I go through all this, Appa? Let me remain as I am!'

'Don't be silly!' admonished his father. 'There is a time for everything and this is the time for you to get married. I have fixed the date. So let us start.'

'But how can we leave the shop and the house? What if someone sets fire to the house again?'

'No one will do that. The king has promised to send three of his men to stand guard over the house. I am also getting someone from Thanu Pillai's house in Madurai to sleep at the house. Ayyanai is also there, of course. I am sure they will all look after the house. Don't worry about it.'

Kalyani did not make the journey as she was still too sick to travel. Subbamma agreed to stay and look after her.

Subbamma was still not free, although the female spirit that had been troubling her had been driven away. As the astrologer had not yet placed the deities on her own yantra in the one in the palace, she still had to worship them daily.

'But who will sing all the wedding songs, if Subbamma does not come with us?' asked Sundaram the priest. The female ancestors gave him a strange answer. They entered Subramanya Iyer himself and the man began singing in the high-pitched voice of a woman. 'Let us start, Sankara,' he said, in the same, female voice.

It struck Sankaran that the voice sounded like that of the Kottakudi dasi. A thought entered his mind unbidden: 'Should I arrange to find another house for the dasi to live in?'

CHAPTER 45

It was not easy preparing for the journey: so many things to pack, so many people to accommodate. When the packing was done and they decided to start on Thursday evening, Ramanatha Iyer arrived from Madras, bringing the news that his son Vaithi and his family, all of whom wanted to attend the wedding, would be reaching Arasur only on Thursday morning. It would be impossible to subject them to another tedious journey that very evening. So Subramanya Iyer decided to postpone the journey to Sunday evening so that the visitors could rest for a few days. Iyer dispatched a letter to the Ambalapuzha family informing them that they would be arriving four days before the wedding instead of a week before.

Weddings were being shortened to three-day ceremonies but Kuppusamy Iyer wanted the traditional four-day celebration. 'Anything less will not be seemly. You must support us and be there to make it a success,' Kuppusamy had begged Iyer. Iyer was secretly pleased by Kuppusamy's insistence on the four-day wedding.

On Thursday evening, Vaithi arrived in Arasur. Both his children were suffering from a fever and his wife Gomati had her period. 'That's all right though,' Vaithi was quick to explain. 'She will have finished with it and had her ritual bath on Saturday, well in time for the trip'

'Why don't you drum the news of my periods to the entire village?' Gomati asked him angrily, but the anger dissipated when she saw Sankaran. She smiled fondly at him.

Vaithi was determined to explore Arasur and took Sankaran with him on a walk through the village. He was a little contemptuous of its size. 'Sankara, this place is just about the length of half a loin cloth!' he joked, but he was impressed by the tobacco shop and its crowd of customers. 'A lot of them come from the villages around us,' Sankaran explained. Vaithi did some quick mental arithmetic to discover that Sankaran was probably making a lot more money out of sitting near the cash box and dropping in the coins than he himself did being a navigation clerk at the Fort in Madras.

When Vaithi was in the shop with Sankaran, the Kottakudi dasi passed by. Seeing Sankaran she entered the shop. Sankaran was pleased to see her. He served her sweet lime juice and betel leaves. More customers popped into the shop simply to see the dasi. She wrote a poem about the wooden doll and a Hindustani song and gave them to Sankaran.

After she had gone, Vaithi nudged Sankaran and asked, 'Who's that good looking wench?' There was a trace of envy in his voice. Sankaran bragged a bit to create the illusion that he and the dasi were close. As an afterthought he added that she was a renowned dancer.

'Rascal! So you have connections with whores?' Vaithi nudged him again.

'It's not like that. She is only a well wisher,' Sankaran replied.

'She really is good looking,' Vaithi went on. 'If it weren't for her hairy arms, she'd be even more beautiful than the angelic white women. Have you seen the white women from close by? I don't think you would have had a chance to, poor fellow! There is no beauty to match that of the white women—their bodies are as creamy and smooth as the insides of plantain bark!'

Sankaran felt like laughing. Unlike Vaithi he very well knew what the white women's bodies were like—but he could hardly say that to Vaithi or Karuthan or Suleiman nor even to Bhagavati Kutti. Thinking of her, made Sankaran feel guilty and ashamed all over again.

The only person to whom he had described in detail his sexual experiences on the ship was the Kottakudi dasi. That night, after telling her everything, his heart had felt really light. If only he could spend another night with her, his body and mind would become refreshed and vigorous again. But that could not happen thanks to that stupid astrologer who, by erecting that yantra in the palace garden, had killed all sexual desire in the dasi. What a clever and talented woman she was, Sankaran thought. How well she could compose poetry! She had told Sankaran that she spent most nights writing poetry, not erotic but spiritual.

'Vaithi Saar, do you like Tamil poetry?' he now asked his guest.

'Why do I need to know poetry to do a clerical job or to bed your Manni?' was the answer.

Sunday dawned crisp and busy. There were so many preparations to make for the trip. Ayyanai arranged for eight large bullock carriages, each capable of seating four persons comfortably. They could even lie down in the carriages—they were so spacious. Gomati Manni's children had recovered from their fever. They visited the shop to see the wooden doll and were so taken with it that they refused to leave it behind and go on the trip. 'If you behave and make this trip, you can pack the doll in a crate and take it with you when you return to Madras,' Vaithi cajoled them. Hearing him, Sankaran thought that if the Kottakudi dasi did not have fuzzy arms, Vaithi would have liked to pack her too and take her with him to Madras.

Just before they set out, Subramanya Iyer went in to take leave of his wife Kalyani and his aunt, Subbamma. When they saw Subbamma, the ancestral women began to wail loudly through Iyer. One of them shushed the others, explaining that as Kalyani had just then gone into an exhausted sleep, they should not make a noise and wake her up. Then they all spoke in subdued voices. Subbamma herself said serenely, 'Do not weep. I will look after Kalyani. Return as soon as the wedding is over. Don't you feel sorry for this Brahmin? Why on earth did you have to possess a man? Could you not have found a woman?'

The ancestral women replied that they were forced to possess Iyer only because they could not find any other suitable and close relative. 'After all, he is our great-grandson. So it is only right that we go with him. But that is not the reason we are weeping,' they said.

'Then what is the reason for your tears? Will all the relatives in the place you go to be well?' Subbamma asked worriedly.

'Everyone will be well, Subbamma,' they replied, in Iyer's now husky, female voice.

Ramanathan peeped in at just that moment and asked, 'Shall we start?'

'You start first, Ramiah,' the ancestral women instructed him. 'Take a coconut with you and break it at the Ganapati temple at the border of the village. By that time Subbani, here, will be with you. Don't take the coconut that they have already kept ready—that is rotten. Take a good one from the kitchen. Everything will go well,' the ancestors told him and sent him on his way.

Subramanya Iyer worried as usual about Kalyani's health.

'Do not worry about that. When Sankaran and his bride come here to get her blessings, Kalyani will be sitting up,' the ancestors assured him.

Subbamma began to sing a festive song. Before she could complete two lines, her voice became husky and she began to cough. Then the ancestors took over and sweetly completed the song through Iyer.

'When you take the couple to reside in the new house, this is the song to sing,' Subbamma told Iyer, whose eyes brimmed with emotion at these words.

'I am so worried about leaving Kalyani behind, Aunt Subbamma. Will she be alive until my return? Will this house be there? Last time I went on a trip, Saama died and the house was burnt down. Is it Kalyani's turn now?' Iyer's voice broke.

Again the ancestral women interrupted him. 'Everything will be well,' they reassured him. 'Everything will grow and flourish joyfully.' Despite their happy words there was an undercurrent of sadness in their voices.

Subbamma stood by the window and watched the carriages leave. She prayed fervently to the deities in her yantra as well as her ancestors that the wedding should go well and that there should be no mishap.

It would soon be sunset. In the evening light Subbamma saw the huge yantra that the astrologer had set up in the palace grounds. She prayed to the deities in that yantra too.

'Subbamma, when it grows dark, light a lamp near the palace yantra. And take your own yantra in its cane box and leave it there. Today is an auspicious day. Let your deities climb on to the big yantra tonight!'

It was Subramanya Iyer, speaking in the voice of the ancestral women. Listening to his funny voice, Vaithi's children burst out laughing. Even Sankaran smiled.

Suddenly Subramanya Iyer began singing loudly from his carriage, 'Should you peep on women while they bathe?'

It seemed to Sankaran that his father was staring directly at him as he sang. It made him nervous. Would the ancestral women have seen everything else that happened with him too? Would they have seen the orgy on the ship? Would they have seen his visit to the Kottakudi dasi? Fortunately, Iyer's voice was submerged by the sounds of the carriages rolling, and the bells around the necks of the bullocks clanging. But Iyer continued to sing: 'Women who bathe…'

'Stop this nonsense, Subbani,' chided Sundaram the priest. He was not a great fan of the ancestral women as he always felt they treated him with great impudence. They reacted now with characteristic irreverence. 'Shut up, cow eyes!' they said, adding, 'Once Sankaran's wedding is over, we will not come here at all. You can be happy.'

Sundaram did not open his mouth thereafter.

When they had broken a coconut at the Ganapati temple at the border of the village and prayed that their journey should go without any obstacles, Annasamy the astrologer joined them. He carried a bag of clothes and a cane basket.

'What's in the basket?' someone asked.

Before he could reply, Subramanya Iyer spoke in the voice of the ancestral women, 'What else? Another yantra! This is for the bride's family, has he not taken a fat fee from them already?'

Sundaram the priest began roaring with laughter.

CHAPTER 46

The night sky had clouded over, obscuring the stars, when Subbamma reached the yantra in the palace grounds. She carried an unlit oil lamp in one hand and the cane box in the other. A cool wind bounced over the plants in the garden bringing the happy tidings of rain. Subbamma stepped carefully so as not to jog the lamp and spill the oil. She could have brought the oil in a separate jar but that meant she would have to make another trip to get the cane basket with her yantra.

Subbamma was still confused about whether what she was doing was right. Although the ancestral women had told her very clearly that she should take the yantra to the palace grounds that very night and set the yantra deities free, she was nervous about doing this without the consent of the astrologer. But what could she do? Annasamy seemed so busy these days. Although she had asked him several times, he had put off setting the deities on her yantra on the one in the palace. Now he had gone to Ambalapuzha to erect another yantra there for the bride's family. Annasamy could probably make yantras for each of the 33 crore deities in the Puranas. At the rate at which he was making yantras, and earning money to buy up land around the village, he would probably run out of deities. Subbamma missed the advice and chatter of the spirits of the ancestral women. Oh, they were a nuisance all right, making her dance to their tunes like a puppet but now that they had gone away with Subramanya Iyer, she missed them sorely.

In a little while the lively deities in her cane box would also depart. She had brought along turmeric, vermilion powder and plantain fruit to give them when she said goodbye to them, just as she would have done for any female guests taking leave of her.

From tomorrow, Subbamma would not have to get up at the crack of dawn and draw buckets of water from the well to pour over her head so as to be ritually clean for worshipping the deities of the yantra. She need not rush to get the milk to feed them. She need not make sure that all the doors of her house were bolted so that no strangers (especially strange men) could enter when she was bathing her deities.

'I am sending you away without the say so of the astrologer. Is that all right?' she asked the deities in a voice close to despair.

There was no reply from the box. Perhaps the deities had gone to sleep. Subbamma placed the box under a flowering bush. She placed the lamp with its five points near the yantra. Then she went back to the box. Somewhere an infant wept.

When she withdrew a small cane bowl containing rice flour from the box, she thought she could hear the infant's wails get louder. Was it a kitten? There was not much difference between the cries of a kitten and an infant. Subbamma drew kolam patterns on the ground before the yantra. A strong wind swept the lines away even as she drew them. Suddenly she heard a voice. 'Subbamma, how are you, girl?'

Were the deities in the box speaking to her? Did they not wish to leave her? Were they playing hide and seek with her? Subbamma lit the five points of the lamp carefully and bent low to touch her forehead to the ground. A gust of wind rushed over the lamp and put it out. What a mischievous wind! What was its rush? Subbamma chided the wind as she removed the yantra from the box.

'Why do you chide the wind, Subbamma? It is only doing what it is meant to do.' The voice was clear now and decidedly female. Subbamma could easily recognise it. It was that of Saama's lover, the woman who had committed suicide. Subbamma began to shiver with fright. It was stupid of her to have brought the yantra over to the palace grounds to get rid of the deities. Obviously this wretched woman had returned to haunt her.

'Why are you plaguing me?' Subbamma yelled into the silent night. 'Have you not done enough harm to everyone? You have taken away my child Saama so that you can have your pleasure with him forever. What else do you want? Why have you come back?'

'Don't be angry with me, Subbamma,' said the voice, gently now. 'I haven't come to harm you. That whoreson astrologer has sent me up through the yantra, never to return. I cannot return to you or to Saama. I am now in the womb, waiting to be reborn.'

'Subbamma, you can chat with her later. Let us out!' clamoured the deities in Subbamma's yantra. 'We have many friends on the Maha Yantra. That dolt the astrologer has separated us from them. Let us out, old woman. We will go and join our folk.'

'Send them away first, Subbamma. We will talk later. I have much to tell you. I feel as if I were choking inside this womb. Kitta Iyer is such a louse that he cohabits with Snehamba every chance he gets, never mind if she is pregnant with me.'

Subbamma felt slightly dizzy. She quickly removed the yantra from the cane box and placed it against the base of the lamp. Then she lit the five points of the lamp again. This time the wind was still and the wicks burnt with steady flames. The deities from the yantra rose up with shouts of joy and Subbamma extended the offerings of turmeric, vermilion and plantain fruit towards them as her parting gifts. The deities, playful as ever, smeared the turmeric and vermilion on Subbamma's face and squashed the bananas and smeared the squash all over her hair. Then they laughed and ran towards the Maha Yantra to climb on to it.

'Subbamma, this too looks nice!' said Saama's lover, observing Subbamma. Again there was the sound of an infant crying.

Subbamma tried to wipe off the fruity mess on her hair with the edge of her sari and folded her hands and prayed to the deities. 'Please let everyone be well and happy.'

'Why do you worry, Subbamma? Every one will be well, no matter what you and I are destined to be.' It was Saama's lover again.

Subbamma was no longer frightened of her. She just wanted to chat, that too from the womb of someone called Snehamba. Who was Kitta Iyer? The name sounded vaguely familiar.

'Don't you remember?' the woman asked her. 'He is the elder brother of Bhagavati Kutti, the girl Sankaran is going to marry.'

Now Subbamma remembered the buck-toothed woman with her squeaky voice and her husband Kitta Iyer. So the restless soul of the woman who had committed suicide had at last found refuge in a womb and would soon be reborn. Whether the astrologer Annasamy had intended this or not, it was all to the good.

'In a while, I will leave all this behind. I will be reborn as a boy. Each of my extremities will have one extra digit. That will make me different. If that old man from Alapat had not fallen on the fire-cracker man and caused him to lose a toe, I would not have these extra toes and fingers. But what can be done? Do I decide these things? Or do you?'

Subbamma could not understand much of what she was saying. Who cared who was born with how many fingers or toes? She was tired. All she wanted to do was to go back home and sleep.

'All of us in our family will convert to Christianity. That will be the next big event!' the woman in the womb informed Subbamma, who could not quite understand any of it but kept quiet all the same.

'Subbamma, do you know that your husband will come back here?'

'What of it?' Subbamma retorted listlessly. It mattered very little to her now whether her husband returned or not.

'When people become ascetics they usually go to the Himalayas. But that bright spark, your husband, chose to go to Guntur, and built himself a hut near a chilli field. For some time he followed all the observances of an ascetic. Then he took up with a Telugu woman and set up a family with her. When he tired of that he reverted to asceticism and is now planning to come back here.'

'I'll slipper that rascal!' exploded Subbamma. 'What does he have to do here?'

'Subbamma, there is reason for thought here,' the woman in the womb advised her. 'If that husband of yours returns here and dies, you will lose your status as an auspicious woman and become an inauspicious widow. That is what the spirits of your ancestral women were trying to tell you. If you become a widow they will not be able to possess you and have fun. The tobacco Brahmin is hardly suitable for them. Already he is in danger of losing his voice because of constantly talking and singing like a woman.'

'Let them all go to hell. I suggest you curl up in your womb like a good infant. Let things happen as and when they will.' Subbamma got up carrying her cane box. She felt irritated but did not quite know at whom.

'Your ancestral women are clever girls, Subbamma. They are trying to instigate the Telugu woman so that she holds your husband back in Guntur. If he dies there you are hardly likely to know. So you will continue to be an auspicious woman. Do you see that?'

'Why should I be auspicious? So as to menstruate for these wretched spirits? Or shake my boobs and buttocks when I walk just because they feel like doing those things?'

When Subbamma began to walk back, the deities in the Maha Yantra had begun to quarrel with each other, using words that made her ears burn.

Then, with an almighty crash, the Maha Yantra fell down.

CHAPTER 47

While Sankaran's wedding procession was taking place, something strange was going on behind the closed doors of the vaidyar's house in Ambalapuzha. Gathered inside were the vaidyar, the son of the chief priest of the temple, a few of his friends and the astrologer, Annasamy.

Watching the bright lights of the fire crackers illuminating the sky, through his window, the younger priest said in an impatient tone, 'Only if all this ceases, can we get on with our work.'

The fire cracker man was limping ahead of the procession. His disappointment in the disappearance of the copper box containing his severed toe (that had grown into a five-toed foot) was written all over his face.

The pipe players in the procession paused in front of a house on the way and essayed a lengthy bit of music. 'As if the procession were not enough we have to bear with this music as well!' cried the priest in frustration.

'Why don't we all go eat the wedding dinner and then return to get on with this?' suggested one of his friends.

'Can't you think of anything but food?' the young priest snapped at him.' Here we have a chance to test a theory. Should we not use it?'

'Hey, who says we can't test it after eating a festive dinner?' his friend laughed.

The priest was eager for dinner himself but the delay this would cause in conducting their experiment worried him.

The whole thing started with the arrival of the astrologer from Arasur. He came as a member of the bridegroom's party. But almost upon entering Ambalapuzha, he had become agitated when he heard that the Maha Yantra he had erected in the palace in Arasur had crashed to the ground. The deities on the fallen yantra had woken him up and complained loudly to him about the yantra.

'Hey, Sozhia!' they called. 'You just dusted the mud off your backside and rode away on your bullock cart without a backward glance at us. Look what happened to the place you erected for us to reside in! As if it was not badly made enough, that old Subbamma (from whom you grabbed a lot of money to make a yantra) brought the deities on her yantra and loaded them on to our space. The trouble those creatures cause! Is it fair?' The deities admonished him so sternly and loudly that the astrologer woke up in unbearable panic. When Kupusamy Iyer and his family members, accompanied by groups of pipe players and drummers, stepped forward to receive the bridegroom's party, they found the astrologer pissing without control under a tree, in full view of everybody.

'Hey, Brahmin, you are not supposed to pollute a public space like this! It is not hygienic!' the chief priest's son yelled at him but the admonition was drowned in the music of the pipe players. The astrologer heard him and looked up. The younger temple priest saw fear in his eyes. He realised that, like the old man from Alapat who began to float because of some physical weakness, the astrologer was behaving in this embarrassing fashion only because of some sudden mental shock. If Kuppusamy's family were to notice his strange behaviour, they would take him away and begin to subject him to the mumbo jumbo of an exorcist; it would be best if he were treated more scientifically. So the young priest unobtrusively drew the astrologer away to the vaidyar's house.

The astrologer was babbling incoherently. The vaidyar checked his pulse and declared that he was physically fine—it was his mind that had been affected. It would be best if he slept a while. The vaidyar prepared a solution of opium in a glass vial and fed it to the astrologer who fell into a deep sleep shortly. The young temple priest looked at the doctor's glass vials with fascination. He felt science was beckoning him. Progress was linked directly to science, of that he was very sure. He was soon going to leave for Kollam to study medicine so that he could be a skilled healer like the vaidyar. He would go, whether he had his father's permission or not.

While the astrologer was fast asleep in the vaidyar's house, the wedding festivities had begun in Kuppusamy Iyer's house. Duraisamy Iyer came to the house where the bridegroom's party was staying, bringing a large container of steaming hot coffee.

'This is a new beverage called coffee,' he announced proudly. 'It has become very popular in these parts. I believe it sharpens one's brain and strengthens the body. People give it all kinds of attributes. Please taste it if you would like to.'

Sankaran was relieved to get the coffee, as were Vaithi and Gomati. The elders followed suit, curious to know what coffee tasted like.

Sundaram the priest, however, refused, saying that he would not drink even a glass of water before having a bath and left immediately for the river. He would have liked to have the coffee after he had bathed, but he wondered if there would be any left for him.

'Where is Annasamy?' he said suddenly. 'I would take him to the river but he is nowhere to be seen!'

No one had seen the astrologer in a while. Uncle Krishna Iyer wondered whether the astrologer had fallen off the carriage on the way. 'Don't say such an inauspicious thing!' Subramanya Iyer shushed him 'We have already suffered much loss of life and property. Only now is something good beginning to happen.'

Just then the younger temple priest came over to have a tumbler of coffee and inform them that the astrologer had taken slightly ill and was resting in the vaidyar's house. He added, without anybody asking him, that coffee was good for the growth of one's intelligence.

The astrologer remained in the vaidyar's house, swaddled in a blanket and babbling his worries. From what the vaidyar could make of his words, he deduced Annasamy's problem and explained it to his students, 'This man has made a copper yantra and erected it on wooden posts in his village in a garden. He seems a good mathematician. But instead of using his knowledge for scientific progress, he has been using it for nonsensical purposes such as imprisoning deities on copper plates. Now, that yantra has crashed to the ground and he has somehow come to know of it. What is interesting is that the information has come to him through the collective force of someone aiming these thoughts at him. Obviously he is going to remain sick until that copper plate is replaced in its original position.'

Annasamy, who was listening, shook his head vigorously and said, 'But there are deities and they did complain to me!'

The young temple priest began an argument to prove to the astrologer that there was no logic to what he was saying. But the vaidyar signalled to him as if to say, 'Don't cross him. Let him talk.'

'Don't worry about anything,' the vaidyar said soothingly to the astrologer. 'Things will soon become all right. We will take the appropriate steps.' The vaidyar prepared another solution of opium which the young priest proudly heated in a glass vial over a flame.

One of the priest's friends came in to tell them that the formal announcement of the wedding was being conducted in Kupusamy Iyer's house. He also said something more important: that the softest idlis, and ginger and coriander chutney were being prepared for breakfast.

As soon as the astrologer fell asleep again, the group left for the wedding and the breakfast. As they walked they decided how the astrologer could be cured: they would feed the astrologer, wake him up properly and then urge him to direct his thoughts to someone in Arasur who would do his bidding and replace the yantra where it belonged. The idea that this could be achieved by the sheer force of the astrologer's thought process was so exciting that they went to breakfast in great good humour.

Their good humour vanished, however, when they returned and Annasamy woke up. He gulped down fourteen of the idlis that they had brought for him from the wedding and blinked confusedly when the vaidyar tried to explain to him the theory of 'sending' thoughts to another person, however far away he was. Finally he said that he might be able to comprehend their theory if they explained it to him mathematically. If that was not possible, he would bathe and meditate for some time. After that he might be in a better frame of mind to understand what they were saying.

After he had bathed and meditated, the astrologer's mind was clearer and he seemed to follow what they were asking him to do. He closed his eyes and began to concentrate on a man who was middle-aged, fat and had a big moustache—the vaidyar, entering the astrologer's mind, gave the others this information excitedly. The vaidyar sat so close to the astrologer to absorb his thought process that he was drowned in Annasamy's foul breath, but he bore it all patiently for the sake of scientific progress. The vaidyar not only absorbed what the astrologer was thinking but also tried to 'send' the thoughts across.

So strong were the thoughts from these two men that, miles away in Arasur, the king, on his way to relieve himself in the backyard, stopped suddenly, as if someone had pulled him back. A moment later, as the thought force hit him in full, he began to splutter with rage. 'Rascal! How dare you stop me when I am in a hurry to relieve myself! Bisons and donkeys fuck your sister!' he yelled at the cook, thinking that it was the cook who had interrupted his walk to the backyard. The cook expressed his displeasure at the king's swearing by scorching the dry fish that he was roasting for the king's breakfast. He also spat on it for good measure.

When the vaidyar, who could see all of this in his mind's eye, described the scene to his students, they burst out laughing. Thereafter, the astrologer thought, in turn, of an old Brahmin woman, a customer at a tobacco shop, a woman who had just sat down to milk her buffalo, a man who was hammering iron shoes on a bullock's hooves, another man who was selling peacock oil in the market place, and so on. The astrologer unable to concentrate on the person for longer than it took him or her to walk four steps. This took all day. By the time the procession of the bridegroom started with great festivity that evening, the vaidyar and his students were at their wits' end. Even as the astrologer was trying to send his thoughts to send Subbamma to the palace, the firecracker man set off the crackers in the bridegroom's procession, thereby ruining the astrologer's concentration. The old woman walked right back into her house, muttering, 'Is it fair, I ask you, you old women, to keep making me wander in and out of my house?' She obviously imagined that her ancestral spirits were being mischievous again.

The young priest and his friends decided that nothing could be achieved until the noise of the wedding procession abated. They heard the sounds of the dance performance beginning. The young men could barely contain themselves when they heard the pleasant sound of ankle bells and the throb of the drum. Deciding that the scientific experiment could wait while they went to feast their eyes on the rounded shoulders and heavy breasts of the dancing girls, the vaidyar's students left to watch the dance performance.

Annasamy asked for a vial of opium solution so that he could sleep while they all went to the dance and dinner afterwards. 'Let me sleep!' he said pleadingly. Obviously, the astrologer was getting addicted.

CHAPTER 48

'Hasn't Kittan turned up yet? Where on earth has he gone? Is this the time for him to do a vanishing act?' Kuppusamy Iyer was yelling to his wife, Visalakshi, in the kitchen. Gomati, Vaithi's wife, came over to get a vadai for her toddler and Kuppusamy stopped speaking.

One of the wedding cooks brought Gomati four hot vadais, placed on a bit of plantain leaf. As she turned to go, Visalakshi asked her, 'Shall I get you some more? Poor child, he is probably very hungry!'

'He refused to eat breakfast, Akka. That's why he is so hungry. Your house has such a huge garden and groves and fields, that he just could not tear himself away from playing outside. In Madras we do not have so much space. If it were not for good salaries and the sea breeze, no one would live in Madras!' Gomati broke the vadai into little bits, blew on them to cool them and fed them to her son.

There was a lull in the wedding proceedings. The couple had gone into the house to the pandal where the actual wedding was to take place. As a prelude to the wedding, the names of the gotras and names of four generations of forebears were being exchanged between the two families. Kuppusamy Iyer's uncle and aunt, who would give away the bride, were there, ready for their role in the proceedings.

The astrologer, Annasamy, who had been feeling much better since the previous night, was there, dressed in white silk veshti and upper cloth, his forehead neatly marked with a red namam. He was back to his normal self, hustling people and speeding things up with great gusto.

Annasamy had solved his problem last night—the sound of the dancers' bells had reminded him of the Kottakudi dasi and he had managed to send her to the palace to set the yantra back on its pedestal. He passed the good news on to the others when they returned at midnight from the wedding entertainment. He went to sleep quietly and woke up completely refreshed. The vaidyar was upset that he had not been around to witness the astrologer actually getting someone to do his bidding from so far away but the very fact that such a thing had been proved possible made him and his students happy. They were able to take part in and enjoy the wedding wholeheartedly the next morning.

'O young man who resembles Lord Vishnu himself, I hand over to you my daughter, who looks like a golden statue, and who is but a playful child yet. From now on she is your wife. May you multiply your family through her and may you, with her help, fulfil all the duties that the deities expect of you. And may this bring you prosperity and joy.'

The priest intoned the mantras for giving away the bride, adding, 'The time has come to give the bride away. All of you should gather here.'

Annasamy lifted Gomati's son and ran towards the pandal, with Gomati at his heels. Visalakshi said urgently to her husband, 'Let's go too. Otherwise everyone will wonder where we are!' Kuppusamy followed her, still very confused and worried about where Kitta had gone.

'With the blessings of the Sun God I receive the water you pour in my hands which are protected by the Aswini Devas. With the water I also accept your daughter as my wife.'

When Sankaran finished repeating the mantra after the priest, Bhagavati lifted her head and gazed at his face for a moment before bending down again.

'The bride's people should weep now!' announced the wife of Snehamba's brother, who had come from Alapat for the wedding.

'Weep at a wedding? What rubbish! We don't do such inauspicious things in our place!' priest Sundaram's wife retorted sharply.

Visalakshi glanced at Snehamba who was sitting with her back to a pillar. Her eyes were brimming.

'Sneha, where is your husband? Why are you weeping?' Visalakshi whispered to her.

'It's nothing. He'll soon be here,' Snehamba replied, wiping her eyes and trying to smile, but she could not hide the fear on her face.

'You are pregnant. Don't worry about anything. It is not good for the baby,' Visalakshi said gently and stroked Sneha's hair before walking forward into the wedding pandal.

'Can we give up our practice of weeping just because you don't like it?' Bhagavati's sister Alamelu was saying rebelliously. Kuppusamy shushed her, even as Visalakshi joined him in the pandal.

'Alamu, if they don't like it, why should we be stubborn and weep? We can do all that when your daughter gets married!'

'Oh, but who knows how long we will have to wait for that?' Alamelu wondered.

Her elder sister Echumi pinched her waist and whispered loudly, 'Let me know what your husband has planned. I will calculate the day and star on which your girl will be born!'

Laughter rose in the pandal, making Alamelu's husband Somanathan blush and squirm.

'Oh saintly Brahmins, give me water unpolluted by death or dirt. Let the drops of water, which hold fire at its very centre, and which fall on this girl's head, protect her and the children I will give her. May this woman have the blessings of all the deities and may she rule my household as its queen. May she protect and nourish the cows and horses in my household and may she be loving and supportive of my parents and other members of our family.'

The mantras Sankaran was uttering flowed through the priest Sundaram's ears to his mind in a pleasing manner. But he resisted listening to them, thinking, 'These auspicious mantras are foreign to me. I should have no interest in them or in anything that is not to do with helping departed souls to cross over to the other side.' It seemed to him that his Guru was there, sending these words into his mind.

When Bhagavati went in to change into the wedding sari for the main ritual, most of the women, including Visalakshi, Gomati, Alamelu and Narayani, went with her. Normally, Snehamba would have gone too. But today she just sat there with her back to the pillar, staring into mid space.

Early that morning when Kitta Iyer had told her that he was going over to the Savakkadu Brahmin's house to get the loan from him, Snehamba did try to dissuade him, telling him that it would be better if he went after the wedding.

'I will not get the money if I don't go now,' Kitta had replied. 'I believe today is very auspicious and the pastor will conduct a special prayer before the money is handed over. That will make the money multiply many times. We will be able to start our eatery in Kollam soon.'

'But how can you go without attending the family wedding?'

'It won't take me more than an hour. The Savakkadu Brahmin's carriage will be waiting for me at the edge of the town. I shall go in it, fetch the money and be dropped back. I'll be here before Bhagavati's thali is tied. Don't worry.'

'Can't you ask for the carriage tomorrow? No one will notice your absence tomorrow when all the minor rituals take place. But today, everyone will wonder where you are.'

'You were the one who hankered to set up an eatery. You were the one who forced me to go hither and thither to get the money ready. Now that we have an opportunity to get money at a low rate of interest, you drag me back and tell me to delay it until tomorrow. Look, the thali will be tied only a little before noon. I will be back well in time for it.' He had reassured her and left unobtrusively on his trip early in the morning. Why was he not back yet?

'Bring the bride! Bring the bride!' Subramanya Iyer's relatives, Krishna Iyer and Ramanatha Iyer cried impatiently fearing that the auspicious hour would soon be over.

One of the younger temple priest's friends drew near Annasamy and thrust a bundle into his hands. 'Hold this carefully. Kuppusamy Iyer said this will be required for the maravanai tomorrow.'

'What is a maravanai, boy?' the astrologer asked. 'Is it a wooden board or a copper plate?' His thoughts were now entirely occupied by the copper yantra he had brought along. When the wedding was over he had to get Kuppusamy Iyer's permission (and fees, of course), install the yantra in the garden and then leave for Arasur.

'Don't you know what a maravanai is? It is the costume for the dancers who have to perform for the bridal couple before they leave for their home the day after tomorrow.' The young man removed a false moustache from the bundle to show the astrologer.

'Who will be sticking this on?' Annasamy asked, just as Bhagavati returned to the pandal dressed in a red, nine-yard-long sari.

'An elderly lady will play the role of the man and an elderly man, like yourself, will play the role of the woman.'

As Annasamy listened to this with interest, someone stamped hard on his foot. It was Kuppusamy Iyer, who was in a hurry to get to Snehamba to ask her about her missing husband.

'Sneha, where is your husband? He will not go anywhere without informing everybody. Is he not in favour of this wedding? Even if that were the case, is this the time to absent himself?'

Snehamba's eyes brimmed over again. Before she could actually sob, the pipes and drums reached a crescendo as an accompaniment to the ritual of the bridegroom tying the thali around the bride's neck. At the same moment, Kitta Iyer could be seen entering the house.

Kuppusamy cried happily, 'There he is! Don't cry Sneha!'

Kitta Iyer entered the pandal, tightening the knot in his veshti at the waist. Inside the knot was a metal cross.

Just one hour before, instructed by the pastor, Kitta Iyer had converted to Christianity in the presence of the Savakkadu Brahmin-Christian.

CHAPTER 49

'*Nandavanattilor aandi...*'

The pipe player was essaying the well known song at a slow pace, so as to enable the elderly maravanai dancers to step carefully.

Alapat Sesha Iyer, Snehambal's father, was dancing the role of the woman. He wore a silk madisar sari, studs in his ears and a wig. Kohl rimmed his eyes. He danced slowly in front of the bridal procession which progressed at snail's pace through the streets of Ambalapuzha.

Sankaran had not wanted the procession. 'We have to leave for home this evening. I don't see the need for a procession,' he had protested.

'But you are not going to be alone in the carriage,' Narayani had enlightened him. 'Bhagavati Kutti will be with you. Whatever you left out saying to her last night you can say to her now!'

Bhagavati's sister Echumi stage-whispered to Nani, 'Are you dumb? They would not have exchanged a word last night. Are nights for speaking?' Her voice could be heard all over town.

It seemed to Sankaran that Bhagavati was blushing more right now than she did the previous night. He felt comfortable and in control of his body (as well as hers). Was it for this he had married her, with so many mantras and rites, with so much expense and pomp—was it all just for their two bodies to lie against each other for all their nights to come?

He felt they would soon become compatible mentally, whether they tired of the wonder of their physical contact or not. The exertions of the previous night had been exhausting for both of them. Their eyes still looked tired.

'Nandavanattil or aandi/ avan nalaaru maadamai kuyavanai vendi...'

'Aandi and tondi are all fine. But keep an eye on that old man so that he doesn't start floating again,' the vaidyar warned the younger temple priest as the two, along with astrologer Annasamy and priest Sundaram, sat on the pyol outside the vaidyar's house and watched the procession. Then the vaidyar set out to the canal to bathe.

The old man from Alapat had arrived only that morning. He had not attended the wedding. Only Snehamba's youngest brother had arrived in time for the wedding. He was known for saying the wrong thing at the wrong time. When they had all sat down to eat the wedding feast, he was the one who noticed that Kitta Iyer had started eating without uttering the necessary mantra.

'Attimber, have you forgotten the mantra, or have you decided that you can postpone it for the next meal?' he asked loudly, embarrassing Kitta and angering Snehamba, who was upset both with her brother, for being so crude, and with her husband, for being careless of niceties. Already there were murmurs that he had not pulled his weight for his sister's wedding. Even Visalakshi, who was not usually given to criticising anyone, said something a little critical of Kitta's behaviour. It was a good thing that he had at least been in time for the muhurtam. Otherwise he would have been the object of everyone's displeasure. As for Kamakshi manni, she would definitely have used it as an excuse for starting her next kitchen war.

Snehamba, however, had too many things on her mind at the moment to worry about the opinions of others. After Sankaran and Bhagavati had gone into their bedroom that night, Snehamba called her youngest brother and told him to get back to Alapat and ask her two elder brothers to come to Ambalapuzha.

The bed chamber of the bridal couple was simply the store room made over. All the grain sacks and baskets of tamarind and chillies had been removed from the room. A cot had been shifted into the room and decorated with flowers. Outside the room, after the couple had gone in, a group of women stood around singing erotic songs in a chorus. Snehamba's youngest brother was completely lost in the songs and in the beauty of Narayani, Bhagavati's friend, who walked hither and thither looking every inch a white-clad apsara. He was reluctant to leave for Alapat.

'You want me to go now?' he asked glumly. 'Every dog will be sleeping soundly. There will be no boatman to take me across the canal. Even if I were to find a boat I am sure I will not find a carriage to drive me to Alapat.'

'If you pay the right price, both boatman and carriage driver will be at your service all night long,' Sneha retorted and, pressing four rupees into his hand urged him, 'Start quickly now!'

The money was from the loan Kitta had brought back from Savakkadu. The rest would go towards setting up the eatery in Kollam. When Snehamba held the bag of money in her hands, she felt triumphant and euphoric, as if the world was at her feet. If Kamakshi ever began a quarrel with her again, she would hit her on the face with this money bag. That would shut her up! Who could raise a voice against the power of money?

On the evening of the wedding, when Kitta told her that he was going out for a while, she remembered that he had not performed his evening rituals or uttered the *Gayatri mantra*. 'What is the matter with you? Have you forgotten your evening rituals, the way you forgot to say your prayers before lunch?' she chided him.

Kitta Iyer came close to her and laughed. Then he removed the metal cross from the knot in his veshti and showed it to her, saying, 'I will only worship this!'

'Oh for God's sake, why are you keeping that thing with you? The pastor has probably put a spell on it and given it to you. Throw it away!' she exclaimed.

Kitta put his hand over her mouth so that she could not speak further. 'Look, we don't have to pay any interest on the loan—all because of this cross! The Savakkadu Christian has even found a place for us to set up the eatery—we can start next week. Only because of this cross! Now I am going out to order the wooden doors for the eatery. Keep this money bag with you carefully. Give me the money when I ask for it.'

After Kitta had left, Snehamba pondered on this new worry. Along with the money had come the cross. Was he a Christian that he had to walk around carrying a cross? A terrible sense of unease swamped Sneha. Just at that moment, Echumi, Bhagavati's sister, invited her to come to the pandal to watch the fun of the nalangu games and drew her away.

When Sneha reached the pandal, Bhagavati was presenting Sankaran with a novel gift, a watch. It had been imported. The watch hung on a long chain. It would also chime at every hour, it was said. It was the vaidyar who had got it for Kuppusamy Iyer, all the way from Tiruvananthapuram.

'Bhagavati, ask your husband what he will give you in return!' Vaithi urged the bride, as he hung the watch from the veshti knot at Sankaran's waist.

Sankaran thought for a long time before he promised to get a Belgium mirror for Bhagavati the next month. He wished he had thought of it earlier and bought it through Karuthan or Suleiman.

'Let the mirror come when it will, Bhagavati,' Vaithi teased. 'Ask him for something right now. Otherwise he will forget all about it and leave for Madras to make more money!'

Visalakshi laughed and interrupted him by saying, 'What our son-in-law has promised, he will surely deliver. Don't underrate him. Sneha, why don't you say something? I seem to be doing all the talking!'

Sneha made a pretence of joining in the revelry by saying, 'Of course! I am sure he can get a mirror in Madras or even in Savakkadu, if he wills it!' But her heart was not in the conversation. She had a terrible sense of foreboding and wanted to have her brothers with her for support when the time came.

Despite Sneha's youngest brother returning to Alapat at her bidding and conveying her request, it was not her brothers who tuned up the next day, but her father.

'Your brothers are all so busy. So I thought I would come over and congratulate you all on the wedding! I am in fine health now,' he said happily.

Snehamba was in no mood to listen to him, as just a little earlier, Kitta had informed her, in a secluded spot in the garden, that he had converted to Christianity.

'Don't worry about it. I will manage it all,' he had said in an effort at calming her. 'In any case we have to be in Kollam in the next ten or twenty days. So start preparing to go.'

His words did not calm Snehamba who was reduced to a state of panic by what he had said.

This was a contingency that the Savakkadu pastor had anticipated. 'John Kitta Iyer, there is no doubt that your wife will be greatly disturbed upon hearing that you have converted to Christianity. It is only to be expected of a woman. It will take time for her mind to accept the truth. When her mind clears and she recognises the life eternal, she will find peace again. Until such time, what you have to tell her is…'

'Sneha, I will be a Christian only until such time as I can repay the Savakkadu fellow's loan. Then I will be back to my old self,' Kitta said to Sneha as he had been tutored.

Sneha did not know whether to believe him but the idea of setting up the eatery and earning a lot of money was tempting. Every one she knew who was in the hotel business was doing well without exception. She told herself that her husband was perfectly capable of making enough money to return the Savakkadu Brahmin's loan in six months and revert to wearing sacred ash as before.

It was as Kitta was telling Sankaran that he needed to go out for a short while that Sneha's father turned up. Kitta greeted him and asked him to eat and rest. The old man, however, was more interested in knowing who was going to dance in the procession. 'Actually, there is no one,' Kuppusamy told him sadly.

'In that case I can dress up as a woman and dance,' said the old man eagerly.

'Can you?' Kuppusamy asked him doubtfully. The image of the old man urinating at the temple flag staff crossed his mind.

'Kuppusamy, I don't float any more,' the old man reassured him. 'Sometimes, when I am asleep, they tell me that I rise up a finger's breadth. But if they put a couple of heavy mats under me I look as if I am flat on my back. I am fine, really.'

They tried to find a woman to dance in a man's costume along with the old man, but no one came forward.

The ancestral women who spoke through Subramanya Iyer asked Sundaram's wife why she could not dance. 'Just for fun,' they wheedled. But the woman refused firmly. Was she Subbamma to do their bidding? Was she crazy that she should tie a veshti over her madisar and jump around on the streets? Peeved by her refusal the ancestral women began to sing, in Subramanya Iyer's voice, a ribald song heckling Sundaram's impotence, when Iyer was dragged away from the venue by the astrologer who complained that the antics of the ancestral spirits were getting unbearable.

Subramanya Iyer promptly turned on the astrologer and snapped, 'Go make a yantra shaped like a vagina. You can install it here and worship it!'

The old man from Alapat had donned his female costume and had begun dancing, leading the wedding procession.

Sundaram, who sat on the vaidyar's pyol, watching the procession, remembered the mantra uttered in the bridal chamber last night at the auspicious hour, 'Into you will I place myself and kindle a fire from which our heirs will be born.' He was too old to kindle any fires. He had no heir who would do the rites to lead his soul to a safe place.

Annasamy was content because he had finished installing the yantra in the Ambalapuzha house. Yantras and machines, they were all the same, he thought. Beside him, Subramanya Iyer spoke in chaste Malayalam. 'There is something boiling in a glass vial. It is important to concentrate.'

In the carriage, Sankaran gently pinched Bhagavati's palm. She reacted by saying in a soft voice, 'That is the only place you have left unpinched on my body.'

Sankaran wanted to dress her in one of those figure hugging gowns that the white women wore, and then have her undress in front of him. Sex seemed to be everything to him at the moment. He must tell those rogues to get him those music discs. He should stand naked upstairs and listen to the music. Sankaran had studied the Sama Veda and then forgotten it. For a moment Sankaran felt himself change into someone else. Then he was brought back by the chiming of the watch at his waist.

The old man from Alapat was singing,

'The Brahmin cook went to Calicut,

He was directed by the man from Savakkadu

To change his religion.

If you want thick coffee,

Or steaming idlis,

Or crisp vadais,

Go to the Christian's shop.'

The old man rose a little from the ground as he sang. 'The ancestral women have possessed him!' said Sundaram to the astrologer.

Running to hold the old man to the ground, the younger temple priest said to the astrologer, in the voice of the vaidyar,' Of what use is a yantra shaped like a vagina to the progress of science?' His breath, which smelled of opium, was soothing to the astrologer.

CHAPTER 50

The house was abuzz with visitors coming to offer their congratulations. The huge quantities of sweets and savouries that had come with Bhagavati's dowry were useful, not only for the family to munch on but also to offer to the visitors.

Subramanya Iyer had arranged for the young couple to start their life in the newly-renovated house in Arasur. It seemed to him that the characteristic energy and joy of his family was only just returning.

Kuppusamy Iyer and Visalakshi had accompanied Bhagavati to Arasur, bringing an impressive dowry of utensils, jewellery, silken mats and other things. Visalakshi liked Arasur. She felt comfortable enough in the village to go unaccompanied to the market place and temple. 'Why is the water in your village pond so red?' she asked Sankaran.

'That is not a pond, Akka, it is a tank,' he replied. 'But the water is sweet.'

'That is true. It is as sweet as candy,' Visalakshi agreed, drinking the water.

'The water smells muddy,' observed Kuppusamy.

'What do you expect it to smell of, the sky?' Visalakshi retorted, laughing.

Watching her laugh, Annasamy's wife observed the she had a lovely smile, as did all the Ambalapuzha family women, including Bhagavati.

Visalakshi as well as Krishna Iyer's wife and the priest Sundaram's wife, had to play host to the numerous visitors, as Kalyani was still not well enough to get up from her bed. Soon after their return to Arasur, Subramanya Iyer brought the couple to her, made her sit up and urged her, 'Bless the children, Kalyani.'

Kalyani gazed at hem vaguely, muttered, 'Look after your wife, Saama. Don't let her catch fire.' Then she flopped down and went back to sleep.

There was one prominent person missing in the welcome committee at Arasur: Subbamma. No one knew where she had gone. She seemed to have vanished without a trace. 'She had promised to look after Kalyani while we were gone. Where on earth has she disappeared to?' asked Sundaram's wife.

Old Ramalakshmi, the cook in the Vedic School, replied, 'Subbamma was suffering from high fever. She was worried that if she stayed here she might infect Kalyani. So she went to her own home. That was two days after you left for the wedding. After that I saw her one night walking down her street, singing as if she did not have a care in the world. That was the last I saw of her.'

'But why was Subbamma singing, when the ancestral women were all with me? She could not have gone with them,' reasoned Subramanya Iyer.

'Her voice was awful,' said astrologer Annasamy's wife. 'I don't think the ancestral women had anything to do with her disappearance. Anyway, Subbamma was walking and singing with great gusto in the rain when we last saw her!'

The astrologer himself was not at all happy with Subbamma for having, without his permission, placed the yantra he had made for her, near the one in the palace garden. What problems that had created for him! It gained him nothing but that soothing concoction that the vaidyar had given him. If the Kottakudi dasi had not obliged him and set the Maha Yantra right, God only knew what further calamities would have taken place. When this thought crossed his mind, the voice of the Ambalapuzha vaidyar interceded and said, 'That is no way to think! You must learn to be rational!'

The astrologer resented the vaidyar frequently visiting his mind and giving his opinions. He wondered what kind of calculations he would have to make to create a yantra that would stop the vaidyar from butting into his mind. The astrologer walked past the Maha Yantra and was surprised to find that it seemed to have shrunk in size.

Sankaran took Bhagavati to his tobacco shop. As they walked down the market street she received more glances than even the Kottakudi dasi.

At the entrance to the shop, the wooden doll nodded its head several times as if to welcome Bhagavati. Bhagavati found it difficult to climb the narrow stairs leading into the shop. She told Sankaran that the smell of tobacco nauseated her.

'What can I do, woman? I have to sell this to support our family. Such is my fate,' Sankaran replied half jokingly. Nevertheless he was relieved that he no longer had to store even a leaf of tobacco in his house. It was all stored in the palace compound. He sent a silent thanks to the elderly white officer for having made this possible.

A customer came to get snuff from the shop. He paused upon seeing Bhagavati and, saying that he would return later, walked away.

'Don't let me interrupt your business,' Bhagavati said quickly and began climbing down the stairs leading out of the shop. Halfway down, she started sneezing and stood there, one eye closed, a smile on her lips. She looked so delectable that Sankaran had to resist the urge to rush down and hug her tight. Instead he called for Ayyanai. When Ayyanai appeared Sankaran remembered that Bhagavati had said that he reminded her of the old man from Alapat. The thought made Sankaran laugh. Without quite knowing why her husband was laughing Bhagavati too joined in the laughter.

'She laughs so beautifully, master. It was this laughter that was missing in our house all this time,' Ayyanai observed on another occasion to Sankaran as they were driving to the shop.

This was when the queen from the palace had come to offer her congratulations. Subramanya Iyer's entire family had been there to welcome her. Sankaran alone left abruptly, saying he had work in the shop.

The women of Iyer's family welcomed the queen warmly, especially as she was pregnant. Ramanathan's and Sundaram's wives sang an auspicious song as they offered her a ceremonial welcome. Everyone missed Subbamma as she would have risen to this occasion with such apt and lovely songs. The spirits of the ancestral women too were missing. Perhaps they had gone in search of Subbamma.

The queen apologised for the king not accompanying her. He was busy looking over the palace accounts with his manager, she explained.

Ramanatha Iyer replied politely by saying, 'I am sure it is not easy to administrate a zamin like this. There must be so many complexities! I have had experience in this sort of thing as, when

I was an employee of the court, I had to deal exclusively with litigations concerning zamin property. '

The queen wondered briefly whether this old man would not make a good substitute for the present palace manager.

Sundaram's wife took the queen around the house. When she was ready to leave she was given betel leaves and turmeric and vermilion. She embraced Bhagavati warmly and kissed her on her forehead. 'Make sure that the space around the well, where you bathe, is private,' she advised Bhagavati. 'Ask them to bring the sloping roof right over the well or make them put a new thatch roof over the well. There are a lot of men coming and going from the palace these days because the tobacco is stored there. Some of them might pry and look at you while you are bathing,' the queen said with concern.

When Bhagavati repeated the queen's words to Sankaran later, he said angrily, 'If anyone even tries to look your way I'll kill him!' but he said this with his head bent low, unable to meet Bhagavati's eyes.

Just when it seemed there were no more visitors left to offer congratulations, Thanu Pillai and his wife arrived from Madurai. They gave the couple a gold sovereign each and rolls of strung jasmine and kumkum from the Meenakshi temple.

Then it was Karuthan's turn. He had also brought with him a fresh consignment of snuff. So his first job was to store the jars of snuff safely in the palace store room. Then he visited Sankaran and told him affectionately, 'Iyere, I meant to come to your wedding but my wife delivered at just that time.'

He gave Sankaran a pair of lovely Chinese silk shawls. 'Is it a boy or a girl?' Sankaran asked him.

'One of this and one of that. My wife gave me twins this time!' Karuthan replied, smiling.

'Bhagavati, this rascal is my business partner,' Sankaran introduced Karuthan fondly.

Bhagavati folded her hands in greeting.

'Run and get him some coffee!' Sankaran told her, smiling as widely as Karuthan.

One of the last visitors to offer congratulations was the Kottakudi dasi. That her name was Mohanavalli was a piece of information that only Bhagavati gathered. She did this by simply introducing herself and asking the dasi her name. The latter was deeply moved and told Bhagavati that this was the first time anyone had asked her for her name. That it was someone as young and beautiful and educated as Bhagavati made it even more special, she added. When Bhagavati told Sankaran that night, he was thinking about the dasi's rounded elbows. When his conscience stung him with the question whether it was right for him to be thinking about another woman while with his wife, he sat silently down on the swing in his house. It was close to midnight then. He could hear the sound of the rain outside.

He wondered why he had not told Bhagavati about the Kottakudi dasi visiting his shop. But what reason did he have to mention her? Perhaps he could have shown his wife the poem she had written on the occasion. But Bhagavati could not read Tamil, only Malayalam, so the poem would have made no sense to her. It would be good if she could learn to read Tamil. He should get her a tutor—not a man, perhaps the dasi herself could come and teach her. He should ask her. He should also ask her what she was willing to teach him.

Bhagavati came and stood close to him. He pulled her to him, laid her gently down on the swing and kissed her softly on her navel. Aroused, she sat up and embraced him and kissed him hard on his lips. When he entered her on the gently moving swing, a thought flashed in Sankaran's mind, 'All this has happened earlier.'

'What a pest you are!' Bhagavati, sitting up on the swing, complained, but her eyes were happy. She tried to knot her loose hair. 'Don't,' he said. 'Let your hair be. In the light of the lamp you look like Rati.'

These words too had been uttered earlier.

'Bhagavati, sing me a song.'

'Are you crazy? How can I sing when I am like this, polluted?'

'Are you polluted because I touched you?' Sankaran asked, pulling her on to his lap.

'You didn't stop with touching, did you?' she retorted softly, giggling.

Then she sat down on the floor before him and began to sing.

And this too seemed to him familiar. He was Saama. And this woman, sitting there and singing, was Saama's lover. The swing was the same as where they had coupled. The same wall behind the swing. Once there had been a painting of the goddess Lakshmi. Here it was that the old white officer had tipped the ash from his pipe. It was outside this house that old Subbamma sat and sang the very same dirge that came out of the music discs. The very same music discs that Saama listened to. The rascals who had brought him those discs would return again. To them Saama and Sankaran were all the same. This house too would one day be burnt down. Then it would be rebuilt and someone else would move on the swing. Everything would go round and round like the music disc and every event repeated.

Sankaran dropped off to sleep lying on the swing. Bhagavati slept on the floor nearby, supporting her head on her arm. It rained all night.

Sometime during the night a thunder clap was heard. In the direction of the neighbouring house something could be seen burning. The king woke up in a panic and looked out of his window. It was not the tobacco merchant's house that was burning but the Maha Yantra in the palace garden. Within seconds it had toppled over and been reduced to ashes. Where the yantra fell there was another spark. A cacophony of squabbling female voices could be heard rising into the air.

'Go back to sleep. This is nothing,' his ancestors told the king.

'It was not a house that burnt, was it?' the king asked them anxiously. If the tobacco merchant's house caught fire again, he would probably have to give up his bedroom for storing their tobacco.

'No, nothing like that,' Bushy Moustache soothed him.

Reassured, the king took out his copper urinal from beneath his bed. At the same moment he saw the smaller yantra fly out of sight like a flaming plate.

Seeing these events in a dream, the vaidyar, in far away Ambalapuzha, clucked in disgust. 'What a nuisance! Damn the Arasur astrologer and his yantra! Who the devil was this woman Subbamma and why should the yantra fly off in the direction she took? Idiotic people! As if mosquitoes are not enough to ruin one's sleep, we now have astrologers!'

When, having vented his frustration, the vaidyar pulled his blanket snugly around himself and went back to sleep, it was almost dawn.

CHAPTER 51

Ten years later, one morning:

'This vehicle is meant for business purposes, not for carrying food for visitors. If the son-in-law hears of it he will be very annoyed. What is the matter with you and your sister—suffering from an overflow of sibling affection, are you?'

Somanathan was yelling at the top of his voice to his wife Alamelu, who cringed and tried to reason with him in soft tones. 'Ayyo! Why would I consider that sinner, Kittan, my brother? After he cut his sacred thread and converted, we have no relationship. My blood boils when I think of that whore Snehamba. I have no wish to feed them. It was Bhagavati Kutti's idea—she has such a generous nature!'

From where she stood, Bhagavati could hear the conversation clearly. She felt sad. But what could she do? Here, the men decided who could have a relationship with whom.

In the last ten years, ever since she came to Arasur as a bride, she had never disobeyed Sankaran. Yet when, for the first time, she had asked him for a favour, he had not been easy about it.

'You know Somanathan—Alamu's husband?' she had begun hesitantly one day.

'What of him? He is fine, running his eatery in Madurai, isn't he?' Sankaran had replied.

Bhagavati had remained silent for a moment. She knew that Sankaran was aware of everything that had befallen Somanathan and was feigning ignorance.

Four years after Kitta Iyer had converted to Christianity and taken his share of the money from the sale of the land and gone away, Somanathan too decided to move to Madurai to set up an eatery, influenced by the rags-to-riches story of so many hoteliers. It had been the month of Vrichika when he had left.

Kitta too had left in the same month, a year before, leaving behind a grieving Visalakshi Manni and Duraisamy Iyer. Visalakshi had wept her heart out and Duraisamy had tried to persuade Kittan to at least postpone his departure until after Duraisamy's annual trip to Sabarimalai. 'Look, I start my annual penance for the trip today. Wait just one day. I will sign any paper you want,' Duraisamy Iyer had begged. But Kittan would not relent. 'I don't care who climbs a hill or starts a penance,' he had retorted. 'I want my money now. Unless I leave right away, I will not be able to open my food shop in Kollam on the twelfth, which is an auspicious day.'

'Durai, let him go. He has decided to go in any case. He is not our Kitta any more, he is John. Let him go in peace. Let him prosper wherever he is,' Kuppusamy spoke, staring at the wall in front of him.

But then Visalakshi began to cry. No one had seen her weep like this before. She was not grieving for Kittan's conversion to Christianity. It was the departure of the fully pregnant Sneha and her two little daughters that she could not bear.

'Akka, do you think I wish to go?' Sneha asked her, putting an arm around her shoulders. 'Especially when I am as pregnant as I am? But this man is so stubborn. Be patient for a while. I am sure we will all return soon.'

Visalakshi hugged her even as she knew that what Sneha promised was not going to happen. The girls would join their father, holding his hand and going to the church. As for the unborn child, girl or boy, it would be born a Christian and grow up as one. Later, Sneha too would join them, holding a cross and attending Sunday prayers at the church.

When their land had been divided and Kitta given his share, he had sold it and taken the money with him. Kuppusamy Iyer's friend, Karunagapalli Sangunni, bought Kitta's land.

The family began to scatter after that. The following year, Kitta's sister Echumi and her husband Ramendran left for Kannur, where a very wealthy land owner wished to hire Ramendran as a cook. Next Alamelu and Somanathan left for Madurai to start an eatery there, but they did not fare as well as Kitta. When it became difficult for Somanathan to support his wife and three children, he sent Alamelu to meet Bhagavati. It was then that Bhagavati went to her husband to ask for help for her sister's husband. And Sankaran was less than cordial in his reply.

'If you can only give him a job in our shop, Attimber will be able to manage his life,' she suggested timidly.

'It is such a tiny shop. There is not enough room in it even for me to fit in.' Sankaran teased.

'When I said 'shop', I did not mean the one here. You haven't appointed a manager in the Madurai shop after the death of Thanu Pillai. Can't you give that job to him? He has studied accounts in school.'

Sankaran wanted to appoint the Telugu Brahmin clerk in Madras for that job. Meanwhile, Suleiman, who had gone off to Rangoon to expand his business there, had also put in a bid for the services of the Telugu Brahmin for his shop there. The clerk's business savvy was such that he was greatly in demand. It turned out that he was not interested in stepping out of Madras. 'If you ask me to continue in Madras, I will,' he said categorically. 'Otherwise I'll quit.'

This worked in Somanathan's favour, and he was shortly appointed as the manager-cum-clerk for the Madurai shop. It took him several months to get the hang of things, but he was now efficient and was enthusiastically making plans to expand the business. Alamelu and he had come to Arasur from Madurai two days ago to take part in the ear-piercing ceremony[14] of Sankaran's second daughter, Kalyani. Within an hour of their arrival in Arasur, a modern carriage rolled to a stop outside Sankaran's shop. For a moment Sankaran thought that the carriage was a new acquisition of his neighbour, the zamindar, whose grant from the government had gone up. He was proved mistaken. Inside the carriage were Kitta Iyer and his family.

This was not the Kitta Iyer Sankaran had known. John Kitta Iyer wore a long shirt, panchakaccham, and a cross on a gold chain around his neck. Every other moment, he seemed to be drawing a cross with his finger in the air. His only son, who had six fingers and toes on each hand and foot and seemed a smart and energetic fellow, began to fiddle with the head of the long defunct and dust-laden wooden doll outside the shop.

'All that dust will give you a cold,' admonished Snehamba as she stepped out of the carriage. She was stouter than before and wore several rope-like chains around her neck. Later, at Sankaran's home, she gave Bhagavati a small packet of vermilion from the Meenakshi temple in Madurai, saying, 'These people never go to temples anymore but how can I be like that?'

She seemed the same as before. Nothing that had happened around her seemed to have affected her. Perhaps, thought Bhagavati, she was insulated by her money.

Snehamba's two daughters had grown tall and shapely. They wore scarves around their heads, and crosses on chains around their necks. Both said they were studying in college. When Sneha chided one of them, 'Don't keep nibbling on that chain!' the girl ignored her. After a pause, however, when she saw Bhagavati staring at her, she let go of the chain. Bhagavati felt like drawing the child close and hugging her.

Sankaran felt it inappropriate for relatives who had converted to another religion to stay in the house so he lodged them in a house four streets away. Sankaran owned a lot of houses in the village now, buying anything that came up for sale.

John Kitta Iyer explained that he was on his way to Madras to take part in an evangelist meeting. He meant to use the opportunity to establish an eatery there.

Alamelu and Somanathan refused to talk either Snehamba or Kitta Iyer.

'God knows what Sneha showed the old man from Savakkadu, he is like a mesmerised monkey and keeps pouring money into her lap. Next that bitch will make her daughters take up whoring too,' Alamelu observed venomously.

Bhagavati put her hand on her mouth to shut her up. 'Akka, why are you insulting them?'

'The whole world is doing that!' Alamelu retorted. 'You should make enquiries in Kollam. The whole town is laughing at them. That is why that ass is escaping to Madras!'

Every town gossiped about its residents, Bhagavati thought. Gossip reached her that Sankaran had a relationship with the Kottakudi dasi. They said he was the father of the dasi's only daughter. The girl went to school with Bhagavati's eldest son, Swaminathan. Whenever she saw the girl, Bhagavati tried to find the resemblance to Sankaran in her face and failed. Could she ask the child who her father was, or even the dasi?

'Girl, all the men in this family have roving eyes—the one I married and the ones I bore. Look after your husband carefully,' Kalyani had told her daughter-in-law lucidly before she died a month after Bhagavati had given birth to her eldest son.

'I am going to Tirupattur on business. When I return in the evening we will leave for Madurai. Be ready. So there's plenty of use for this vehicle. It is not meant to serve useless people!' Somanathan shouted instructions at his wife before he left.

Bhagavati heard his words clearly and returned to the kitchen to ask innocently, 'Akka, what is going on?'

'Why, I believe you wanted to send food in the carriage to that whore and her family? I know that the food, the carriage, the bullocks and the hay they eat are all your property and you can do what you like with them. But should you not ask your husband his opinion before deciding what you should do?' Alamelu said cuttingly.

'I don't know if it is right or wrong, Akka. But they are our guests and there are children there. Can we starve them?'

Bhagavati did not wait to listen to Alamelu's reply. Instead she went to the front of the house and called her son. 'Saama, take these containers of food in Ayyanai's cart and deliver them to…'

Even before she finished speaking, Saama stopped playing and set out eagerly.

'Athai, let me also go with him!' begged his playmate.

'No, Marudayya, your mother will scold you if you leave here. Go home to the palace now.'

Marudayya was the king's delayed offspring, as unexpected and precious as unseasonal rain. If it had not been for the child the government would have taken over the zamin for being heirless. It was small wonder then that the king and queen doted on the child. The result was that he was completely overfed and was growing to be a giant, but a sweet-natured one.

'My mother won't say anything!' he told Bhagavati now. 'Why should you tell her about it?'

He ran, chuckling, to Ayyanai's cart, pushed Ayyanai aside and began driving the cart himself.

'Marudayya, my cousin, whom we are going to see now, was able to set the wooden doll at our shop right. It can nod its head again now,' Swaminathan told his friend proudly as they sped to his uncle's place. It had taken just one day for him to get close to Medhaiyar, John Kitta Iyer's son.

He added another piece of information. 'Know something? He has six fingers on each hand and six toes on each foot!'

'What about below his waist—does he have one there or two?' Maruda Iyer queried interestedly.

'Is this any way for children to talk?' Ayyanai chided the two of them. Then he had a fit of coughing and leaned back against the frame of the cart and dozed off.

'He can speak four languages. And he knows Kalari, a kind of fighting. But he is very afraid of bats!' Swaminathan went on about his cousin.

Then Maruda Iyer pulled the reins of the bullocks and the cart stopped outside the house where Kitta Iyer and his family were lodged.

CHAPTER 52

'I have finished writing about Arasur.'

My ancestors were not impressed.

'What have you written? You have just started!' they observed.

They rose again from where they sat and clung like smoke to the edges of my table. They spread like mist across the screen of my computer and stopped its functioning. Their smell remained in my empty coffee cup.

I cannot quite tell what kind of a smell that was. A bit like snuff, something like the sands of the Vaigai river, a smell of bats perhaps, the odour of a white woman's armpits, the smell of moss from an old well, the stench of pigeon droppings, the acrid smell of fire crackers, the perfume of attar.

'Hey, it's nothing like that. It's just your imagination,' said the Banian Brothers as they rose.

'What's your hurry? What war are you rushing off to?'

That sounded like the king—the voice was authoritative.

'The flower festival approaches. We have to make our collections. A new tahsildar has come to the village. So we have to go meet him.'

'Are you going to sell him music discs too?' the elderly man with the big moustache asked.

'Is he the king's father-in-law?' I enquired.

'There is no king, how can there be a king's father-in-law?' came the retort from the man with the bushy moustache. Why the fellow had ropes of strung jasmine wound around his wrists so early in the morning, I could not fathom.

'Did you think the king a buffoon or what?' the man spoke again. It seemed he was teasing me.

Someone else answered him. 'Why, the boy has not written anything wrong. He has had only good things to say about everybody!'

'The queen did not commit arson. Remember that!'

The woman who said this looked like royalty. But I will not call her the queen. She will probably deny it.

'What happened to the king's descendants?' I could not help asking. I needed to know why the palace was in ruins.

'Why do you say 'his' descendants? You should say 'ours', shouldn't you?'

'Really?'

A man with a tuft above his forehead exclaimed with more surprise than I. As he rose like smoke and covered my computer screen, it came alive again, featuring geometrical shapes.

'I have installed seventeen deities here. Now your machine will work without any problem,' he said.

'No, I am not astrologer Annasamy,' he said in reply to my question. 'I am the chief temple priest's descendant in the fourth generation. As for the astrologer, he has had several births and is currently an Arab running ostrich races in the Gulf.'

'What happened to Subbamma?' I asked.

'Sinner! How dare you call her by her name?' The man did something else to my computer and the screen filled with red squares. The computer seemed to be in danger of crashing.

'Don't be angry with me,' I said in a placatory tone. 'I am eager to know what happened to that elderly lady.'

'She went to Kasi and haunted the ghats where the corpses burn all night long. She sat there singing what she called Hindustani ragas and made such a noise that an elderly Muslim took pity on her and took her away and made a small hut for her to stay, outside his house. Subbamma called out to her ancestors with her dying breath that he was her long lost husband. But they had no time to listen to her as they were in a hurry, as always, to get to a venue where auspicious rites were being performed to placate ancestral spirits.

Another man intruded into our conversation at this point. He smelled of attar and a pigeon perched on his shoulder. He looked around my room and asked me about the value of my house. I told him that it was not for sale.

'You don't know who Subbamma was,' he told my other informant. 'She was wandering around in Madras where she was spotted by Theresa, the elder daughter of John Kitta Iyer. It seemed Subbamma was looking for the address of the retired navigation clerk, Vaidyanatha Iyer. Theresa, who taught at the university, took her home and kept her there, teaching her to pray the Christian way and to sing good evangelist songs.'

Even before he could finish, an anaemic looking woman interrupted, saying that nothing like that happened with

Subbamma. 'I know, because I should have been born to Theresa, but she had a miscarriage and I died before birth,' the woman added. She also said that Sankaran's son Swaminathan married John Kitta Iyer's second daughter, Amalorpavam, although she was older than him, and eventually converted to Christianity.

'Nonsense!' cried another woman who had the squeakiest voice imaginable. 'They did marry but the wedding took place in the temple of Vadakkunathan. Her name was Kamala, not Amalorpavam, and she had to eat ten grains of rice as a rite to reduce her age before she married. One month before the wedding, in the month of Vrichika, we flung the Savakkadu Brahmin's money at his face and returned to our own religion!'

The squeaky-voiced woman was displayed faintly on my screen. Then the image morphed into a mundu wearing, bald headed man who was selling lottery tickets. 'Saare, want lucky tickets, government lottery tickets?'

'Don't trust this bald headed fellow, none of those tickets will win a prize,' announced a middle-aged man fanning himself with a palm leaf fan and belching at periodic intervals.

'What happened to the tobacco shop?'

The Banian Brothers replied to this question. Sankaran's son Swaminathan did not like to run the shop and went off to Madras to study in the university. His sister Kalyani and her husband, Narayana Iyer, continued the business.

'The business continued for another two generations. Then the family produced mostly bank and government clerks and the business died a natural death,' added a dark-skinned, stocky man, and the taller of the Banian Brothers exclaimed, 'Is that so?'

'Don't pretend!' I chided him. 'Is there anything that happens in town that does not come to your knowledge?'

'Actually, we know little more than arranging festivals, collecting funds, visiting and paying our respects to important persons and some minor trading. We hardly have time for anything else. In fact, we hardly know if we are going to make enough money for our next meal or to fill petrol for the car,' they replied sadly.

'If you get on to a ship with your camera, you will make plenty of money,' came the pert observation from a woman who had six digits on her hands and feet.

'We pledged our camera to Karu. Peri. Chokkanatha Chettiar, the money lender, and could never get it back,' the Brothers said, with sad expressions.

'What happened to Sankaran's son, Swaminathan?' I asked.

The woman with six digits answered this question. 'Swaminathan followed his friend Maruda Iyer to the university in Tiruvananthapuram as a lecturer. Both were known for their knowledge of mathematics and English.' She added that Swaminathan did convert to Christianity but did not marry a girl older than him.

Another voice added, 'The queen would not leave the palace, even after she had become old. So, when Maruda Iyer left with his family for Tiruvananthapuram, he left his mother in the care of Bhagavati. Bhagavati as well as her daughter Kalyani and her husband, Narayanan, looked after the queen with as much love and care, as if she were their mother. Even after the death of the queen, the palace continued to be used for storing tobacco.'

The Banian Brothers approached me and whispered, 'None of these people belongs to the Arasur line. They have just come down for a chat. So don't waste your time on them. Get on with your work.'

'But what about my grand-uncle who ran a tobacco shop in Ambalapuzha? Isn't he here?' I asked.

'I am he!' replied a little girl. 'I will tell you the remaining story of the Arasur family,' she said, running round me energetically.

'But, lady, you would have been born much later. How would you know what happened earlier?'

'What is the use of all that information? Must every event be recorded from the beginning to the end like the links of a chain?' The girl dissolved in air. With her, the others vanished too.

'It's getting late. Don't you want to contribute to the flower festival?' the Banian Brothers extended their note book towards me.

'I'll give you money tomorrow,' I replied, as always.

Only when I had shut down the computer and left the room in order to have a bath did I remember that I had not found out what happened to Suleiman. I would have to ask the Banian Brothers when they visited next or my ancestors when they came down for some coffee tomorrow morning.

Suppose they were not my ancestors at all?

Never mind. Surely, they would also know of a Suleiman or a Swaminathan. There would be an Arasur family too. Perhaps the name would be different and even the place, in a different time. But they would tell me about someone, somewhere, who lived and was happy or otherwise, and of events that took place or did not.

I will listen to them and then write it all down.

Glossary

Aavaram	A kind of wild flower
Agraharam	Brahmin quarter
Akka	Elder sister, or older woman
Ambi	Younger brother, or a small boy; popular nickname
Amma	Mother
Anna	Elder brother or older man
Annapoorani	An incarnation of goddess Parvati, believed to nourish and feed the universe
Appam	Pancakes made of rice flour and jaggery and often used as a substitute for the sacramental wafer in churches in Tamil Nadu
Apsara	Heavenly beauty
Aswini devas	Celestial beings who bestow good health
Athai	Aunt

Attar	Perfume
Attimber	Elder sister's or aunt's husband
Ayyare	A form of address, referring to the Saivite group of south Indian Brahmins or priests
Ayyo!	An exclamation of dismay or fear
Baccha	Child (in Hindi)
Banian	Inner vest made of soft cotton cloth, sometimes with short sleeves
Besh	Bravo!
Bhogam	Pleasure, in this case, the pleasure of sex
Chatram	A large stone hall built along the highway to house wayfarers and travellers
Chennamangalam	
Devi	One form of worship at this temple is a chorus of laughter keeping beat with claps
Chettinad	An area in Tami Nadu populated by the rich merchant community of Chettiars
Chidambaram	A temple town, about 250 km south of Chennai
Chottanikkara	A temple town in Kerala; the deity here, Bhagavati, is said to have powers to cure the demented
Darbha grass	Also known as Kusa grass, it is used in its dried form in most Hindu rituals
Deepavali, Kartikai...	During both these Hindu festivals, lamps are lit in hundreds to light up homes
Dhatu	The name of a year in the Tamil calendar. The Tamil calendar is cyclical and consists of 60 years. Each year has a name

Diwan	The chief minister in a king's court
Dosai	Rice and lentil pancake
Dost	Urdu for friend
Dua	Prayer, in Urdu
Dubash	Interpreter, very powerful during the British Raj
Ede	A familiar term of address in Malayalam
Edo	Malayalam word, meaning 'Hey' or 'Look here'
Eriseri, puliseri, milagoottan	Vegetarian dishes special to Kerala
Gayatri mantra	A mantra chanted by Hindus as a daily ritual
Ghee	Clarified butter
Gosai	A group of wandering north Indian ascetics
Gotra	All Brahmins are said to descend from one of the ancient, Brahmin ascetics like Kasyapa, Bharadwaja and Kausika. A gotra is the name of the line of descent of each Brahmin. People do not marry within the gotra as they are considered siblings
Grantha	Ancient writings
Guntur	A town in Andhra Pradesh
Guruvayur	A pilgrimage centre in Kerala dedicated to Lord Vishnu (Narayana)
Halwa	An Indian sweet made of wheat flour boiled in sugar syrup and flavoured with spices and nuts

Hanuman	Lord Rama's devoted lieutenant in the *Ramayana*, the monkey god
Homam	Sacrificial fire
Hundi	Promissory note or bill of exchange
Idli	Steamed rice cake
Javvadu	Solid perfume made from the excretions of the civet cat
Kali Yuga	The present epoch, according to Hindu mythology also known as the age of darkness, said to last 432,000 years
Kasi	The original name of Varanasi
Kesari	A soft sweet made from sugar syrup and broken wheat
Khus khus	Cooling scented grass
Kolam	Decorative patterns made on the ground with rice flour outside homes and temples
Korma	Spicy gravy made in Muslim households
Kottakudi dasi	Dasis or devadasis were dancing girls dedicated to the local deity. Kottakudi is the name of a village
Kriti	Musical composition with lyric
Kshatriya	A member of the warrior caste
Kudumi	Tuft of hair at the back of the head
Laddu, jangiri	Sweets
Land of Parasurama	Kerala, said to have been created by Parasurama, an incarnation of Vishnu
Lingam	The symbol that denotes the Hindu god, Siva. Here, Sankaran has confused Lincoln with Lingam

Madisar	A sari, nine-yards long, worn by married Brahmin women
Malayalam coast	Present-day Kerala
Mami	Literally aunt; the term is used to address Brahmin women
Manasa sancharare	A well-known composition by Brahmendra that translates as 'Where does my mind wander?'
Manni	Elder brother's wife
Meenakshi	An incarnation of goddess Parvati. The Meenakshi temple remains, to this day, Madurai's best known landmark
Melshanti	The chief priest of a temple in Kerala
Menaka	According to Hindu mythology, Menaka is a celestial dancer, a woman of incredible beauty
Milecha	Sudra or those belonging to the lowest caste
mudali	One of the upper castes in Tamil Nadu
Muhurtam	The auspicious hour during which the significant wedding rite takes place
Munde	A swear word directed at a woman, referring to her as a shaven-headed widow
Mundu veshti	Veshti worn in the Kerala style
Nalangu	A marriage ritual during which the bride and groom play games to get better acquainted. Had its origins in child marriage
Namam	The caste mark of Brahmins who worship Vishnu
Nambudiri	Kerala Brahmins

Narmade, Sindhu, Kaveri...	Three of the seven sacred rivers of India (the other four being Ganga, Yamuna, Godavari and Saraswati)
Navaratri	A nine-day Hindu festival that celebrates female deities
Paan	Betel leaves, filled with nuts, condiments and tobacco
Paatti	Grandmother
Pallanguzhi	A board game played with cowries
Panchakaccham	The formal south Indian dhoti
Pandal	Canopy / a temporary shed with a roof made of plaited coconut leaves
Pandi	Pandia Nadu, the land ruled by the Pandia kings. This region around Madurai in Tamil Nadu is adjacent to Kerala. 'Pandi Ayyans' refers to Tamil Brahmins
Panguni	The Tamil month corresponding to March-April
Pasu, sisu	Although pasu means 'cow' and sisu means 'infant,' here the words are used playfully only for the rhyme
Poli	A sweet pancake made of flour with a jaggery and lentil filling
Prasadam	Food offered to a deity, it is later distributed among devotees
Prasnam	A form of astrology in which cowries are used to predict the future. Prasnam means 'question'

Punkah	Manually operated ceiling fan consisting of a pulley on which cloth is hung to create a breeze when the pulley is operated with a rope
Punyam	Good karma
Puranas	Ancient epics of the Hindus
Pyol	Platforms flanking the entrance in rural homes
Rasam	South Indian soup
Rati	The beautiful wife of Manmathan, the God of love
Rishi	Ascetic
Sabarimalai	The hill temple of Lord Ayyappa in Kerala
Sadasiva Brahmendra	An 18th century Tamil saint-singer
Saibu, bhai	Terms of address specifically for Muslim men
Sakkiyar koothu	A folk dance-drama performed by a lone actor-narrator mainly in the temple precincts of Kerala
Salem	A town in Tamil Nadu famous for manufacturing very fine quality cotton veshtis
Sama Veda	One of the four Vedas, the other three being Rig, Yajur and Atarva
Sambar	Delicacy from south Indian cuisine
Samskaras	The rites and duties prescribed by the Vedas for the four castes of Hindus

Sarkar	Government or a reference to the British who ruled India till the mid-twentieth century
Sarpakavu	Literally, the 'grove of snakes'. Snake worship is common in Kerala and, traditionally, every big household, dedicated a grove (kavu) in its grounds to a shrine for the snake god (sarpam)
Sastrigal	Priest
Satyagrahi	A freedom fighter, part of Mahatma Gandhi's non-cooperation movement
Shaitaan ka baccha	Child of Satan, in Hindi and Urdu
Slokas	Verses of prayers
Sozhia!	A derogatory term for an astrologer because some astrologers used cowries (sozhi) as an aid to forecasting
Srardha	Rites performed every year in memory of an ancestor
Sri Rama Navami	The celebration of Lord Rama's birth anniversary
Suar ke bacche	Sons of pigs, in Hindi
Sucheendram	Well-known pilgrim centre in Tamil Nadu, close to the Kerala border
Swami	A respectful term of address
Tai	Tamil month corresponding to January-February in the English calendar
Tanpura	Stringed instrument that a singer strums to keep tone and pitch
Taravad	Nair household and family

Thali	A chain, usually of gold, worn by married women; mangal sutra
Tambiran	A form of address with respect
Thinnai	Raised platform at the entrance of a house on which you can sit or lie down
Tirumeni	Term of address for Nambudiris
Uruli	Shallow, brass bowl used for storage and cooking
Vaappa	Father, (among Muslims)
Vadai	Fried savoury made of lentil dough
Vaidyan	(Ayurvedic) doctor
Vallarai lehyam	A herbal paste said to relieve constipation
Veena	Stringed instrument
Veshti	A long unstitched lower garment, similar to a sarong, worn by Tamil men
Vettiver	Fragrant root used to perfume the air and flavour drinking water
Vibhuti	Sacred ash
Vrichika	Malayalam month from to mid-November to mid-December
Yakshi, neeli	Female spirits said to entice men into compelling but disastrous sexual relationships
Yantra	A copper plate, etched with symbols and images that have been invested with the power to bring good and repel evil
Yellow rice	Rice grains stained with turmeric are considered auspicious and are showered on people as blessings

Zamindar	Landlord or minor chieftain
Zamindarval	Manner of addressing a zamindar or local chieftain
Zari	Woven gold lace

Endnotes

[1] Pollution room — In Brahmin households, there was a separate room in the backyard for menstruating women of the family. The belief was that menstruating women were a source of pollution

[2] Cut short his life. — There is a traditional belief that when a woman utters the name of her husband aloud, his life is shortened. Even today, in many Hindu homes, the wife does not refer to her husband by his name

[3] Selling food... — In the time referred to in this book, public eateries were uncommon, it being considered a sin to sell food, especially to pilgrims. Free food was served to pilgrims in most towns. A Brahmin engaging in professions other than that of a priest or scholar was considered a sinner, more so if he sold food

4 Plantains and sesame seeds...	Raw banana and sesame seeds are important ingredients in funeral and memorial rites
5 Confluence of three oceans	The point where three water bodies—the Indian Ocean, Bay of Bengal and Arabian Sea—meet. The Indian town, Kanyakumari is situated at this meeting point
6 Exchanged betel leaves	All over south India, a betrothal requires the two participating families to exchange plates of betel leaves and nuts, fruits and coconuts, to seal the agreement
7 Firecrackers for worship	A custom peculiar to certain temples in Kerala, firecrackers are burst during the main puja in the temple as a ceremonial offering
8 Chennai Pattinam	The city of Chennai; for long Chennai was known simply as Pattinam, as it was only city in Tamil Nadu that qualified for that title
9 Turk	Here, Muslim. At that time, Muslims were called Turukiar or Turk in Tamil
10 Excommunicated	Until the turn of the 20th century, Brahmins believed that crossing the seas to another country would pollute them forever; those who did so were exiled from the community
11 Eclipse	According to Hindu mythology, an eclipse is not just a celestial happening. The myth is that two demon serpents, Rahu and Ketu,

swallow the sun and the moon during the eclipse, and spit it out at the end of it. When the eclipse takes place on a day governed by a particular star, all those born under that star are said to be adversely affected. Priests are invited to perform propitiation rites to ward off the ill effects of the eclipse

[12] Rice-feeding ceremony	Known as annaprasanam in Sanskrit, this is the ceremony at which a one-year-old baby is fed its first mouthful of rice
[13] Vikramadityan	Legendary king known for his courage and razor-sharp intelligence that helped him accurately judge all disputes and puzzles brought to him
[14] Ear-piercing ceremony	In most south Indian families, when an infant turns one, a ceremony is held during which its head is tonsured and its ears are pierced

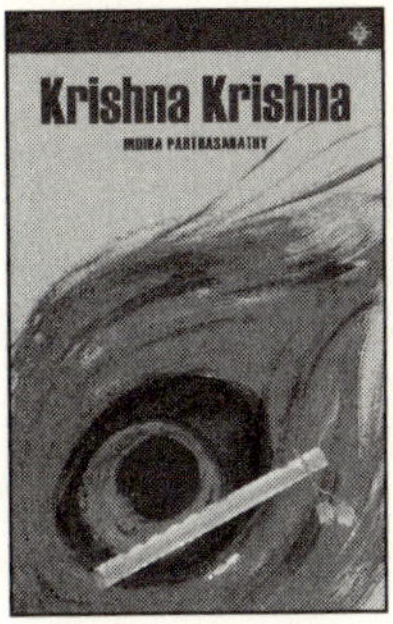

Krishna Krishna, Indira Parthasarathy

He may be the most charismatic personality in Indian mythology, but this is the first time Krishna is the hero of the story. Narada narrates it in an excitingly contemporary voice.

ISBN : 978-81-8368-284-8

Price : 200 Pages : 248

Star-Crossed, Ashokamitran

Ashokamitran's *Star-crossed* is a novel about the world of Tamil cinema minus the glamour. It exposes the daily trials and tribulations of a cast of characters none too familiar to those who equate the world of celluloid with the proverbial dream factory.

ISBN : 978-81-8368-283-1

Price : 150 Pages : 144

I, Ramaseshan, Aadhavan

Aadhavan's *I, Ramaseshan* traces the emotional evolution of an adolescent growing into young adulthood. Written with humour and insight, the novel touches on the gaps in generations trying to understand each other.

ISBN : 978-81-8368-282-4

Price : 200 Pages : 216

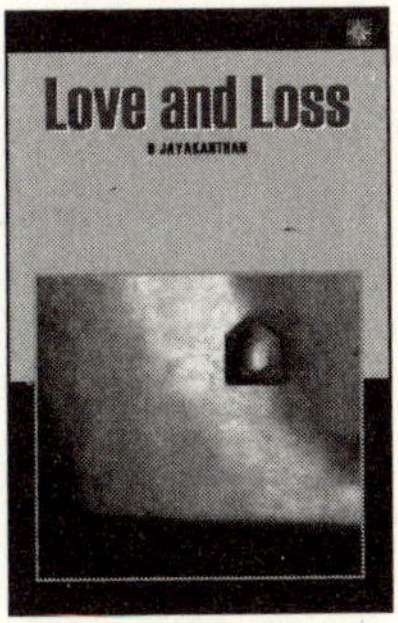

Love and Loss, Jayakanthan

Jayakanthan's *Love and Loss* is a sensitive 'slice of life' story that explores the lives of Thangam, a construction worker and her son Chitti. The squalid slums of erstwhile Madras, now Chennai, form the grimy background to the tender drama of a woman trying to find an anchor to her life.

ISBN : 978-81-8368-285-5

Price : 150 Pages : 160

A Home in the Sky, Vaasanthi

Vaasanthi's *A Home in the Sky* is the story of the brutal repression of an innocent child by his self-righteous father and the tragic outcome it brings about. Two women, with their love and compassion, help end this story on a positive note.

ISBN : 978-81-8368-351-7

Price : 200 Pages : 240

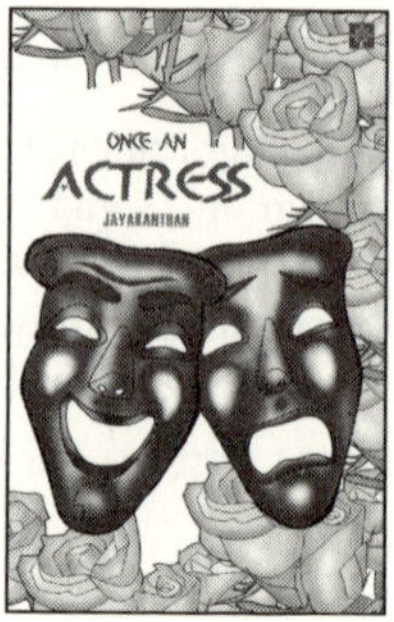

Once an Actress, Jayakanthan

A sensitive stage actress and a brilliant journalist come together in an intense interplay of emotions in a relationship punctuated by intolerance, separation and eventual reunion.

ISBN : 978-81-8368-352-4

Price : 200 Pages 232

Wings in the Void, Indira Parthasarathy

Indira Parthasarathy's *Wings in the Void* explores the wheeling and dealing, ambition and greed that rule the lives of countless upwardly mobile Indians caught up in the intrigues of the political and diplomatic circles of Delhi.

ISBN : 978-81-8368-353-1

Price : 200 Pages : 224

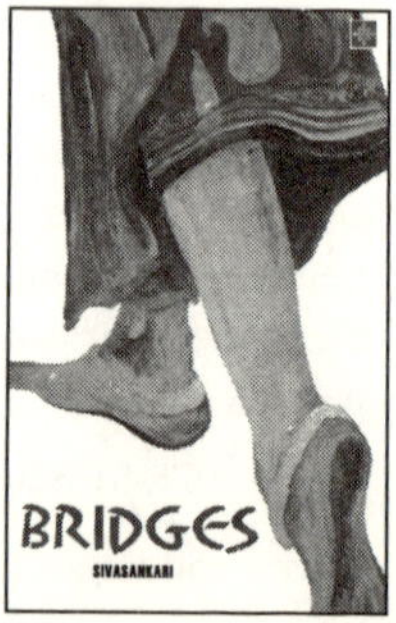

Bridges, Sivasankari

Sivasankari's *Bridges* is a saga of three generations of upper caste Tamil women. It gives the reader rare glimpses into customs and traditions typical of each period it covers—with an unjaundiced eye, great attention to detail, compassion and humour.

ISBN : 978-81-8368-354-8

Price : 200 Pages : 288

Rishi Moolam, Jayakanthan

Jayakanthan's two protagonists are helpless victims of psychological maladies. The author discusses themes such as suppressed libido and the Oedipus complex—areas Tamil writers generally dared not enter in the 1960s.

ISBN : 978-81-8368-382-1

Price : 150 Pages : 144

Paper Flowers, Aadhavan

Aadhavan's *Paper Flowers* explores the psyche of several individuals playing superficial roles in their daily encounters with life in a largely metropolitan setting. Their insecurity and sense of alienation prevent them from realising their potential.

ISBN : 978-81-8368-383-8

Price : 300 Pages : 408

Today, Ashokamitran

Ashokamitran's *Today* raises serious questions about the validity of the value systems governing our lives in an increasingly complex world. It is without doubt a trailblazer in post-modern Tamil literature.

ISBN : 978-81-8368-384-5

Price : 100 Pages : 88

The Temple Elephant, P S Sri

The Temple Elephant is a bestiary with a socio-political and spiritual message. Set against the backdrop of the British Raj, the novel takes its readers on an odyssey from the beautiful jungles of South India through the opulence of palace life to the serene simplicity of an ashram.

ISBN : 978-81-8368-385-2

Price : 100 Pages : 104

Twice Born, Vijay Raghavan

Vijay Raghavan's *Twice Born* is the tale of a man who embarks upon the conquest of unhappiness; and then on the conquest of happiness. He is helped on his voyage of self-discovery by a deus ex machina in the form of Dr Hekyll and Mr Jyde, two splinters of his fractured self.

ISBN : 978-81-8368-469-9

Price : 200 Pages 200

Into this Heaven of Freedom, Indira Parthasarathy

Indira Parthasarathy's *Into This Heaven of Freedom* is set in New Delhi at the height of Indira Gandhi's reign. It captures the intrigue, suspense, manoeuvring and one-upmanship that characterise politics.

ISBN : 978-81-8368-470-5

Price : 200 Pages : 216

Where the Lord Sleeps, Neela Padmanabhan

In this beautiful novel, Neela Padmanabhan has captured the soul of Trivandrum and laid it bare for us to see. Through the life of Anantan Nair—the humble hero of this novel—we experience the tragedy of princely Kerala, caught in a whirl of vulgar modernisation.

ISBN : 978-81-8368-471-2

Price : 200 Pages : 240

Ashes and Wisdom, Indira Parthasarathy

Indira Parthasarathy is at his sardonic best while dissecting the hypocrisies of Indian society. In this novel he lays bare the double standards of fiercely competitive men in the business world and their women forced to live in their shadows. Humour and compassion soften the blow and the reader is left with empathy for each of the characters.

ISBN : 978-81-8368-492-7

Price : 150 Pages : 160

Lizzy's Legacy, Hephzibah Jesudasan

Lizzy's family is caught in a bind. Once the first family of the village, they now have nothing but their 'respectability' to fall back on. As members of other castes begin to overtake them in wealth and position, the men folk of Lizzy's family feel threatened. Change comes, but at the cost of many innocent lives.

ISBN : 978-81-8368-493-4

Price : 150 Pages 168

Blood Ties, Yuma Vasuki

Yuma Vasuki's *Blood Ties* is a harrowing tale of domestic violence and terror. Set in a small town in rural Tamil Nadu, it deals with a joint family of three brothers sternly presided over by their widowed mother. Intertwined with graphic accounts of violence are scenes of everyday life of the children of the novel, made bearable by the presence of mind and calm of the eldest of them, a girl.

ISBN : 978-81-8368-491-0

Price : 300 Pages : 424

Deception, Sivasankari

Giridhar and Durga live a picture-perfect life until Giridhar is sent to the UK on work. Durga endures the separation but becomes increasingly worried as letters from Giridhar dry up. However, a final revelation sets her on a journey she had never thought she would undertake. A journey for truth.

ISBN : 978-81-8368-490-3

Price : 100 Pages : 120

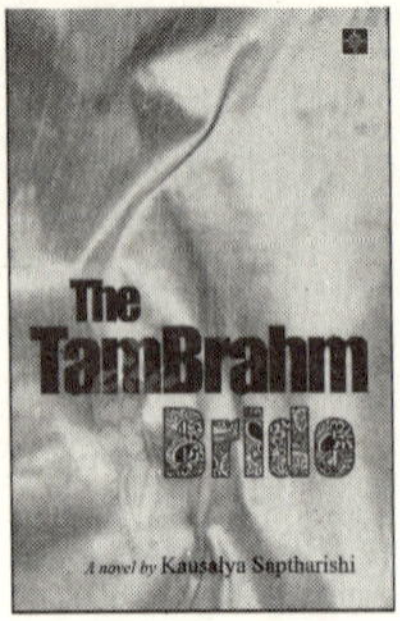

The TamBrahm Bride, Kausalya Saptharishi

The TamBrahm Bride is a light-hearted journey through the dizzying world of south Indian arranged marriages predominantly populated by astrologers, matchmakers and NRI grooms. Rivettingly told, the story may be set in the Indian context, but has a universal appeal that echoes the sentiments of a global audience.

ISBN : 978-81-8368-583-2

Price : 200 Pages 248

Sons of the Sun, Sa Kandasamy

Chelliah is a proud young lad who overcomes a troubled childhood amidst rural deprivation through self belief. Bullied at school and at home, surviving his mother's anxiety and lack of confidence in him, he finds a role model in auto mechanic Ramu. His work takes him to the big city, where he finds friendship and betrayal, love and loss, challenges and triumph. Sa Kandasami's tender story climaxes in Chelliah's election as an office bearer in a workers' union.

ISBN : 978-81-8368-584-9

Price : 200 Pages : 256

Surrendered Dreams, Indumathi

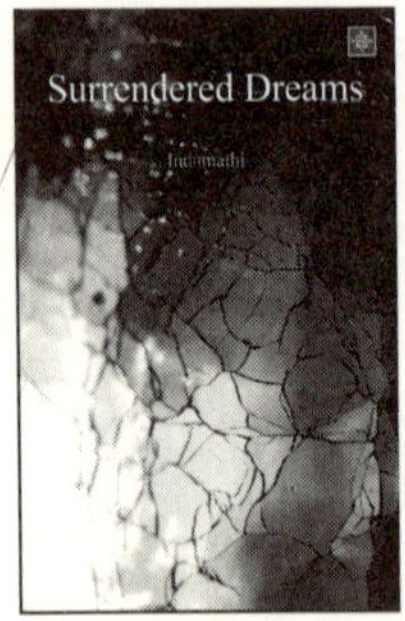

Indumathi's *Surrendered Dreams* is a coming-of-age story, sensitively and sympathetically written. Bound by a sense of filial duty, Parasu, the eldest son of Jagannathan, gives up his dreams of higher studies and settles down to a safe and secure government job. Viswam, his younger brother, also dreams big, but when reality hits him, Viswam is forced into a deeper understanding of the way we want life to be and the way it really is.

ISBN : 978-81-8368-585-6

Price : 100 Pages : 120